Chosen as one of the Best Books of the Year by *Newsday, Los Angeles Times Book Review, Chicago Tribune, The Village Voice Literary Supplement, The Hartford Courant, St. Louis Post Dispatch*, and *Publishers Weekly*

Praise for *The Ordinary Seaman:*

"A marvel of a book—vast, literate, human and entertaining."
—Oscar Hijuelos

"A portrayal of the ingenious complexity and resilience of human nature in its most essential form. It is rendered with tremendous vitality, intelligence and sweetness. That combination alone makes it rare in modern American letters."—Mary Gaitskill, *Salon*

"I can't recommend this book highly enough. . . . *The Ordinary Seaman* does credit to the novelistic form, yielding up mysterious, vivid worlds, seldom seen but always there. It's just great. I loved it."
—Carolyn See, *The Washington Post*

"Goldman, author of *The Long Night of White Chickens,* is one of the most exciting and ambitious novelists currently exploring the form, and his second novel successfully runs thrilling narrative risks. In its electric verbal intensity . . . as well as in its sheer storytelling power, *The Ordinary Seaman* is a remarkable novel."—Claire Messud, *Newsday*

"Goldman's art lies in the juxtaposing of ordinary desires and extraordinary circumstances to create a pattern of wonderment; he has written an epic of the misplaced and misguided . . . a novel . . . with a rare largeness of heart. Here many apparently disparate things get acquainted, as happens in port cities. Goldman brings Spanish and English into a beautiful partnership. His descriptions of sex and bodies somehow evoke both the epicure's taste and the starved lover's raging appetite."—Scott L. Malcomson, *The New Yorker*

"Goldman's extraordinary second novel, *The Ordinary Seaman,* [is] a book that approaches mythic dimensions. . . . A fascinating, relentless story of psychological and moral complexity that confirms his stature as one of the brighter lights on the literary scene."

—Thomas Christensen, *San Francisco Chronicle*

"An imaginative tour de force, a spectacular achievement by any standards . . . Powerful . . . intelligent and engrossing."

—Charles R. Larson, *Chicago Tribune*

"Absorbing and moving . . . touching and provocative."

—*The Atlantic Monthly*

"A strange and suggestive historical novel of the present moment . . . *The Ordinary Seaman* turns out to be a surprisingly optimistic book—a story of escape, not confinement, an adventure instead of a disaster. The crew's ordeal almost fades in the bright light of Esteban's discovery of America—an America of immigrants still alive to its original potential."—Edwin Frank, *The New York Review of Books*

"A magnificent novel, delicious to read, impeccably handled . . . A narrative masterpiece comparable, in my judgment, with the great classics of the genre . . . The skillful cunning with which Goldman weaves his plot reminds me of the best moments of *The Long Night of White Chickens*. This is a young author with the robust maturity of a master."—Alvaro Mutis

"A tightly wound narrative of hardship and survival . . . a powerful exploration of human behavior . . . As dazzling as it is exactly right . . . and memorably so."—James Polk, *The Philadelphia Inquirer*

"Francisco Goldman does what few can: he creates a world so real that when you have turned the last page, you say, 'I've been there, and I will never forget it.' . . . Often very funny and ribald, riveting because it is so generous and inventive . . . Here, a corner of Brooklyn becomes the exotic and foreign experience, and through Esteban's eyes it is as mysterious and alluring as Tangiers."

—Sandra Schofield, *The Dallas Morning News*

"By turns absurd, moving, comic, and bawdy. *The Ordinary Seaman* tackles the genre of the seafaring novel as it hasn't been done in New York City since Melville."—Allen Lincoln, *Time Out New York*

"Keenly observant and brilliantly unnerving fiction . . . a tale of almost surreal intensity."—Donna Seaman, *Booklist* (starred review)

"Stunningly good . . . [a] powerful novel."

—Jeff Baker, *The Oregonian*

"Powerful . . . a searing picture of human vulnerability and courage . . . This novel should establish [Goldman] securely on the literary map."—*Publishers Weekly* (starred review)

"A tightly woven tapestry . . . Goldman's powerfully charged writing brilliantly limns this allegory of immigration and abandonment."

—Harold Augenbraum, *Library Journal* (starred review)

"Francisco Goldman is a state-of-the-art, contemporary hybridist . . . [a] deep evocation of the tormented entanglements of world capital and banana republic . . . .Goldman's playful, tense-switching narration . . . gets so deep inside his character's memories that you feel their collective nausea, which, like the shaky start of a peyote trip, is a prelude to the unfolding of painfully beautiful truths."

—Ed Morales, *The Village Voice*

"Goldman's acclaimed debut, *The Long Night of White Chickens,* proves to have been no fluke; its successor is an equally compelling saga. . . . Even more memorable is Goldman's fresh and moving take on such matters as longing, love, cruelty and fellowship, probed in a poignant and original narrative."—*Kirkus Reviews* (starred review)

"*The Ordinary Seaman* is a contemporary odyssey, the chronicle of a journey that will not occur . . . brilliantly imagined. . . . The most striking aspect of *The Ordinary Seaman* is its language, a baroque Espanglés . . . which Goldman so deftly handles . . . the story of how a society comes into being . . . a Latino version of the settlement of America."

—Alberto Manguel, *The Independent* (London)

THE

ORDINARY

SEAMAN

ALSO BY FRANCISCO GOLDMAN

The Long Night of White Chickens

THE ORDINARY SEAMAN

FRANCISCO GOLDMAN

GROVE PRESS
NEW YORK

Published simultaneously in Canada
Printed in the United States of America

Library of Congress Cataloging-in-Publication Data
Goldman, Francisco.
The ordinary seaman / Francisco Goldman.
p. cm.
ISBN 0-8021-3548-X (pbk.)
I. Title.
PS3557.0368073 1997
813'.54—dc21 96-47626

Design by Laura Hammond Hough

Grove Press
841 Broadway
New York, NY 10003

00 01 02 03 10 9 8 7 6 5 4 3 2

For Veronica

and in memory of Robert Rosenhouse

Passa, lento vapor, passe e nâo fiques . . .

Passa de min, passa de minha vista,

Vai-te dentro de meu coração,

Perde-te no Longe . . .

Pass on, slow steamship, pass on, don't stay . . .

Sail away from me, get out of my sight,

Get out from inside of my heart,

Lose yourself in the Distance . . .

Oda Marítima by Fernando Pessoa

MIRACLE

When Esteban finally reached the airport in Managua it was nearly three in the morning and the airport was closed and he sat down on his suitcase on the sidewalk in the humid, buggy night to wait for it to open. Doña Adela Suárez had told him to be there at six. For the second time in two weeks, he'd ridden a bus all the way from the Pacific port town of Corinto to Managua. The colectivo from the bus stop had cost more than he'd expected, and he thought now that maybe he should have walked, though Sandino Airport was a long way from wherever it was he'd gotten off the bus in that invisible city of sprawling night that didn't seem to have any center or outskirts, here and there a cow standing at the edge of the highway, a stretch of slogan-decorated wall, the disc jockey on the colectivo's radio dedicating romantic ballads to the wide-awake war dead.

He sat on his battered cowhide suitcase listening to the predawn racket of the birds and roosters crowing nearby and others that sounded as faraway as the stars and chewed manically on his thumbnail and tried not to have too many thoughts. As a way of turning off the light on something that had just come to mind, wincing his eyes shut and then opening them wide to stare as if blindly into the dark seemed to work. Sometimes he took his thumbnail out from between his teeth and quietly said, "Chocho." Several times he took her watch out of his pocket to look at the time: her watch, until she'd given it to him. And then he'd put the watch back into his pocket, and light another cigarette, letting the first exhalation mix with a long sigh while he silently spoke her name. Once he even said, out loud and emphatically, "Today you start a new life." And then he felt excited and nervous in the pit of his stomach again, just as he had been off and on for weeks, ever since the afternoon he'd sat in Doña Adela Suárez's office in Managua and she'd told him he could have the job.

It was still dark when a double column of soldiers stomped by on a predawn run, calling out in unison. And then, just when the sky was beginning to lighten behind the palms, the first of the airport workers, men and women, many dressed in green fatigues, began drifting in; and then they came more steadily; while travelers began arriving with mountains of luggage, entire families and others traveling alone gradually forming a long line behind Esteban; workers swept the sidewalk, gardeners marched out with their machetes; food and chiclet sellers, taxi drivers, beggar children, police all appeared out of the murky dawn to take up their positions. And he sat watching as if it was a performance meant just for him, thinking it was all like one of those parable-plays about the creation of the world according to the Indians. When the sole entrance to the airport finally opened, it was manned by soldiers, and he tried to explain his situation to them but lost his privileged place in line anyway because Doña Adela Suárez hadn't arrived yet with his papers and passport. He retreated on the sidewalk and set his suitcase down. Within seconds an old man with silvery, receding hair who'd been waiting in line just a few places behind him stepped out too. The viejo, wearing a white guayabera and pressed tan pants, carrying a dark vinyl suitcase, walked limberly towards him with a preposterously excited smile lighting up his face and a bright, expectant look in his eyes, and said, "Until I overheard you at the door, chavalo, I was worrying that maybe I had the wrong day!" He laughed, his smile somehow became even wider, and he put out his hand and said, "Bernardo Puyano, a sus órdenes."

"Esteban. Mucho gusto," he said warily, shaking the happy viejo's hand. He didn't like being called chavalo.

"You've been to sea before?"

"Pues, no," said Esteban.

"Claro que no, a cipote like you—"

"Esteban," he corrected him.

"Sí pues. I'm the waiter," this effusive viejo went on, nodding. "Apparently there isn't going to be an officers' waiter—pues, my usual position—but just one waiter for the whole ship. Vaya, in times like these, a job like this, it's like a kiss from God, no? And for a chavalito like you, what good luck!" The viejo lowered his voice and tilted his face closer so that Esteban could smell toothpaste mixed with coffee and something sour when he spoke: "Leave this shitty country behind. Vos, it wouldn't surprise me if you found yourself in the arms of a blue-eyed, blonde gringita tonight, your very first night. Chavalo, you'll see what it's like to be a handsome young marinero set loose in the world!"

"What if we both have the wrong day?" asked Esteban.

"It can't be," he said. "I know Doña Adela said Sunday. And when I went to mass yesterday, it was definitely Saturday. The archbishop has personally blessed our voyage, patroncito."

Esteban is nineteen, a war veteran, of course he doesn't consider himself a boy, but Bernardo will never call him anything but chavalo, muchacho, chigüín, chico, patroncito, and, most annoyingly, cipote.

Doña Adela Suárez, a secretary with the shipping agency Teccsa Corporación in Managua, had interviewed and hired the five Nicaraguans, including Esteban and Bernardo, who were to leave from Sandino Airport that morning, headed to New York City to meet the *Urus:* the old ship's waiter, a middle-aged galley cook, and three ordinary seamen, the latter without any previous shipboard experience whatsoever. When Doña Adela finally arrived at the airport, she was carrying their passports and U.S. Embassy–issued seamen's transit visas. It was the twentieth of June, and the *Urus* was to sail from New York four days later carrying, according to Doña Adela, a cargo of fertilizer to Puerto Limón, Costa Rica. She wore big, clear-plastic-framed, octagonal, pink-tinted glasses, aquamarine slacks, and a white blouse with the English words *over the* followed by a colorful little rainbow printed all over it. To Bernardo the pattern on her blouse couldn't have seemed more apt:

"Mi Reina de la Suerte," he enthused, thanking Doña Adela yet again for his ship's waiter's job and giving her a clumsy one-armed embrace at the tiny airport bar, where the puffy-faced, slit-eyed cook had rum with his coke and the others just coke and Adela paid. "The

Queen of Luck" was the sister-in-law of Constantino Malevante, a Greek ship captain who'd worked for many years on the Mameli line when the dictator Somoza owned ships, and who now lived in Miami making his living outfitting flag of convenience ships with Central American crews. Twenty-three years before, Bernardo had worked as waiter in Capitán Malevante's officers' saloon.

"And what is my new capitán's name, Doña Adela?" asked Bernardo at the bar.

Doña Adela frowned behind her cake-plate glasses for a moment; then said she couldn't remember, though she was sure Capitán Malevante must have sent it to her.

"Greek, I suppose," said Bernardo, disguising his dislike of Greek capitanes, including Constantino Malevante, which over his last eighteen years of landlocked nostalgia he'd been exaggerating as much as he had the virtues of English shipmasters.

Esteban was the tallest of the five. His brown skin had a smooth, saddle-soaped luster, and his build was so slender and bony that his jeans and white, short-sleeved shirt seemed tenuously hung from his hip and collar bones. He wore the same pair of black combat boots that had accompanied him through two years of war.

One of the other two ordinary seamen was a coppery skinned teenager named Nemesio, who looked as if some unattached mass of superconcentrated gravity must follow him around everywhere like chewing gum stuck to the soles of his shoes: mournfully drooping eyes, forehead slanting into a massive nose descending at almost the same angle, hulking but sagging shoulders, chubby, squashed legs, his stone-washed jeans zigzagging down to his shoes, and a portly panza hanging over his belt—later, onboard the *Urus,* Nemesio's nickname would be Panzón, though not just for that reason. Esteban quickly established that Nemesio had been in the army too, serving as an aircraft spotter right there in Managua, standing on a bald hill all day with two other soldiers taking ninety-minute shifts watching the horizon through binoculars, boring as hell; so far aircraft had only attacked Managua once during the whole war anyway. Which is why, Esteban suddenly thought, Nemesio's eyes are so droopy: staring through binoculars at the white hot sky day after day, they'd melted.

The other ordinary seaman, Chávez Roque, nearly as tall as Esteban and even darker skinned, looked older than his twenty years, his cleft chin swarthy, chest hair brimming up through the collar of his blue polo shirt. He wore black jeans, old cowboy boots. Chávez Roque said he hadn't been in the army, not exactly. He'd worked on a government road-building crew along the Costa Rican border, in the jungles of the Rio San Juan, but he'd been given militia training and an AK to carry, but he'd only fired it in "combat" once, when a tapir bursting from riverbank foliage startled him . . . missed it, pues.

"I was in a BLI," said Esteban, lighting a cigarette. He was sure he saw respect still their expressions like the fleeting shadow from an airborne hawk. He didn't have to say anything more. He'd been in one of the irregular warfare battalions.

"Maybe the war's over now," said the former aircraft spotter.

"Maybe," said Esteban neutrally. Chávez Roque, turning his head to watch an hembra in tight jeans and stiletto heels walking past, said, "Saber, vos." Onboard the *Urus* his nickname would be Roque Balboa.

When they'd boarded the plane, Esteban was disappointed to find himself seated next to the happy viejo. After the takeoff he craned forward for a glimpse past Bernardo at the airport military installations below, thinking of helicopters he'd ridden at the front. He saw five green military ambulances parked in a row, rear doors open, canvas stretchers on the tarmac, figures in fatigues and medical whites standing around waiting . . . So helicopters and planes were still flying mangled and bullet-punctured bodies in heated, vibrating pools of blood over jungles, mountains, and plains. Despite the cease-fire and all the talk of peace. The ambulances shrank to a row of capsules and vanished from sight, the corrugated metal roofs of hangars turned into huts, palms became weeds, the green and brown landscape plummeting, plummeting downwards like a whole country flung off a high cliff. Bernardo suddenly turned to him with an ecstatic grin and said, "Once again, chavalo, the old wolf to the sea!"

Then he sat back, remonstratively patted the armrests as if making sure they were really bolted in, and stared straight ahead, smiling beatifically into the air over the mounded tops of passengers' heads, all this, Esteban supposed, in some further display of gratitude to his Queen of Luck. A profusely perspiring middle-aged steward, bulging cheeks, goatee, was wheeling the jingling liquor cart down the aisle. The scarlet-lipped stewardess, her hair a maelstrom of oiled, ebony ringlets, was still giving her safety lesson, her hands wagging the pinkish tubes—the voice on the intercom said to blow into these—protruding from the deflated life jacket bladders over her breasts. The blast of sun in the window turned Bernardo's broad, spotted forehead as silvery as his hair, and Esteban reflected that he really did look like some benignly crazed old wolf: his chin was angular, and his lips looked as if they reached ear to ear, two long, thin, contented-looking seams.

The liquor was free. "Chivas?" said the steward grouchily, over and over, sliding his forearm over his slick forehead, underarm dark with sweat. And wine from France. Up ahead Esteban saw the cook reach out for another rum and coke, a gold chain bracelet dangling from his thick, hairy wrist.

Poured into clear plastic cups, flashing in sunlight, the wine looked like candlelight inside dark red glass. Or like bear's blood.

"I've never drunk wine," said Esteban. Not even in church. The men in his family, his tíos and primos, didn't go to church, though his mother did.

"All ship's capitanes take wine with their meals, bueno, on Sundays at least," said Bernardo. "Greeks, every night. I'll try to sneak you a glass now and then, patroncito."

"Bueno," said Esteban flatly.

"The English prefer beer," the viejo went on. "Every afternoon at three Capitán Osbourne would say, *Beer O'clock!* But he was never drunk. A grand man, chico. Capitán John Paul Osbourne was his name, but his friends called him *Hay Pee*."

Bernardo took only coke with his peanuts, so Esteban did the same, though he felt entitled to drink whatever he wanted because this was a significant day, the start of a new life, and the airline ticket had cost him so much. He owed his tíos the combined sum of the ticket and the fee charged by Doña Adela Suárez for getting him the job. After two months on the *Urus* he'd be able to pay them back and there'd still be four months to go; then he'd be able to sign on for a whole other year, provided his capitán was happy enough with his work.

"The best years of my life, muchacho . . ." No major port on earth, apparently, where Bernardo hadn't walked with the long, loping steps and sinewy smile of a lighthearted and elegant officers' saloon waiter. But he hadn't been to sea in eighteen years, not since Clara, his second wife—Clarita was only twenty-nine when she died, he said. Of tetanus, horrible. She was German on her papi's side, chavalo. And he was left with three little daughters to raise on land. All of them light skinned, just a little plump like their mother, and one, the youngest, even has blue eyes, though her mami didn't. Raised them in the same neat little cement house with a cement porch out front that they all still live in now, in Managua, in Colonia Máximo Jerez. A house paid for with two decades of saved-up officers' waiter's wages and a loan from Clara's much older cousin, a customs inspector in Corinto, like a father to her. Perhaps you know the family, muchacho? No, you wouldn't, you're too young, he's in Panamá now, left right after El Señor Somoza did. Never paid him back, never a word of recrimination. María, Gertrudis, and Freyda, muchachas maravillosas, educated, prepared. One a teacher, the other a secretary in the Trade Ministry though she keeps out of politics like all her sisters, and little Freyda still a student. María's novio and Gertrudis's eight-year-old cipote live at home too, a crowded little place, crowded but always neat and clean—Pues, he's never produced a son of his own. But he has three grandsons, three little cipotes, Gertrudis's hijito and two whom he's never even seen, though it's his dream to. Because he has two daughters from his first marriage too. The younger, who disgracefully has never married or forgiven lives in Greytown now, with her mother and mother's new husband, an evangelical Protestant pastor, but the other, Esmeralda, restless like her papi, lives in Jerusalem. Sí pues, in Israel. In Israel, Esmeralda became a Beauty Queen, chavalo! Married an Israeli policeman, they have a daughter and two sons. The Israelitas are the oldest and most noble race on earth, don't listen to the lies they tell in our poor, hate-demented little country, muchacho. How many times has he sat on his porch in the evenings grieving over the state of our beloved Nicaragua, wishing for Israeli commandos to fly in and do away with our Nine Comandantes the way they did those terrorists on that hijacked plane at the airport in Africa!

Bernardo looked directly at Esteban, the forced vehemence of his expression contradicted by the clouded softness of his wide-open stare. Esteban merely returned it until the viejo looked away. His tíos always talked like that, if not quite as screwily. What was it to him what viejos thought, except, chocho, why did they always seem to think he needed to hear strong opinions, and that he must be full of strong opinions about the same things they always had strong opinions about?

Seething, he barely listened while Bernardo chattered on about his years working as a chauffeur in Managua, the families he'd driven for, including one related to the Petrocelis. Bernardo hadn't touched the lunch that had been served in the middle of his life story—Esteban had glumly passed up wine again—but now the viejito punctured the wrapping of his crackers with his plastic fork, carefully peeled yellow wax from his tablet of cheese, and cut the cheese into thin slivers, which he arrayed over two crackers. It was all he ate. Then he was talking about his daughters again. Esteban, devouring the gravy-soaked beef that was as mushy as eggplant in just a few forkfuls while his stomach roared with hunger, wondered what the viejo's youngest daughter looked like, and who'd fixed the middle one, leaving her with child when she was what, fourteen or so? Bernardo said that his daughters' paychecks were worthless now, vaya pues, like everyone's. He felt he'd become a burden to them. Disgracefully, he hadn't had any work in nearly two years, since the last family he'd worked for had suddenly gone to live in Venezuela. But he'd been going to see Doña Adela Suárez once a month ever since, pleading with her to convince Capitán Constantino Malevante to find a place for him on a crew despite his age. With the money he earns on this voyage, muchacho, he's going to buy two chicken incubators! Then he'll no longer be a burden to his daughters; he'll have a dignified old age, because people always need chickens and eggs, especially now, when sometimes in Managua you can't buy a chicken or even an egg anywhere:

"Son of a million whores, have you ever heard of a country running out of chickens?" He brought his fist down onto the armrest and fell silent a moment. And then he deftly switched the two meal trays, saying, "Here, take mine." Esteban picked up the pineapple cake and began to eat it. Bernardo said, "All the meat that doesn't go to the Comandantes or Cubans or Russians and I don't know who else goes to the soldiers."

Esteban had heard this so often he merely shrugged. He didn't know where all the meat went. But his battalion, a BLI, rotated into the jungle for three-week stretches with a week at base or bivouacked outside some town in between, had rarely been supplied with anything to eat, never mind meat. The few campesinos they ran into in the depopulated war zones might have bananas to take, or even an ox, but never nearly enough chickens to feed a battalion. Otherwise they lived on fish from rivers and streams, hunted birds and rodents, macheted down makengue trees for the sopping, breadlike pulp at the heart of the trunk. In the jungle everything was always dripping wet, but sometimes you couldn't even find a limón to suck; sometimes the nearest river or stream might be days' march away, but there were insect-clouded bogs of undrinkable black water everywhere . . .

"You know what we learned to drink in the jungle? We called it refresco."

"You were in the army? A cipote like you?"

"Can you guess what we drank?" He felt really irritated by this viejo now, his soft eyes intently fixed on him as if he'd asked him something much more personal.

"From coconuts, imagino pues."

"That far in from the coast?" Esteban laughed. "No, the juice inside a monkey's stomach. You kill a monkey and take out its stomach and poke a hole in it"—and he lifted his hands to his lips and mimed holding a wobbly sphere, which he slowly deflated in his long, spread fingers. Monkey stomach juice tasted like sweet fruit pulp blended with urine and grass.

Bernardo zipped an angry line in the air with a finger. "To send young muchachos like you off to die, brother against brother. How can it be?"

"Muchachas too," said Esteban matter-of-factly, staring down at his tray. Now this annoying viejo was going to want him to explain war too.

"No sé." Esteban sighed. He picked up a sugar packet, bit off a corner with his teeth, and poured some sugar on his tongue.

After a long moment, Bernardo said, "The first time you get seasick, you know what to do? . . . Go forward, and bite the anchor."

"Bueno."

"Or drink gasoline."

They didn't talk much after that, though neither pretended to sleep either. The movie was eliciting an almost unbroken riot of yelping laughter and swooning squeals of *Ay qué lindo* from the passengers. Esteban put on his headphones. A huge, slobby dog was in love with another huge, slobby dog wearing a pink bow in her collar, and because the two dogs didn't want to be apart, the smiling, teary-eyed families who owned each dog had to decide what to do about this awkward situation, but then the dogs ran away together. They all lived in that usual America-land of big white houses, each in the middle of its own tree-shaded park. The enemy is the government and its warring policies, not the American people, no? When Esteban removed his headphones, Bernardo immediately turned to him and asked: "Have you fathered any children?"

"Pues, no." Esteban scowled.

Eventually even the light in the window had paled. Esteban forced himself into a long, methodical daydream of female flesh and lovemaking. It didn't work; he felt miserable, not at all aroused, trying to remember her and the way it had been in Quilalí, the last girl he'd fucked and one of only three he'd ever fucked but the only one who'd ever let him do it up the culito, buried in jungle earth now, something of him still inside her scientifically if invisibly still inside her mixing into the rotting earth, verdad? In another half century he'd be this old waiter's age. Puta, would it have stopped by then? This death blotting out love whenever he tries to conjure love, totally fucked up: like with that whore in Corinto last week, when she was naked on her burdel bed and suddenly all he could think of was *her* perfumed, satiny flesh and blood ripped apart sprayed through green underbrush while on her bed she rolled over on her belly like a dog thrusting hard round smooth little buttocks up at him, *No te preocupas, amorcito, no pasa nada chúpame aquí*—smiling! If that putita had known what he was thinking, it would have been *her* getting the hell out of there as fast she could, no? *No pasa nada.* Ni verga. No pasa nada, mi amor . . . Was there a girl in one of the ports they'd be stopping at, maybe even someone he'd meet over the next few days in New York, or someone out there in their voyage along that part of the world where city and ocean air intermix, where people live caressed inside and out by opposite kinds of air and breezes, which is why they're incapable of keeping things in, of keeping love hidden, no? Was there a girl who was going to bring love back to him, fill him with love as he swallowed the warm breath of her kisses, who was waiting for him right now in a shimmery haze of hot city and ocean air without even knowing him yet? He sat purposefully and suspensefully still, trying to imagine her. Should I make her older or younger? Rich or poor? Light or dark? What's her name? What language does she speak? Should she pull her shirt off over her head herself, her chichis suddenly blooming and bouncing from under her elbows going up in a band of cloth, or will I unbutton . . . He turned his head away, staring down at the aisle so the viejo wouldn't see the hot, wet stinging in his eyes—I'm ruined, no good for anything . . .

Later, when there was turbulence, Bernardo told him about chairs lashed to the legs of the officers' mess dining table during rough seas and that the way to keep plates and glasses and silverware from sliding off was to soak the tablecloth with water, and even better than that, water that rice had been boiled in, if the galley cook had had the discipline and foresight to save it.

"A man who plans ahead is worth two, muchacho. But not this one. This cook drinks too much. First day on the job, and look, he's arriving drunk. Have you seen how many rum and cokes he's already taken?"

Maybe I'll get a tattoo, thought Esteban. Should I get a tattoo? Up on my arm, not all over like prisoner tattoos. Elegant, with meaning, a sailor's tattoo. Something that says, I'm leaving the earth to be reborn. A skeleton climbing a ladder up into the stars. Or navigating a ship through the stars. Otílio de la Rosa has a yellow fish outlined in red tattooed on his chest and a hummingbird on his arm and at the beach that chavala said, What are you, a pet store? and just like that he learned what a mistake he'd made.

On the way to Miami, where they cleared customs and immigration, the plane had stopped in San Pedro Sula, Honduras, where among the passengers who boarded and filled the remaining seats were ten more young seamen on their way to New York to meet the *Urus*. But they wouldn't all come together until Kennedy Airport, gathering around the gargantuan, hairy-shouldered American in basketball shorts who met them in the arrivals area, a cardboard sign that read *"Urus"* in scratchy black marker held from the bottom in two hands against his chest. After that day they'd never see him again, but whenever the crew had cause to recall him, they'd refer to him as El Pelos, The Hairs, or just Pelos. He had black hair cut short like a yanqui soldier, wore work boots with bright orange laces and a sleeveless T-shirt with his shorts, and his muscular arms and broad shoulders were totally matted with bristly black hair. "Hi. How are ya," he said over and over as they gathered around, scrutinizing them with gray eyes as quiet and watchful as a mistrustful child's. When he'd finally counted to fifteen he said, "All here? OK, let's go."

He led them outside, this odd and uneasy American, into a late afternoon heat as stupefying as any which mundanely withers Nicaragua's coastal plains, and left them, faces burning, standing on the sidewalk while he went for the van. A moreno porter wheeling an empty cart back inside shouted at them, "Qué vaina? Son equipo be béisbol, no? Campeones!" and raucously laughed. Is that what they looked like, a baseball team? Sun and clouds had dissolved into a haze the color of boiled, yellowing cauliflower. The airport, a vastness of sooty concrete and glass and traffic, was all by itself the biggest, noisiest, and most unfamiliar city Esteban had ever been in, though it wasn't as if he'd never seen such places on television or in movies. He stood gaping at the endless clamor of yellow taxis pulling up in a flurry of shouts, doors and trunks flapping open, slamming shut, roaring off—yet the air, for all the commotion, the constant, ripping thunder of takeoffs and landings overhead, felt utterly still; humid, petrol-fumed air and a faint rankness of old crab shell, the ocean somewhere nearby.

Behind the open trunk of a radiantly polished red car, a blonde stewardess in a crisp white blouse was tightly entwined in a ravenous kiss with a handsome young man, mouths deeply tunneling. Her honey-hued elbows and arms shifted around his neck; she seemed to be trying to press herself ever more tightly against him, hip to hip, head tilted back, hair falling down like poured, shimmering grain. The man dropped a hand from her waist to her nalgas, her starched skirt denting like soft tin around his big-knuckled fingers, cheeks underneath springing back, wobbling the shimmering fabric around those flagrant indentations. They went on kissing while the crew watched, each in his own way sharing the sweltering heat between the two clamped bodies, running their tongues over their own sweat-salted lips, feeling their own humid shirts clinging to their skin. Then the lovers broke apart as if they'd agreed to do it for exactly so many minutes and seconds; he shut the trunk, they walked to opposite sides of the car, got in, and the car drove off. "Hijo de la gran puta," one of the crew inevitably growled, others clucked impressed assent, they stood marveling and grinning as if they'd all just had their first providential taste of life at sea.

They shook hands, exchanged names; there really wasn't much more to say, they'd be spending the next six months together and maybe more, so what was the hurry? Nearly everyone struck a pose of friendly reserve, serious and casual, as if to say, I'm a good guy, but don't think I can't be a cabrón. Though a few seemed stuck in wary surliness, or seemed to think they were superior. The cook, squinting through swollen, reddened eyes, stinking of sweat and rum, put out his hand to everyone. "José Mateo Morales. Soy el cocinero." "Marco Aurelio Artola, electrician." "Tomaso Tostado, ordinary seaman"—Tomaso Tostado had a gold tooth. Bonnie Mackenzie, the one moreno on the crew, a wiry and cherubic costeño from Puerto Cortés, was an ordinary seaman too, and, despite his name, said he doesn't speak much English, bueno, un poco, *mon, fock, brother;* knows the words to eight Bob Marley songs, but, brother, take the lyrics apart, try to use a word here and a word there to speak his own thoughts in English, it comes out sounding like a parrot making senseless noise. Regarding Esteban's qualifications as an ordinary seaman, Adela Suárez had asked him if he was literate and if he knew how to use a paintbrush, and that was almost all she'd wanted to know.

The van was like a small bus with four rows of seats, hot and airless despite the air-conditioning. The cook sat up front with El Pelos, whose shoulders rose over the back of his seat like the tops of folded, hairy wings. Esteban sat by a window, with the irritating viejo squeezed in beside him.

Marco Aurelio Artola, the Honduran electrician, a freckled, twenty-year-old mulatto whom they'd nickname Canario because of his high, twittering voice, said he'd thought New York City was going to be pretty flat, *planito planito,* with just one building rising over everything, the Jehovah's Witness Watchtower. All his life he'd been seeing the Watchtower on the cover of the Jehovah's Witness publications a proselytizing barber in his pueblo was always pressing on customers.

So that was funny, the crew's first shared laugh: how could he be so bobo? "What, you never watch television?" one of them scoffed. "You never watch *Kojak*?" When the teasing subsided, Bernardo turned to the fuming electrician and asked if he'd ever been to sea before, as if such unworldliness were impossible in a seaman.

"No. I'm an electrician, I worked in Tela. Y qué?"

"And for that you were hired to work on a ship, chavalo?"

"Bueno, what's a ship, a building that floats, no?"

"Pues, no."

"Last month we fixed this old hotel, so fucked up the wires still had cloth insulation, all shredded, worn out. We rewired it top to bottom, ve?"

The one they would call Cabezón because of his immense, gourdlike head, had been hired as an engine room mechanic, but in

Honduras he'd worked as a mechanic in a fish canning factory that also produced fish bouillon cubes from offal: turbines, boilers, diesel engines, there wouldn't be such a difference. Except on the ship he'd be earning more than a dollar an hour and saving every cent, while in Honduras he'd earned five dollars a day. The moreno from the coast said that wasn't so bad, he'd earned three. And in Nicaragua? No jodas, grumbled the cook from the front, people weren't even paid with real money anymore, even frijoles had become rich people's food.

It turned out that everyone but Bernardo and the cook had been hired based on qualifications only conjecturally related to shipboard ones. The crew included two electricians, two mechanics, a cook, a waiter, and nine ordinary seamen; nine Hondurans, five Nicaraguans, and one Guatemalan. The Guatemalan was the other electrician, his last job with an oil exploration company in the jungles of the Petén—like so many chapines, he had a reserved demeanor, and because of that and also because it's a well-known joke all over Central America that Guatemaltecos are only born to give their army more people to murder, his nickname onboard would be Caratumba (Tomb Face). The other mechanic, the pretty boy they'd call Pínpoyo, had worked with heavy construction equipment, Caterpillar diesel engines. While everyone in the van chattered on, Esteban saw Bernardo looking worriedly at the back of the cook's head, as if willing him to turn around and say something about this.

"It's having experienced officers onboard, a good chief engineer, that matters," said Bernardo firmly. "Everyone else just does what they're told."

The van rushed along the elevated expressway, bounced and vibrating. Esteban had only felt this way in helicopters before, not even in IFA trucks, sweating and slightly nauseous and trying to see everything. He saw a cemetery so vast and withered it looked like a whole miniature, firebombed city. How could anyone be happy here, living in an endlessness of factories, refineries, windowless slabs, who knew what it all was? He peered down into side streets as if into the bottoms of suddenly snatched away boxes, dirty brown brick, yellow tienda signs, figures walking along serenely like drunks at dawn through yellow-brown air; he saw people sitting in chairs by sidewalk cooking fires, some in their underwear apparently like at home, but they were so quickly past. Was that corn growing on that rooftop? He would never walk down those streets at night, never. The expressway curved, and skyscrapers filled the van's window on the other side; he rocked and craned trying to see, glossy gray skyscrapers looking like they'd be blinding in the sun. The van swerved, El Pelos hit his horn, shouted, "Fucking Chinese," words Esteban understood, though the rest of Pelos's sullenly muttered invective was lost on him. Bernardo murmured in his ear, "They're going to have to be good teachers, these officers, chavalo. It's lucky the Atlantic doesn't make itself truly dangerous until October, bueno, generally."

The Island of Skyscrapers and lights in the sky like fireflies before dusk and the behemoth bridges hanging in a sudden openness of ocean and sky. Tugs, barges, traffic streaming alongside the river. A gleaming white freighter berthed by a neat row of rectangular, blue warehouses down there, but that wasn't where they were going: the expressway bent downwards and away, soon pulling them through an endless row of iron girders supporting traffic overhead, the van filling with shadows. Industrial buildings, a row of narrow, dilapidated houses, a gasoline station, a pink sign with the black silhouette of a naked woman kneeling like a mermaid, hands clasped behind her head. Morenos in sleeveless T-shirts and hats on a corner, children on bicycles; a long row of dull brown brick buildings, trees growing between them. They turned down a street lined with immense old brick warehouses. They drove along the long brick marine terminal yard wall.

El Pelos handed an envelope to a uniformed man in a booth, who waved them through, into the stilled complexity of the port. Here and there masts, derricks, and the bristling tops of monumental ships' superstructures protruded over the roofs of numbered terminal buildings. Motionless cargo cranes against the sky. Parked truck cabs. Sheds and warehouses with aluminum siding. A man driving an empty forklift out from behind a long row of containers. It was Sunday evening;

perhaps that was why there didn't seem to be much going on. But El Pelos kept on driving for a surprisingly long time, deep into what seemed to be a deserted and apparently defunct end of the port, where the buildings were much older, abandoned looking, made of crumbling brick and concrete. Sandy wastes of weeds and built-up earthworks suddenly opening on a patch of beachfront fronting a long, broken pier. A smashed, hollowed-out car chassis in a rubble-filled lot. They passed a small, listing old freighter apparently resting in eternal dry dock inside a fenced in, overgrown, scraggly-treed yard, leafy squirrel nests in the conning tower and a squat black dog barking at them from the bridge, an inner tube hung with rope from a bridge wing. An elephantine warehouse built of tattered gray wood, an emptiness of darkening sky and water glowing like a movie screen through huge, gaping doorways.

Esteban was conscious of Bernardo's breathing next to him in the now quieted van, his emphatic, almost rhythmic exhalations. They came to a pothole-ripped parking lot partially enclosed by brick wall, a rusted chicken-wire fence lying on its side all the way across it like the undulating spine of a long-dead dragon. At the far end was a cluster of sheds and low buildings with smashed and boarded-up windows, a ruin that looked like a row of concrete-encased rolls of toilet paper that had been pounded down with a giant sledgehammer, and in front, a tall, concrete, rectangular structure—an old grain elevator—towering against the bands of coloring sky low on the horizon behind it: "Ve? Ahí está, el Watchtower," said the twittering electrician, but now no one laughed. They drove over a flattened portion of the fence and around the front of the grain elevator and onto a paved finger pier with a freighter berthed on one side, blocking most of the covelike basin from view.

The crew got out of the van and stood on the pier with their suitcases, looking up at the darkened and silent ship looming over them like a cold canyon wall, breathing the familiar stench of stagnant waterfront rot. The immense, rust-smeared hull seemed suffused with an almost lavender glow against the hot dusk's powdery blue sky streaked crimson and orange. Around Esteban his crewmates' faces all seemed to be glowing too, their eyes and teeth, their short-sleeved shirts and white guayaberas.

El Pelos had stayed in the van's driver's seat, his long, hairy legs protruding from the open door, smoking and listening to rock music on the radio. They were waiting for el Capitán.

"Bueno, es un barquito, no?" said Tomaso Tostado after a moment, sounding quietly elated, his gold tooth flashing. Some brought out cigarettes and passed them around, smiling. Well, it *is* a ship, thought Esteban, surprised he felt so relieved to have arrived, at the end of this long day, to at least this certainty of a ship. He held cigarette smoke inside himself and looked up at the ship, feeling tired and satisfied. He slapped a mosquito away. A perfectly regular-looking ship, sturdy and capable, and he was going to work on it. Who cared that it was berthed in the middle of desolation? What difference would that make in a few days, when they'd be out to sea?

It may have been a modest-size freighter by modern standards, 400 feet long, floating well above its load lines, but it looked enormous to Esteban. Three derrick-rigged King masts protruding over the long main deck. *Urus* painted high up on the prow against a dark smear covering up what must have been its previous name; *Urus, Panama City* on the stern. But there were no lights onboard; everything looked painted with shadows. The deckhouse, whitish, speckled with dark gashes, was back near the stern; two rows of black portholes visible beneath the bridge and wing; a smokestack. The ship's ladder was up. Water rustled heavily against ship and pier, slapped pilings. The heat still held itself over everything like someone at the very end of holding his breath.

Then Esteban heard Bernardo whispering in his ear that the ship was nothing but a broken eggshell, chavalo. Esteban stared straight ahead into the iron hull. What made the viejo think of an eggshell?

"No lights," whispered Bernardo. "No electricity. It's a broken eggshell, chavalo."

Esteban looked at him: Bernardo was holding his cigarette between two fingers as if it were some fine Cuban cigar, seemingly studying it even as he said, "The mooring lines don't even have rat guards, ve?"

It was nearly dark when a car, headlights on like cat's eyes, came around the grain elevator and onto the pier. A sleek black Mazda. El Capitán, pues. They could see the back of his head inside the car, a strikingly oblong head with small, close ears. The door opened, and the man who unfolded himself from the driver's seat was so tall, skinny, and angular he looked like an elongated shadow of himself rising on a wall. His head was shaved nearly bald; he wore neat jeans, a black belt, and a white T-shirt, shiny black rubber-soled shoes. He stepped back and gently closed the door, turned and looked at them with tender sheep's eyes. In his thirties, probably. A high forehead and a prominent nose and small, thin lips puckered as if they were scornfully kneading a mouthful of thread even as he looked them over with his spurned lover's eyes. He looks like a priest, thought Esteban. Some young Spanish Jesuit who shaved his beard off yesterday.

"Hola, bienvenido," called out el Capitán. "Espero que no fue demasiado cansado el viaje." His voice had a youthful, slightly querulous timbre. He stood with one hand thrust straight down into his front pocket, elbow tucked against his side. Then he said, "Momento," and walked slowly over to the van, one long arm loosely dangling. Well, he speaks Spanish anyway. He wasn't what Esteban had imagined a capitán would look like, but he seemed formidable enough, no? A certain gravity. Educated seeming. Carries himself well enough. Esteban glanced at Bernardo—was the viejo going to call el Capitán chavalo and cipote too? But Bernardo was staring up at the shadowy deck, his expression rapt and sardonic, lower lip curled. Poor viejito, thought Esteban, he's let all his frantic good hope collapse over nothing because he's so used to everything always going wrong, all that grateful mierda about good luck just a desperate hoax.

El Pelos had turned his radio off and sat listening, mouth open, to el Capitán. And then el Capitán pulled his wallet from his back pocket and paid Pelos without counting the bills and slid the wallet back into his pocket just like that. Esteban liked the way el Capitán pushed the door closed for Pelos and then stepped back, watching as Pelos started the van and lifted his hand in a wave—el Capitán merely nodded—and backed off the pier, waving again at the crew as he went past, his pallid face looking swollen and ghostly.

There was someone onboard, maybe that was what Bernardo had been watching. They heard a sudden clanking and, looking way up, saw that a man in white pants and untucked shirt had just stepped out through the gangway, onto the still-raised aluminum accommodation ladder running parallel to the bulwark and rail. The man walked out along the ladder's length almost like a tightrope walker, with careful, emphatic steps, his weight slowly sinking it. But when he reached the end of the ladder, he was still high above the pier, the ladder only slightly slanted downwards—then they heard him laugh; it must have been a laugh, but it sounded like some faraway bird squawk or monkey shriek, coming from up there in the dark. Clasping both railings, the man on the ladder bent at the knees and began vigorously jolting himself up and down, over and over, stomping-jerking the ladder down in an uproar of quaking aluminum, screeching hinges and winch cables, stomping it all the way down until the bottom step was just a foot above the pier. They could see him clearly now—black, curly hair, big smile, lively eyes, about the same age as el Capitán. He kicked at the platform folded up against the ladder's railing until it was horizontal, but instead of stepping down onto it, the man glanced at the crew on the pier and called something out to them in English and then started immediately back up the ladder. What had he said?—they were words Esteban knew, it had sounded as if he'd said, *I love* and then something else . . . not *you,* it couldn't have been *you,* some other word, no? *I love you?* It had been some other word. Watching the man hurry back up the ladder, Esteban suddenly saw a dog, eyes glinting through the dark, crouched as if frozen in midyawn-stretch near the top, forepaws extended down over two steps.

When the crew carried their luggage up on deck, the grinning man was waiting for them, and the dog, a German shepherd, was standing by his leg, the second German shepherd Esteban had seen that day. For the second time that day Esteban was suddenly and sickeningly reminded of Ana, the East German tracking dog his company had spent an experimental few days following through the jungles of the Río Coco region along the Honduran border; Ana had led a point squad right into a fatal ambush and had just had the time to tear out an already wounded contra's throat before being torn apart by bullets herself. Though the German shepherd at Miami Airport, leashed to a uniformed officer, padding around the baggage carousels sniffing, as if with feigned nonchalance, at everyone's luggage, had seemed much more Ana-like. This German shepherd stood panting loudly, long tongue hanging down, dripping silvery filaments of drool into a puddle between its paws.

The curly haired man was shorter, paler, and stockier than el Capitán, with a full mouth, a short neck, and restless, sharp, brightly dark eyes. His pants were baggy, frayed at the hems over dirty white sneakers, his untucked, short-sleeved shirt mostly unbuttoned over his hairless chest. He held a long, yellow-rubber-encased flashlight in two hands in front of his waist.

El Capitán introduced him as Mark, el primero oficial, or first mate. Then el Capitán did a strange thing; he told them the dog's name before he'd told them his own: Miracle, which he even translated, milagro. Mark stood smiling at them, his eyes beaming cheerfully.

"Y yo me llamo Elias," said el Capitán. "Y soy tu capitán."

Probably Greek, thought Bernardo bitterly. Claro. Scavengers and perverts of all the oceans. The crew stood in a group by the portside rail, backs to the collapsed skeletons of piers and smashed terminals, Capitán Elias, el primero Mark, and Miracle facing them from the gap between plank-battened holds. There were no lights; ship and cove were like a blacked out city, the deck a long expanse of, to Esteban, mainly indistinguishable shapes.

"Be very careful where you walk, muchachos," Capitán Elias said, leading them across the beam. He was so tall, skinny, and erect that in the darkness he looked a part of the ship itself, a long piece of spar that had detached itself and come to life. "There are still some unrepaired spots on deck you can fall through, all the way down to where we won't even be able to hear you calling for help," he said, and for the first time, he laughed, a brief, low titter rising from his chest, fluttering out through his teeth.

Behind the stern, past the grain elevator, and over the port, looking much closer than they could possibly be, Manhattan's clustered skyscrapers glowed, giant rectangles of refrigerated light in the hot sky.

Capitán Elias said, "I'm afraid I have to apologize about the lack of lights and plumbing." There'd been, he said, an accident when the ship, purchased by its new owner, was en route to Brooklyn from a place called New Brunswick, in Canada. A small explosion in the crankcase, causing a fuel line fracture, sprayed fuel, hitting a hot exhaust pipe, which had started a fire. Capitán Elias said the fire had done a *wonderful* job on the ship's electrical wiring and cables. The cables and wiring were connected to the ship's generators, which were connected to the switchboard, which distributed power to the ship's circuit breakers, radar, winch controls, steering gear, plumbing, ventilation, to the hydraulic pumps driving the diesel engine and everything else, nearly all of which, he said, was perfectly shipshape otherwise. So it wasn't really as bad as it sounded. They were still waiting for some spare parts, new circuit breakers, due to arrive any day now from Japan, isn't that right, Mark? In other words, hombres, until the wiring was repaired and the ship was brought up to class and could be newly insured, they would be delayed in port. Lots of deck work to be done too, rust removal, painting, welding, nothing out of the ordinary, it wouldn't take long.

Capitán Elias spoke in a calm, straightforward way, explaining everything meticulously, a man who wore his authority lightly, who wanted to be trusted rather than feared—he reminded Esteban of a certain kind of army officer soldiers trust because they know he's careful, telling them what they need to know instead of trying to inspire them with noisy heroics. But Bernardo was aghast, couldn't believe his ears, because he'd detected a clipped, subdued echo of Capitán J. P. Osbourne's British accent in Elias's perfect nautical Spanish, of a jovial but restrained condescension that inspires respect and obedience rather than resentment—unlike the cynical disdain of Greeks, their boorish capitanes no better than truck drivers. Impossible that this skinny gargoyle dressed like an adolescent could be an English shipmaster! It must be a trick, a nostalgic hallucination summoned by the billowing dread fogging his eyes and ears . . . But in the coming weeks the rest of the crew would realize that Capitán Elias spoke the way he did, saying "Nicara-goo-wah" and "Mana-goo-wah," because his accent *was* British, though tempered by years of living amidst other languages and accents; and his Spanish, especially when he was excited, they would notice, was often peppered with odd bits of slang, mainly Mexican, though soon el Capitán would be adopting theirs' too. *Güey* was a word he would use a lot. *Way*-y-y. "Pinche güeyes." José Mateo, the cook, would say that he'd often heard younger Mexican seamen use that word, which usually didn't seem to mean anything more particular than "you" or "you guys," though sometimes el Capitán would also say, "Don't be such a *güey*."

Capitán Elias said, "The *Urus,* I have to acknowledge, was delivered to its new owner in less than ideal shape. But Mark and I wouldn't have accepted our commissions, hard as maritime work is to come by these days, if we hadn't felt confident about this ship. The engine, the hull and holds, the cargo gear, this is all in excellent condition. If it hadn't been for that fire . . ." and he held out his hands and shrugged. "As soon as she's repaired, we'll sail, with the usual complement of additional officers and crew, who have already been hired and are waiting for us. So this is *our* job, caballeros. The *Urus* is a ship we're all going to feel proud of."

From far out in the harbor came the long blast of a ship's horn, and Capitán Elias paused, seemingly relishing the sound and then the silence, suddenly interrupted by the rising and subsiding yauling of cats coming from somewhere out there amidst the rubble of the cove. Miracle whined. And el Capitán said:

"One more thing. I know you're all tired and want to get to bed, but I think this has to be explained. The *Urus,* of course, has a Panamanian registry . . ."

And he told them to think of it like this: *onboard* they were in Panama, contracted seamen protected by that country's sovereign laws. *Onshore* they were in the United States, where, of course, for the next four days, until their seamen's transit visas expired, they were perfectly legal. But they all knew what rough places port cities could be, and this was one of the most dangerous, especially once they left the port yard and entered the streets around "los proyectos." They didn't know how often the police found murdered seamen on the sidewalks and in the alleys or in abandoned warehouses or floating down some harbor channel at dawn, stripped of wallets and papers, no way for the police to know who they were or where they came from or how to contact their families, they ended up buried in an anonymous pit on a paupers' cemetery island in the harbor while their ships sailed away without them, their crewmates and officers probably assuming their missing mates had just jumped ship, certainly a common enough circumstance.

Capitán Elias said, "Oiga! If you want to jump ship, try your hand at life in New York City, go right ahead, I'm not going to try to stop you." And then he laughed, one of those brief, lugubrious titters. "But please leave us a note or tell somebody if you do, OK? Just so we'll know what happened."

Then el Capitán quickly translated what he'd just said for Mark, and Mark grinned down at his shoes, shaking his head. Some of the crew, including Esteban, forced themselves to smile too.

"Los proyectos," said Capitán Elias, "son problemáticos." The projects ran parallel to this end of the waterfront, on the other side of the wall beyond those trees over there, block upon block of government housing for the very poorest people, with different heavily armed drug gangs controlling different blocks of buildings and stretches of street. They didn't like strangers wandering through, said el Capitán, though of course they saw a foreign seaman as the Golden Goose, wads of shore leave money stuffed into his pockets and not knowing where in hell he was going. Capitán Elias said he would avoid los proyectos entirely if he were them. Drugs onboard, of course, would result in immediate termination of employment. And if you pick up a woman, be sure to use a condom. He looked forward to six months of profitable tramping, hopefully more, who knew where they'd be headed, all over the Caribbean, South America, Europe, the Mediterranean, ports a lot livelier, with a lot more to offer and a lot cheaper, than Brooklyn's.

Then Capitán Elias said that was enough for now, Mark would show them to their cabins. And Mark switched on his flashlight and began to walk towards the deckhouse, the dog following.

As soon as Bernardo and Esteban were alone in their sweltering cabin, the viejo said, "This isn't a miracle. It's a disaster." Later, when the old waiter would adopt the stray cat and teach it to sit like a dog by his side while he sat at his daily chore of sifting and plucking roaches and roach shit from rancid rice, he would even counterbalancingly name the cat that, Desastres. But Miracle would live on, and Desastres would end both disastrously and somewhat miraculously . . .

Mark's flashlight had briefly illuminated a scarred steel box with paint-peeling bulkheads, mattresses laid on the floor, bedding folded on top. Their deck-level cabin, like all the cabins and everything else in the first two stories of the deckhouse anyway, had been stripped of all furnishing or decoration. Even watertight doors and many of the porthole covers had been removed. In the galley and mess el Primero had beamed his flashlight into the dense darkness of an iron cave, showing the cook and waiter a butane gas two-burner stove on a table, some pots and pans and utensils, a hefty wood-paneled water tank mounted on a high steel shelf.

They heard the Mazda start up and drive off the pier, taking their officers and Miracle back to wherever it was they spent their nights. Mosquitoes whined around Esteban's head.

"El Capitán wears a wedding ring," said Bernardo as they made up their beds, both sweating profusely in the airless dark. Esteban, kneeling, leaned back for a moment and laid his palm into a warm puddle where the dog had drooled.

"They both seem buena onda," he said, furtively wiping his hand along the bottom of his mattress. They seemed cheerful, sincere, no?

Their porthole held a broken slice of dirty pane, though no breeze or soft ray of diluted light penetrated its open half. Bernardo pushed the porthole cover all the way open. Then they lay on their beds, unable to see each other. Esteban felt the longing for sleep throbbing through his body, but his mind stayed wide awake. How strange, he thought.

This morning we were all in Nicaragua or Honduras, and now here we are, left alone on a ship with no lights or plumbing on the other side of the world, in the middle of nothing, in *Bruklin,* Nueva York, not far from people supposedly disposed to murder us for money we don't have. He listened for some far-off sound of malignant life from los proyectos, but what he mainly heard was the viejo's dilapidated breathing and heavy sighs.

After a while Bernardo, as if he were talking out loud sadly and only to himself, said, "But luck is this way, verdad? It's not for everybody, no?"

"When the ship is fixed, we'll sail," said Esteban vehemently. "We're still getting paid. Vos, we're getting paid to work, y qué?" It was stifling! And the mosquitoes!

"This ship is a broken eggshell," repeated the viejo flatly. "It's ready for scrap. No lights or plumbing or fans! And el Capitán, I see no capitán there, he's just a deluded niñote, with the air of a pervert no less."

"Why would they have us come all the way up here to work on a ship that's a broken eggshell? Where is the logic in that . . . Bernardo?"

A pervert? He couldn't bear him! He shut his eyes and then opened them again and stared into the darkness and didn't even look over when he heard the old waiter's quiet, wheezy weeping. Why did they have to share a cabin! He clenched his teeth, listened to the silence that wasn't silence at all, to faint scrapings and pattering through the fathomless expanse of floating iron—iron and not, hijueputa, a floating eggshell!

Well, at least the viejo isn't a pato, he thought. His tíos had warned him, but he already knew that ships' crews were supposed to be full of hardened patos. Years of long, lonely voyages leaving them twisted, still wanting women on land, boys at sea. A muchacho like you has to be ready to fight like a cornered tiger in defense of his *physical integrity,* his tío Beny had warned. Watch out for the patos buying you a beer in the mess, dropping a sleeping pill in. But it didn't look like there was going to be any beer for sale on this ship—and no one had ever even been to sea before, except the cook and this weepy old waiter. *Chocho,* viejo! Tranquílase, you'll get your chicken incubators!

In the morning Esteban was the last to wake. He went out on deck and found the rest of the crew gathered at the portside rail, drinking the instant coffee that José Mateo and Bernardo had brewed in the mess and served in plastic cups. There was nothing to eat, Bernardo informed Esteban in a portentous tone, because rats had gotten into the carton of donuts their officers had left them the night before. The coffee burned their fingers through the plastic, so everyone was gingerly balancing his cup on the rail while they stared out in appalled, sleepy silence at the blighted landscape surrounding them. A pile-lined earthen barrier, topped with gravel, enclosed one side of the cove, but to portside the cove was lined with the abandoned, wrecked shells of old warehouses, offices, and shipping terminals—one terminal, its blue paint eroded by age and salt, looked like a giant circus tent, sky showing through its broken slats, faded lettering in English, French, and Arabic over its broad doorways: "Wienstock Spice Co." They saw gulls balanced on one leg atop the stumps of collapsed piers. To stern stood the defunct grain elevator with its cracked, discolored whitewashed facade, and the rubble of the old grain terminal behind.

DESASTRES

1

Now, one hundred and eleven nights later, Esteban lies awake shivering in two rank T-shirts and jeans and rotted socks under his thin blanket on his mattress on the floor, thinking, Oye? What if he just takes the lifeboat? Rows away somewhere. Vos, like that Dutchman who fled Corinto in a rowboat. Row where? Row away or run away. Where?

The cabin's mine-shaft darkness hides the viejo, but Esteban can hear him sleeping or waiting to sleep, his steady but softly sputtering breathing like barely percolating coffee in an old enamel pot. Often Bernardo sleeps with his eyes open, like a mule. The October night's damp chill fills the pitch dark cabins like wet smoke. But only Esteban, though he doesn't realize it, has the beginnings of an asthmatic respiratory condition, caused by so many months of breathing paint fumes and solvents and powdered rust and steel and wet weather and bad, sparse food and that soaring September fever and croupy cough. He doesn't wheeze, his throat doesn't close, and though at times his breathing feels terrifyingly shallow, he exhales freely, so it isn't that kind of asthma. Every time he starts to drift off to sleep, a rebellious spasm in his breathing wakes him to quivering lungs that feel full of cold, bright light, spreading from there into all his nerve endings with a tingling phosphorescence . . .

Chilled nerves aglow and tingling, he thinks, Tonight I escape. Then, hijueputa, why doesn't he get up and move? He needs to visualize this escape in a practical and encouraging way, except he's missing the details, he might as well be planning an escape into the Milky Way as into the city; and so it's just another insomniac fantasy, not even soothing, though few of his nighttime fantasies, thoughts, scenarios are ever soothing. Where will he go in the city?

And what does Bernardo see, sleeping with his eyes open? Happy things or sorrowful? Though Esteban can't see him in the dark of the cabin, the viejo sleeps and dreams that way now, eyeballs like glimmerless frogs' heads protruding from black, still water in a jungle-canopied bog. Bernardo is dreaming that he's in the officers' saloon pantry on a ship steadily approaching a great port; he's finished washing up the officers' silverware, and now he's laying bananas into a wicker basket for the morning. Though the engines have been slowed, the ship's bulkheads vibrate from the propeller's churning the too shallow water of the channel. Tugs bump up alongside, softly jolting the ship. He lays out a new tablecloth on the officers' dining table, sets it for breakfast. The officers' smoking lounge, the gleaming galley are both deserted. He steps out into the corridor, and hearing the sound of dominoes slapped down on a tabletop coming from the crew's mess, looks inside, sees dominoes arrayed over a table, four empty chairs. He climbs the stairs to his cabin to change for a night onshore, seeing no one. He goes outside onto a rear deck for a smoke, and glancing up at the bridge wings, he's surprised to see no one there either, no harbor pilot or shipmaster or officers. He climbs the steps to a wing and finds the bridge completely empty too, wheelhouse panels and radar screens glowing, no one manning the quivering wheel, a lamp on over the nautical charts table and no one there. Directly beneath the wing a tug, at a skewed angle like a feeding pilot fish, churns alongside the hull. A long, narrowing, double row of red and white buoy lights marks the channel through the placid, wide waters leading to the city illuminated on the horizon . . . When the ship is finally settled alongside a pier, he sees mooring lines flung out from the deck, snaking through the air, but he sees no one tossing them, no one on the pier to catch them. Cargo cranes like long-necked, petrified dinosaurs rising in the quiet night over warehouse sheds, the cluttered yard, but he sees no stevedores, no parked vehicles that could belong to waiting shipping agents or immigration officials. Yet when he goes down on deck and descends the accommodation ladder to the pier, he finds a yellow taxi waiting there. There's a driver at least, a moreno with a thick, wrinkled neck, though he never speaks or turns around to glance at him as they drive into the city, nor is there any reflection of the driver's face in the rearview mirror. They drive through the poor people's neighborhoods beyond the port, darkened, shabby buildings and streets, no traffic, no one out walking. Suddenly they pass a small, whitewashed building with strung lightbulbs around the door and along the roof, the parking lot crowded with milling moreno men in white T-shirts holding paper cups and bottles in brown bags, and then it's dark and deserted again, and there isn't even a driver anymore, the taxi is driving itself, the driver must have gotten out to join the other men back there. Now quiet panic floods his chest. The taxi pulls over to a curb, and he opens the door, gets out, and the driverless taxi drives off. He's on Bourbon Street, in New Orleans; of course he's been here before. But everything looks closed, though here and there he sees illuminated neon signs protruding over the sidewalk, colors softened by the mist hanging over the street and the streetlights' wreaths of silvery vapor. He walks down the long row of shuttered restaurants, bars, stores, signs displaying nude women. He feels neither happy nor sad now, neither frightened nor at ease. But he's glad he didn't have to pay for the taxi. And he has an adamant erection. The ship leaves in a few hours, he doesn't have much time to enjoy his time onshore, that's what he's thinking. He finds a bar, its front open to the street, glowing beer signs, a jukebox, racked glasses and bottles behind the long, empty bar. He sits at the bar, but there's no bartender. He sees himself sitting there in his clean, fresh clothes, with this unsated and hopeless though nonetheless pleasing erection in his pants, his expression satisfied and patient over having found at least this one place still open. After a while he gets up and goes behind the bar and pours himself a draft beer and carries it back to his stool and sits there slowly drinking it, looking out at the graying, neon-tinged street. He realizes he's on the very verge of comprehending something, that there is something he's always believed to be true that in fact is not, he feels it in his chest, this new yet still wordless certainty suspensefully dawning . . .

A frog, an ear, a worm, a tic, a beast, a black marketeer and speculator and a pato—the Dutchman owned a hardware store with a house attached near the Corinto port gates, and La Turba came and painted his walls with those insults, then stood out in the street chanting and screaming them. And the Dutchman came out of his house and walked right through La Turba, eyes burning straight ahead, face and even bald head glowing red with fury and humiliation like some just defrocked priest, walked all the way down to the beach while the jeering mob and excited children, including Esteban, followed and the Dutchman pulled a rowboat off the sand and into the water without even taking off his shoes or rolling up his pants and got in and started to row. While he was still close to shore he looked ridiculous, a splenetic and exaggerated Dutchman rowing, but the more he dwindled from sight, the more his emphatic dignity seemed to grow. Everyone watched until he was just a fleck against the sunset, the color-enflamed sky seeming to proclaim his radical strength. And when night swallowed the Dutchman up, even the darkened ocean seemed fretful with chastened worry. Esteban had thought it an almost magical act and confused himself, ardently hoping a passing ship or fishing boat had eventually picked the Dutchman up or that he'd at least reached an island and hadn't rowed into a mine. But even back then he knew to keep such thoughts to himself in front of his tíos, who accused La Turba of murder, his tíos who were modest bisneros, dollar hoarders, speculators, and black marketeers themselves. That was the year la CIA mined the harbor, blowing up that Japanese freighter and another, Panamanian like this one, and attacked and burned the oil storage tanks, black smoke and flames billowing into the sky like a volcanic eruption . . .

He'll row out to sea like the Dutchman did. Just sit in the lifeboat waiting out there for a real ship to pass like the Dutchman must have, pick him up, give him work, wash dishes, anything, get his life going again just like that! The *Urus* has a lifeboat, and another embarkation deck where another lifeboat should be. Not like they'll be needing lifeboats anytime soon, no? One afternoon a few weeks after they'd arrived, Capitán Elias suddenly ordered a lifeboat drill. They'd already spent much of that heat-torched day repairing the jammed, rusted winches that cranked the lifeboat davits forward and back over the embarkation deck—and finally succeeded! Seven ordinary seamen, including Esteban, hands, arms, and clothing black with warm lubricating grease, crowded in and sat in the boat waiting like nervously grinning astronauts for it to drop. But el Capitán stood by the release lever just watching, his lids partly lowered over something like contemptuous amazement in his eyes, thin lips pinching a paper clip smirk into his cheek, until an oppressive suspense filled the boat with a weight heavier than water. Capitán Elias, who was usually so polite and even friendly! Suddenly helpless rage had flooded Esteban like waves of nausea before vomiting: in a flash he'd understood that Capitán Elias had only ordered them into the lifeboat because he was frustrated and bored and for some reason had decided it would be amusing to see them sitting there—as if seeing them sitting there like that somehow confirmed some idea he already had about them! But the crew had been excited and eager to test the lifeboat because they were frustrated and bored too, and at least they'd fixed the winches! Capitán Elias then coolly said that that was enough, what did they think, that he was really going to drop the lifeboat? How were they going to bring it back up? Did they want to dive into that steamy muck and swim around, haul it out and carry it back up themselves? And when el Capitán turned away, he laughed, a high-pitched, short yelp of a laugh. They remained sitting in the boat, humiliated and stunned, as if each was privately wondering what he could do to recover his pride *right now* and coming up with nothing. Then, without uttering anything but a few low curses, they climbed out one by one . . .

Sometimes, when Esteban is alone in the cabin and is sure that Bernardo is busy in the mess or with some other chore, he reaches into his suitcase and pulls out the dirty green sock which by now is his cleanest and most intact sock but which he has sacrificed to the wristwatch he keeps hidden inside—when capitán or primero isn't there, it's the only working watch or clock onboard now, the two clocks the crew has left being useless since they have electrical cords attached. It's a little Mickey Mouse watch, with a red plastic strap, and though it still works, he's never even adjusted it for the time zones passed through flying to New York. Sometimes he stares at the time as if at a mildly interesting insect wriggling in the palm of his hand. Usually he lies back on his bed and holds the watch to his nose, his lips, the worn-smooth plastic back of this watch, which holds no lingering scent or taste of her though it rode against her skin for however long she owned it before she gave it to him. Just as the time it counts, ticking forward, holds no trace of her either. Often he goes more than a week without taking the watch out and looking at it. Sometimes he just reaches into the suitcase, squeezes the sock, thumbs the hard little shape inside.

Sometimes it drizzles for days at a time, the sky a cold sponge of gloom pressing down on the ship, frigid puddles seeping into their cabins—they miss the warm, sudden downpours of summer falling like hammer blows all over the ship, the thunder and lightning that made them feel as if they were in a savage storm at sea on a ship so sturdily navigated that not even a tidal wave could lift it or make it roll.

Sometimes they see hawks and falcons circling, colorless, sharp specks high in the sky; they've never seen one dive towards the cove, but they've seen them doing so farther away, beyond the blocked horizon, out over the harbor. And in the sky over Brooklyn, they regularly see faraway, tight flocks of pigeons swooping and dipping like giant kites. Gull shit rains down on them.

Sometimes at night Esteban hears brief crackles of gunfire in the distance, thinks of ambushes that are over in the time it takes a column of bodies to fall down, in the time it takes for a column of troop-jammed trucks to turn into an immobile wall of torn and twisted steel, smoke, blood, and screams . . .

No one is quite the same person he was when he arrived in June, not on the outside, certainly not on the inside: time fills them like the stagnant air in a flourishing mushroom cellar.

A dead ship, a mass of inert iron provocatively shaped like a ship, holds no snug dreamers at night, just fifteen fucked up marineros shivering and waiting for sleep. Every night they send themselves out on the same forced marches through the same interior landscapes of recalled, imagined, and reimagined pleasures, mostly having to do with love. But even the most pleasing and arousing and seemingly reliable love scenarios become harder and harder to bring to life after too many visits—though these keep smiling invitingly as if nothing has changed, smiling as if they really wish nothing had changed and are maybe even denying to themselves that they've grown bored and just don't desire their lonely marinero's callused touch anymore, they say tomorrow night it will be OK again but then it's even worse; they fade, turn coldly reluctant and finally exasperatingly dull; they break your heart a little, when you just can't bring a favorite love scenario to spectral life anymore. Then you have to, just have to turn to something or somebody else . . .

But insomnia is also like another person lying in bed beside you, verdad, Esteban? It's yourself, keeping you company. Your mind, lying brightly awake beside you, while you turn away from it, burying your face into a stinking mattress, your body exhausted from being exhausted. Insomnia is a woman lying perfectly still beside you while you toss and turn, Estebanito, sometimes she reaches out a dry, cool hand and caresses your pene so stealthily that not even the viejo sleeping with his eyes open will notice; or sometimes she reaches out a hand and touches your shoulder, reaches out all the way from that warmly lit, yellow-painted room in León; she's one of two sisters who shares it, although, Esteban, she's also lying right there beside you at the same time. It's a school night and they're listening to El Amante Loco de La Loma's radio show. For all the manly Castilian butter of his voice, they say El Amante Loco is actually a Spanish dwarf who came to León with a Mexican circus and then stayed behind. But what a voice! She told Esteban once that just hearing it made girls shiver and smile. All you men out there, listen to what El Amante Loco de La Loma has to tell you: A woman doesn't want your resentments, jealousies, your crazy bad thoughts, save that for the cantina, compañeros, or for that sad song you're going to write, set it to music and then pretend it doesn't belong to you. A woman wants joy, happiness, pleasure, and if she tells you she wants you to be that new modern man, to open up that sad birdcage in your heart and let all your complaints and worries and misfortunes come hopping, squawking and flapping out, don't do it 'manos. Listen to El Amante Loco, he's never wrong, never milks the wrong leg, amputates the wrong cow, pollinates the wrong train, boards the wrong flower, and now for this marvelous old bolero from Bola de Nieve . . . La Marta sits on the bed combing and combing her hair while the bolero plays, solemnly frowning as she forces herself to remember all the brave young compañeros fighting at the war fronts, her sister sitting on the opposite bed with an examination book open on her lap, lightly obliterating with her pencil eraser some equation she's just realized she set down wrong. Both sisters wear long, loose, white T-shirts to bed, and lately Esteban lets himself briefly savor the smooth, sturdy curve of her bare thighs leading back into the shadowy crevice, a glossy centimeter of scar tissue on her gleaming shin like a foreboding amidst soft, brown angel's hair. How long do we have left to live, sister? How many months and days left to you, to me? It will happen twenty-three days after the true love thing. Shhh, grosera, good night, turn off that ridiculous Amante Loco. Do you think he tells the truth? Leave the light on so Esteban can watch us. He doesn't need light. His brain and lungs are full of light . . .

Esteban pushes off his blankets, sits up gasping cold air. He's never told Bernardo, never told anyone onboard, about the volunteer nightmare battalion from León, about la Marta and her sister. Once he told the viejo about Ana, the German shepherd tracking dog, and he kicked up such a hysterical fuss Esteban swore never to mention war to him again.

He sits at the edge of the mattress tying on his boots with electrical wire laces and moments later steps from the short passageway out onto the deck and looks up at the lights of small planes scattering like mercury beads into the far corners of the night. A helicopter banking towards the glowing skyscrapers, abandoning its futile search for some sign of life from the *Urus* and her crew buried somewhere down there in the darkness. The decanted thunder of yet another descending airliner. The night sky is always busy, always awake too.

2

THEY FOUND A RAT SKELETON AT THE BOTTOM OF THEIR WATER TANK THE first time they took it down to refill it at the spigot at the foot of the pier, that's why everyone but Panzón and Miracle was so sick those first few days in June; even Capitán Elias and Mark, but everyone knows *they* went to see doctors. But Capitán Elias brought them a clear plastic jug filled with something watery and almost tasteless to drink; it made everyone's diarrhea worse and then left them constipated for three days. Sometimes, they've noticed, Mark, with a touch of friendly mockery, calls Elias "Doc." Capitán Elias seems to know almost everything about the mechanical workings of ships, and el primero Mark seems to know almost nothing, though they can't know this for sure, since he doesn't speak Spanish.

By the end of that first week onboard, nearly everybody already had a nickname: Panzón, sagging stomach so strong he was the only one who hadn't gotten sick from rat water; burly El Barbie, after the doll, because he's so loud, ugly, and macho; El Tinieblas, his hard, thin body covered with prison tattoos, a vivid black scorpion on each forearm, always speaking in whispers as if hiding in dangerous Darkness; Cebo, radiantly good-natured and built like an Adonis from so many years of deep-sea free diving for lobster, no one was sure exactly why Tomaso Tostado had decided to call him Fish Bait, but it seemed hilarious the first time and stuck; El Faro, the Lighthouse, wearing glasses and smilingly nodding and agreeing with whatever anyone says; Bonnie Mackenzie, El Buzo, his skin like a skin diver's wet suit; Cabezón with his big head; Chávez Roque, Roque Balboa; Caratumba, the only Guatemalan; Pínpoyo, the pretty boy electrician; Canario. They'd tried Rambo on Esteban, and then El Piricuaco or El Piri, which means Rabid Dog, which the Hondurans knew was what la contra called their enemies in Nicaragua, but both names always made him look befuddled-crestfallen and later they'd come up with El Nieto because he was like the viejo's grandson, but that wouldn't stick either, maybe Esteban is slippery with nicknames (though in his BLI he'd eventually had one which made him blush and grin like crazy . . .). With a name like Tomaso Tostado, Tomaso Tostado doesn't need a nickname. Bernardo is just the viejo, and José Mateo is just the cook, Cocinero.

Throughout that first month Capitán Elias and el primero Mark were still coming to the ship every day, even Sundays, to share and guide the crew's labor. They worked right alongside the crew from morning until dark and often later, their commitment to the task of repairing the ship setting a tone of concentrated urgency and optimism: they were in a hurry. They didn't have all the time in the world. The port berthing fees were costing the owner a fortune. Soon the ship would sail. On hands and knees under the barbed sun, the ordinary seamen scraped, sanded, and chipped, scrubbed with wire brushes; and so did Mark, melting with sweat, cheerlessly and silently grimacing like a man clawing a tunnel out of prison with his fingernails. Orange extension cords and pneumatic cables ran from the generator and compressor on the pier up onboard, powering the few disc sanders, chipping hammers, grinders, and blowtorches they took turns using; plumber's lamps for working below deck. All day long the industrial shriek of tools blasting iron numbed their ears and doubts. Capitán Elias, the electricians and mechanics immersed themselves in the engine room, attacking the dead forest of wiring and generator at their scorched roots, huddling over el Capitán's small library of well-thumbed, grease-stained engineer's and electrician's manuals . . .

Capitán Elias and el Primero always lock up the generator and compressor on their pier and take the keys with them when they drive off at night with Miracle in the back of the Mazda. Mark, when he and Miracle come alone—Miracle is Mark's dog—drives a maize-colored Honda. Where do they go at night? Where do they live? They live *in the city*. Capitán Elias says his wife is an artist and a university professor—"An artist first," Esteban heard him say once, "a professor second, and a wife, though she does love me, a distant third, soon to be an even more distant, over the horizon let's say, fourth"—el Capitán's wife is "expecting a baby." El Capitán says his wife's belly "is like a melon." Hmmmm, qué rico. Why doesn't el Capitán ever think to bring them a few melons? Even one melon. It would be great to eat a melon.

Sometimes, when he's in the mood, Capitán Elias becomes curious about the crew and politely asks them all sorts of questions about themselves, his tender sheep eyes so attentively fixed on their faces as they answer. And sometimes they question him. Capitán Elias says his father is British and his mother Greek, and mainly he's lived in London, right here in New York, and all over Latin America, in the Amazon even, that's why his Spanish is so good. He studied mechanical engineering, engine room mechanics, and ship design before switching to navigation and officer's training at a nautical academy in Greece. He also studied medicine in London for a while. He's tried his hand at lots of things, he's very educated and worldly. This is the second time he's been hired as a shipmaster. He says that someday he would like to open up a first-class Greek restaurant in New York, and own his own small fleet of cargo ships, and spend part of every winter in the Aegean and summers in Wiltshire, which is in the English campo. Personal questions always make Mark grimace; he never tells them anything about himself, hiding easily behind his lack of Spanish. Though Mark's private life seems to be a constant topic of conversation between him and Elias, with el Capitán always seeming to give advice, which Mark eagerly or miserably accepts, nodding, ruefully smiling, frowning, or wincing. When Capitán Elias talks to Mark, he talks very fast, one hand hatcheting up and down, his vivid eyebrows fusing close together over his suddenly narrowing eyes, and sometimes, when he seems excited about the point he's about to make, he pauses, then launches it in a surprisingly high, almost whinnying voice while his eyebrows arch up too. A few times el Capitán has turned to whichever crewmen might be standing nearby to translate what he's been telling Mark and to ask what they think, and then laughed at Mark in a delightedly mocking way, while Mark scowled and rolled his eyes or grinned with embarrassment. Esteban was standing nearby the time Capitán Elias said that about women not wanting to hear a man's resentments, jealousies, and crazy bad thoughts: "Mark has to learn not to whine in front of his women, no matter how much they love him, am I right, Esteban?" el Capitán asked. And Esteban taciturnly agreed, then spent the day pondering the advice. Though it didn't seem to apply to any way he'd ever yet behaved, it seemed worth remembering. There's something very unrelaxed and unhappy about el Primero, even though he smiles a lot and doesn't ever seem mean-spirited the way el Capitán occasionally does.

Capitán Elias keeps access to the bridge, officers' quarters, and wings locked at night too, though they've all been up there in the day, where everything has been stripped bare of the teak paneling and brass fittings Bernardo says would usually cover the walls of the officers' quarters on such a ship. Capitán Elias and Mark keep a table, a few chairs, a radio–cassette player, and two mattresses up on the bridge, though they never stay the night. The only remnant of the officers' quarters' presumed former luxury are three black-and-white tiled, nearly square, sunken bathtubs, each in its own cabinetlike little room. These are Japanese, Capitán Elias has explained, they work something like steam baths. Let's fix the electrical problem, muchachos; once we have plumbing again we'll get these baths going and then we can all sink our bodies down into those boxes of hot water and steam, have Japanese baths. Won't that, el Capitán adds in English, exaggerating his usual accent, be bloody fucking marvelous. So the ship's previous owners and officers, according to Capitán Elias, were Japanese. That explains the leftover sacks of roach-infested rice and the musty box of chopsticks they found in the galley, the rotted crates of rusting sardine cans left behind in a deep corner of the hold.

From the starboard bridge wing they can see all the way across the harbor to the opposite shore: ships and fragile-looking cargo cranes in the ocean-hazed distance, oil refinery and storage tanks, factory smokestacks, bridges, church steeples, smoky hills beyond; looking south over waterfront warehouse and terminal roofs and trees, they can see the upper portion of the Statue of Liberty out in the harbor, green, oxidized arm in the air.

The first time he climbed up there for a look Bernardo said, "When that statue walks, chavalos, this ship will sail."

The viejo never passes up an opportunity to remind them.

Throughout the hot summer months, until just a few weeks ago, noisy groups of teenage morenos often came late at night to sit at the end of the pier, under the *Urus*'s prow. Los blacks was what Capitán Elias called them, and soon most of the crew began calling them that too. They were the only people during all those months that the crew saw from the ship at night, though sometimes cars drove into the lot behind the grain terminal's ruins, stayed awhile, drove off into their own wobbling tunnels of light. Usually los blacks had two or more music boxes, all tuned to the same radio station; they drank beer from quart bottles and passed marijuana cigars, listening to their booming, shouted music. Sitting well out of sight up on the darkened deck, the crew always felt aroused by the sweetly pungent smoke—sometimes marijuana smelled like deliciously roasting meat—it made their taste glands tighten, faintly drifting up through harbor rot mixed with burning tobacco leaf, radio music and deejay crowing, laughter and shouted speeches. City life and sexiness happening just under their noses, down there on the pier! The crew tried to avoid any mention of the one night they'd left the ship and cut through los proyectos on their way into Brooklyn and Capitán Elias's warning had come true; it was too depressing to talk about, the humiliation and their own cowering terror still popping away like camera flashes inside them whenever they thought about it or even imagined the possibility of lowering the ladder and trying to join the parties on the pier. Sometimes los blacks smoked something else in little stems they held like toy whistles to their lips, though the odor didn't seem to reach them. Capitán Elias said it was "crack," and in the mornings he'd often pause to idly kick the little glass vials this drug came in off the pier.

When los blacks left the pier at night, walking off with music boxes carried on their shoulders like high-caliber machine guns, they liked to stop and hurl their empty beer bottles against the hull. Whether they were still out on the darkened deck or already in bed, the crew heard the soft smashes far below as if from a mountaintop; the sounds recalled them to the immense emptiness of iron their deck rested on. And the silence after somehow left them feeling even more left alone.

The afternoon's blazing sun and heat languished in the mess and cabins at night like an invisible fever patient, so they ate dinner outside, sitting along the four raised coamings of the cargo hatch closest to the deckhouse, backs to the open hold, most of them shirtless and barefoot, oblivious of mosquitoes. But they rarely took off their heavy, paint-sweat-grease-and-grime-saturated pants: they looked down a little on men who wore shorts—though Mark and even el Capitán sometimes wore shorts—never mind those who went around in rotting underwear, and anyway, most had stopped wearing underwear. They still had razor blades to share then but used and reused them sparingly, shaving with cold water and soap down on the pier—only twice since has Capitán Elias remembered to bring them a bag of plastic, disposable razors. Blood dribbled constantly from chins cut by worn blades. They washed every day, but it was as if their skins were becoming unwashably filmed over. By late summer they were no longer taken by surprise by the sight of one another: increasingly sad eyed, shaggy, and dirty as young corpses risen from graves.

They'd worked until well after dark one night, and by the time dinner was ready, los blacks were already out on the pier. Bernardo carried the metal plates out from the mess two at a time, finally bringing out his own and the cook's. Rice and canned peas fried in cooking oil, sardines mashed in, that was what they were eating, plates on their laps, the night the first bottle smashed into the deck near where they were sitting. They stared at the spray of barely glimmering shards. Some stood up with plates in their hands, cursing softly. Seconds later another bottle shattered like a handful of hard-flung coins against a wheelhouse window.

So now, along with the usual bombardments of gull shit, this new problem of bottles falling out of the sky. And now they had to keep their shoes and boots on at night too, their burning, suffocated toes and feet infuriated.

Then los blacks began holding contests, trying to hit different parts of the ship with bottles, aiming for the bridge or the masts. They heaved bottles as high into the air as they could, arcing them over the hull and onto the deck, shouting and disputing amongst themselves over how close they'd come to hitting their targets. It was strange to sit there, laconically staring off or talking quietly as usual, a few huddled around Pínpoyo's dominoes, while others passed around the rice pot to scrape up a handful of el raspado, the crunchy rice seared to the bottom—in those months, they sometimes even had sugar to sprinkle over it—and then a bottle suddenly smashing and raining glass from above or hitting the deck, crew members jolted to their feet, covering their heads with crossed arms, Desastres the cat speeding off to hide. It plunged them into miserable silences and tirades of cursing, sent waves of adrenaline coursing through helpless limbs and spirits. The bottles always broke; they couldn't even pick one up and hurl it back. What should they do, throw wrenches down at them instead? In the engine room they have wrenches as big as tennis racquets. Without even having to discuss it much, the crew knew that shouting, Oye, stop throwing bottles up here! would probably only incite even more bottle throwing. It was a good thing that los blacks usually drank beer by the quart and quickly ran out of bottles.

One night Tomaso Tostado and Cebo swore they saw a bottle plummet through a small, square hole in the deck, about two feet wide, one of those they hadn't patched and welded yet, heard it simultaneously break and splash down in the boggy bottom of the hold, the sound so muffled that those who hadn't seen the bottle fall through the hole didn't even lift their heads or ask, What was that?

When los blacks were on the pier the crew avoided standing by the rail and spoke among themselves in near whispers. As far as they could tell, los blacks were unaware that there was anyone onboard, or at least they didn't seem to care. The ladder was always up, the ship always silent and dark, a dead ship on its way to scrap, a target practice ship, one more waterfront ruin. But there were also nights when los blacks didn't throw bottles, not up on deck anyway.

Sometimes they lost themselves in long, nearly serene dance parties, trancing rhythm burning away the pumping, angry vehemence of much of the music like sun a layer of mist. Most of the crew, even Bernardo some nights but never the cook, would climb the nine rungs of the two steel ladders to the foredeck, get down on all fours, and crawl to the gunwales, raising their heads up under the rail just enough to watch. Spidery, beautiful, hypnotic, often wicked-looking dances. Girls slowly rubbing their own crotches to the music and letting everybody see, one arm extended and flapping, the boys taking on one powerful, sexual, or magically robotic pose after another; they looked like bodies endlessly stepping out of their own bodies to become other bodies. And dances that looked almost like extravagant games of hopscotch, dazzling footsteps, hopping sliding hopping and arms flailing. Some of them had amazing haircuts, with designs and even words that looked branded into shaved skulls; girls with hair braided into mop strings and tentacles. They wore big, loose, unbuttoned shirts that billowed like Arabian robes when they danced and sweatsuit tops unzipped over thin, muscular chests and stomachs; some went shirtless, flashes of gold, basketball sneakers like Mark's, baseball hats worn sideways, backwards; some of the girls wore skintight, sleeveless tops or short dresses, the brown gleam of bare limbs and shoulders against black water and night. Sunglasses in the dark.

But one night when the crew was watching, a muchacho wearing a tight black T-shirt, fatigue pants, and combat boots suddenly broke away from the others and came silently and exaggeratedly high-stepping on tiptoes like a circus clown down the pier, then stopped directly underneath them and stared up, his muscular arm rigidly pointing. He held that outraged stare and statuelike posture, pointing up at them, for a long time. Some of the crew slid or rolled away backwards, but others, including Esteban, stayed in frozen crouches at the rail. And then this muchacho started to shout, enraged, crazy shouting, as if maybe he was just playing at being angry, *fucks* and *mothuhfucks* but otherwise they couldn't understand a word he was saying. Then some of the others—looking up from the end of the pier or walking slowly towards him, eyes up to see what he was pointing at—began to shout and laugh too. A bottle smashed against the anchor windlass, near where Canario and Roque Balboa were crouching, glass spraying over their backs. Everyone pulled back from the rail when another bottle whizzed overhead. Esteban had been trying to picture the facial features of this one muchacha down at the end of the pier. It was too dark and she was too far away for him to see what she really looked like, but she'd so prettily hopped and flopped around, awakening something inside him that was screaming for prettiness and hopping and flopping, her eyes bright, her braids flying, sí pues, she'd really gotten him going for a bit, imagining the love affair, inviting her up into his cabin and finally running away with her into a new city life of hopping and flopping and fucking and everything else— But look, there she is screaming up and laughing at us too, I could drop a wrench right down into her mouth, smash those white teeth like glass too. In Nicaragua we end up not just screaming and throwing bottles, we slaughter each other. And they give us the best weapons on earth to do it. Y qué? What does any of that have to do with this?

Some of los blacks seemed to come to the pier every night, and others came now and then or maybe even just once; they never came when it rained. The crew didn't recognize anyone from the night they'd been attacked while crossing los proyectos—the one Esteban watched for was fat and wore a small gold loop in each earlobe. But now that they'd been discovered, los blacks grew more and more interested in the crew, actually seeming to absorb the crew's silent, furtive presence up there on a darkened ship into what they came to the pier to do at night. Almost nightly at least someone took a turn shouting taunts up at them, usually incomprehensibly, though sometimes they understood, *"You fucked you fucked you po mothuhfucks fucked . . . ,"* on and on like a chant. Then at least El Barbie shouting back that they could go fuck their putamadres and suck on their putamadres' farts, always something elegant like that. Los blacks seemed to know something about the *Urus;* it was as if they'd somehow figured out what the crew's situation was.

They spray-painted DEATH SHIP on the grain elevator, and skulls over crossed bones, and another night someone even wrote, CAGUERO DE LA MUERTE, which seemed to mean "Shitter of Death," though they probably meant "Cargo Ship of Death," leaving out the *r* in *carguero,* but, the grain elevator being the crew's latrine, maybe they did mean that. They scribbled with spray paint all over the generator and compressors' shields.

Esteban and the others talked it over at length one night. "This thing that is happening to us here," said Esteban, trying to imitate the slow, somber, reasoning-out-loud tone of his political officer in the BLI, "seems funny to them. But it also seems to make them angry. Why? Bueno . . . ," and his index finger froze pensively over his lips—chocho, there was an impressive word his political officer might have used to explain this situation, what was it?

"Because what is happening to us here, vos Piri"—El Barbie sneered—"is very funny, but it also makes them sick to live on the same planet with a bunch of helpless losers who don't know how to fight back. The stone fits the frog, no?"

The cook growled, "That is unjust." And El Faro, squinting around at everybody without his eyeglasses and excitedly nodding, exclaimed, "Sí pues! Fight back!" While Bernardo glared at El Barbie the way he always does whenever anyone taunts Esteban with the name Piri.

But Esteban was sitting on deck with his index finger still curled against his upper lip, because he'd suddenly remembered the words *lumpen proletariat,* and they had made him feel even more apathetic and pointlessly far away from himself.

"All this fucking broken glass everywhere! It just doesn't go with me, to do nothing back," said El Barbie. "Omar Usareli doesn't take shit from anybody!" El Barbie's name is Omar Usareli.

"That's why you live with your tongue up el Capitán's culo, eh?" said Bernardo. "Who are you to talk about fighting back?"

El Barbie stared threateningly at Bernardo, and Tomaso Tostado put up his hands and said, "Ya! Stop talking babosadas! Hijo de la gran puta, we're all in this together!"

And sweet-natured Cebo suggested lowering the ladder and inviting los blacks up for a talk, and everyone gaped at him.

"Why not, why not try and talk to them?" said El Faro.

"Hombre, are you crazy?" said Roque Balboa. "Remember what happened en los proyectos? You've already forgotten how you lost your glasses?"

"Qué mariconada," said El Tinieblas, picking up a length of rusted chain. "Look at all the shit we have up here to hit them with. And that night, we didn't have anything."

"And if one of them has a gun?" said Pínpoyo. "Remember that scene in Indiana Yones, the guy with the big sword is ready to cut off his head and Indiana Yones pulls out a gun and shoots him!"

"It's true, vos," said Caratumba, the terse Guatemalteco. "Some of them will probably have guns."

"Why don't we just send El Buzo down to talk to them?" said El Barbie. "He's a mandingo."

El Buzo, leaning on the rail with his curly goat's beard and chin resting in his hand, looked at El Barbie with a deadpan gaze for a moment, then said, "Brother, yo no me meto con nadie." That's one of El Buzo's favorite refrains: even when playing a double domino he always says that he doesn't get in anyone's way.

"They're just cruel delinquents," said Bernardo.

"Vos, son lumpen!" Esteban suddenly exclaimed, and everyone looked at him curiously, waiting for him to say something more.

"Lumpen jodido," he added. "Fucked lumpen, just like us."

"Y qué?" said Roque Balboa.

"Y qué," said Esteban. "I know."

"What's lumpen?" asked Canario.

"Pobre Esteban." Panzón chuckled, giving him a soft clap on the shoulder. "Still a communist."

One night El Barbie, obsessed with the idea of turning a bottle into a Molotov cocktail and pitching it back, stood on deck for hours with his eyes trained on the sky, hoping to catch one before it landed. He didn't even come close, since there was no way of telling when or where the next bottle was coming, but he almost broke his face tripping over a chock. Esteban hoped Barbie would run right into one of the holes on deck and disappear.

At first, in the mornings, Capitán Elias interrogated the crew about los blacks. What do they do, what do they want, what do they say? He seemed desperate for more information, but they had little to add to what they'd already told. Capitán Elias obviously didn't like it that los blacks were coming to the pier at night, but Esteban noticed he didn't seem to know what to do about it. He noticed, for example, that Capitán Elias didn't mention calling the police or even port security. Then el Capitán stopped asking about los blacks altogether, though he still went out to the end of the pier every morning as soon as he arrived, kicking the glass vials into the water whenever he found some there; and whenever he found even a shard of glass on deck, he scolded the crew for not having swept up.

Los blacks all came, they imagined, from los proyectos, that labyrinth of brown brick buildings that begins opposite the port yard walls and the trees and the block of mainly warehouse-lined streets parallel to the waterfront. Few streets cross los proyectos, though there are sidewalks and a grass mall and trees and park benches, and at night the brick buildings with their lights on seem to run on in serene, shadowy repetition forever. They'd only been "delayed in port for repairs" a little more than a week the night they'd decided to disregard el Capitán's warnings. They wanted to see Brooklyn, they wanted to go for a walk, post some letters, buy some beers. José Mateo, the cook, had been in Brooklyn, years ago, must have been somewhere around here, he remembered a bar whose Puerto Rican owner would drive him and his crewmates back to their ship after the bar closed so they wouldn't have to walk back; it was dangerous back then too. But who was going to attack fifteen marineros? They were more worried about running into Immigration Police, ending up in one of those underground cells el Capitán had told them about, put to work cracking walnuts open with their teeth.

It was another humid, moon-smothering night. They stood around the spigot at the foot of the pier and a rusted barrel filled with water scummed by soap, grime, insects, their decrepit oasis, stripped down to wash, though Esteban felt that all soap did was grease the layers of stickiness all over himself enough to swirl them around a little. They jogged naked back up the ladder, clothing bundled in their hands. In their cabins, many dressed in their best. Pínpoyo's cologne was called Siete Machos, and he splashed some into Esteban's hands, stinging his blisters. Pínpoyo is handsome like a puppy-eyed pop star, like Chayanne, looks much younger than his nineteen years, carries himself like a baby-faced galán, that's why the crew calls him Pínpoyo. The pressed white trousers and the shirt that looked like fireworks against black sky were still in dry-cleaning plastic when he unfolded them from his suitcase. His immaculate white leather cowboy boots had been kissed by lipstick-smeared lips over both narrowing tips. The woman and Pínpoyo had been in bed, both naked except for him in his boots, when she reapplied her lipstick and kissed his boots right there with her juicy chunche right in his face like this, that's what he told Esteban in his cabin, smiling, hands out by both sides of his face grasping invisible nalgas, eyes bright with the memory and now the telling. Esteban stared at the kisses on the boots and exclaimed, "No jodas!" Pínpoyo said he'd only worn the boots that once; his idea was to have them completely covered with kisses by the time their tour was up, collected one woman at a time, port by port, wouldn't that be putamadre? "No jodas!"—he'd heard and seen a lot of crazy things in his life! But for some reason this reminded Esteban of Rigoberto Mazariego, who brought his novia's childhood doll to war with him, a naked plastic doll with blue glass eyes and a wild tangle of reddish hair, took it everywhere, on patrol, into combat, charging up jungly slopes cradling the doll against his ribs with one hand and his AK out in his other, flopping down under fire, charging back up, calmly setting the doll down beside him when he needed both hands to aim and fire, he and the doll did great, neither ever wounded, not even during the ambush on the Zompopera Road, slept with it, ate with it, bathed it. But was Pínpoyo's thing with his boots like that? Or was it more like Otílio de la Rosa's fish and hummingbird tattoo, which was now an embarrassment to him?

Too bad for Canario; he picked the double-six domino, he couldn't go into Brooklyn, someone had to stay behind and stand watch . . .

They decided to cut across los proyectos rather than risk dark, empty streets with faraway figures waiting on unlit corners to drag foreign seafarers down alleyways at the point of an Uzi, verdad? Looking back on it, the lack of people outside in los proyectos on such a hot night should have seemed ominous. A whole noisy barrio happening indoors: the night air like a sizzling frying pan full of all kinds of music mixed together, merengue, salsa, rap, reggae; voices pouring from windows, a woman tiredly braying, "Pepinoooo Pepinooo" in a low foghorn voice that sounded Cuban to Esteban, television, telephones ringing, the rattling whir of electric fans, air conditioners rumbling. And down below, nobody out, all stillness and shadows. They'd walked quietly, crossing the tree-bowered lawns, through the shadowy caves between brick buildings, young men lounging in open, graffitied stairwells turning to look at them, someone shouted something from a window. And as if that unintelligible shout from a window in the dark gap between two buildings had somehow warned them, they'd quickened their pace, and then it was like walking into lightning, the sudden, brief stampede of footsteps behind and then blurred lead pipes cracking against skin and bones; within seconds the crew sprawled as if napping, hearts pounding into the cool dirt and grass. Morenos and a few Latino-looking trigueños with moreno hair, one of them clasping a tiny pistol at the end of outstretched arms: *Stay down, don't move, shut up,* that's probably what they were saying. Roque Balboa said, "No dispara!" and the one standing closest kicked him in the head. But Roque's saying don't shoot like that suddenly made Esteban think of Guardia forcing people to lie facedown before shooting them in the back of the head and his fingers dug into the earth and he watched their feet, almost all of them wearing those big sneakers like Mark's. Then one of their attackers spoke in Spanish, warning, "Tranquilo, tranquilo, muchachos, y no les va a pasar nada." They were in a hurry, moving now as if they'd just snuck into a farm patch to gather vegetables growing from prostrate bodies, stepping among them in their silent, big sneakers, yanking wallets and money from pockets, bending to undo watches . . . Esteban saw Bernardo pushing himself up, trying to kneel, out of it, his forehead pouring blood—one of them whacked his piece of pipe against Bernardo's shoulders and Esteban sprang towards the viejo and instantly felt himself grabbed up and his arms pinned to his back while a muchachón with earrings in each ear and a piratical kerchief and his big, flabby upper torso bared stepped forward and punched him five, six times in the belly in the face splitting his lip filling his head with acid-tasting fumes. Esteban was let go of and slumped backwards onto the grass. Now there was laughter all around. Then someone else was standing over him, wide eyed, his mouth a small, silent *o,* slowly waving a long blade over his face . . . mierda, *his* knife, Soviet Army issue, he'd been allowed to keep it after the BLI. They ran off into the night with his knife and everyone's money and watches, including the cook's gold one and his gold bracelets, even necklaces and crucifixes yanked from necks, one with Pínpoyo's once-kissed white boots tucked under each arm. And the four folded five-dollar bills, one from each of Esteban's tíos, that he'd had in his pocket. He'd left his watch back in his cabin, but, chocho, he felt like crying about the knife. The crew lay there as if a grenade had gone off among them and they were only now beginning to stir from the sleep of the dead. Where's my arm? Has anyone seen my head? It seemed to Esteban that he didn't recognize anybody, had no idea who they all were. All those personalities that had already been tagged with nicknames seemed to have fled into the night too, leaving moaning, whimpering bodies behind on the ground, bodies beginning to stir now and grope for scattered wallets and letters to mail: Look, this is me, on this ID card, that's my photo, and this letter's addressed to my novia, can't forget her name. There was Bernardo, his eyes closed and flickering in a mask of blood, barely conscious. Esteban tried to lift him up by the shoulders, but his own legs felt so weak and wobbly he fell down sitting with the old man sprawled over his lap. Hijueputa, in all the war I only got hurt this badly once. And never lost my knife. He sat there looking around, his lips and nose looking like one big, bloody hole in his face, wanting to tell everybody that they had to get up and go, that the blood was nothing, especially when it was your own, that it was wonderful to be able to taste it, feel it filling your own mouth, you fat black pato hijueputa with your earrings and flabby tits . . .

They retraced their steps back to the ship, Cebo and El Barbie, the two strongest, making a seat for Bernardo with clasped arms and his arms around their shoulders. They cut across the withered futbol field and small park kitty-corner from a corner of los proyectos; and then down a short, brick warehouse–lined street blocked at the end by a chicken-wire fence with an open gate, which led past brick walls and a canal lined with liquid storage tanks and desiccated trees on the opposite bank until the road curved away, running directly behind their cove and the lot: it was the same road they'd taken that first night with El Pelos in the van, but from the opposite direction.

They washed around the spigot and barrel on the pier. The others silently waited their turns while Bernardo lay propped back on his elbows with his head directly under the splashing water, looking like some ancient polychrome saint who'd climbed off his church pedestal and flung off his robes to wash two-millennium-old martyr's wounds, blood-dyed water running in a sheet over his face and thin, bony chest, dividing around his small, cannonball belly and bladed hips, pooling under driftwood thighs and wrinkled old man's testicles sagging onto the pier. Canario came running down the ladder and onto the pier, twittering "Qué pasó? Qué pasó?" but knew as soon as he saw. Some went to bed that night holding the blood-soaked rags that had been their best shore leave clothes to cuts on their heads, grateful, for the first and last time, for the torrid shelter of iron bulkhead walls. Bernardo had a muddy bump on his head for the rest of the summer, and the cook limped for weeks from a blow to his knee. El Faro had lost his eyeglasses, and Tomaso Tostado two bottom teeth, but not the gold one on top.

The next day unfathomable sadness and listlessness and shame disabled the crew even more completely than the stomach ailments from drinking rat water not even a week before. They put down their tools and went and sat stuporously in the shade under the deckhouse.

Capitán Elias and el primero Mark saw their bruised and cut faces and figured out what had happened right away, of course. So impatient he was jittery, talking at them in a fast, terse tone of righteous concern, Capitán Elias demanded that they tell him exactly how it had happened. But the crew had already agreed not to tell him a thing. No sé. Nada. No pasó nada. They stared down at the deck.

"You see? Didn't I tell you?" He laughed with exasperation and looked from one crewman to another with rapidly blinking eyes, his nose probing the air like an offended ostrich's beak. "Are you muchachos expecting to get paid for today? How many days have we spent just lying around now?"

But the rat in the drinking water was *his* fault, and el Capitán *knew* it. What had he and el Primero done, filled it without looking inside first, was it a Japanese rat? They'd gulped down water constantly and heedlessly those first sun-susurrated days, and when they'd taken it down to refill it for the first time, there it was, an eyeless and earless rat evaporated to its skeleton, teeth, and claws, scraps of wet fur clinging to bone like the last shreds of a disintegrated shroud.

"Take it easy today, OK?" said el Capitán. "No work, we'll start again tomorrow. Vaya, muchachos, now you know where you are. Stay in Panama from now on, it's safer, despite what you read in the newspapers."

Qué *qué?* What newspapers? Moments later capitán, primero, and Miracle drove off the pier in the Mazda.

And Bernardo said, "Chavalos, when that statue walks, this ship will sail."

And no one even said, Shut up, viejo.

3

AT FIRST THE EARNEST GULLIBILITY WITH WHICH THE CREW PLUNGED INTO the slave labor of repairing the *Urus* appalled Bernardo. From the very first night onboard he'd cursed himself for not even having the money to buy a plane ticket home, bitterly told himself he would've gotten back into the van with El Pelos and headed right back to the airport if only he'd had a few hundred dollars to his name. At night he indulged fantasies of strangling the smug young capitán, worms exploding from that smirking baldie's eyes and ears, out his nose and mouth. As fervently as any praying child he wished for amnesia to come and erase all memory of the life which had brought him only to this; but perhaps, he thought, amnesia never comes to the rescue of old men who want to forget, its hungry mists enfolding only those with so much they want to remember, like vultures preferring a fat cow to a withered mole.

The muchachos didn't know what a true ship, a true capitán, was like and acted as if they had no choice but to believe that when the ship was fixed, she'd sail. Look at all the tools onboard! The hundreds of cans of antirust solvents, primers, and paints! What's it all for, viejo? Why else are we here?

He couldn't answer. Bernardo racked his brain and couldn't think of why else. As the weeks, and then months, dragged on, Bernardo would become ever more aware of the black wind of disaster gathering invisible force in the night, getting ready to sweep them away like crumbs off a table, until finally he'd stop trying to figure out *why else*. While the crew would grow even more reluctant to relinquish their belief in the promise. It was as if their stranded hope and his pessimism would finally bring them to the same conclusion: as if they too would feel ready to die on this ship rather than go home, still in debt, with nothing to show for their months at sea but their own blameless gullibility gaping like gory holes gnawed open in their breasts by sharks.

There wasn't even a dining table in the mess. Down on the pier, inside the grain elevator, through a smashed little doorway in back, was their toilet. No washing machine and dryer for clothes, no work boots or overalls for the crew, never mind a waiter's uniform—yes, two dozen pairs of work gloves were supplied, but most of these soon wore out, were never replaced. Capitán Elias hadn't even given them shipping articles to sign, which he should have done their first day onboard. But the muchachos didn't even know about shipping articles, didn't understand that the contracts they'd signed in Nicaragua and Honduras were merely like baggage claim tickets accompanying them to New York, saying, Here is the crew Constantino Malevante has procured, here are the more or less standard terms of employment the shipmaster will need to legitimize through shipping articles if he wishes, legally, in keeping with the custom of the sea, to claim his bags. But not even the cook had complained, telling him, "You haven't been to sea in twenty years, viejo, everything has changed. Corner cutting everywhere, the profits aren't the same, and you don't even *expect* to know your ship owner's name anymore. Certainly I've never seen anything this bad, but owners can get away with a lot now." He shrugged in his hard-eyed, laconic way. "But we're not here working to turn a ship into a bus, eh? It's a ship, there'll be inspections, and they still have to pay us if they want to sail."

Their third Friday onboard Capitán Elias let them quit work before dusk, announcing a meeting and—surprise!—a barbecue. While tools were being stored, cables hauled up and coiled, capitán and primero went down to the Mazda and Honda—each had driven his own car that day—and carried a wheeled barbecue grill up the ladder, and then brown paper bags full of groceries. Slim, fatty, red cuts of steak in bloody supermarket packaging, fresh corn still in husks, plastic tubs of "potato salad," long loaves of bread, Oreo cookies, three bottles of green chili habanero sauce from Mexico, and two ice-packed coolers filled with soda and beer. Usually, in those days, the officers still provided the crew with meat for their dinners: packages of thin, graying pork chops, hot dogs, chicken liver or thighs, small fish, heads still on, packed with bones and guts. Canned vegetables. The refrigeration in the food lockers didn't work, of course, these were boxes of fetid heat, so anything perishable had to be eaten the same day it was brought onboard. Food left out went to the rats, who scoured the mess for crumbs at night, eating through anything, even clock hands apparently, that wouldn't break their teeth.

So the barbecue was special, and the crew took it as a sign that Capitán Elias was pleased with their progress after the slow start. The meeting, they thought, was going to be an upbeat assessment of the work left to be done, and would undoubtedly address the matter of their salaries. They knew they should have been paid, in a combination of bank checks and cash, at the end of their first two weeks; when payday had passed without the officers even mentioning it, the crew had assumed that they weren't going to be paid for the days lost to rat-water poisoning and the beating after all. When they were talking it over amongst themselves that night, Bernardo had said that was unjust, and most of the crew had agreed, if silently; but who was there to protest to? After all, el Capitán had warned them not to go into los proyectos, and they all still felt ashamed and chastened over what had happened there.

They all went down to the pier to wash, Capitán Elias and el primero Mark too. The crew in naked clusters around the spigot and barrel, scooping water over themselves from the barrel and kneeling by the spigot, soap passed hand to hand. The grain elevator looming over them, a bleak, malodorous windmill without arms, increasingly graffitied with the night's snake-tongued messages. This was always a melancholy time of day: the workday washed off but left their skin still tinged, ever grayer, as if with exhaustion and unease. At night they woke to their darkest worries and fears, and washing on the pier, it was always as if they were trying to hold night off a bit longer, mainly with jokes and banter to entertain el Capitán. Meanwhile Miracle lapped thirstily at the soap-foamed, pooling water full of whatever had washed off them, while Mark kept saying, "No, Miracle," rolling his eyes with exasperation and pushing the dog away with his foot. Mark always kept his underpants on when he washed and often didn't undress at all, an inhibition the crew, without giving it much thought, ascribed to el Primero's rigid and unsurprising sense of hierarchy more than to anything else. It seemed normal enough for him to endure his griminess until he got home. He was not a boss who bathed naked with his workers, like Capitán Elias. He didn't want to touch the insect-and-soap-scummed water in the barrel. Mark tended to keep his distance and in this way, Bernardo often reflected, behaved more like a true capitán than Elias, though this did little for el Primero's air of authority. Capitán Elias, perhaps without even meaning to, undercut Mark's authority every day, simply by the way he treated him, affectionately teasing as if to a younger brother, a little haughty or impatient, a certain tightening of el Capitán's lips when he listened to his primero, the suddenly speeded up jackhammer way he had of answering him sometimes. Bernardo had his own nickname for Mark: El Hipnotizado. Something faraway and soft in his eyes, for all his automatic and boyish smiling. As if his private thoughts were like a long, slow-moving train he rode on all day, gazing unseeingly out the window. Often they heard him humming broken bits of jingles to himself, over and over.

Capitán Elias, like Mark, got to go home at night, bathe in hot water, change into clean underwear and clothes. But Capitán Elias always stripped naked to wash with the crew anyway, even when it rained. He towered over them like a huge plucked stork, rubbing himself all over with soap as if trying to cover himself with a new coat of sudsy feathers. Down on all fours, he held his nearly hairless head under the spigot, exaggeratedly snorting, loudly fluttering water in and out of his mouth, long fingers groping along his scalp.

". . . You tie a rooster to the bed," El Barbie was saying that evening, supposedly advising Cabezón with a well-known prescription for his wedding night, but really performing for el Capitán, "and the first time it crows, you sit up, wave a finger at it, and say, Va uno, eh? And the second time it crows, Van dos, eh? The third time you get out of bed and kick it to death. And the first time your woman gives you any shit, look at her, wave a finger, and say, Va uno, eh?"

The naked capitán giggled; he folded his sinewy arms across his hair-shagged chest, lowered his chin, giggled some more. El Barbie beamed proudly while Capitán Elias translated the story into English for Mark, wagging his finger in the air, practically shouting that last Va uno, eh!

And Mark shook his head skeptically and said, "Yeah, right, Elias. Tell it to Kate." And then, looking around at the crew with an amazed expression in his eyes, his face suddenly a jumpy-browed mask of exaggerated mirth, he pointed at Elias and exclaimed, *"Tell it to his wife!"* and laughed all by himself.

El Buzo said that his older brother had tried that. Except the rooster didn't die, and his brother spent the next two weeks nursing it himself, feeding it popcorn, peanuts, even shrimp by hand, and little spoonfuls of milk. "Ay mon, he was sick to his heart about that rooster," said El Buzo.

And Capitán Elias said, "And that güey's wife's been walking all over him ever since!"

He'd said that in Spanish, but Mark shook his head again and grinned down at his own feet, said, "Yeah, right, Elias. Gimme a break." And this time el Capitán briefly glared at him, his lips tightening.

Capitán Elias and Mark, in his underwear, carried their work clothes to the trunks of their respective automobiles and changed into T-shirts and jeans. And the crew carried their clothes back on deck, where some put them back on, and those who had something cleaner to change into left them in muddy clumps outside the mess for Bernardo to launder. At least, during those summer months, the clothes Bernardo laundered down on the pier and laid out on the rear deck dried quickly; eventually it would come to seem nearly meaningless whether their saturated rags were laundered or not.

On deck, in front of the deckhouse, Capitán Elias filled the barbecue grill with charcoal and balled up scraps of brown paper bag, doused them with lighter fluid, lit a match, and danced it over the mixture. Flames rose with the sound of flags flapping in a stiff wind, quickly subsided. While Capitán Elias and Mark fanned the coals with flaps of cardboard and bent down with puffed-out cheeks to blow over them, the crew milled around watching and sipping from cold cans of Budweiser, wincing at the cold bubbles of flavor tearing deliciously at their parched tongues and mouths; it was as if they'd never tasted beer before, just a few sips left them dizzy, faces pleasantly numbing.

"Hijo de cien mil putas!" exclaimed Panzón. "I've never had beer in a can before. Está búfalo!"

"Búfalo!" assented El Faro with unfaked happiness for the first time since the night of the beating in los proyectos, when he'd lost his glasses.

Esteban, who'd been to war, and El Tinieblas, who'd been to prison, didn't let them themselves get too excited about the beer—going three weeks without what you're used to was nothing new to them, their postures seemed to say. I feel like drinking eighteen, thought Esteban. He imagined himself home in Corinto, drinking with his friends on the beach, savoring the memory more than the beer. But then, the last time, they'd gone from the beach to that burdel—where she'd rolled over on her belly and thrust her smooth little nalgas up at him, looking at him over her shoulder, and right there he'd hallucinated that she'd turned into a fiendishly grinning dog, and now a heavy sigh poured out of him, he stared down sadly at the can in his hand, told himself, Fuck it, ni verga, it was right for him to be trapped on a broken ship with fourteen other males.

There was enough beer for each member of the crew to have two. When José Mateo reached into the cooler for another, Tomaso Tostado announced that he was saving *his* second beer for after dinner. El Faro said that was a good idea. And Pínpoyo said, "Why not?" And everyone looked at the cook crouched over the cooler. Mesmerized as they were by the pleasure of that first beer, the second loomed as an immense problem—suddenly it seemed terrible to have no more beer left if they had two so quickly, a beerless barbecue, meeting, and night stretching ahead—which Tomaso Tostado had just solved. He's smart, always knows just what to say, Tomaso Tostado; with jowly cheeks and solemn Indian eyes in a square head he looks like a pensive rabbit, one with a daffy smile now, gold tooth over missing teeth. José Mateo grunted, dropped the can back into the cooler, and trudged back into the mess, where Bernardo was husking corn and taking small sips from his beer, letting it chill and then slowly warm his mouth before swallowing. The water in the battered aluminum pot on the little two-burner butane stove was taking a long time to boil. José Mateo picked up Bernardo's can and took a long, greedy drink.

"You can have the rest," said Bernardo. "But I get one of your ears of corn."

The cook drank down the rest of the beer without even answering.

Outside, on the horizon, clouds were massed into the shape of a long, opaquely black bow tie, half a mottled moon protruding over the knot in the yellowish gray sky. A breeze, faint and odorless, strained through the brackish harbor heat, the new smell of burning charcoal, like a ghost stepping through a wall.

Capitán Elias said to let the charcoal cook for another twenty minutes or so; each taking a beer, their first, the officers went inside to the corridor, climbed the switchback stairs to the bridge. The crew stood around the barbecue grill anticipating steak as if deliciously seared, crunchy steak fat was already melting down to nothing inside their salivating mouths, empty stomachs growling and crumpling. So they didn't even notice the first slow dollops of rain. José Mateo came out of the mess for another beer just as the rain began pelting down faster. He glanced at the others with slit-eyed disbelief, wheeled the grill into the passage under the deckhouse's second level, went for his "second" beer. Then the hungry daydreamers woke up, hurrying for cover and into the mess. Thunder rumbled low in the sky, and as if this was the signal for all the dancers in the chorus to charge out from the wings at once, stiff and steady rain swept over the ship, clattering against the deck, steaming off the jumping water in the cove.

When the officers came down from the bridge, Capitán Elias was carrying the Coleman lamp and Mark the radio–cassette player that they usually kept locked up in the wheelhouse; encased in black plastic, this music box wasn't as large as the ones los blacks brought to the pier at night. Mark set the music box down on the floor in a corner of the mess, tuned it to a Spanish-language station, stood up and smiled, looking around as if he wanted to say something. All eyes focused on the music box, its beady red light glowing, as Spanish, so familiar yet unfamiliar, roared like a separate small storm in an iron corner of the mess: a manly, rolling baritone playing the part of a mouthwash battling the quickly vanquished and squealing nemeses, Placa y Ginjivitis. Next, barely audible above the roar of rain outside, came the mournfully hushed, feminine tones of "Cruz de Navaja" by Grupo Mecano, a song Esteban had frequently heard over the radio and on jukeboxes in Nicaragua: he sat back against the bulkhead, eyes shut, immersed in the soft, floating voice more than in the lyrics of betrayed love and murder, the female, whispery singing like a voice long lost inside his own memory . . .

Outside, in the shielded but puddling passage between deckhouse and rain, Capitán Elias barbecued the steaks while José Mateo stood by his side, giddily enfolded in the embrace of oncoming inebriation. He'd traded his steak away for Bernardo's second beer too, and was feeling happy, repentant, and sentimental all at once: the story his newly aroused blood was telling him had somehow awakened a warm and unfamiliar wave of self-love in the cook.

"Tengo un problemita con alcohol, mi Capitán," José Mateo announced, in a swollen-chested, decorous tone. "Y el problemita es este: La verdad es que, pues, lo quiero mucho."

Capitán Elias glanced at José Mateo with a bemused smile, said that while he liked alcohol too, he probably wouldn't go so far as to say he was in love with it, though who knows, sometimes you don't realize how in love you are until it's too late, no? And the cook cackled, nodded his head, and said, "Así es, mi Capi." Elias went back to his busy barbecuing, shuffling partly cooked steaks onto a pile at the edge of the grill and pulling others over the red coals.

José Mateo shrugged his shoulders heavily, folded his arms, cocked his head to one side, and narrowed his eyes; then he raised his chin and said almost defiantly, "Two bottles of rum a day, or of tequila, as much beer as I could hold, that was never a problem for me . . ." Claro, he'd been in too many drunken brawls in cantinas when he was younger but had survived them all more or less intact, blown all his money on puchilachas in brothels now and then, woke up lying on some sidewalk in a foreign port city without his wallet a few times, that was all. But always a ship waiting for him, a place to sober up and sleep it off and get back to work, he could always count on that, mi Capitán. But the last job he'd had, on the *Tamaulipas,* there was a radio operator, a Mexican called El Peperami, híjole, as bad a drunk as me. The ship spent two days taking on cargo in Vancouver. And he and El Peperami, they'd been into the city, drinking all through the night and into the morning, but they made it back somehow. And as the ship was still loading, they got another bottle of tequila and a fishing rod, went and sat at the end of the pier, behind some containers piled up there. When their crewmates finally found them, they were both passed out cold. They loaded them like two large sacks of cement onto the prongs of two forklifts, which two dockworkers drove back to the ship. And then they were put inside a cargo net and hoisted up on deck at the end of a cargo hook. And that's where he woke up, out on deck at night, shivering with cold, El Peperami snoring away beside him, both of them still inside that net, the ship plowing out to sea . . . Until that hijueputa of a Norwegian capitán came by, told them they were fired. They were put off at the next port, Anchorage, Alaska. Carajo, qué humiliación. For all he knows, El Peperami is still there, working on one of those offshore fish-canning factory ships. But he used up the rest of his money flying back to Managua, a big mistake, mi Capitán. Has a little house there that he lets an old aunt and her daughter live in; he'd had hopes of marrying that cousin but, bueno, it hasn't worked out. Has a small fortune in now totally worthless cordobas in the bank . . .

José Mateo laughed a harsh cackle from the back of his throat.

And the barbecuing capitán smiled and said, "Esa es una trágica historia, Cocinero."

"Pero lo que te quiero decir," stammered José Mateo, "es que . . . este . . . Pues, bueno," and he stopped. He stared out at the rain through heavy-lidded, slitted eyes, his pupils two dots of murky bewilderment. Then he looked at Capitán Elias again and said, "Putamadre mi Capi—este barco es único."

Capitán Elias tonelessly replied that it was definitely a unique ship and asked José Mateo if he'd mind telling the muchachos that the meat was done.

The crew ate sitting on the floor in the mess—dark but for the coppery light radiating from the Coleman lamp, barely casting a glow on rust-hued bulkheads—plates between their legs, on their laps, balanced in one hand under their chins. They chewed and chewed, for the steak was tough, with faraway looks in their eyes or eyes squeezed shut, murmuring, groaning with pleasure; washed the meat down with cold cans of soda; sopped up blood and grease with clumps of bread. A slowly widening puddle of rainwater was seeping in through the mess door. Brassy music, mainly salsa, blared tinnily from the music box in the corner now. They devoured their corn, surprised at the softness and diminutiveness of the kernels on this gringo corn, the delicate sweetness smothered in chili habanero sauce; buried meat and corn under heaping portions of gooey potato salad. José Mateo gnawed fiendishly at his ragged, denuded corncob, held it against his teeth noisily sucking moist air, biting into the cob as if that might release a little more—feeling sorry for the cook, Bernardo gave him back half the steak he'd bartered away; passed the other half, along with his extra ear of corn, to Esteban. By the end of the meal they all felt so stuffed they couldn't even eat all the Oreo cookies.

Then, when everyone but Bernardo and the cook had finally started in on his deferred second beer, Capitán Elias stood in the middle of the floor and said he had a few things he wanted to talk to them about. But Tomaso Tostado interrupted, rising to his feet to thank the officers for the meal and the beer, clearly a tiding of better times ahead on the *Urus,* and everyone applauded and cheered, El Barbie blowing shrieking whistles with his fingers in his mouth, while Capitán Elias stood there curtly nodding, a small, rigid smile on his face, his T-shirt dark with sweat over his chest, under his arms, the crown of his high forehead slick and gleaming. Just as they'd anticipated, he began the meeting by telling the crew that he was satisfied with their progress so far. "Everyone has been working hard. I can't ask for more than that," said Capitán Elias. The owner was very pleased, and, anticipating a reasonably imminent departure, was reinitiating his search for a new cargo to carry. "But I'm afraid I have some not so good news too, caballeros." Due to the longer than originally expected delay in port, the canceled cargo, the mounting berthing fees, the price of all equipment and materials, the cost of reinsuring the ship . . . the owner was having a cash flow problem. As soon as the ship was declared seaworthy and the new cargo contracted, they'd be paid, of course. He and Mark were forgoing payment too—and him with a baby on the way, bills up the culo to pay, his wife wasn't too thrilled! But there was a bright side to all of this, no? What did they need cash for in Brooklyn? They were illegal once they went off the ship anyway. Wouldn't it be better, for themselves and for their families back home, to be paid all at once as soon as the ship was ready to sail? Hadn't they all come here for a chance to better their economic circumstances and help their families? Better that than blowing their pay on televisions, watches, radios, and other junk in Brooklyn, verdad?

When Capitán Elias was finished, the crew sat and stood around the mess in sullen silence, warily watching him as if waiting for something more. El Capitán stood with his hands deep in the pockets of his jeans now, looking from face to face. Mark, leaning against the table that supported their stove, fidgeted with his car keys. Miracle lay on the floor, head on paws, as if depressed by the lingering odor of steak in the closed, muggy air.

Bernardo was the first to speak up. "Capitán," he said, and el Capitán looked over. Pausing to gather his thoughts, Bernardo nervously rubbed his nose. He said, "To me, this sounds unjust. Pues, sí." He nodded emphatically. "Let's not hide the truth, Capitán, this ship is a swamp of safety and maritime labor violations, and now this, *un gran insulto*! I think these muchachos know how to manage their own money. A trip into Times Square to see a movie, a hamburger at McDonald's, that would not be a wasteful spending spree. Instead, Capitán, you ask us to be slaves—"

"No, Bernardo!" Capitán Elias jumped in vehemently as if to smother any echo of the waiter's words, eyes suddenly shiny and intense. "That just isn't true!" He said that was absolutely the wrong way to look at it, a purely emotional reaction, *Bernardo*. Because slaves don't get paid, but they were going to be paid every cent they were owed! So how could Bernardo say such a thing, him with so many years of maritime experience? Shipboard violations, pues claro, but wasn't that what they'd all been hired to take care of? Every day there were fewer. "Can you tell me what else it is you think we're all doing here, Bernardo?" Certainly, a hard job, a tough situation. Capitán Elias said he'd never been through anything like it either. But laws protected them. Panamanian law. International laws. United States laws covering every ship in port, regardless of flag. "The ownership has to pay us or this ship doesn't move. It's as simple as that! Isn't that true, Bernardo?"

When Capitán Elias was done, Bernardo looked down at his hands clasped over his waist, at his wrist as if he still wore a watch there, and then up again.

"Espero que sí, Capitán," he said firmly.

This part of the meeting went on a little longer. Various members of the crew forced themselves to find new ways of asking, without sounding too childishly plaintive, if el Capitán really was absolutely certain they were going to be paid; again and again, they received the same patient assurances. Finally, when Capitán Elias asked again if there were any more questions, he was met with averted gazes and silence.

"OK," said Capitán Elias. "Bueno, caballeros. I think we all deserve a party, no?" Then he pulled a wad of white cloth, like a fat handkerchief, from his back pocket, slowly unfolded it, and held a scissored square of bedsheet up for the crew to see: EL BARBIE'S BAR written in black marker across it. El Barbie, flattered and reddening, laughed loudly while Capitán Elias fastened the banner under the water tank on the high shelf at one end of the mess. He turned around and made a forlorn face, put out his hands, apologized for the lack of women, smiled, and then looked over at el Primero and said, "Mark, can you go and get the beer now? A bottle of rum. Coke. Ice . . . ," and lifted one shoulder in a light shrug.

"Come on, Elias, it's raining," said Mark.

El Capitán looked at him coldly. "What the hell, Mark?" And still looking at him that way, he pulled out his wallet. "While you're gone, I'll tell them about the promotions—if you have no objection."

"Great," said Mark. And he went and took money from Elias, then left the mess followed by Miracle.

"Al Primero no le gusta la lluvia," said Capitán Elias and asked if they'd ever heard of a seaman afraid of a little rain—no, Mark was just impatient to go and see his new chica, that was what it really was, these single guys, how they suffer, no? Capitán Elias was already explaining the promotions when they heard the Honda start up on the pier. The promotions were to make their labor even more efficient, to streamline the chain of command. As far as he was concerned, they all deserved to be promoted to *segundo oficial*—or even higher! But a crew of all second mates, that probably wouldn't work out. So Cabezón and Caratumba were promoted to first and second engine room officers, respectively; Canario and Pínpoyo, first and second electricians. And El Barbie was named contramaestre, or bosun, in charge of overseeing the ordinary seamen's deck work and communicating the officers' instructions. They needed a purser, someone to keep a better record of the crew's working hours and wages—Who was good with numbers? Elias wanted to know. When no one asserted such a talent, el Capitán posed a mathematical problem: A pig, a wolf, a sack of corn on a riverbank, and a farmer who can only transport one at a time across the river in his small canoe. If the pig is left alone with the corn, the pig will eat it; if the wolf is left alone with the pig, the wolf will eat the pig. So how do you get them all safely across? . . . Qué? El Capitán repeated the problem, but no one could solve it, the pig was always left alone with the corn or the wolf with the pig, and the crew, baffled and suspicious, wondered what el Capitán was up to now . . . Until Panzón's lugubrious expression suddenly lightened and he said to take the pig first, mi Capitán, then bring the wolf but take the pig back *across* and leave it there, come back with the corn, then go back for the pig. Capitán Elias told Panzón he was the purser and that he'd bring him a ledger book tomorrow (and, the day after the next, he did).

"The ordinary seamen," Capitán Elias said, "should now consider themselves able seamen." Because they'd certainly learned as much in three weeks on the *Urus,* he said, as they would in the year they'd need to spend working onboard any other vessel to qualify for able seaman certificates.

Capitán Elias paused a moment; perhaps he was waiting for Tomaso Tostado to lead another round of applause for the new "able seamen." But it didn't come. Most everyone was openmouthed—they were vulnerable to this, after all, aching for it, any dose of triumph, anything bright to write home about—until Tomaso Tostado's hissed "So where are the certificates?" which apparently el Capitán didn't hear, instantly opened a trapdoor under their brief surge of buoyancy. Then El Tinieblas, staring down, whispered between his raised knees, "And a raise? Más nada encima de nada?" and giggled weirdly. Capitán Elias, uncomprehending but suspicious, looked over and was apparently placated by the smiles he saw breaking out on the faces of the others seated near the tattooed former prisoner. He smirked back at them as if he too understood and felt himself equally entangled and fatalistically amused by this farce of "promotions" he was somehow being "forced" to perpetrate. But then he heard El Buzo from another corner of the mess suddenly singing, in English, with low, soft, perfectly inflected mimicry, *"Oh pirates, yes they rob I . . . ,"* and when he looked over El Buzo glanced innocently away. Then everyone saw el Capitán's pallor actually darken, and he held himself perfectly still for a moment, staring into some anger-letting void somewhere over El Buzo's head, his lips pressed thin.

"I meant what I said," Capitán Elias finally said, fiercely; but then he smiled sadly, his eyes softening. "Of course it can't become official until you've served a year, I know that," he said. "But I think we find ourselves in a situation far enough outside the norm that we can write our own rules, for now, and stand by them. So consider yourselves very able ordinary seamen. You deserve at least that much."

Capitán Elias let that sink in a moment, and then he said, "You're probably wondering why I didn't name a segundo oficial," and focused his gaze on Bernardo with what seemed skeptical warmth, mirth slowly seeping into his expression like water up through footprints on a beach. "I think you've already appointed yourself to that role, Bernardo," he said. "But I'm afraid your work detail isn't going to change. You're el segundo oficial, at least until we sail and the real segundo boards. Of course, you're still the waiter too."

It was as if Capitán Elias had delivered the punch line to a very long, very straight-faced routine which had finally become pretty funny: for the first time since the meeting began, nearly everyone succumbed to laughter over the notion of the waiter being promoted to second mate. If the crew had felt confused by el Capitán's esteem for El Barbie and his apparent assumption that they shared it, that seemed less baffling now in the context of el Capitán's joke on the old waiter, which finally seemed as much a joke on himself as it was on all of them and this whole jodido ship. But Bernardo stared stonily at el Capitán and a moment later leaned over and muttered near Esteban's ear, "Este niñote, qué pendejo es." It wasn't until days later, as they pondered the full meaning of the joke, that they suspected that Capitán Elias had actually begun his speech on the promotions in earnest, and then, sensing that his ploy—well meaning? deceitful?—was floundering, had simply changed course and improvised a comedy. By then the able ordinary seamen would be feeling fully ordinary again, the reality of their days too plainly what they were to be lightened by any new label.

Mark, rain-wet curls sticking to his forehead, came back, asked for help bringing his purchases up from the car: six six-packs of beer, a jug of Bacardi rum, paper cups, two plastic gallon bottles of Coca-Cola, two bags of ice, a carton of cigarettes, that was what Cebo and Roque Balboa carried into the mess. No limes.

The radio was turned all the way up. Esteban stayed sitting beside it well into the "party," knees up, chewing his thumbnail, occasionally taking a drink of beer. There was a grumble of thunder, a loud crack of lightning nearby, rain like celestial debris. Rum, beer, tobacco smoke, sweaty, steamy air, music, loud, boasting voices; Capitán Elias said he felt like he was back in one of those Amazon backwater cantinas, sort of place where everyone drinks to pass out, güeyes falling backwards off their chairs and splitting their heads open on the floor while bleary-eyed drunks stumble around tracking the blood all over; cockroaches as big as his foot . . . Later Bernardo, from where he stood with the others grouped around José Mateo listening to the cook's ribald, rum-stoked stories, looked over at Esteban. Sometimes the chavalito just goes off, he thought, his heart going out to him. After three weeks he recognized the state all too well: Esteban relentlessly chewing his thumbnail, his burning, faraway stare aimed out over rocking knuckles, holding his breath inside himself and letting it out all at once through his nose, loudly, almost sputteringly, like an angry otter.

José Mateo, animated tonight for the first time in three weeks, was telling about the bule bars of Santos, Brazil. How you spent all night buying drinks and dancing and kissing and feeling up some splendid, big-assed, big-breasted puta, and then you got her back onboard and into your cabin and undressed her and, hijo de cien millones de putas, mi Capitán, she turns out to be a macho! But he never knew a more degenerate, vice-ridden putero than his friend El Peperami, radio operator on the *Tamaulipas*. Discovered his puta was a puto and decided he didn't care, even told them all about it the next day, how he'd thought to himself, All the money I've already spent, all the time I put in, and here we are naked in bed and I've got a hard-on and I'm drunk, bueno, in love as in war, ni modo, every hole is a trench!

And then everyone laughing and repeating the punch line and some of the chavalones wrinkling their noses, shouting, "Nooo! Nooo! Ay no! Qué asco!"

El Barbie looked over at Esteban sitting by the radio on the floor and shouted, "Piri! Oye, Sandinista! Is that true, in love as in war, every hole is a trench?"

And Esteban gaped up at him.

"Is that what you piris do in the jungle, every hole a trench?"

"Qué?" asked Esteban, looking irritated and confused.

"Barbie," said Bernardo. "Ya."

"Este Estebanito, mi Segundo," said El Barbie, a beer in one hand and a paper cup of ice and rum in the other, turning away, "you can't joke around with him about anything."

Capitán Elias was translating the cook's story for Mark, who was sweating profusely like everyone else, his shirt completely unbuttoned. Mark took a step back from el Capitán as if he didn't like it when he stood so close, as if el Capitán had been spraying his face with spittle, and said, "Uh-huh, I get it. Fucking-A!"

So it was strangely like all the other midvoyage shipboard drinking parties Bernardo remembered from twenty years before. Though it hadn't turned violent yet, and probably wouldn't so long as the officers were present. Stories like cooped up, alcohol-lathered bulls breaking through midvoyage monotony and nostalgia. Brothels and whores, brawls, clever escapades with contraband, screwy capitanes—does anything else of interest ever happen to real seamen? Wives sometimes, but wives don't usually make for good shipboard stories. Despite himself and the persistent, sweat-stung throbbing of the bump on his head, Bernardo was enjoying it—he had happy and strange memories too, he wanted to tell a story too . . . Which one? Waking up in his cabin in a friendly port, sunlight streaming through the porthole, the screeches and ship-jostling knocks of derricks hoisting cargo and the shouts of stevedores, the harps and guitars of jarocho music playing somewhere and a faint trace of perfume infiltrating the muggy air of the cabin and raising an appetite like the smell of eggs and bacon frying and suddenly the knock on the door and a voice, "Mujeres! Quieres mujer?" announcing that the good-morning whores have boarded the ship . . . Or that stuck-up braggart, Capitán Yo Yo, who was bringing his wife and two teenage daughters (all capitanes, by the way, name their daughters for stars and constellations, did you know that, chavalos?) to see his ship, but the guard at the port gate thought they were putas and asked for a bribe, and Capitán Yo Yo began to beat the guard, who pulled out his pistol and shot Capitán Yo Yo in the belly in self-defense; Capitán Yo Yo died with the hot tears of Maia and Merope drip-dripping on his face

. . . El Tibio, whose gonorrhea got so bad his whole pene turned black and green and revoltingly leaky, and they were still a week from the nearest port, where doctors would undoubtedly have to amputate it, but the second mate took a band-saw blade from the machine shop, long, sharp, and thin, sterilized it, then drove it all the way down El Tibio's urethra, gouging and twisting it around, serrating and scraping the diseased flesh out while El Tibio's screams turned a whole ten-thousand-ton cargo freighter into a trembling, frightened niñita cringing in a corner . . . Entering the port of Hong Kong on a rainy night, the huge bow crushing a fishing sampan that couldn't get out of the way, the brief screams of fishermen far below, the brittle clatter of smashed boat pulled by wash under the ship into the propeller; there was an accident in the engine room almost immediately after, a piston cylinder cover flew loose and smashed a Burmese oiler in the face, shattered both cheeks and the bone over his upper lip; the Burmese engine room crew and many of the Latino seamen became convinced that the ghosts of the Hong Kong fishermen had somehow climbed onboard and put a curse on the vessel; they wouldn't work, the ship couldn't leave port, their Greek officers even began beating some of them, until finally a resourceful "ship visitor" from the local port chaplaincy came onboard to help resolve the standoff, went away and came back with a Catholic priest and a Buddhist monk of some kind, and they conducted ceremonies to exorcise the vengeful spirits . . .

But Capitán Elias was telling a story about when he was master of the *Seal Queen* two years ago, bringing her into Yokohama. Ship traffic was really backed up, it was going to be a long wait outside the harbor, but the pilot boat had already come out to meet the ship, and the pilot had climbed up the drop ladder and was waiting, sitting on a couch in a corner of the pitch dark wheelhouse, when el Capitán went back up about three in the morning. Capitán Elias greeted the pilot in the usual manner, offered a cup of coffee, made small talk about the delay, was struck by the pilot's polished English and highly feminine, somewhat lisping voice: Sounded like some pampered Oxford-Malaysian rubber-plantation-scion poof, if you know what I mean, voice like seductive smoke in a long silk sleeve. The pilot's a bloody maricón, he thought, a total fruit! Nothing against, you know, but a harbor pilot? Usually you expect gruff retired captains, or inbred union types with the bearing of New York cops. He thought it was pretty humorous, was all. He couldn't see the pilot's face in the utter dark of the wheelhouse, what with the polarized windows and all, just a faint glow of black hair, a white shirt collar protruding over zipped black windbreaker. He went out onto a bridge wing to have a smoke, count the lights of ships ahead. The pilot came out a moment later. Now, with a little moonlight, he could see the pilot, and you know what?

The pilot was a young woman. He actually gasped. And she smiled at him disapprovingly, as if she knew what he'd been thinking back there in the wheelhouse. This really cute Japanese girl, just adorable, sexy face! Her hair short like this, just under her ears, the long nape of her neck deliciously bare. She was even wearing a black necktie. Yoriko was her name. Only twenty-four. A capitán's daughter, her father now retired from merchant ships and working as a pilot himself. I shit you not, güeyes. Yoriko had wanted to be a ship capitán too, studied in England, graduated from the world's best nautical academy. But it's still hard for a woman to become a shipmaster; there are only a few in all the world! Though she'd passed all exams, was technically Capitán Yoriko. Her father had gotten her into the pilots' association, the pay was great, better even than what most shipmasters make, and she was playing in a rock band too. Do you like sports? she asked. No, I hate sports. Do you like rock and roll? Uh-huh, I certainly do. You're young to be a master. You're young to be a harbor pilot. She pulled a tangerine from her pocket, wrapped in a white napkin. They shared it. Did you see any whales? she asked. No, not this trip. Hombre, you know? It was just in the air, they both knew. This rapidly accelerating and naughty air of infatuation. There was no one in the wheelhouse but the helmsman and el tercero, sleeping at the charts table—but el Capitán, already fantasizing about what might be about to happen, went and slid the door shut anyway. You know, he's a believer in fidelity, he doesn't mess around on his wife. And he'll tell them all something, he's not really very good at sex. Don't laugh, he's serious, how many of you think you're really good at it anyway? He enjoys *thinking* about sex, can easily spend a whole day in bed like when he has the grippe or something doing absolutely nothing but *thinking* about sex, but when he actually has to do it?—well, hardly ever, güeyes. But el Capitán and his wife love each other, so it's different. But whenever he's with anyone else he feels a certain insecurity, always thinks he can see in her face that she's thinking of someone who does it much better. He's kind of repressed, is what it is. Let's say he's just another repressed pervert, a stress on the repressed, OK? Oh, you don't believe! His limbs are too long, takes his blood too long to get from one end of him to the other, maybe that's what it is. So he doesn't move around much. It takes him a long time to get hot. His hands are always cold, they don't like that. Go ahead, pinche güeyes, laugh! He's not ashamed of it. But there on the wing, el Capitán began to kiss Capitán Yoriko. Unzipped her windbreaker, undid her tie, unbuttoned her shirt. She undid his belt. Blew him awhile. Hombre! Pulled her own jeans down wriggling. They sank to the floor of the wing. Wrestled around pulling off boots. Right there, they did it. In short, fucking great, her on top, him looking up at her face, and the stars . . . —But short. Spontaneity, romance, and lust all in one rocket booster leaving one short vapor trail in the sky. Done. She lay on top of him a long time, though, whispering and nibbling. Finally got up without a word, pulled on her pants, her boots. He could have gone to sleep right there. But he got up too, went into the wheelhouse, brewed a pot of coffee. When he came out with the coffee, it was as if nothing had happened; they sipped the coffee, smoked, leaned against the bridge wing's flank, talked ship talk a bit. He figured she hadn't liked it as much as he had after all. Oh well, what else was new? He'd treasure the memory anyway, always be grateful to Capitán Yoriko the harbor pilot. It was dawn before the ship was ready to move, when he turned the ship over to Yoriko and she expertly guided the *Seal Queen* through the channel, calling out commands in her lisping and sophisticated, sweet voice. And when the pilot's boat came out to pick her up, she went down, told them she'd be staying onboard, came back up into the wheelhouse, and stood beside el Capitán, just her arm lightly touching his. Softly told him she had the next two days off. A miracle. They hardly left his capitán's quarters except to dine one night in the port, rented some Japanese porno for his VCR, bought wine—that's right, Japanese porno, muy sofisticado y sucio, güeyes. Had pizza and sushi delivered to the ship. Fell in love with her, he most definitely did fall in love with her. Promised to see her again. Never did, of course. Bueno, así fue, caballeros, Capitán Yoriko, qué mujer! Totally unforgettable couple of days, really. Well, you know how it is, he's married. Loves his wife. Loves her. Absolutely loves her.

Capitán Elias, with a funny, almost rueful twist to his lips and a shy-seeming softness in his eyes, stiffly basked in smiles warm with alcohol and astonished admiration—even Bernardo, who'd always known el Capitán was perverse but had never suspected a timid perversity that could be revealed so ingratiatingly, felt oddly won over by his revelations and story. And though Elias had told his story in Spanish, Mark, swaying slightly, approached him with his hand out, and el Capitán lightly clapped his own hand down on it.

"Yoriko, huh?" said Mark, and he chuckled.

"Yoriko," said Capitán Elias, with a nod.

"Brill, huh?"

"Definitely brill, Mark."

"Fucking-A, Elias! You're too much!" el Primero grinned drunkenly, and el Capitán suddenly scowled and turned away.

Then Bernardo told his story about being on a ship sailing from Istanbul carrying, among its cargo, hundreds of crates packed with bagged, red-dyed pistachio nuts. "Chavalones, the crew couldn't keep their hands off those pistachios. The whole crew addicted! Sneaking down into the hold at every chance, ripping open crates and bags, stuffing their pockets with pistachios. All these marineros macho going around all day with their fingers and lips colored bright pink with pistachio dye!"

Mark loved that story more than anyone else, laughed until he had to go and lean sluggishly against the bulkhead, eyes squeezed shut, laughing as if surrendering to an invincible tickler.

Later Esteban looked up and saw Mark drunkenly swaying, grinning goofily at Bernardo, and shouting, yet again, "Pink lips and fingers! Muy funny, man!" Esteban took a drink from his warmed beer. Cebo was using a broom to sweep water out the mess door. El Capitán and others were gathered now around El Tinieblas, who'd taken off his shirt and was showing off and telling about his prison tattoos; from where Esteban sat, in the umbral corner outside the lamp's dim, coppery glow, he could see a Mickey Mouse waving a white-gloved hand from the dark, thin flank just under El Tinieblas's rib cage, among all the other images and symbols tattooed all over him. And José Mateo pulling up his shirt to show the marinero tattoo on his chest: helmsman at the spoked wheel, Jesucristo with one hand on the helmsman's shoulder and pointing the way ahead with his other.

And Esteban went back to thinking about la Marta and the horrible day a few months ago when he'd taken a bus from Corinto to León for the Juventud Sandinista commemoration in front of her house on the first anniversary of her death. Marta Llardent—*Presente!* Honor to the revolution's immortal dead. Verdad? Ni verga. La Marta. There was a small band of musicians in green fatigues and black gloves marching up and down in front of her house, and a girl in a silvery drum majorette's uniform, her baton clumsily twirled in black-gloved fingers too, and a bass drummer who took big, high steps and pounded out the rhythm and turned smartly on his heel in the steamy mud to march yet again past the big pink stucco house which took up half the block. Marta and Amalia's parents and little brother Camilo didn't even come out to watch, windows shuttered behind iron bars, door closed; up and down the uniformed musicians marched. And then, at the end of her street, at the muddy edge of a grassy lot with some tall jicaro trees in it—parakeets teeming in upper branches, which shone lollipop green in the last light of the sun evaporating into a graying sky; the excremental stench of split-open jicaros rotting on the ground—they planted a small boulder painted red and black, MARTA LLARDENT in white, BON 77-65, her volunteer battalion, and the date, there to remain for ever and ever, like an infected eye staring up at the sky, open to sun and rain, pissing dogs and drunks. Her sister still vegetating in the military hospital in

Managua a year later, though soon to be sent to Cuba for more operations, rehabilitation. Her parents, who wouldn't come out or watch and who had no interest in the boulder; they would have been my in-laws, who knows, maybe they'd even be abuelos by now. We'd be living in León, I was going to try to start university, and she was going to work and finish her studies part-time . . . Y qué? Speak to me, Martita . . . What am I supposed to feel? What do I owe you? Why this nothing inside?

And then the man on the radio said, "Nicaragua . . ." Esteban stayed hidden in his own thoughts at first, as if it was himself who'd spoken. But then he heard "Nicaragua" again: the man on the radio was saying that despite the Sapula agreement and the cease-fire, both sides were quibbling over terms and supposed violations, and then he heard a short burst of nasal-fulminating English, the U.S. president, quickly drowned out by Spanish translation requesting full renewed-funding-arming-training of the Nicaraguan Freedom Fighters. Esteban saw Capitán Elias's long legs suddenly standing in front of him, and looked up and saw El Barbie poised behind el Capitán's shoulder, still with a drink in each hand, his chubby, small-eared bat's face, his eyes blearily alert, a queer, gaping dog grin, and the other Nicaraguans coming over, drawn to Nicaragua on the radio. Capitán Elias shouted, "That fucking idiot! Wants to start the war up again. I don't see why we can't leave Nicara-goo-wah alone. Such a fucking tiny country!" And then everyone was talking all at once, the usual mierda: the viejo was saying he didn't approve of the war but the revolution a shitty betrayal. And el Capitán was loudly asserting that the United States caused the betrayal of the revolution's ideals by suffocating it with an illegal war, saying, "That's the problem with fucking Americans, can't deal with being an imperial power and so they fucking deny they are one, just don' fucking want to know, do they?" And now el Capitán looking down at Esteban again and saying that back in '79 during the insurrection against Somoza he'd really wanted to join the Sandinista International Brigades fighting on the Southern Front but he'd had a business in the Amazon going, and then he said, "You were a soldier, Esteban? Is it true you were right in the middle of it?" I'm not going to say a word, thought Esteban, looking up at the fishy underside of el Capitán's chin, but he nodded anyway. "I'm honored to have you onboard, Esteban," said el Capitán. "Truly, I am. You muchachos kicked culo on an army backed and trained and led by the greatest military power on earth!" Sí pues, the viejo was saying, the cubs sent to do all the fighting are fine chavalitos, both sides full of wonderful young people fighting for democracy, so then why is there a war if la contra are for democracy and the Sandinistas are for democracy? How can there be this war, starving everyone who doesn't fight, giving business only to the coffin builders? Because the leaders on both sides are liars, hypocrites, traitors, and puppets! "Do you feel betrayed, Esteban?" asked Capitán Elias. "No, señor," said Esteban. He lived, didn't he? Sí pues, *kicked culo,* so they say. It's over. Came home to shitty ration cards and no work and his bocón uncles and his mother boiling shark bones or crab shells for caldo and moldy Polish potatoes—and democracy. "Wasn't it la Revolución that taught you to read, Esteban?" Chocho, este capitán. "I went to school," said Esteban, hitching his shoulders. Go outside and get some air even if it's still raining, but he couldn't bring himself to move. And El Barbie saying, "You can't talk about politics with a piri, mi Capitán. He was just another brainwashed, rabid dog. That's what the communists do, isn't that true, Capitán?"

"Comemierda," said Esteban listlessly. Eat shit, Barbie.

"Come muchísima mierda, Barbie," said Panzón, jovially-clumsily clapping the new bosun on the back.

"Oiga, mi purser, it was all fine with me, all those luscious young Nicaraguan whores flooding into Honduras." And Barbie threw back his head, laughed up into the air like a whale.

"Put you mother out of work, pendejo." Roque Balboa giggled.

And everyone laughing. And the group finally trudging away. And Esteban already chewing his gritty thumbnail until cold sparks shot through his teeth. Before turning away Capitán Elias put his big hand down on his head, ruffled his hair. Comemierda, Capitán . . .

Now what's going on? Howls of laughter. Something about a drinking game El Barbie used to play back in La Cieba. Some of the crew lying, sitting on the floor. So many staggering around it looked like real rough seas. Pínpoyo stumbling out the door to vomit. El Barbie almost fell down pulling the butane stove off the table, and now Barbie lining Oreo cookies along the edge of the table. "Rompe la galleta, mi Capi!"

El Capitán protesting, "No no, Barbie, we have to go now."

And Mark slurring, "What? What's going on?" while El Barbie explained about breaking the cookie. "What?"

"With your dick, Mark," said Capitán Elias. "The game is called Break the Cookie."

El Barbie standing unsteadily over the table undoing his fly, pulling out his pija, shouting, "Winner gets the last beer!"

And he leaned against the table with his pija in his hand, waggled it up and down as if taking aim, closed his eyes, opened them again, and then he forcefully slapped it down onto an Oreo cookie and the cookie jumped in the air but didn't break, El Barbie shrieked, with hilarity or pain, spun away, and barely got out the words "Your turn, mi Capitán!"

"No fucking way," he answered.

And then this happened: Mark moving towards the table as if wading against a waist-high river current, undoing his pants, pulling it out, expression strenuously wide eyed with brutish concentration, and he thwacked his doughy pene down hard onto the table, missed the cookie completely, and stumbled backwards, two, three crumpling steps, and landed on his ass and then lay back with his arms out laughing.

And everyone who hadn't passed out yet grinning and gaping with stuporous amazement at Mark, while the dog came and sat sturdily by el Primero, panting over his face, and Capitán Elias shaking his head, his smile contemptuous and bemused, saying, "Well fucking done, Mark. Well done! Willy full of splinters now, isn't it. That's going to feel *good* in the morning."

El Capitán helped wobble-legged Mark out the mess door, looking back over his shoulder, saying, "Take the day off. Take tomorrow off, güeys. Fue una gran fiesta!" No one went out to raise the ladder that night; and the next day the mess was covered in rat-shredded husks and cobs and other barbecue debris and stank of rancid beer and vomit, and Mark's Honda was still parked on the pier, and it was at least a hundred degrees out, the low tidewater in the cove stinking and bubbling like some rank cow pasture puddle in the tropics, and the smashed wooden terminals seeming to sigh in the steam heat; nothing to bury the queasiness in their stomachs and their hangovers with but sardines and rice fried in cooking oil, nothing to drink but water from the spigot on the pier . . .

4

WITH A GLANCE AT HIS LEDGER BOOK, PANZÓN CAN TELL EACH CREWMAN what he's owed down to the last cent: the mechanics, electricians, and cook earn $1.33 an hour for a sixty-hour workweek, $0.33 more per hour of overtime; the "able" ordinary seamen earn $1.22 an hour, $0.22 more for overtime, and the waiter earns $1.06 an hour, with no fixed overtime rate, since why should a mess waiter have to work overtime? (Despite the promotions, of course, no one received a raise.) Capitán Elias and Mark wear wristwatches, but when they aren't there, there are no watches around, no working clocks onboard: everyone on the crew who'd worn a watch had it stolen that night in los proyectos, except for Esteban, who'd left his back in his cabin. Canario has a clock radio with an electric cord attached, and the cook's clock has to be plugged in too, so these are useless. But Roque Balboa had brought a battery-operated clock, and Pínpoyo a somewhat larger plastic wind-up clock that ticked like an angry skeleton dementedly pounding its hollow skull over and over against the inside of a coffin lid.

At first Roque Balboa's clock was kept next to the stove on the table in the mess so that everyone could know what time it was, but Desastres—still a kitten really, a skinny runt with orange fur that had just appeared in the mess one day and been adopted by Bernardo, who said she was a female and would be good for hunting rats and named her Desastres to rolling eyes—pawed it off the table, the little clock shattered against the iron floor, and that was that. Then Pínpoyo's wind-up clock was brought into the mess, but they put it up on the high shelf with the water tank where Desastres wouldn't be able to get at it; for about a week the clock's ticking ate at José Mateo's nerves like termites. Until one afternoon the cook and waiter heard Desastres meowing desperately in the mess and found the cat crouched on the high shelf anyway, panic-stiffened tail swatting back and forth, batting-twirling the clock closer towards the edge with every swat right before their horrified eyes. Bernardo jumped on a crate and reached up just as the clock toppled over into his hands. So José Mateo put the clock inside one of the two walk-in food lockers whose refrigeration doesn't work and where he would no longer have to endure its maddening, hollow-plastic ticking. Whenever anyone wanted to know what time it was, he had to go to the food locker, yank with all his strength on the handle until the door opened in a burst of hot, rancid air and flaky debris, and there was the clock, on the rotted wood-planked floor, loudly ticking away, phosphorescent green hands and numerals faintly glowing in the dark. But one morning Panzón opened the food locker and saw the clock lying on its side near the back wall, and when he went inside and picked it up, he saw that it was exactly five past one, which was impossible, the workday was just beginning, the morning sun low in the sky. The clock's hour hand was missing.

Panzón carried the still loudly ticking clock out on deck, into the sunlight; the crew crowded around. Who would do that, snap off the hour hand? Why would anyone do a thing like that? The thin, flat metal ring that had been the hour hand's base was slightly wrenched forward, minusculely jagged and glinting where the hand had broken off. The minute hand still ticked along, though its base was slightly scarred too; the middle of the plastic clock face was scratched. It was as if, instead of just snapping off the hand, someone had mutilated the clock with a fork or bottle opener, something like that. But who would have gone into the food locker and, even in a lonely fit of nerves and angry fidgeting, done that to the clock? (Estéban? The sulky thumb chewer?) The crew was stupefied. Someone had broken their only working clock. Someone had done something very peculiar. They looked around at one another, feeling bewildered and miserable. (Had Esteban—?) How fragile their confidence in each other was after all! It all depended on a person not doing strange, upsetting things like this—who knew what a pendejo like that might do next?

When Capitán Elias and el primero Mark arrived, Panzón showed the officers the clock. "Well, it's just a shitty old clock," said Capitán

Elias unflappably. "I'll bring you a new one." Mark said, "Wow. That's totally weird." El Capitán frowningly studied the clock for a moment, then plucked the minute hand against the clock face as if it was a banjo string. Pulled on it, let it slap back. He pulled on it again, and this time the minute hand snapped off—it really was a slender, brittle thing. "You see?" said Capitán Elias. "Piece of shit." Then Cabezón had to go and open his mouth and say that he could repair it; maybe if he hadn't said anything el Capitán really *would* have brought them a new clock. Cabezón did try to fix it, at his workbench down in the engine room he soldered the minute hand back on, then the new hour hand he'd sheared and shaped from a strip of hammered tin, and the hands did move, though not to the tempo of time, not even close.

But even Capitán Elias, apparently, couldn't get it out of his head, going home at night and pondering why anyone would have broken the hour hand off his crew's clock, searching for an answer in his vast library of technical and nautical manuals and encyclopedias, no doubt. Because the next morning he took Panzón aside and said he thought he knew now what had happened, said, "Panzón"—el Capitán liked using the nicknames the crew had given one another—"abordo tenemos algunas ratas, no?"

A ridiculous understatement. Lying awake in their cabins they often heard rats scratchily moving behind bulkheads, under floors, and over ceilings. They flooded into the mess late at night when no one was there, ate any food left out, they'd torn at their already roach-infested sacks of rice until cook and waiter found some steel tool lockers to store them in, scattering rice mixed with rat droppings all over the floor, which Bernardo had swept up and thrown overboard, miserable about the waste of food and his own wasted and ill-fated life, the two calamities seeming hideously connected . . . Very late one night the rats had even flooded into Bernardo's insomnia. Tormented by the idea that the rats were going to eat Desastres, he got out of bed, hurried to the mess, and stood at the doorway gawking in horror at the revolting black shapes and minutely sparking eyes swarming like lumpy, rippling black lava all over the floor. Even in his anxiety over Desastres he hadn't imagined there were that many rats! And then he found the cat's glowing eyes blinking on and off in the dark: Desastres was sitting untouched in the middle of the floor like some miraculous rat deity, turning her head this way and that, observing her loathsome worshipers groveling all around. He called out, "Desastres!"—and the cat gave a little chirp and ran out of the mess, tail straight up with a live cockroach the size of a man's thumb clamped in her mouth. After that even the cat seemed to know to stay away from the mess late at night, cuddling up against Bernardo's feet to sleep, confining her nocturnal prowling to the deck. Who wanted to look at so many rats! But of course they'd told el Capitán about the rats at night. Capitán Elias was always saying something like, You know, before we sail, we'll have to get those rats exterminated, don't want rats nesting in the cargo, do we? So when Capitán Elias brought up the clock and suggested that they had a few rats onboard, Panzón said, "Sin duda, Capitán, hay ratas. Bastantes."

Capitán Elias leaned over Panzón's hunched, sagging bulk, talking like a man in a panicky hurry to get his argument across before he lost its fragile thread: Rats liked shiny objects for their nests, and in the dark of the food locker the clock's glowing hands must have looked especially shiny, no? And since the food locker has a musty wood floor that definitely must still smell like food to rats and probably even has bits of old food tamped down into its cracks, the food locker is definitely a place that would draw a rat wriggling up through those floorboards—Capitán Elias's voice rose breathlessly: "No ves, Panzón? Qué chinga, cabrón! Fue una rata!" That rat, he said, had coveted those shiny clock hands for its nest, had gnawed, pulled on, and finally broken the hour hand off! So now the hour hand was part of a rat's nest! Capitán Elias, tightly smiling to himself, went and got his flashlight, and Panzón followed him into the food locker.

In the food locker el Capitán frowned and said, "Ve? Mierda de rata por todos lados. No lo hueles?" Must be one full-of-shit rat, shitting all over the place like a hundred rats, Panzón almost said out loud. But the rat droppings seemed to have dampened el Capitán's mood. Without a doubt, he said almost forlornly, waving the flashlight's beam in a slow circle over the floor, there are rats.

Esteban knew that he should offer his wristwatch to Panzón so that he'd be able to keep track of the crew's working hours. But he couldn't bring himself to, didn't want to. The watch was his secret. A strange secret to possess, "the time," one wasted on him because what difference does it ever really make to him whether it's 4:37 A.M. or P.M. or any hour? Vos, telling the time over her grave. A piece of the empty air over her grave folded inside his sock. Guilt burned through his blood whenever he thought of it. What kind of compañero was he, hoarding his watch, making a fetish of his watch like some religious old widow?

Though Panzón quickly discovered, to Esteban's relief, that he didn't need a watch or clock to tell time by after all. Hadn't he just spent a year on a hilltop outside Managua as an aircraft spotter, staring at the sky through binoculars, internally timing his staring to ninety-minute shifts? The habit was now so ingrained that Panzón just had to look at the sky and he knew how much time had passed since the last time he'd looked, practically down to the minute, even on overcast days, his sense of the sky innate as any ancient mariner's. There was a clock inside him now, automatically counting ninety-minute hours, and that was all he needed for his bookkeeping.

Panzón tries to be a diligent and accurate purser. But he counts the days when neither of their officers comes to the ship and they do no work at all as full workdays now too—and even adds on overtime, trying to keep this within reason, no need to exaggerate, el Capitán knows how long their workdays tend to be. It was Bernardo who'd first suggested the measure to Panzón, arguing that given the conditions onboard and the fact that they'd yet to see even a centavo in wages, it was only fair that every day count as a workday whether they did any work or not since, vos—wasn't it obvious?—it was work just being there.

The crew passed Bernardo's motion by unanimous vote, then unanimously agreed that the old waiter was entitled to as much overtime as everyone else. Just as Capitán Elias had said, Bernardo's daily routine hadn't changed now that he was "el segundo" too, though the joke went on reverberating through the old waiter's hopelessly ingrained sense of shipboard order. As the highest ranking "officer" onboard when capitán and primero weren't there, Bernardo should have served himself first at every meal; which of course he never even thought to do. Otherwise the only thing that bothered him about having to adjust his serving to rank—the engine room and electrical "officers" were decent chavalos, and insisted that he stop being so exagerado—was having to serve El Barbie, el contramaestre, fifth. Aside from the purser, who at least had an actual new job to do, El Barbie was the only one who took his elevation in rank seriously, posturing as boss of the ordinary seamen while ignoring their increasingly irritated disdain. As soon as Capitán Elias or Mark or both arrived in the mornings, El Barbie would ask if they had instructions for the crew that day—to which Mark would respond with a baffled grin or a flustered wave of his hand; El Capitán would usually tell Barbie to just have the crew finish whatever they were doing yesterday, or, if there was something new to be done, would explain it to them himself; then El Barbie would go around all day parroting whatever it was el Capitán had said.

Bernardo had first found the cat, an orange female stray with a white chest and a nose the color of raw steak, standing in the middle of the mess one afternoon in July, meowing as if complaining over not having been fed yet. The cat must have stealthily scaled the ladder, unseen, while everyone was busy working. A ship should have a cat, he'd thought right away. Shipboard cats, these are practically a tradition. They hunt mice and rats. There are even those who believe they frighten shipboard ghosts away. Bueno, something soft to touch, a fleeting diversion for callused hands and hearts, nada más.

In the afternoons, Bernardo and José Mateo usually sat on crates outside the mess with pots on their laps sifting rice for dinner from the sacks the Japanese had left behind, plucking out live cockroaches and the husks of dead cockroaches and dropping them into a pile by their feet, carefully crushing the live ones under their heels, sweeping and wiping the viscous mess up when they were done. Desastres usually hovered nearby craving a handout; she was always in the mood to toy with and eventually eat a cockroach. Desastres had a habit of jumping up onto Bernardo's or José Mateo's lap to rake her paws through the rice, and once, when the cook swatted her away too brusquely, she scratched him, leaving vivid red stripes on the back of his hand.

So Bernardo began patiently teaching the cat to obey the command to sit: "Siéntate, Desastres!" and he'd push down on her haunches with his hand. In less than two weeks, the cat was responding just as Miracle would to the same command in English, anyone only had to say "Sit!" to the dog and it would; but Desastres obeyed only Bernardo, and not only that but would remain seated for the longest time, at least until fed a cockroach, or a pinched little ball of bread—when they had bread—soaked in sardine oil. Mark and Capitán Elias said they'd never seen or heard of a cat that could do that, said cats aren't supposed to obey like dogs, or even like lions and tigers, said that's why you never see a troupe of common house cats jumping through hoops at the circus; they even spoke of putting Desastres on television to perform this "stupid," they called it, trick. Sometimes just the sight of Desastres obeying the command to sit and then primly holding the posture was enough to make Mark double over with squealing laughter, arms folded over his stomach, laughter that seemed to gnaw deeper into his stomach the longer the cat sat.

Once Capitán Elias asked Bernardo why he'd named the cat Desastres.

"Because I couldn't think of any other name, mi Capitán," Bernardo answered. It was the first time the old waiter had ever referred to him by that respectful formality, *mi* Capitán.

Desastres liked human company—why else had she come to the *Urus,* hardly a perpetual banquet for a cat, when out there around the cove there must be mice, moles, baby birds and squirrels, bits of fish dropped by gulls, all manner of insects?—liked sitting on the crewmen's laps, playing roughly with their hands, chewing at the base of thumbs, leaving small scratches and bite marks; liked planting herself between their legs as if trying to trip them. Cebo, the former lobster diver, paced the deck with Desastres cuddled in his muscular arms, hand tucked gently over the vibrating pebbles of her purr, or rubbing her padded little paws between his fingers, lullabying over and over,

Mira la niñita,
ninguna más bonita . . .

So here on the *Urus,* according to Capitán Elias and Mark, was a cat that could do what no other cat on earth could do. If the officers said so, was it true? But el Capitán is a knowledgeable young man, full of worldly experience, and the cat clearly thrilled him: no one doubted that if el Capitán could only have coerced Desastres into obeying him as she did Bernardo—and he tried, bent over cooing, "Siéntate! Siéntate, Desastres!" wagging a cockroach pinched between his fingers while the cat sniffed and pawed at it and finally darted away—he'd have claimed the cat for himself, whisked her off to that television show, brought his treasure home to live, shown the cat off to his wife's artist and professor friends. So that was another of the cat's wonders: minus Bernardo, Desastres was just another trickless, scrawny waterfront stray, though one unusually friendly to humans. No one could recall ever having seen a cat that obeyed the command to sit before, though in uncertain asides most admitted to never having paid that much attention to cats anyway, cats which, after all, inhabit every dark nook and cranny of the tropics, scratch any shadow and a cat will come slinking or scampering out. Here on the *Urus*! You'd think that the first time the cat sat for Bernardo the sky would have opened and a long, silvery beam would have shot down and anointed them both in miraculous light. Pues, argued Bernardo, when St. Joseph of Cupertino flew up to the rafters of his church in Italy, there was no such light, people mainly said, Look, there goes that fat, smelly, retarded little priest flying again; they laughed at his fat, hairy ass from under his cassock, and that was a far greater miracle than this. And when the Madonnas in Nicaraguan churches weep actual tears over the country's dishonor and mounting dead, where is this ray of light or any other celestial fanfare? So what's a cat that sits? It's not as if she flies. Even if she is the only cat in the world that can do it. But imagine that, the only cat out of how many trillions of cats in the world, puta Bernardo! Just think of all the thousands of merchant ships plying all the waterways of the world at any given moment and all the cats on those ships and that here, in this shitty little corner of Brooklyn on this shitty ship that doesn't move, this one cat—like the rarest gem set into a flip-top ring! Yes, that's miracle enough, vaya pues, enough. And so the small pop of giddy delight that materialized as if from a silent firecracker in the very air every time Desastres obeyed Bernardo's command to sit and then just sat was even more thrilling than an extraordinary run of luck and skill at dominoes, which could be happening on any other ship out there at the very same time and in the very same sequence and would still be less remarkable than the singularity of this cat; and was pleasing in a way oddly similar to—yet different from, by virtue of being shared—a happy dream recalled in the morning and silently savored for days until the sandpaper of longing wore that away to nothing too. The crew especially liked saying the cat's name, "Desastres! Desastres! Ven gatito! Psst! Ven!" liked that it obviously and increasingly annoyed el Capitán. Bernardo smiled to himself whenever he heard the name echoing from far reaches of the ship like some subversive war cry, "Desastres! Desastres! Desastres! Desastres!" liked to think the chanted name woke Capitán Elias sweating and gasping from his sleep at night . . .

But, after all, men shouldn't allow themselves to get too attached to a cat—cats come and go; nor should anyone feel too sorry when, just as someone is in the surliest mood, the cat gets tangled in his legs and he kicks her away, sends the cat sliding and hissing across the deck . . . though luckily, never down a hole. There are countries, José Mateo reminded them, where people eat cats; he'd heard of Chinese ships that carried cat carcasses frozen in their food lockers just like any other meat. All the Nicaraguans had heard stories of hungry neighbors eating cats, dogs, even pet parrots, *arroz con loro,* sí pues, the revolution's sole contribution to the national kitchen, no?

Desastres was a wanderer, a prowler, like most cats. A clever and independent cat, for hadn't Desastres broken away from mother and brood?—the cats they heard raising such a hysterical, incestuous clamor almost nightly from the wreckage around the cove like demon souls fighting and reveling in a haunted cemetery. Sometimes Desastres disappeared for a day or two at a time—lost in the bowels of the ship, hunting water bugs, other insects, baby rats, who knew what?

About six weeks after Desastres first appeared in the mess, she vanished again, and didn't come back. As the days went by, the mood of quiet desolation the cat's disappearance caused was palpable. It felt a bit like the days after the beating in los proyectos, that fragile, helpless, bewildered mood again. They searched the ship, every corner of the two-level engine room, went down into the hold, looked behind the ballast tanks, climbed the steel rungs of the narrow ladders inside the masts; Cabezón even descended into the keel duct with the officers' flashlight, crawled along the long, dark, flooded tunnel at the very bottom of the ship calling out, "Desastres," climbed into the propeller shaft. But Bernardo knew Desastres was dead. When cats don't come back, he told himself, it's because they're dead or have found someplace more hospitable to live, not likely out here. Well, you can't let yourself get too upset about losing a cat. We're grown men after all—or, in some cases, nearly grown, anyway, and growing much older by the day, poor chavalitos. For all we know, one of those hawks or falcons in the sky dive-bombed when none of us was looking, snatched Desastres up, and took her to some rank lair of fish and rodent bones. Or the rats got her after all . . . One more thing to grieve over, make you sigh in the night, nada más. Bernardo missed the cat, that was for sure, and so did everyone else. But it was just a cat, one with a singular talent that had cheered everyone up, though it couldn't *really* be called miraculous, could it? A cat qualified to go on television to do her stupid trick. More than once Capitán Elias had said he was going to bring a video camera to film Desastres sitting, because otherwise no one would believe it, and he was visibly frustrated with himself for not having done so before the cat disappeared.

5

JUST THIS EVENING PANZÓN TOLD ESTEBAN THAT SO FAR, FOR HIS hundred and eleven days onboard, he's owed one thousand and seventy-three dollars and forty-four cents—more than enough to pay his tíos back for the airfare and the hiring fee. Gracias, tíos.

Capitán Elias always says that he and Mark haven't been paid yet either. But Capitán Elias talks on the telephone to the owner, who tells him that as soon as the ship is up to class, as soon as the cargo is chartered and she's ready to be on her way, they'll be paid. Anyway, el Capitán sometimes reminds the crew, they're free to go when they want, the U.S. Immigration Service has nothing against illegal aliens *leaving*. They've voted on it a few times, why don't we all just leave? But who wants to go home after all these months of work without a cent and still in debt? And who has the airfare? Who wants to turn himself in to Immigration, sit in prison until they finally make up their minds whether to foot the bill for your deportation or not? At the beginning some sent letters home, giving them to el Capitán and el Primero to mail, letters in which they for the most part disguised their plight, until it became impossible to do so—how to explain letters still mailed from New York after so many months?—so they stopped writing, and hardly anyone has even the money to buy a stamp. Esteban has a handful of Nicaraguan coins and no one he really wants to write to anyway. The other day Cabezón and Panzón risked carrying letters they'd written to their novias all the way down to the working end of the port yard until they met up with some Chinese—or Korean, or Japanese, how were they supposed to know?—marineros strolling back to their ships and tried to give them the letters to mail from wherever they were going next, communicating with sign language: the sailing hand with raised-thumb smokestack, swooping backhand gesturing towards "far away,"—who knows what the Chinese or whatever they were understood? They just smiled stiffly as if at a couple of ragged beggar lunatics, turned on their heels, and walked away.

The *Urus* does look better now. The entire deckhouse has been newly painted—white, with patches of red primer still awaiting coatings—though not the hull, or portions of the deck where months of work with sanders, chipping hammers, grit blasters, and portable grinders have been demolishing layers of old paint and rust down to new gleaming steel; many of the holes in the deck have been plated and welded. And new cables and wiring have been threaded up and down the ship's length like a whole new set of veins in an old body. But the ship still has no self-generating electrical power. Something about hard to replace circuit breakers, ordered but somehow lost en route from Japan, new ones supposedly arriving any day. But maybe it's still the wiring after all; they're working on that again too.

The leaves on the summer-parched trees beyond the port yard walls and the cove are turning yellow, and the other morning the deck was frosty. They build fires on deck every night now, collecting wood from the ruins around the cove. The chilly morning air makes everything smell different, sharper, the cold smoke in their clothes, their own skins, they hold their arms and bare shoulders to their noses and breathe it in. A cool, swampy odor billows up from the holds. Even their garbage and their shit loosely covered over with dirt and lime and petrified grain dust inside the grain elevator has a newly refrigerated smell. Supposedly, when the weather gets really cold, the rats will leave the ship, el Capitán says they'll look for someplace warmer. Capitán Elias and Mark come to the ship less frequently now, and not always together. They say they spend their days scouring scrap yards for circuit breakers. They never bring enough food, though there are still sardines, and rice.

That night Esteban stands at the rail in the dark, looking down at the pier, the generator and compressor locked away under graffiti-smeared, yellow shields. He thinks, Lower the ladder and leave it down, walk away. Just walk away! Walk where? He crosses the beam to the other rail and leans forward on crossed arms, staring at the long, jagged outline of a collapsed pier, the black water swift and rippling in the incoming tide . . .

He yawns, begins absently to pace, down the long length of the ship to the stern and up through midships to the prow, and then back. Maybe if he had a bottle and some music, he'd dance. Dance and drink all by himself out here on deck until he felt tired enough for sleep. Or even, puta, just a bottle.

Pretty soon someone will be coming out to take a piss over the side. For a while last month, in September, most were too frightened to do even that. One night someone hiding in the wreckage across the cove fired three gunshots at the hull, the bullets hitting like iron hailstones, followed by the hull's faint, half-imagined reverberation. The day after the next some were lowered over the side in bosun's chairs to probe for where bullets had hit in the iron vastness, but they were able to find only one shiny dent, which looked like it had been left by a ballpeen hammer smashed into soft steel. There were no more gunshots fired at the ship after that, but at least a week went by before anyone could even joke about it. Even now everyone but Esteban and El Barbie is too frightened to shit out there at night, preferring to hold it in until morning, when they can go down into the grain elevator rather than hang like some obscene monkey by both hands from the rail, toilet paper or rag clutched in one hand, bare ass exposed to the cove . . .

Esteban clasps a mooring line tied tightly between gypsy head and bitts, synthetic rope thick as his arm, stands looking down at his hand closed over it through the vapor left by his shallow breathing in the chilly air. He can shimmy down it if he wants. It's how the rats got onboard, presumably how they'll leave when the temperature drops even more. Over the side the rope droops slackly, running midships towards the stern, down to the pier. Rope climbing is something he knows how to do, one of the first and only things taught to draftees in training before they were sent out to learn war by instinct. He walks to the foredeck. Here the length of rope is much longer but tauter all the way down, suspended over the gap of water opened by the prow's curving away from the pier. This one. Why not?

He walks all the way back to the makeshift toolshed between the smokestack and the engine room pit aft, roughly hammered pine walls and door and a corrugated polyurethane roof; inside it's pitch dark. Standing unsteadily on coils of rope and chain and winch cable and bundled tarps, he gropes along the loose shelves.

A paint scraper. A knife for splicing wire. A short, heavy marlinespike. He puts the knife in one pocket, the spike in another.

Walking back he sees Cabezón across the deck at the rail, pissing soundlessly over the side. No jodas, he wants to get going; maybe he can sneak past before Cabezón sees him, but Cabezón turns his big head and looks at him over his shoulder. "Qué onda?"

"Pues, nada."

Cabezón is already zipping up. All their pisses are this brief. Their bladders are turning to rust. Esteban always finds himself pushing and pushing, trying to get a little more out, yet he feels a swollen itch to piss all day long. Sometimes he dreams that he's urinating as abundantly as an elephant.

Cabezón's head looks necklessly propped in the collar of his grease-stained sweatshirt like a fortune-teller's big crystal ball, magnified, hair-fringed face sleepily and convexly peering out. Esteban slides his hands into his pockets to hide the tools as Cabezón crosses the deck towards him and then leans on the rail with folded arms.

"I've been thinking about what we talked about the other night," says Cabezón, sounding almost drunk.

What had they talked about?

"You were right, vos. I'm going to buy the pink horse."

"Ajá," says Esteban. He's never heard of any pink horse. Delirium. Or else Cabezón must be sleepwalking, dreaming about a pink horse. Is this the perfect final conversation to be having on a phantom ship or what?

"That'll be the good part of being paid all at once, no? When I get back, I'm going to buy the pink horse, just like that."

"What are you going to name it?" asks Esteban, fascinated despite his impatience; he's never conversed with a sleepwalker before.

"The Pink Horse." Cabezón shrugs. "It's a good name. Like I told you, Natalia's mother's cousin owns it. But he's moving to Roatán. Said he'd sell it to me cheap and give me plenty of time to pay. Natalia and I can live in the back and run it together and I can still work as a mechanic in the day. Pues, why not?"

"It's a cantina or something?"

Cabezón looks at Esteban a moment and, keeping a straight face, says, "What are you talking about? It's a pink horse. You've never seen one?"

Esteban waits by the rail awhile after Cabezón has plodded chuckling off to his cabin. Then he walks swiftly back to the foredeck, steps over the rail, and hangs on in a crouch, looking down between his legs at the rope emerging from the mooring pipe and the black water underneath and in one motion pushes off and grabs the rope to his chest as he falls and wraps his legs around it, finding a center of balance after a few scary lurches. He slowly shimmies backwards down the mooring line, descending the wall of the hull, pausing several times to shove restless tools back down into his pockets. At the end he turns himself around to pull himself up onto the pier.

He stands looking up at the ship, lungs and hands tingling, trying to picture himself still up there, lying awake in his cabin near the viejo as he has night after night. If he climbs back up, will everything stay the same? It will be like cutting a person out of a group picture in a newspaper, one you can take out or put back in whenever you want.

Now what? The whole unknown city. The pale gold skyscrapers on the horizon. What if by this time tomorrow I already have a job? Can I go looking for a job dressed like this? Where will I sleep? In that park with the horses that's always in the movies. I'll find the United Nations, and then the Nicaraguans there, tell them I fought in a BLI and ask them for clothes. But will they think I've done something wrong? Send me back?

A white slice of moon hangs over the breakwater forming the harbor side of the cove. In between, sequined wavelets ride the current, licking pilings. Someone else might come out on deck. He walks swiftly off the pier and around the grain elevator and into the lot behind, and hesitates there as if at a confusing crossroads in the middle of nowhere. Pues, he can go anywhere now. What will they say in the morning, when they see he's gone, and the ladder still up?

But instead of into Brooklyn, his footsteps pull him towards the ocean. It isn't fear, more like a self-protective yearning leading him this way. He doesn't want to lose what he feels in himself right now, wants to get to know it instead of taking the chance of squandering or ruining it in some disastrous adventure he hasn't thought through.

The immense old terminal of mouse gray wood, shaped like an airplane hangar, stands on a stretch of beach and tumbled pilings and rubble, between the road and a field of high weeds. He crosses the field, a fried landscape of dry stalks and brittle, silvery leaves, towards the terminal, hears the faint tinkling of buoy bells out in the harbor night. A brambly tumbleweed suddenly lifts across his path like the ghost of a porcupine. Inside, the terminal feels as spacious and empty as a gutted cathedral with a floor made of sand, a dizzying sensation of airy pitch darkness soaring up all around. He hears the beatings of invisible wings and cooing high above, looks up through the dark at the muted glow of night sky through tatters in the roof. And he sits down right in the cool sand; it's as if a flood tide had carried the sand inside and, receding, left it smoothly and evenly distributed over the terminal floor. The solitude, this sudden fact of himself, of being Esteban Gaitán and all that he's lived through and kept pent up inside for so many months, he could almost weep from this bewilderment and wild mix of emotion he suddenly feels. He stares straight ahead like some campfire-stunned jungle animal at the edge of a clearing, through the terminal's immense pier gates at night sky over the blackened harbor. He lies back in the sand. It was raining softly in Quilalí the first time he saw her—she and her sister, waiting outside the church door in the rain-misted glow from the light inside, she sitting on the steps facing him and her sister standing at the edge of the doorway watching the yanqui padre with the unpronounceable last name finishing up the evening mass. Across the street, in an adobe-walled poolroom lit by a single weak bulb, men in white cowboy hats leaned over their cue sticks. An old man on a white horse with long, rickety legs lightly cantering down the dirt street and on into the dark leading out of town. Esteban and his friend Arturo were in uniform, AKs slung over their shoulders. Their BLI had spent the last three weeks moving through the mountains in a triangle between there and Wiwilí and the Río Coco, mostly in coordinated pursuit of a contra column finally caught in a pincer, driven back across the border; his and another company were now bivouacked just outside the town, waiting for the battalion to re-form. He and Arturo weren't really looking for girls when they decided to take a walk into town, though of course they'd said they were. Quilalí was unlikely to offer much but awkward campesinas who wouldn't even be fun to talk to after the first few minutes, and though militarily secure, it was supposed to be full of contra sympathizers anyway. But then they saw the girls in green fatigues in front of the church, and the one sitting on the steps looked up as they approached, long, black hair falling around her shoulders, and her luminously large eyes saw right into him with the swift, soft tumble of a twirled open lock, seemed to reach in and lay invisible, soft hands around his heart. At first he thought she looked owlish, but then he realized she was beautiful, her soft, round face was beautiful, so melancholy and serious, and she met his gaze as if she knew him and wasn't at all surprised to see him. The other compita, curly and short haired, lighter skinned, hand propped on one hip, buttocks swelling her fatigues, turned and looked at them over her shoulder. He looked at the first one again. What was she doing here? He asked her that.

"Waiting to talk to the padre," she said.

"Why?" He didn't have any special reason for asking, just couldn't think of anything else to say. He noticed that there was a piece of thread tied around her little finger, and that the thread led up to the unbuttoned opening in her shirt and disappeared into the triangle of softly swelling skin inside.

She looked at the other girl, and then back at him, and shrugged. "We have to talk to him," she said.

Arturo butted in. "Who are you with?"

"BON Seventy-seven–Sixty-five," answered the other girl.

"What's that?" asked Arturo.

"It's a Batallón Voluntario Juventud Sandinista from León," she said. "We're from León."

"I didn't think they still had those," said Arturo.

"They do."

Esteban's girl—she was already his girl—cupped a hand over her shirt between her breasts, and looked down at her hand.

"What do you do? Coffee harvesting? Medical work?" asked Arturo.

"No, we've been in the mountains," said the short-haired girl.

"Going after la contra?" Arturo said it as if that couldn't be what they'd been doing.

"Sí. Pues . . . To tell you the truth, they've been going after us. It's been more like that."

"They let women fight?"

"Sí. Bueno, except for us, it's all compañeros."

"I'm Arturo, this is Esteban. We're with a BLI."

And the girl standing said, "I'm Amalia, and that's Marta. We're sisters."

They sure seemed serious. Well, joining a volunteer battalion, what did he expect?

"What's that thread, Marta?" asked Esteban. He wanted her to lift her eyes and look at him again.

But she only seemed to peer even more intently down at her shirtfront, just her nose protruding from the waterfall of hair over her face. Her hands nudged something up from inside her shirt, cupping over the open collar, and then she was holding a small squirrel, thread fastened around a rear leg. The squirrel had silky, red fur and crouched tremblingly in her palms, then wrestled itself around so that its tail was raised towards Esteban. She held the squirrel out to him, and he stepped forward and bent down and cupped his hands over hers and took the animal into his, her tied finger crooked as she lifted her hand a little, following the thread.

"Qué tal," said Esteban to the squirrel, feeling his voice quaver as if he felt exactly the same way the squirrel seemed to. He asked her where she'd found it.

"In the mountains," she said.

"Did you kill many contra?" asked Arturo.

"No. Not one, to tell you the truth," said Marta after a moment, her eyes on Esteban's hands, her hand still raised as if offering it as a perch to a flying bird.

"But they killed . . . well, they killed a great many of us," said Amalia, her voice rising. "The day before yesterday they killed the compa leading us. We're here waiting for a new officer, supposedly."

Esteban, lying on his back, watches the sky slowly lightening through the tattered terminal roof. He's been listening to their cooing all night but now he can see mourning doves perched like mauve bowling pins on the rafters under the ruined ceiling. Now and then one of the doves flies into the graying air, wings beating, circling under the roof before landing on another rafter.

He kissed her for the first time that night, hours after the sisters went in and talked to the padre while he and Arturo waited outside. He held her tightly against him while she sobbed against his chest, soaking his shirt with salty tears and drool, the squirrel back inside her shirt, tucked between her breasts. By the end of that week everyone in the battalion was calling him Ardilla, for that squirrel.

"Three nights in a row," she said. "We set pickets out on the perimeter of our camp. And found them in the morning with their throats slit, all stabbed up, mutilated. The third night they got Beto. Amalia and I had known Beto since, *ufff*—before primary school. He'd made the decision to join up with us. And when he was told it was his turn to stand guard, he cried, he knew. But he did it. They scooped out his eyes, as if with spoons. They have this instrument, Esteban, it's as if they can light up the jungle at night, see through trees. But they'd just shout insults and threats at us, say things about us so that we'd know they could see us, shoot off a few rounds . . ."

"Vos, they don't try that mierda with us," he said finally. "Their toys. They run from us. We chase *them*."

"They could have finished us off," she said. "All of us. But they didn't. Instead they just followed us around. They were playing with us. *We* were their toy."

Later she told him that if their officer had insisted on posting guards the fourth night they were prepared to kill him themselves if they had to. But then that very day, out of nowhere, a bullet had smashed through jungle, splintering branches and leaves, and killed him, taken away a piece of his head. And they'd left him there, hiked out to a road, and walked all the way to Quilalí.

When Marta and Amalia's new commanding officer arrived in Quilalí a few days later, he put a hand-lettered cardboard sign up over the door of their temporary quarters in some old stables: THE GREATEST VICTORY IS THE BATTLE WE AVOID HAVING TO FIGHT. No training can prepare you for death, though war does that almost better than it does anything else, until finally you realize you have a good enough chance to get through it alive and your body turns into terror and joy. After his battalion left Quilalí a week later, he thought about that little cardboard sign every day, fervently trusting in la Marta's new officer, formerly a mailman and militia leader from León, to keep his cautious or noble or whatever they fucking were words.

After a while he gets up and walks towards the wide pier gates at the front of the terminal and sits down on the cracked timber frame, looking at the double row of blackened, barnacle-coated pier stumps extending into the pink-tinged expanse of flowing, rough, gray water. He can see the whole statue now, standing on her own island. Close to shore the water is almost the same shade of green as the statue, and sudsy-foamy, the bank a piled rubble of stone, driftwood, broken pier debris, litter, a length of rotted yellow mooring line winding through it all like a giant princess's braid. The ringing buoys, lights glowing palely in the dawn, run in a diminishing line across the harbor. Two long barges cut slowly, in opposite directions, across the buoys. The skyscrapers immensely walling one end of the harbor. A tugboat passes so close he can hear the loud chugging of its engines and the water parting around it and see a man at the wheel behind greasy glass. He watches it plowing towards the long bridge at the other end of the harbor. Out there, just beyond the bridge, waits a huge ship with an orange-and-black hull, a tanker probably. Gulls swooping and skimming the water with their grinning cartoon-villain faces, wings out as if wired to coat hangers.

He walks back through the terminal, early morning sunlight slanting at awry angles through the roof. What do the doves feed on? Mice? He imagines doves roasting on a spit over a fire on deck. Would it make his crewmates sick? He'd have to catch at least a dozen anyway. Bueno, he's eaten pan-fried hummingbirds, each no more a mouthful than a peanut inside a grease-soaked shell. Make a net and build some wings and float around up there snagging doves, vos, ni verga . . .

6

CLARO, ESTEBAN'S BED IS EMPTY, HIS BLANKET A JUST VISIBLE KICKED-OFF lump in the cold, grimy cabin, the same leaden gray dawn he's just watched from his barstool on deserted Bourbon Street filtering through the cracked porthole along with the sobbing of gulls. What a dream this is, chavalito, it just goes on and on, but what does it mean? And why does he feel that he'd rather not wake up from it? The ghost ship stone silent, but isn't it time to leave, shouldn't the engines be running? It would be comforting if he could get up and look out the porthole, see shifting furrows of foam-striped, gray, empty ocean all the way to the horizon, know that the dream would last at least as long as an Atlantic crossing. Then he could go about his work serenely, setting the officers' saloon table three times a day for no one, serving no one, mopping the floor in the officers' quarters corridor for no one, diligently sewing a lost button onto the uniform shirt of his invisible capitán, polishing his empty shoes. But then who would pay him? Bueno, if it's true that on this ship, as on the other, no one ever comes to pay you, then, all things considered and weighed, I'll stay on this one, muchísimas gracias . . .

Except, as every morning, every part of his body asserts its own distinct ache or chilly discomfort. Kidneys left out over night in a cold iron pan. Fingers made of chalk. Crushed can knees, and swollen ankles—every morning, until his ankle joints begin to loosen, he shuffles around as if his feet are serving trays. Chest heavy as a dead elephant lying on its side in a pit of wet talc. Dios mío, what desolation. But at least long stretches of this dream have been peaceful and even pleasurable, an untroubled journey, bringing me closer to something, knowledge, a recognition, algo.

There are three color snapshots propped against the bulkhead by his mattress on the floor, images blurred behind the fogged plastic he keeps each tightly wrapped in. Right now a giant cockroach is crawling up the veiled ladder of the cargo freighter *Mitzi*—that is, crawling up the plastic over the picture of himself holding Clara's hand in front of the *Mitzi*'s ladder, her hair, skin, and dress bright as a daisy in the eternal tropical sunlight; in another split second a now forgotten crewmate will lower his camera, while he himself will let go of Clara's hand and climb the ladder with a taste of her lips on his which will have to last nearly a year. Another snapshot is a fairly recent one of his and Clara's daughters and grandson on their front porch in Managua—his motherless daughters impossibly grown up now, glad to have him out of the way, but expecting him home in another year or so, their unconsoling investment in his airfare to New York having paid off, his pockets wadded with redemptive dollars. The third snapshot is of Esmeralda, his daughter from his first marriage, when she was a beauty queen in Haifa. He hasn't heard from Esme in thirteen years now, and as far as he knows neither has Florencia, her mother, remarried now to an evangelical Protestant pastor, moreno like herself, in Greytown. Not a single letter. He has no address for her.

Santísima Virgen! so many years ago! when he was little older than Esteban is now, and Esmeralda was a baby, a grinning chocolate elf with freckles and dimples, living in Managua with Florencia, her sister and grandfather, Don Peter Cooper, from Bluefields, a tailor who worked at home, people would ask, "Where's your papi, Esme?" or "Who is your papi, Esme?" and Esmeralda would point at a hat, any hat that happened to be nearby, a souvenir capitán's hat from Veracruz, a baseball hat, one of her abuelo's straw fedoras hanging from a peg. She would point at that hat. Whenever she sees a hat now, does Esme still think of her papi?

Her papi el viejo lobo de mar, a hat lying in bed, dreaming with eyes open, waiting to wake up on a dead ship named *Urus*.

Bueno, if you believe that the earth, everyone and everything in it, just as it all is, really is proof of God's will, does that help you make sense of anything? Because at least you can tell when Luck is out to fuck you, but who can bear to think that God is? God treats each person's life like a tedious game of solitaire, indifferently laying down the cards but determined to reach the end, no? Or maybe it's more like this: God and Luck are two old friends drinking in a cantina, taking turns buying, growling like two pompous Spaniards, "Yo invito ahora," after every round.

For example, let's say God brought Esmeralda to Haifa to be a beauty queen, knowing what that would probably mean in the long run. But then Luck decided that Esme's crown, rather than being the prelude to a long career as just another fading dockside, exotic dama, should serve to entice a lonely Israeli policeman.

Or take José Mateo, the cook, who won fifty thousand cordobas in the lottery and was about to retire from ships and buy himself a cantina when the revolution happened, so he prudently decided to go to sea again until the situation settled, and now his banked cordobas are worthless. Fired from his last job for outrageously excessive drunkenness. Now he finds himself cook on the *Urus,* frying mashed sardines and rancid rice.

And so you see, chaval, it isn't only when you gamble that you lose. Bad luck brought me to this ship, because God had no reason to do that to me. Once here, He decided that my purpose should be to look after these muchachos, especially Esteban, like a son. So I've told myself.

But the chavalo's bed is empty. And I'm a ludicrous old man traveling an abandoned earth on a ghost ship, unloved and uncared for, already forgotten, and look, instead of upsetting me, this truth fills me with placid peace. That's the dream's message, sent to console and resign, softly coercing me into relinquishing my vanity along with everything else. At last, I must begin to see things clearly. One of youth's vanities is that you go on mattering, pues, to the people you've cared for, however inconsistently or ineffectively. That loving forms eternal ties, stronger than time, even when as dormant and quiet as the shade under a tree. So today this silly young man in an old man's body is going to wake up old on the inside too, is that it? Vos, ready yourself, viejo lobo. You're already forgotten. Even poor Desastres is gone. Desgraciado, stop trying to entangle others in your vanity. Do you really think you make a difference to these muchachos, who are fucked with or without you? Did you really think chicken incubators, a little business of your own to run in your last extra years, earning you enough to pay for your own portion of whatever gets dolloped onto your plate at meals, was going to bring a flicker of respect or affection to your daughters' eyes, simply because their papi el viejo lobo de mar went to sea one last time to be able to sell eggs wrapped in newspaper cones to neighbors? The shit-flecked shells smudged by newsprint trumpeting the virtues of a squalid fratricidal war that has bled the country even of chickens and eggs, turning everyone but the Comandantes into heartsick paupers, sí pues, Nicaragua has no luck either, you would think that no country should feel lucky in a war or while at war but of course this isn't true, even in Nicaragua there are many who believe themselves lucky for this chance to stuff themselves with glory while everyone else starves.

"Chocho!"—the boy's voice obscenely exploding his reverie. So he's not alone on a ghost ship after all. Esteban has stepped over the rat-damming iron panel laid across the cabin door's lower portion and stands in the underwater gloom looking at him with an openly mocking and bemused smile:

"Vos, heating up your head up with a picture of your daughter? Don't you think that's disgusting?"

Bernardo looks wonderingly at the picture he'd been holding up between two fingers in front of his own face, the plastic peeled back as if he was getting ready to eat it. Ever since he got that bump on his head that night he's been doing things without noticing himself, mind like a television screen fading to black and then after who knows how much time suddenly and impertinently blinking back on—and there's Esmeralda, green-dyed ostrich feathers pluming from a little gold cap on her head, hair straightened and bobbed, lips scarlet and plump as a split-open pomegranate, a tiny gold-sequined leotard, and her limbs bared, arms out in the air, one long thigh turned towards the camera, knee slightly raised, golden high heel propped on tiptoe, "Look, Papi. I'm a Beauty Queen! Love, Esmeralda. Haifa, Israel, 1964."

Esteban reaches down, plucks the snapshot from his hands, stands over him looking at it. When Esteban came in he had a funny, feverish glow in his eyes, private and aloof like a cat's, and look, all over his pant legs, little bits of straw and burrs, grains of sand, as if he's been lying down in a field . . .

What was he doing, lying down in a field? And with whom? What field? He sits up suddenly and swallows his question the wrong way, explodes into a coughing fit, hawking and heaving and gasping for air while Esteban watches suspiciously. And then when he's quieted, sitting there panting like a thirsty Miracle, Esteban hands the picture back, smirks. "Bueno, I can see why that policeman went for her. But, vos, don't you think it's a little strange, a girl sending her father a picture like that, and her father carrying it around for years and years?"

"It's the only one I have of her. Florencia kept the rest. But it's a good picture. To her mother, its meaning was even biblical."

"Sí? Cómo?" And he laughs. "Puta, I'd like to see that Bible." Esteban sits down on the edge of his bed, undoes his electrical wire laces, pushes his boots off with his feet, lies down fully clothed, and pulls the blanket over himself. "So why is it biblical?" he asks after a while, turned on his side facing away.

"Where were you all night?"

"All night? Here. Where else?"

"You have campo on your clothes. This ship has not suddenly turned into a farm."

"I was here, but I couldn't sleep. I went for a walk."

"A walk."

Esteban suddenly sits up, glares at him with perplexed affront. "To look at the ocean. Oye! Qué te pasa?" Finally his expression softens. "You know what I did? I went down the mooring line, and then back up. Nobody saw me. So don't tell anybody." The boy holds his eye a moment longer, then flops back down.

Bernardo ponders this. Sí pues, that goes with Esteban, it's something he'd get it into his head to do. Climb down and then back up a mooring line—like some stowaway who decides he's gotten off in the wrong port. Why? Why did he come back?

"Then why did you come back?"

Esteban says nothing.

"You're going to leave." Halfway through this sentence turned from a question into something close to a command. And suddenly Bernardo feels excited, wonders how he couldn't have thought to suggest it before! Wouldn't a real father have thought of it long ago?

"You should go, Esteban. Take your chance, chavalo. Me, I'd rather die than go home empty-handed after all these months, owing my daughters money."

And he thinks, It's true, I'd rather die.

"Who says we're going anywhere? They'll find us here in a thousand years, and your skeleton will still be holding on to that picture, and, vos, they'll put you in a museum, the primitive viejo lobo pervert."

"You should leave," he persists. "The way Esmeralda did. For her, taking this chance, it was a triumph."

"Bueno. I'll be an Israeli beauty queen too."

"Think of it this way, patroncito. Luck bought the last round, and so here you are with the rest of us"—but Esteban is a complete atheist—"so now it's your turn."

"My turn to *sleep*."

Does he want to end up like me? He left the ship and now he needs to go farther, like Esme, who triumphed. Why should the poorest wetback sneaking across the border have more daring when he couldn't have more hunger? Trouble is, Esteban is loyal, to the idea of what he came here for and of who he is, to all that won't ever pay or repay him, is that it? I have to be convincing, lay down this argument paving stone by paving stone.

"She went from Nicaragua all the way to Israel, chigüín, a bold girl, no one can take that away from Esmeralda, she even changed her religion. You know what her mother thought? That in her own way, Esme was living almost the whole story of the Bible." That Esmeralda had strayed so far into Satan's domain—that picture, Satan's beauty queen!—that God fought back by planning a back-door escape for her, going all the way around, practically, to the beginning of the Bible to build her a little door, lead her through it into heathen Golden-Calf-without-a-cowbell wanderings in the desert so that she could find the One God in the unlikely form of a lonely, somewhat lost and lusting, but basically stable, hardworking, and decent Israeli policeman of frankly dark North African features, a family man to lead her to the land of milk and honey. Didn't it happen that way? It came to pass, pues, that God next situated Esme and her blossoming family in Jerusalem, holy to Christians and Mussulmans too, claro, a strategic maneuver, because here, according to Florencia, Esme was destined to embrace the Messiah along with all Rome's idolatrous perversions, this just a stepping-stone to salvation's last stop, the True Path, the Purified Word, et cetera. Florencia had shed her own never very devout Catholicism by then; he'd come home from the sea one year and found himself married to a fervent Protestant, fundamentalist, pentecostal, and evangelical. You can't imagine, chavalo, the grip this howling salvation had on her. A troubled time. As bleak as this one now, in many ways. Denouncing the wayward, irrefutably vice-ridden, and worldly ways of the seafaring life night and day, begging him to stay home, renounce that life, accept the Lord's Call. She vacuumed all the love that was left from his heart with her incessant Lord, Satan, Doom, and Paradise, until he only wanted to get away. Blaming himself for what his years of desertion had made of her, he fled to sea again and never came back, not to her . . . The money he'd been saving for years so that one day he and Florencia could move out of her father's, buy a little house of their own, this was destined to go to another woman, other daughters.

"Bueno, so that was what Florencia foretold for Esme. And when Esme named her first two sons Moisés and José, Florencia thought these were providential signs, divining José the carpenter, not the coat of many colors. So when the girl came, muchacho, shouldn't she have been named María, or at least for a saint? Instead Esme named her Chiniche. Chiniche? I think this is an African name . . ." He'll probably never know now why his Israeli daughter suddenly chose an African name for her daughter.

Esteban lying still on his stomach, facing away—has he been listening? Bernardo lifts a hand to his head, softly strokes the still sensitive, grape-skinned bump with a finger. Was that clear? Has he made himself understood?

"So it didn't happen, you mean," says Esteban finally, sleepily.

"It didn't happen . . . Who knows? I haven't heard from Esmeralda in thirteen years. But I hope it didn't. Esme decided to convert to her husband's religion, and ve? She was happy and fertile, three children in less than five years. Maybe she's had even more? She can name them for the Moorish kings for all I care. She's forgotten us, but why shouldn't she have? Her mother pestering her like one of those screaming preachers, like the one she's married to now. Her father a hat on a chair, and of even less use to her. But when lucky people take chances, luck rewards them, that's what I think. You made it through that war. I don't think luck is through with you yet, chavalo. Maybe it's just a matter of going down that rope again, and not coming back up."

He looks over at Esteban, not even stirring, sleep as silent as smoke on a ship made of smoke; the morning light wet smoke colored and just as soft, in the cracked porthole; the corridor in the doorway still dark. A querulous and hungry squawking nearby, not gulls, a raven?

What should he tell him now? Sadness like a chimney, smoky words and memories pouring from it . . . Clarita curled up, withered and stiff as a dead spider on her hospital bed from tetanus . . . Esteban has never even been in love, at least has never mentioned having ever felt either the euphoria or the infernal consequences of love; all he thinks about is that fucking war, which has robbed him of everything a chavalo his age should be so vulnerable to . . . Florencia . . . When he first met her. As fresh and shyly full of life as any niñita but already a sturdy woman's body. She'd been to school, was working in a bakery in downtown Managua. A bakery that, like the rest of downtown, isn't there anymore, destroyed in the earthquake of '72. "Florencia was standing in a bakery window the first time I saw her, chavalo, a bakery that isn't there anymore . . ." She stood in the bakery window, in her clean, white uniform, setting little white plastic swans into the blue frosting waves rimming the tiers of a very grand wedding cake. There, on the other side of the window, stood her future hat on a chair, just home from his first long and lucky voyage at sea, having embarked from Panama City as a lowly crew's mess dishwasher and janitor nearly two years before! And lucky to have found even that job. Begging marineros for a hint of work from bar to bar, his paltry saved-up-to-go-to-sea money nearly gone, but he had a little girlfriend, a cimarrona named Miriam Monróy, who snuck him food, worked in a little cantina–seamen's brothel in the Casco Viejo owned by a raucous, skinny, long-limbed woman, part Syrian, part Chinese, who'd seemed ancient to him then but undoubtedly would seem young now, she was the lover of a Greek capitán named Gorgo, whose ship had been in port for repairs three months already—what was her name?—her skeptical and shiny Oriental eyes coming back to him now, the small, lipstick-smudged mouth, the loose skin drooping under her chin, her nervous, cigarette-winged, dragonfly fingers . . . Gorgo had given her a port pass so that she could get past the yanquis and come to his ship whenever she wanted, and she lent it to him on the condition that while looking for work he'd also distribute mimeographed flyers advertising her "Seaman Bar," boarding as many ships as he could, leaving flyers in little stacks by the gangways. Which is what he did; how he was hired, not by Gorgo but by another Greek whose ship was in port, Aristotle Voulgaris, master of the *Opal,* one of a small fleet of cargo vessels owned by one Señor Fedderhoff, a gringo living in Panama City. A good, busy, and profitable ship. Five months into the voyage, they departed Veracruz with a cargo of garbanzos bound for Barcelona, sailing into a mid-Atlantic Christmas. An obese and nasty-tempered Panamanian named Zacarías Rojas was the officers' saloon waiter. And would you believe it, chavalo?—the day before Christmas Eve, Zacarías Rojas was in the meat locker with the mayordomo, both of them struggling with all their might to pry a frozen Christmas turkey loose from the ice-coated rack the turkey was ice-welded to, when Rojas suddenly fell over dead from a heart attack. He had family in Panama, a wife, children. Señor Fedderhoff radioed the ship that they should bring Rojas home. In other words, leave him there, right where he'd fallen, sparing the crew the grotesque effort of having to drag his manateelike bulk up on deck for a burial at sea. For the rest of that voyage, which eventually took them through the Suez Canal and down the Red Sea to India and the Orient, Rojas lay unmourned in the meat locker, frozen under a frozen sheet, hard as concrete, his skin turned an iridescent, turbid blue. His timid and repentant ghost never bothering anybody. For seven whole months, until they docked in Panama again. With crowbars and boiling water Rojas was pried loose from the floor, delivered to his family. But guess who'd been promoted to the officers' saloon the day after Zacarías Rojas ceased to exist? Christmas Eve. No older then than you are now, chico! (While a green ordinary seaman who'd discovered he hated deck work began a new career in the crew's mess.) More coffee, mi Capitán? Sugar on your toast, mi Primero? Sí, jefe, your liver without onions. He never had to ask twice, always remembered what they wanted and how they liked it, rode their whims and caprices and sullen midvoyage torments smoothly, elegantly, never scowling with aggravation like Rojas, who had often refused the low-ranking officers dessert if they asked for it even two minutes after the meal hour had passed! In roughest seas, chavalito, he was a sweet-tempered circus plate juggler. Instinctively knew how to make a Greek boor feel like an English admiral, well before he had the unforgettable experience, in 1969, of serving Capitán John Paul Osbourne as personal waiter and valet. Bernie, Capitán Osbourne used to call him, and sometimes *Old Bean*. How couldn't he have felt lucky? In all the merchant ships sailing all the seas, was there another officers' saloon waiter so young, so well liked and appreciated? And not badly paid, no. Bueno, a burning Managua sidewalk, Panama hat tilted back over forehead, hands in pockets, cigarette in mouth, basking in the vision of this young morenita's poise and beauty, fluid limbs and shapeliness and a clean, white uniform, fingers dipping into a small cardboard box perched on her ample hip, pulling out swans. Ask any seaman, Santos, Brazil's bule bars have no rivals, but if he'd confused a taste for African skin with their squalid enchantments, this vision of a happy-eyed Florencia and cake, as seductively deranging as any Santos siren, disinfected his lust and left his desire intact, left him standing there strangling on a need to possess not for one night but for a lifetime! Impulsive, sí pues. But often seamen who want to get married don't get much time on land to make up their minds! Which is why, claro, they make mistakes, why it takes them so many years to realize these mistakes, realize that they themselves are the mistake, carajo. She looked over her shoulder, saw him watching, left him stuporously rooted with her direct, utterly blank, green-gray stare, went back to swanning her cake, looked over at him again, and then suddenly, a shy and flustered smile like a sunny, snowy island rising on the horizon . . . He went right into that bakery, said he wanted to buy that cake. She giggled, said, Aren't you going to let me finish? Who's in such a rush to get married? And he said, Me. With you, queen of my life. The boldest moment of my life, chavalo. An electrical charge still jumps his heart, his belly, when he remembers it. She looked at him incredulously, her eyes glinting with what he thought was a proud girl's haughty affront, and then her tongue went *tch!* against her teeth, and she said, Are you a marinero? Yes, he said, but not that kind of marinero, I'm no womanizer or liar. And she laughed, said she didn't mean it that way. You see, Florencia had recently been to see some old woman, an hechizera who could read the future in cigarettes. You brought this witch a cigarette, she lit it, puffed on it a bit, twirled it slowly between thumb and finger in front of her eyes while it burned down, and in the pattern of burning paper and ash, she could read the future. The love of her life was going to be a marinero, this brujita had told Florencia. Young and handsome, who would marry her and then leave her alone at home with children for years, but that she shouldn't worry because when that marinero finally came home for good he was going to be as rich as Petroceli . . . "Florencia believed that, cipote, and so did I. How couldn't I have, I mean to say, back then? Sí pues, back then! The way—"

"You both got what you deserved, viejito." Esteban's emphatic, pillow-muffled voice breaking in and surprising him, and he says, "Qué?" and bird-cocks his head, and the boy says it again, louder, his body not even stirring. "She got what she deserved. Vos, you both did. Believing a thing like that, the future in a cigarette, hombre, no jodas! And you're always calling *us* gullible."

* * *

Throughout his life, of course, Bernardo has heard countless stories about people seeing ghosts, sensing and hearing phantom presences, though it has been exactly half a century plus one year since he last suffered such an experience, the year before he left for the sea, when his own mother's ghost appeared to him, an incident which then terrified and grieved him since he'd understood that his mother's showing herself to him like that meant she was unhappy, her spirit in distress. But he hasn't thought about his mother's ghost in years, nor has he ever received such a visitation even from poor Clarita, even though he used to pray for one, willing silently into the night for her to come and reassure him of her forgiveness and love. He believes he's long lost whatever it is that makes a person seem receptive enough to such apparitions that they appear, and assumes it must have something to do with age—why should a spirit hurry to see him when he'll be among them soon enough?—or with the tarnishing of his own soul by misdeeds and guilt.

Yet at the very moment when Esteban was sneaking off the ship for the first time last night, he was dreaming of being on a ghost ship. The dream's lonely suggestiveness has lingered into the day, as such dreams tend to. This queasy mood, a languid, hollowed out sensation at odds with the excitement he feels over his new secret obligation—Esteban must leave!—an immanence out there, like the sense of a still-faraway change in the weather coming, his tattered nerves straining to pick it up in the chilly October air. Thus a certain receptivity to ghosts.

He's doing some laundry down on the pier, his pant legs rolled up, his hands numbing in the cold water from the spigot as he rubs uselessly at stained rags with an evaporating sliver of soap, and glancing up he sees them coming around the corner of the grain elevator, arm and arm, an old couple helping each other along, two ancianos: the old man in a green gabardine overcoat, black beret, and dark glasses, the old woman in a pink woolen coat and a flowered scarf knotted around her head. They're the very first people he's seen close up, besides officers, crew, and los blacks on the pier, since that night in los proyectos—and they've come on foot? His first shocked impression is that they *are* ghosts, that somehow he's fallen back into last night's dream and this is some new twist, an impression abetted by the anciana's powdery-papery pallor, her wrinkles shining like sprinkled sugar in the sun, her smeary raspberry red lipstick, and the wafting scent of her perfume, heavy, florid, and sweet enough to drown any trailing odor of the grave.

The old woman speaks first, and Bernardo, gaping up at them like a frog from his midpuddle crouch, stammeringly answers in Spanish that he doesn't speak English. And the anciana's thin, painted eyebrows rise, and she says that it is certainly a pleasant surprise to run into a Spanish speaker out here, yes, what a pleasure it is, mi buen hombre, to meet you; she uses the formal usted.

"Gracias, señora," says Bernardo, turning off the tap and rising to his feet. "Mucho gusto, a sus órdenes. En que te puedo servir? Dígame." And he rolls down his pants and dries his hands against the legs, and has the uncertain impression that the two, even the old man behind his dark glasses, have been frowning at his accent.

For a moment more the couple stand looking expressionlessly around them at the rusted ship, out at the dilapidated remains of long ago thriving piers and terminals; at the obscenities and skull and crossed bones spray-painted on the grain elevator, the rusted remnants of scaffolding and chute dangling beneath its high window like broken sticks from an old eagle's nest.

"Somos de Argentina," the anciana says, adding that they've lived in Brooklyn for many years now; she doesn't ask where Bernardo is from. They are truly old, he thinks, at least ten years older than I, and the anciana, maybe more!

"Mi buen hombre. Can you tell me? Is this the so-called Grain Pier?" asks the old man, his voice a bit hoarse though with a polished, politely demanding timbre and enunciation; and he smiles, pulling his lips back, showing pink gums and all his yellowed but orderly teeth.

Bernardo answers that he guesses, with all due respect, that it's been a long time since anyone has called it by that or any name, as you can see, señores, there's not a lot going on, just this old ship, which we're trying to repair, though, if you want my opinion, when that statue over there walks, that's when this ship will sail, sí, señores, not until then! No! Not until that statue walks! And he stands emphatically nodding at them, feeling embarrassed by himself over this sudden outburst . . .

The anciana looks at him openmouthed, her light brown eyes looking filmed over with blurry, transparent amber. "A strange notion," she finally says.

The old man seems a bit vexed by Bernardo's words, his arms rigid at his sides, and then, as if finally finding the internal strength for a hiccup to release an uncomfortable pocket of air, he says, "*Well.*" And then, in Spanish, "I am looking for a certain shipping clerk I was told worked here, a man named . . . ach, but it's terribly difficult to pronounce, *Ponds-and-berry*. Francis, and this terrible last name, *Ponds-and-berry,"* and he chuckles dryly, showing his gums and teeth again. "Something like that . . . You've never met such a man? Francis *Ponds-and-berry*? In Spanish he would be Francisco Lagunas y Baya, which I suppose is not of much help, since that is not the caballero's name, hmn?" and again, his soft, repressed chuckle.

"No," says Bernardo, feeling strangely impressed by the old man. "No, we never meet anybody here, señor." They remind him of a couple he once worked for as a chauffeur in Managua, a hermitlike sugar plantation owner who liked to play fandangos on the harp every afternoon and his doting wife, whom he used to chauffeur to mass every evening in a red De Soto two-seater sports car with a cream convertible top; they'd given him a pale blue jacket to wear despite the heat and, daily, a white carnation to put in the lapel . . .

"Ah," says the man, his lips tightening as if making an effort to restrain his disappointment.

"My husband has a very rare illness," says the anciana, "and his doctor told him that this man—"

"Ponds-and-berry!" interrupts the old man, as if it cheers him up just to say it.

"This man is the only other man who suffers from it," she says. "Well, perhaps not in the world, you understand, but the only other man our doctor is acquainted with."

"A very rare disease of the blood, which I'm afraid has no cure," says the old man, "though it progresses so slowly I'm sure something else will finish me off first. Be that as it may, my doctor thought it would be good for us to get together, this Ponds-and-berry and I, to talk about it, compare notes, you see."

"But he's not here," says the anciana.

"I don't believe so, señora."

"In my youth I used to love to go down to the Río de la Plata and watch the ships coming in and out of the harbor," she says a moment later. "Do you know Fernando Pessoa's *Oda Marítima*? Do you understand Portuguese?"

"Perdón, señora? . . ."

But she is already reciting, the Portuguese familiar enough after so many unforgettable stopovers in Brazilian ports and enough like Spanish that Bernardo can pick most of it up, Pass on, slow steamship, pass on, don't stay, pass away from me, get out of my sight, out from my heart, lose yourself in the distance, in the distance, God's mist . . .

And when she's finished she says, "A grand, extravagant ode to ships and men who go to sea, declaimed in the voice of one who likes to go down to the harbor and watch. Bueno, it goes on like that for many, many stanzas."

But the words she has recited remind Bernardo of his dream, he's even about to say so, but suddenly the old man shouts out:

"*Fifteen men on the dead man's chest! Yo-ho-ho and a bottle of rum!*" and chuckles deeply again.

And the anciana is staring down at the soaked, blackened vagrants' rags clumped around Bernardo's feet. "But what are you doing here?" she asks.

"A little laundry."

The women puzzles over this a moment. "Is this a very modern ship?" she asks.

"No, señora, not very," says Bernardo.

"How does it, what is the word, navigate?"

"They go by the stars and use a sextant, Maruja!"—the old man grins—"just like Cristóbal Colón, no?"

Bernardo smiles. "Sí pues. With a sextant and the stars."

And she asks Bernardo to please name some of the stars and constellations most useful to seafarers in plotting their course, and, bemused, Bernardo names the first that immediately come to mind, Orion, the Pleiades . . .

"You can always find Polaris by holding your fist out in front of you, over the Great Bear's hind feet, and then move five fists over, fist after fist, to the left," says Bernardo, putting up his hands to illustrate how he would do this against the sky if it were night.

"Qué maravilla," she says happily, "now I know I shall never again be lost. But those are all Northern Hemisphere constellations you named, mi buen joven. And when you are in the Southern Hemisphere?"

Bernardo's mind goes blank. He can't think of a single southern constellation right now . . . And he decides to change the subject.

"Perdón," he says, "since you are here, pues, bueno—I must tell you. I think this ship is in violation of every conceivable maritime law and regulation. The truth is, we're stranded here, as much as any shipwrecked sailors on some remote island. Do you think, when you get back into Brooklyn, you could inform someone of our situation? The name of this ship is *Urus,* and the capitán is a young man named Elias. That's all I really know. There is an owner, but we don't know his name."

And then he feels bad about what he has just done, since he has no right to presume his crewmates would want him to do this; they would insist, as always, on putting it to one of their interminable votes.

The two look at him blandly. He can see his reflection in the old man's sunglasses. The anciana, Doña Maruja, looks up at the ship again, and so does Bernardo, wondering if anyone else is witnessing this encounter, but he sees no one. She looks back at Bernardo. She has yet to even ask him his name.

"My husband, el maestro, is a semiretired piano and voice teacher. And I have no worldliness. Who should we speak to?"

"Bueno, Doña Maruja," says Bernardo. "Usually, in most big ports, there is a church that looks after seamen, something—"

"Religion!" interrupts the old man jovially. "I shit on it!"

"Shhh, Jorge, don't be vulgar!" She looks back at Bernardo. "Of course, I'll look in the telephone book."

"Gracias, señora. That would be very kind." He has a feeling they're not going to do anything anyway. They might as well be ghosts.

"I'll tell them you're at the Grain Pier."

"Describe it to them as well as you can . . ."

"I will then."

"Señora," asks Bernardo after a moment during which they have all fallen silent, "how is it you know so much about the stars?"

"I am an astrologer, it's been a lifelong hobby. That and other pursuits of that nature. Palm reading, tarot cards. What sign are you, joven?"

"Bueno . . . I have to admit I don't know." It seems to him that once upon a time he knew the answer to this. The woman pulls a small black notebook from her purse. She asks him his birthday, and he tells her, and she writes it down, and then asks what time of day he was born, and Bernardo shrugs helplessly and says, "In the morning," which he somehow feels is true, that he once knew that too, from his mother . . . And the anciana, Doña Maruja, seems to lose herself in her own thoughts for a long moment, apparently doing mental calculations, her raspberry lips tremulously and slightly moving, and then she stares at him in such a way and for so long that he begins to feel uneasy.

"You're a Sagittarius, of course," she says, finally. "You are in some pain. Do your knees bother you?"

"Everything bothers me, Doña Maruja."

"I can tell you with certainty that had you been born a woman, you would have had trouble with your ovaries."

"*Ponds and berries!*" exclaims the old man, seeming impatient now, "*Woods and fairies,* that's what I say!"

And after a few more pleasantries—"*Bon voyage . . . bonne chance!*" —the old couple say good-bye without offering a hand to shake or a polite kiss on the cheek or having asked him his name; and they go on their way, passing out of sight quickly, despite their slow, twinned pace, off the end of the pier and around the corner of the grain elevator, and now Bernardo hears the sound of car doors opening and closing and an engine starting up and catches a glimpse of a yellow taxi driving off from behind the grain elevator and through the lot. Strange that he hadn't heard the taxi arriving. Pues, the splashing of water from the spigot must have drowned it out while he was absorbed in the laundry, in his thoughts.

Bernardo picks up the cold, wet laundry in his arms and climbs the ladder to the deck, where no one is doing any work today, and no one has witnessed the old couple's visit or even heard the taxi. And he thinks, Nowadays life on the *Urus* almost feels like the middle of a long ocean crossing on a real ship—the lassitude, people keeping to themselves, bored with one another, not much to do but play dominoes and tinker around or endlessly chip and paint. He lays the clothes out to dry on the rear deck, trying to remember the words to the poem Doña Maruja had recited. Pass on, slow steamship. Don't stay. Get out of my heart. Lose yourself in the distance . . . Sí pues, in God's distant mist.

Then, as every afternoon, he sits down on a crate in front of the mess, while José Mateo sits beside him, and begins sifting through rice. This was the time of day when he used to teach Desastres to sit, when he and the cook would exchange sea stories, and often the others would gather around to listen and watch the cat sit; but they have very little, perhaps nothing, new left to tell each other nowadays. Bernardo feels like talking though.

"In La Spezia, Italy," he says—he's sure he's told José Mateo this before—"you find the laziest, most cabrón stevedores on earth, no? Whenever we had to load or unload cargo there, it took twice as long as anywhere else, half the time spent with our crew and those Italians screaming and insulting each other and even getting in fights. But their union is de puta madre. They give them very beautiful work gloves, made of soft, brown leather. Chamois, I think, rabbit fur on the inside. Every time one of those Italians would get careless and leave his gloves laying around for a second, one of our marineros would come along and snatch them right up!"

José Mateo narrows his eyes, nods, says those huevones haven't changed a bit, he was in La Spezia just two years ago.

"But they understood contraband," says Bernardo. "If we just passed them a few bottles of good rum while they were unloading coffee sacks, they'd make sure they used their hand hooks to tear open the burlap of *uuuf!* hundreds of sacks! We'd collect the spilled beans, sell it ourselves later."

"You hardly see that anymore, viejo"—José Mateo yawns—"what with so much moved in containers now. Drugs, now that's something else. These muchachos bringing their own coca and mota onboard. Right before we'd get into a port where the dogs were going to come on sniffing, you know what they'd have me do? Burn chilis in pots, until they were charred black, the smoke billowing, carajo, until it was like fire in your lungs, made you nearly blind. And they'd carry these pots all up and down the corridors and into the cabins like priests with their smoky censers. And when the dogs came onboard—Ayyy, tu madre, it made those dogs crazy, it was like they wanted to jump off, noses down, right into the water."

It is late afternoon when Bernardo gets up and goes to his cabin, and he's about to step over the rat-damming panel across the doorway when an overpowering sensation of fear roots him and he feels something pass swiftly through his legs as it bounds over the dam, a shadow, a blurry, translucent, dimly orange shadow now hovering over his bed; he shuts his eyes, opens them, but it's still there—isn't that colored shadow shaped something like a sitting cat? He feels the ache in his shoulder and the fear inside that won't let him move, and he shuts his eyes again and is sure that he hears the low, radioactive crackle of the cat's purr in a corner of the cabin. It's Desastres, he thinks. I must be going mad. How can a cat have a ghost? . . . He hasn't seen a ghost in fifty-one years, since one day a year after his mother died when he came into their old house in Rivas and encountered her there just like this: a pale-colored shadow, her face a brown cloud, her dress a yellow haze, this blurred but recognizable impression and then the terrifying certainty that it really was his querida mamita, sitting on the floor, arranging hairpins in a circle around her. A restless soul enters through the shoulder, in that way makes its presence felt and allows you to see it, he knew that then. And he knew also that he was supposed to shut his eyes and pray as hard as he could for her spirit to find peace, apologize for not having mourned her deeply and constantly enough, promise to have a mass said, to put out flowers in a vase once a week just like you always liked, mamita, beg her to evaporate again into the diffuse spiritual matter of the eternal afterlife. And so he stands in the doorway praying, with shredded concentration, wondering if it was simply a ray of sunlight flashing in and out of a cloud, beaming through the porthole . . . But he felt the shadow moving through his legs before he even saw it, felt the pain in his shoulder blade and the terror enter him there. Wondering Dios mío what does this portend . . . and if Desastres is now just a little pile of bones sharing a rat's nest with a clock's hour hand . . . And if maybe he did the wrong thing, not telling the chavalones about the cat he knew about in Rivas as a little boy that belonged to a well-off campesino who lived outside town, a cat that could do anything a dog could do except bark, not just sit but fetch sticks and lie down and roll over and the campesino even trained the cat to help herd his milk cows, the cat would follow him into town on Sundays when he went to get facedown drunk in the cantina, would sit at the campesino's feet; as a little boy his own father took him there more than once to see this cat, and everyone thought this campesino must be St. Francis of Assisi returned to earth until he was caught smuggling U.S. cigarettes and whiskey by mule train over the border from Costa Rica . . . Vos, was it so wrong? I didn't tell them, Desastres, so that they would love you more . . . He prays, Go away, Desastres, I won't forget you, I'll leave food out, find peace, gatito . . . And when he opens his eyes again the cat's ghost is gone. And, hijo de cien millones y novecientos miles de putas, he can smell cat pee, it's faint but he can smell it!

He leaves the cabin and walks out on deck, sits on the crate again, though he is finished with the rice. His shoulder still aches, the back of his shirt drenched with cold sweat. How can it be? What sign is this? His hands are trembling as if from palsy. And after a while his fright feels mixed with a sensation of muted joy, almost of relief, because why, after fifty-one years, would a restless soul come to him again, now, to provide this proof that there is something after this life on earth after all?

What a day this has been, viejo lobo. He won't tell anybody about this, not even Esteban; they'll think his brain has finally flown off like a bird. He should set some food out for Desastres, but what? How do you set out a plate of live cockroaches? He'll leave an empty sardine can out later, in a corner of the mess, maybe Desastres will come and lick out the oil before the rats do. But why didn't I think to say, Siéntate, Desastres?

For the next ten days, with the same commingling of eerie joy and dull dread that makes everything seem like a portent during these last, crisp days of limpid October light and yellowing leaves and frosty mornings and mountaintop nights, he won't be able to rid himself of the otherworldly sensation the shock seems to have let inside him. He won't see Desastres's ghost again, but he'll feel the cat's presence, will be certain he can smell cat urine in random corners of the ship, though no others will mention that they smell it too.

AS IS, WHERE IS

IN ANOTHER SIX WEEKS, IN DECEMBER, AFTER A NIGHT OF FREEZING RAIN, the Ship Visitor will find them. He'll board a ship whose name and port of registration will have recently been painted off the prow and stern. As a ship visitor he boards some twenty or thirty ships a week, will have been doing so for almost two years, he knows how to size a situation up right off. He'll have seen abandoned crews and ships before, but this will be the first time he'll be struck by the image of a rusted old freighter whose sole cargo is dead autumn leaves. Beyond the enclosed basin where the ship is berthed stand trees that will have been stripped of leaves by the night's storm, and looking up, he'll see a few still tumbling against the overcast sky. Just like in *The Birds,* he'll think, those last ominous birds still up there in the sky. He'll see wet, brown leaves snared in the conning tower and pressed flat to the bridge windows; clinging to stays and shrouds running from the masts as if caught and shriveled by high-voltage jolts in the galvanized wire. He'll see ice-stiffened wads of leaves amidst haphazardly massed garbage and litter in every windward nook and cranny of the deck; leaves scattered over the flooded and icing bottom of an open hold, and, looking down through an uncovered hatch aft into the deep pit of the engine room, leaves over and around the machinery and boilers; blown into the abandoned cabins. Here and there, inside shiny, slightly indented spots on deck where grinding tools have demolished rust, a flattened leaf inside a shadow-thin puddle of ice. Be nice to bring one home to her, he'll think, a leaf inside a slice of frozen puddle, hold it out to her in a gloved hand like some rare jewel, let her lick it, lay it on her brightly bare, arched belly and watch it melt until just the tawny, wet leaf is there like the shadow of a small hand on her glistening skin . . . He'll not so much will her from his thoughts—because he can't—as snap her off like a piece of candy or dry stick.

"Oyen, ustedes." Look at them, the poor fucks. *But look at them.* "Cuanto tiempo llevan aquí?"

"How long? Six months!" he'll nearly shout. And he'll stare out at the bombed-looking cove opening onto a channel streaming out into Gowanus Bay . . .

The crew members who'll have lowered the ladder and then met him up on deck, after the Ship Visitor called up from the pier, will strike him, on first impression, as strangely incurious, or maybe just shy, or totally lost in benumbed stupors. Smoky smelling, black-smudged khaki blankets tugged around their shoulders for warmth over torn and stained clothing, and for all the boyishness of their faces, grimy and unshaven, with soft little beards. A few hard-eyed stares, others vacant, dazed. Almost mutely they'll follow the Ship Visitor as he strides the ripped up deck, inspecting as a ship visitor must while futilely bantering away in banal Spanish, the situation already explicit, appalling. Central Americans. Young. Practically boys! Just a bunch of filthy, fate-stunned boys! They won't smile, won't laugh at anything he says. And they'll seem to be losing their footing, almost falling down, with every step they take on the ice-sheened, dangerously ripped apart deck, not even the calcareous ridges of frozen gull droppings everywhere providing traction. Torn, colorless sneakers, a few cheap work boots, ragged loafers with thin, hard soles. Almost obstinately, humorlessly, no bemused or even embarrassed smiles, they'll be slipping and sliding all over the place as if in some show of belated or purposeless pride they refuse to adjust their manner of walking for ice, twisting their feet sideways like skaters into chocks.

He'll find the rest of the crew still sleeping or lying awake in hunched postures under blankets on the floor of the rust- and smoke-darkened mess, skin showing through rips in blackened socks.

All of them kids, except for one, a middle-aged guy—not really elderly, like that Argentine lady will have said. A Sagittarius, she'll have said. Sixty-eight years old, she even knew his birthday. Well, she's a nut anyway. With her wacky, stilted English: My good man, some weeks ago my husband and I happened upon a most peculiar ship, and a most distraught elderly man was down on the pier . . .

Christ, six months! And if it hadn't for the nutty Argentine—"Good thing she found you, huh?" he'll say to the older guy, the one just introduced to him as the cook.

But the cook and the others gathered around will gape blankly, and finally the cook will narrow his eyes and grunt, "Quién?"

"Tu sabes, the Argentine señora, the one who—an Argentine woman who met you down on the pier?"

And everyone will keep looking at him like that, and some will shake their heads no.

"She said she met a man, an older man, doing laundry on the pier."

And suddenly one of the kids will smile, displaying a gold tooth over a gap of missing teeth.

"Bernardo," he'll say. "Sí pues. Bernardo. No. Ya no está."

"He's gone?"

"Sí pues. He was taken to the hospital, and that's the last we saw of him."

"The last you saw of him?"

"Se fue, pues. Pa' Nicaragua. El Capitán sent him home, right from the hospital. And that's the last we saw of him."

"He was lucky, no?" another kid will say, shrugging hulking shoulders. "He got to go home, sí pues."

Later that morning the Ship Visitor will drive his van off the pier again and into Brooklyn to do some quick shopping for the crew: food, heavy-duty plastic sheeting to put over the open mess portholes and doorway, and six packages of tube socks. And then he'll spend the rest of day onboard, listening, huddled with them in the frigid mess and then around a small wood fire on deck until the daylong wintry dusk finally begins to darken to night. He'll politely decline their offer to stay for dinner. And then the gold-toothed kid will make a ceremonious little speech, thanking him, "our estimable new friend," for the pork chops and peas and Coca-Colas and plastic sheeting and socks. And all but a few of the crew will stand and look at the Ship Visitor with solemn expressions, briefly but intensely applauding. The Ship Visitor will have been spending his days, five days a week, amidst men and boys almost always more or less like these—if hardly ever as fucked over: men and boys, also women and girls, from the poor continents, on the move, crewing ships that sail all the world's oceans and seas and that occasionally stop at this great port, where he has a job visiting ships. But he'll still feel touched and surprised, a little disturbed, by the earnest solemnity of that round of applause.

And then he'll drive his van off the pier and through the marine terminal yard, headed out of Brooklyn and through the tunnel under the river to the Seafarers' Institute in Port Elizabeth, thinking, It really is much easier to get away with hiding a ship out here than over on our side. The newer New Jersey container terminals and tank farms are thriving. But the Brooklyn waterfront's hundred-year-old wastes, its massive brick ruins and miles of collapsed piers and rust-devoured train tracks going nowhere and rank barge canals just don't look remote enough from present-day energies to be so abandoned and empty now. Hard to believe nothing more apocalyptic than just time has happened here.

It will have been a long day, like most days. The day before yesterday it will have been the suicidal Filipina cruise-liner laundress threatening to guzzle a bottle of Clorox, hysterically repeating over and over that she has a high school degree, that she's a singer, that she'd been hired as a shipboard *entertainer* and then they put her in the laundry! Some kind of sexual harassment apparently going on too. Of course the cruise liner will have been sailing to the Caribbean that very evening, usual story. No time to be of real help, to do much of anything but coax the bottle of Clorox away and calm her a little, then go back to the office and log it. Phone ahead in the next few days to the port chaplaincy or seamen's center in the liner's next port of call to ask them to look in on her, if they can. Hope she didn't just take a nighttime dive off the deck—happens, and no one ever knows or cares. Anonymous as mice.

Not bad work if you can get it, being a ship visitor. Well, this might be different. These muchachos are here for a while. Maybe there'll be time to do *something*. He'll take some of them in to see a lawyer tomorrow, get the process going to take out a lien on the ship for unpaid wages. See where it leads, hope for the improbable best . . .

At the Seafarers' Institute, amidst silent offices—everyone but the night service staff having already gone home and Reverend Bazan out to the inexpensive little Uruguayan-Italian restaurant nearby, treating five homesick seafarers from the Maldives to dinner—he'll phone Reverend Roundtree at home, leaving a message on her answering machine, and then log a brief report into the computer. On the Seafarers' Institute's ground floor there's a cocktail lounge for seafarers—there's a chapel too, and in the basement, a cafeteria, and on the second floor, a gym and a TV-VCR room and a small library and a dozen dorm rooms, and up another flight, the offices—and after pausing in the cocktail lounge for his Absolut martini on the rocks, he'll ride the PATH train from New Jersey to Manhattan and take a subway uptown to the university, to Ariadne's apartment. (The Ship Visitor has an apartment in Brooklyn, but she doesn't like it there, finds it, logically enough, inconvenient.) Well, I've sure as hell got a story for her tonight anyway, the Ship Visitor will think. And he'll feel glad about that, arranging himself on his long evening journey home to Ariadne around his anticipation and relief of having a story to bring her (if not an ice-encased leaf).

But when he finally gets there, he'll let himself into her little apartment in the sky and find her not home. A note on the living room's only chair, asking him to meet her "F.a.c.c.o.p."—Fast as can, custom of the port—in a certain bar downtown, though no later than 11:30. Ariadne will lately have developed a thing for shipping terms. Christ, he's exhausted. He'll sit in the chair facing the night-sheened glass of the sliding glass doors at the small living room's front, staring through at the glowing white rail of the little balcony out there. By day these glass doors provide an unobstructed view of the Hudson River, the cliffs of New Jersey, the George Washington Bridge to the north. Ariadne's apartment, which she won in the university housing lottery, is on the penthouse floor of an eighteen-story graduate-student dormitory. Here the thirty-five-year-old Ship Visitor will have been living since August with his love, thirteen years younger than he (at the edge of the very campus where visiting professor Kate Puerifoy, this past term, has been conducting her twice-a-week course in postmodern conceptual photography and theory, The Eye That Doesn't See, though she's recently given birth to a baby boy, just in time for the long winter break. The Ship Visitor won't know that or have any reason to know. Though today one of the Central American seafarers will have mentioned that their capitán's wife "es una profesora y una artista, así dijo el Capitán, pues," a bit of information that would have seemed totally unremarkable had the ship been in less scandalous shape. Instead the Ship Visitor will have skeptically asked the gold-toothed Central American to tell him what else he knows. She and el Capitán just had a baby, Gold Tooth will have replied. No, has never come out to see her husband's ship. And will have had nothing else to add.)

Hard December winds will be buffeting the glass. Nightly these winds off the river thrash and howl around the exposed building while he and Ariadne grip each other under the white quilt in the bedroom, which is barely larger than the bed. Movie winds, she calls them. Making the world sound ominous and lonely, helping to turn a familiar tight embrace into something that feels both cozier and like a solemnly accepted fate. Winter is going to be good for love in an apartment like this. The polluted sunsets across the river will fill the glass wall even more lividly, in starker contrast to the wintry landscape underneath. He'll imagine billowy gray skies and purplish winter twilight, lamps coming on in the park below; a wall of wind-whipped snow. If there's a blizzard, they'll pull ships in from the harbor and anchor them in a long line up the river. And if the river freezes, the ships will be stuck there for a while, and maybe Ariadne will get to watch him through the glass doors on a polar expedition of mercy, making his way to a ship aboard a Coast Guard ice cutter.

Poor kids, he'll think, must be hell out on that ship tonight. But they have their fires, and plenty of firewood around, they won't freeze to death; and they seem to have been getting their hands on a bit of food. Not much even the Coast Guard can do unless conditions onboard are immediately life threatening. Probably just be bringing them warm clothing, blankets, more food, as usual, until it all gets legally resolved, hope it doesn't drag on too long. The most humane thing to do, of course, would be to take them off the ship and fly them home, let them wait there for whatever a court action might bring. A couple of times in the past that's what the reverends have pushed for, but the Seafarers' Institute's very secular and conservative board has refused to set a precedent by shelling out the money. Having just struck a match, the Ship Visitor will suddenly yawn, pulling the cigarette away from his mouth, yawn for so long and so deeply the burning match singes his fingers—"Ouch!"

The telephone will ring, but the Ship Visitor won't get up to answer, will let the answering machine take it. Ariadne has many friends, nine-tenths of them male, many of them wealthy foreign students like herself, her tumbling circus of besotted admirers laying patient, friendly, courtly siege. So much of the world still so polite and well mannered! Everywhere but here in New York, it often seems. Even if one takes the people a ship visitor meets boarding ships as a wide enough sampling of humanity. Even that ship he's boarded twice in the last year when it's come to load scrap iron, crewed entirely by internationally wanted criminals and escaped convicts who sail the seas and supposedly never go ashore (though they must, in far-flung ports less well policed than New Jersey–New York's), working practically for free in exchange for their highly restricted freedom, that ship of floating homicidal manic depression—even *they're* polite! Ariadne's callers leave her long, jovial or suavely low-voiced messages, usually in languages he doesn't speak, and though they rarely acknowledge his existence, they manage to carry off even that slight politely. Ariadne speaks six languages (not counting Latin, which makes seven), though she is most and equally comfortable in French, Spanish, and English.

"Jawwwn? You there? It's Kathy. I'm—"

Reverend Roundtree. He'll snatch up the phone, and she'll want to be filled in regarding the message he left about that ship in Brooklyn, the one that old Argentine woman will have phoned a couple of times about. And he'll tell her everything he was able to learn that day:

"Another abandoned flag of convenience crew, I guess is what it comes down to."

"Indeed, John. And many unanswered questions—"

Detective Reverend Roundtree, the Port of New Jersey and New York's Father Brown. Vodka in the freezer. A drink would be nice.

"Uh-huh. As usual. Just another magical mystery ship." He'll walk the phone into the kitchen, stretching the cord to its full, tautened length, groping with outstretched arm and wriggling fingers for the freezer door and not quite, just not quite reaching, millimeters short . . .

"A bit more than usual," she'll be saying. "Wouldn't you say? Trying to repair that ship for six months? Why?"

"Overly optimistic owner? Thought it would be doable and then it wasn't."

"Well, *that* doesn't get him off the hook. I think we have time to get to work for a change. We have him right where we want him, don't you think?"

"It'll be freezing out, snowing out pretty soon, Kath. Any day, maybe. Can't leave those kids on the ship then. You really want to try to bust the owner?" Come on, Kathy. The Panamanian Registry, like most flag of convenience registries, an assiduous protector of shipowners' anonymity; anonymity built right into the system. Some twelve thousand vessels flying the Panamanian tricolor. And nowhere near the manpower to enforce Panamanian law on their ships, even if they really wanted to. Especially as pertaining to the rights onboard of international seafarers. Phantom owners are hard to identify down here on earth, yet we know they exist, because if they didn't and if the flag of convenience ships they own didn't, if cheap Third World crews and low registration, incorporation fees, and tonnage taxes and every other related convenience didn't exist, exports would lag, throwing many Americans out of work, and imported products would be much more expensive and not so abundant—Ariadne, your four-hundred-dollar French skirts, your La Perla underthings, so many of our favorite beverages, so much of this comes to you by ship!

"Well, I wouldn't be surprised if this one's being run right out of New York," the Reverend will say. "This captain and his friend, they must be in some kind of cahoots with the ownership. They drive to the ship, they come and go. Suddenly they paint over the name and registry. Maybe *they're* the owners, John. You think?"

"Yeah, if they're total dolts. Otherwise I don't really see their stake, except a salary. I wouldn't necessarily presume felonious activity here anyway, Kathy. Incompetence, bad luck, a bad deal. Probably just went broke. Bet that ship's already up for sale. As is, where is. End up being sold or auctioned off for scrap, most likely. That ship isn't going anywhere."

"Well, *someone* thought it was going somewhere. You really think those guys have been getting paid?"

"I'd guess. But they tell the crew they haven't been. All in this together and so on. But they've pretty much stopped coming out, it sounds like, so if they *were* getting paid, I bet they're not anymore. I don't know, we'll see how they react once the lien's posted. Maybe they'll sue for back wages too."

"Or they'll stay away for good. Vanish. John, you watch. Now, what happened to that old man?"

"Sent back to Nicaragua. End of October that was."

"But what did he go to the hospital for?"

"Hot cooking oil spilled all over his leg. Cooking out on a deck over a wood fire. The captain treated him with something or other, supposedly he has some kind of medical training. Seems commensurate with his maritime training. Then he just sat there for a few days until this first mate guy took him to the hospital. I guess I still have to get a clearer version of what went down—"

"No pardi, not on a ship like this." She'll mean owner's protection and indemnity.

"On a ship like that, strongly doubt it."

"So let's see what we have here. No electricity, cooking out in the dark, not getting him immediate medical care. Then that's under the Jones Act—"

"Unless the captain really is an M.D. or something. *Ha*."

"Owner's negligence leading to serious injury. John, we *can* get them in federal court on that. If this doesn't come under the Jones, I don't know what does."

Just about the only thing you *can* get an owner on. She'll probably be right, of course. Though, as usual, the Reverend's overexcited and so often disappointed enthusiasm will make him reach for caution like an umbrella.

"Yeah, OK, maybe. But we don't know the whole story yet—" Like maybe the cook got mad and threw hot oil on the old guy and no one's talking.

"I want to reach that old man, John. Get a deposition. I want to know who paid for his plane ticket home. I want to see his medical records."

Kathy's going to use this case, the Ship Visitor will think, to test the limits of her interest in ministry to seafarers, isn't she? The case we've all been waiting for. A chance to push the institute's board, see how far they'll let us take combative advocacy of seafarers' rights, strike a small but resonant blow, for once, against malefic shipowners. Lately, Reverend Roundtree will have been expressing a certain frustration and restlessness with the job, wondering if she really wants to forgo the chance of having her own parish somewhere, preferably right here in the city, to be a port chaplain the rest of her life, bringing Christian hospitality and the Good News to seafarers.

"We'll go back out there first thing in the morning."

"First thing?" The Ship Visitor will groan silently—if he meets Ariadne downtown, and he will, he won't be getting to bed until at least three. "Yeah, all right."

"How's that swank lady of yours?" Swank? Just the other day, Ariadne will have been that "dangerous" lady—potentially dangerous, the Reverend will have feared, to his future psychological and spiritual well-being. Now why should a Protestant reverend be troubled by, or even compassionately worry about, just awesome, total passion and love?

"She's fine. We've been getting along really well lately." Which will be true enough. Will feel himself hooked, as usual, to a yearning to talk about it but stop himself—it's only been a few months since Reverend Roundtree broke up with her "intended," a shattering event for her. Divorced admiralty lawyer (like the Ship Visitor was going to be, once upon a time, before he decided he'd rather be a ship visitor), played big-time hockey in college. A much more probable, befitting, and seemingly enduring match, supposedly—and it wasn't after all.

After hanging up, the Ship Visitor will pour himself a vodka on the rocks, wash a lemon, carefully shear off a strip of rind with a paring knife, run it along the rim, and plonk it in. Rarely has more than one drink a night when Ariadne is home. There's a British captain, fiftyish, about a decade older than Kathy, who always comes in for a drink in the institute's cocktail lounge whenever he's in port, always cajoles Kath down for a drink. Conservative, self-consciously proper type. Father a bus driver; votes for Thatcher. Calls Kath Bishop, of course. Talkative, with a submerged, typical air of lonely, void-washed (the ocean, the ocean) melancholy. Likes to probe Kathy for the great meaning of things. Seems to be trying to fix just the right look of respectfully adoring attentiveness on his face as he listens, almost like he's rehearsing them both for what he thinks it might be like, eventually retiring from the sea to live full-time with a woman for the first time. On many things they would disagree, which he pretends to like, certain of his principles and unapologetic about any lack of cosmopolitan experience, after a life like his, spent mainly on ships. He'd like to attach himself to her, to her respectable sophistication and intellect, her other kind of worldliness. Or unworldliness. So the Ship Visitor will have been suspecting. Might work out, who knows? Solid guy, seems to be. Of course you never know what lies underneath—with anyone, but these guys especially. Onboard always the captain, usually an introverted way of life, yet every port offering a stage to try out a different self for an audience that's never seen your very own particular act before and doesn't need to know your name . . . Awful not to have all this stuff—what stuff? marriage, money, who the fuck you finally are, and so on—worked out by a certain age. Probably doomed if you can't, though late rallies are not unheard of. But here I am, risking a lot on this *girl*. And liking myself for it, right? Though sometimes this inner voice wheedling, What's she doing loving a prolish ship visitor thirteen years older anyway, how long can that last? Or, I'm in way over my head. More intelligent than he, zillion times better educated, stronger willed even, all blazing temperament, braininess, and wild, gifted body. Though she certainly has her faults, her, umm, vulnerabilities, her temper, at times, like a snapped high-voltage wire fallen to the ground, snaking and zapping. Gladly offer my love as a kind of national park where her neuroses can run protected and free. "When we're married . . ." Ariadne will even have said, twice already, prefacing a passing speculation on the nonexistent future. ("When we're married maybe we'll live in Lisbon, it's a port, you can be a ship visitor there, Johnny." "When we're married my father will definitely disown me.") She with her fifty-grand-a-year trust fund (nearly twice what the Ship Visitor earns) outside all tuition and boarding costs, which her father (who will not have phoned her even once in the four months he's been living with her) pays.

Often Ariadne sits at her desk studying at night and the Ship Visitor pulls a book from her shelves, curls up on the carpet to read or pretend to, waiting for her to take off her reading glasses, switch off her desk lamp, come over and lower herself to his side, smiling her most unabashed and delirium-inducing smile . . .

"What is it about a love that needs such watching over?" Will have found that a few weeks ago, browsing through, of all things, *The Brothers Karamazov*. "Othello wasn't jealous, he was trusting."

After Reverend Roundtree's lover of three years left her in October, you know what she will have said in the office one afternoon? "My father liked to say that a good man always marries a woman superior to himself. Always? Well, he was, with all justification, referring to my mother. Otherwise, I suppose he was no worse than most. But like I've told you many times, my family was a drinking family, totally given over to nonstop mythomania!"

"She says she wants to meet a real American guy, she's sick of wimps in suits and Eurotrash—though aren't we all?"

"Me?"

Daughter of a Colombian-French financier, venture capitalist of some sort, fortune rooted in a family coffee empire dating to the last century, offices and homes all over Europe and Latin America, and a French-Polish mother, a suicide in Paris when Ariadne was fourteen. Educated in European boarding schools and at the Sorbonne. And beautiful. Looks kind of like a tall, white Eurasian girl. All this his second cousin Belle Carbonel, an editor at the glossy women's magazine where Ariadne had a summer internship before starting grad school in the fall, had told him.

"Anyway, Belle," he said, "guys in suits *are* real American guys, and so are wimps. I was a suit not so long ago."

For all the usual whimsy of her voice, Belle was, also as usual, earnest, blunt, and overreaching in her opinions about everything: "Well, we know you have a romantic wimp in your closet, Johnny. And a secret sybarite too. But don't think I tell anybody, though I think it's glorious."

"Don't you think I'm a little too old for her?"

"Oh come on! Just take her out and see what happens. You're cute enough, I promise. Both from totally screwed-up families and backgrounds. She'll figure you out."

"Well, that's not necessarily good."

"It'll take her a while. And you'll *never* figure her out, but you know what? I bet you'll have a helluva time trying."

Well, a pretty blatantly romantic wimp at times, though not lately. And the sybarite even a secret from himself, if the dictionary definition was what Belle meant.

His divorce from Mona was finally finalized just before New Year's, though they hadn't lived together in three years. Mona was already living happily with another man; but she'd insisted right to the end that she *liked* being his wife, not that either had any notion of their getting back together. Sweet Mona O'Donnell, a brassily cheerful performer, but with any scrap of sentimental provocation tossed her way—her favorite TV weatherman in a car accident, a phone company commercial where a yuppyish brown woman with a foreign accent surprises her peasant mother on the other side of the world with an unexpected-good-news call—her face would redden and her usually wit-sharp eyes wellingly cloud and she'd sink back into her cave to chow down on the emotion, whatever it was, maybe even have a good bawling cry. So at the very mention of divorce the past swamped her present: but she *likes* being his wife! Cost him a thousand dollars that he could barely spare, the uncontested divorce, and what it bought him was the new sensation of knowing he was telling a complete truth whenever he told someone he was single. More than a relief. Partial truths can nag worse than a lie, like an untied shoelace in a nightmare, one you keep reaching for and missing, have to keep walking around with your shoe untied no matter what. And so he'd been out with three different women since the spring—conquests! Feeling almost like a ladies' man, a rare period in his life. He was coasting, waiting for the right woman, in no big hurry, not letting himself get all hung up over some fetching nut like he usually did. A man feeling sturdy about his life, with nothing to hide. Shoes tied. A man who likes his job.

And along comes this first date, a blind date, with Ariadne, on a hot, rainy night in late June, the very week that the *Urus*'s crew flew up from Central America to meet their ship. Never forget it. What kind of girl shows up two hours late for a blind date and actually expects the guy still to be waiting? Even bothers showing up, two hours late? What kind of guy waits? Not fair, he wasn't waiting. Nothing else to do. Ball game on the TV over the bar, a hard summer rain outside. And a weird and terrible day at the office, in fact. Forgot all about his blind date, well, didn't feel aggrieved anyway, maybe even a little relieved. Just sat there nursing his drink. He'd spent part of the day in a Port Newark hospital, sitting by the bed of a recuperating Colombian stowaway—he and three friends had hidden themselves inside a coffee-sack-stuffed container loaded onto a ship sailing from Buenaventura. So when the customs inspectors and the DEA guy opened the container down on the pier, this skinny kid in just his underwear popped out and took off running. The Ship Visitor had been up on deck with the crew when he sensed a change in the pitch of the stevedores' shouts amidst the clanging commotion of cranes and hoisted containers, and saw the crane operator in his cable car–like cab wrenching around in his seat to look down at the pier while riding a container off the deck. He went to the rail and saw customs officials and stevedores jogging in the direction of a nearly naked brown body pinioned as if by wind against the hurricane fence, and others gathered around the open end of a container, holding their hands over their noses and mouths, some reluctantly clambering inside. Lifting out the first of the contorted, twisted bodies. Left the other two inside, for the ambulance drivers to deal with. Three dead from suffocating heat, hunger, and dehydration, hunched and sprawled amidst the coffee-bean-stuffed sacks, stiff with rigor mortis. And one survivor with enough energy left to take off in a wild sprint at the first splash of air and daylight . . .

No one else has a job like mine. That's what he often tells himself, taking satisfaction from it, whenever in that kind of Manhattan bar. The sort of bar where guys who look more or less like himself congregate, who all look like they might have gone to college together. White Boys, in the current, annoying parlance. Lawyers, like he almost was, or business, media, or publishing types, artists of one kind or another. Funny how he never meets any doctors in these places. He fits right in. And then he always tells himself, Yeah, but no one else has a job like mine.

Not exactly well paid, but good benefits. In the heart of winter, when everyone else starts looking pale and scaly, it keeps him ruddy, ocean-wind-scrubbed, feeling strong. No doubt about it, the job will have improved his overall demeanor, his self-confidence; so many times a day climbing the gangway onto a ship where nobody knows him, then trying to win the crew's trust, gauge their situation as quickly as possible, often by reading furtive glances and postures more than by what they actually say—few speak English, never mind Spanish. Captains and officers often not very glad to see him. Lots of floating squalor out there, but many good ships too. Roaming the ports and waterfronts in his van and on foot, he'll have learned to feel as comfortable and alert in his solitude as some hard-boiled detective; this mixed with the easy camaraderie of his colleagues at the end of the day, the conversation of reverends and the other staff, of the seafarers and ships' officers from all over the world who stop into the Seafarers' Institute cocktail lounge when their time in port allows them to, the shipping agents, chandlers, tugboat men, stevedores, government guys, the samurai fraternity of harbor pilots.

She came into the bar, out of the steamy rain, more than two hours late, came walking down the aisle folding and fastening her collapsible umbrella, glancing expectantly at the faces of men at the bar, sitting in booths. Red raincoat, red lips, a matte-pale, soft face, like milk with just a touch of brown sugar swirled in, long, lustrous, black hair cut in a fringe over her nearly black eyes; skitterishly bright, this first time he saw those eyes, with anxiety and high-spirited mischief, as if mortified to have arrived so late but deeply bemused by herself too. Knew right away this was Ariadne, though his smile must have been dumbstruck as he caught her glance, waving up from his seat. She sat down smiling, without subjecting him to any protracted scrutiny, simply said, "Oh, you're still here!" and laughed. "The dinner I was at went on and on forever. I'm so sorry, but thank you so much for waiting. I thought I'd take a chance!" She'd shrugged off her raincoat, was wearing a simple sleeveless black dress. Just a kid. The slightly Frenchified singsong of her accent. French lips, shaped by the way they kiss their language when they speak it, drawing her soft cheeks forward (why so many French guys look poofy). Dazzlingly pretty and alive. You're going to break my heart someday, he'd thought then and there. And later that long night, he even told her that: "I better be careful. Or you're going to break my heart someday," blurting it into the giddy, drunken haze enclosing them, and she leaned closer and laughed. "You're probably right. But come on, it's no fun being careful."

". . . Biology, luck, how the hell else can you really explain it?" he told her that night, recounting the Colombian stowaway's story, the first of all the ship visitor's yarns he'll bring her in the coming months. "He lay there in his hospital bed trying to come up with a reason. His faith in God. Always a hard worker. His sense of himself as a guy with an especially strong, stubborn character. His strength of will."

(Lay there with IVs pumping saline solution into his veins and looking like he couldn't even have lost much weight, no slackness in his face, just a shocked glitter in his eyes. All that just to get to the U.S. of A., and he was going to be deported as soon as he was released from the hospital.

(And how could he ask what he wanted to ask? Couldn't, of course. What was it like? What were you all thinking? How did you know when the first one died? Was there a sound, a sigh? And then the other two? He finally asked, How did you not go mad? Left it at that.)

"But I believe in the will, Johnny, don't you?" she nearly chirped. "I believe there must be something else, besides luck or biology, that makes him different. Consider torture, men who break under torture and men who don't. I've always told myself that I could only marry the kind of man who wouldn't break under torture."

Many such preposterous opinions. An idealized sense of life, full of high but untested principles. Should hear her when she gets going on her philosophies of love! But this mixture of youthful unreality and daffily heroic convictions charmed him from the start. Better, even more intellectually arousing, than listening to the reverends, who you weren't dying to sleep with at the same time too.

His stories about his occupation, death tinged by the day's events, enkindled her imagination somehow; perhaps seduced her darker side a little, she with her own appalling history always crouched like a trembling madwoman in her attic. Anyway, gave him, in her eyes, that romantic, manly aura—just what she was looking for, right? A real American guy, not office bound but free in the manner of a movie detective, in touch with darker things but with the spiritual too, the open spaces of port and sea, and reverends. That's how Ariadne saw him that night. A guy who'll come home at night with ocean salt in his skin, and a story to tell.

"You're comfortable among other men," she said approvingly when he came back from the bar with another round—that was all it took, promptly returning to their table with a couple of drinks. She said the men she knew often weren't; trying to press through the "burly crush" of a bar to order drinks intimidated them, they just stood there timidly at the edge, wagging a hand at the bartender, usually she ended up getting the drinks herself (as if any bartender was going to ignore *her*). This burly crush—in *this* bar? Ariadne actually thought they were all *blue-collar workers*.

"Hmmmm, I like that," she said and gave his erection, propping up his boxer shorts, a playful swipe. He'd just gotten into Ariadne's apartment mate's bed; she'd gone to Boston. (An Iranian F.I.T. student, boyfriend studying in Boston—Ariadne would move into the graduate student tower in August.) Ariadne wouldn't sleep with him, said she never slept with a man the first night. Though they'd kissed, in the bar, out on the street, in her living room. It was nearly dawn, too late to go all the way back to Brooklyn, wasn't it? And then sent him to the Iranian girl's bed, and went off to her own, and woke him hours later, sliding in naked beside him. They won't have spent a whole night apart, not one, since. (Tries to get to his apartment in Brooklyn once a week, pick up mail; still paying rent on the damned dump.)

There'll have been plenty of rough stretches, of course. For a while Ariadne will have been bitterly, obsessively—insanely, practically, considering how he felt about Ariadne—jealous of his ex-wife. Somehow, according to Ariadne, he'd polluted his own soul back then, marrying before experiencing a love as great as theirs. He'll have started it all that time, early in their relationship, when he carelessly let slip that he hadn't felt anywhere near this way since he'd first fallen in love with his former wife. Infuriated her—Ariadne doesn't want to be compared with any other woman, not in that or any other way! Oh, this boring American honesty and fairness and reasonableness! What does reasonableness have to do with love? Fairness towards the past has no place in the kind of love she wants. She has a past too, doesn't she? How would he like it, she'll have taunted, if she was just as honest about her past as he was about his? Though really, she'll have told him plenty, hardly less than what he'll have told her. The nearly forty-year-old French television actor she went out with when she was sixteen and seventeen, who'd given her a key to his apartment, taken her to the most decadent parties and clubs, on holidays in the Caribbean, Greece, and Bali, who raged and seethed like a spoiled brat if a single night passed without her consenting to sex, the man she grandly claimed had corrupted her. Her father had become extremely cold to his only child after her mother's death. She hated her father, she'd never forgive him for not having protected his young, starstruck daughter from this sordid affair. Her father should have killed him if that was what it took! That's what *you* would do, Johnny, isn't it, if it was your daughter? The past *has* to stay in the past! What's fairness have to do with it! If I say something hurts me, then it does. And it doesn't matter if you think it's unreasonable or neurotic and *unfair,* if it hurts me, and you love me, then I expect you to protect me from it!

"I'll protect you, I promise, from anything you want," he'll have promised.

"Oh yes, the great protector. But I'm not a poor sailor, Johnny," she'll have said. "Who's going to protect me from you, and your callous honesty and fairness?"

She'll have returned his baffled, wounded expression with a serious one of her own, and then, finally, broken out in a wide, mischievous smile . . .

Somehow, his job as a ship visitor will have become integral to the organic chemistry of their small, dual world—her way of conceiving of it as a strangely fantastical yet heroic occupation, which he can share only with her. But he'll never have realized the degree to which she felt that way until that night in the bar downtown, the night of the day he'll have found the *Urus* and her abandoned crew. She'll have arrived ahead of him for once, Ariadne, four young men, and another young woman seated on couches and stuffed chairs around a low table in a darkened nook. Three of the men he'll recognize as university friends of Ariadne. Very European, the way they look, the mood around the table, you'd know it at a glance. Or rich South American, same thing practically. All smoking. That relaxed, placid sociability. The other woman, reddish hair cut in a page boy, slender legs in silky green slacks hooked over the high back of her chair, torso twisting down like a mermaid's, elbows propped on the sea rock of an armrest. Roberto, from Milan, a law student, also a concert pianist, will scoot over on the stubby couch without uncrossing his long legs so that the Ship Visitor can squeeze in next to Ariadne, whose hands will lightly clasp his biceps as he turns to receive her lipstick-perfume-tobacco-martini-flavored kiss. She'll briskly wipe the lipstick from his mouth with a cocktail napkin, saying, "We've been discussing the fall of the Berlin Wall, Johnny." But he'll soon be feeling ill at ease, big and clumsy, in this company, as he knows he pretty much should, as he knows doesn't bother her in the least, so long as he doesn't make a noisy, defensive fool of himself, which he never really does, unless he's drunk too much. Roberto will still be wearing Ariadne's tan cloth raincoat, which she lent him one afternoon when he dropped by to visit and it started to rain. Apparently he won't have taken it off since—testament to his otherwise unremonstratively, painfully, politely borne unreciprocated love. Wearing it to class, outside in weather too cold for its scant protection, probably to bed. He absolutely will not give it back. Which Ariadne will have been at least pretending to find amusing, Roberto not having any idea that it's just this kind of silliness she's seen enough of and finds pathetically boyish. The raincoat is many sizes too small, the sleeves stopping many inches above his wrists and long, pale, effete strangler's fingers, bunching ridiculously under his arms. And yet it won't look nearly as ridiculous on him as it should. Everything underneath Armani or some damned thing, cashmere scarf around his neck, Adam's apple peeking over it, his smooth face of a young hawk, brilliant blue eyes, sensual-petulant lips, slightly mussed, dirty blond hair. Just the kind of boy anyone else might expect Ariadne to fall for, which, bless her, will be exactly why she hasn't. Which must seem terribly unfair to Roberto. The Ship Visitor, just as invisibly and defiantly smirking back at them, will know they—Roberto and the other two, the French philosophy grad student and the Argentine economics grad student—think he represents just some passing lunacy of Ariadne's, that someday he'll be gone and they'll finally get to say, "Oh, Ariadne, how could you have?"

The other young man, who'll turn out to be a Swiss investment banker with a Ph.D. in German literature, will suddenly get up and do a handstand, one hand on each armrest, over the mermaid, who'll smile and kiss him while he's upside down like that, one hand on each of his cheeks.

". . . Fast as can, custom of the port," the Ship Visitor will find himself explaining, having hit upon without even really trying to a certain gruff and drawling intonation that isn't really his, in response to this unprecedented interrogation from Ariadne's friends about the nature of his work, which will have been going on for quite some time already, prompted by his observations on how the sudden breakup of the East Bloc was affecting ships from those countries . . .

"F.a.c.c.o.p.," Ariadne will interject, anxiously leaning forward, hands on knees, slightly chewing her lower lip.

"Ships just don't stay in port as long as they used to, it's too expensive, and with containerization, roll on and roll off and everything else, they don't have to. It used to take days to unload and load a ship, but now they're in and out in less than twelve hours if they can be. So there's not so much of that old kind of port life, not in a big, modern port like we have here. The people who crew ships now, apart from the captains, some of the deck officers, just don't get to go ashore nearly as much as they used to. It's a drearier life for them now. Cooped up on their ships."

And then the Swiss investment banker will remark on Plato's dislike of sailors and the sea: A bitter and briny neighbor, he'll say, quoting Plato, breeding shifty and distrustful souls, the hucksters, usurers, rip-off merchants of ports, and so on. (Will make a mental note to tell Reverend Roundtree about Plato.) And then that Roberto will say, "But there's still a great deal of truth to that, isn't there? Aren't ports especially home to the criminal element?"

"Sure, there's crime," he'll answer. "Contraband. Drug smuggling. All kinds of fraud. Also a new kind of pirate, truck hijackers. Containers get loaded onto trucks, and they drive out of the port and bang, sometimes within minutes, they get hit. A lot of the stuff you see getting sold on the streets of New York? Comes from stolen containers—"

"No, no, I don't arrest anybody," he'll answer again. "I guess I mainly deal with crimes, if you want to call them that, against seafarers. People working on ships have so few laws protecting them, really. Every flag has its own laws. Every port has its own laws. And there's no really strong or consistent or enforceable set of international maritime labor laws. Middle of winter, you'll get a ship in with a Bangladeshi crew, ice and slush all over the deck, and they'll be going around in just sandals—"

"Johnny brings them shoes and socks," Ariadne will interrupt, glumly. "And sweaters."

And he'll answer, "No, I wouldn't call it charity work, though, sure, that's a part of what we do. Interceding, negotiating, mediating, I do a lot of that. Trying to figure out what's going on between, say, a Greek captain and officers, Punjabi Sikh engine room guys, maybe a Filipino or Latino crew. Maybe there's been brutality by the officers. Or even a murder the Yugoslav captain and shipowner want hushed up—what's it to them what their Egyptian ranks do to each other? and supposedly the dead guy was asking for it, and they don't want to be held up in port. Or an arrest has to be made, and I'll end up liaisoning between the feds or the Coast Guard, the captain and ship's agent, whichever national authorities have jurisdiction, and the seafarer who's going to be arrested, extradited, whatever. Though it's hardly ever that dramatic. Their pay's being stolen, or not sent home to their families like it's supposed to be. Or some seaman's been ripped off by a fraudulent shipping agency in Tuvalu, has paid a fee for his job and all his savings to fly to New York to meet a ship that doesn't even exist. Or a guy really needs to see a doctor and the captain won't let him off the ship, doesn't want to have to pay for it. Abandoned crews sometimes, like the one I found today. Or the ship isn't seaworthy—maybe no ventilation, or plumbing for the crew. Stowaways. Or something simple but important to the crew, like bad food. Or religious problems. When the second engineer hired on, he was promised a Muslim diet, and now they just laugh at him when he demands it. Or something to do with beliefs and superstitions a crew from Kiribati has but their Polish captain just doesn't get, thinks they're a bunch of sissies and shirkers. Political tensions. Sometimes you'll get six nationalities, all speaking different languages, on one ship. Maybe they've come in from a bad crossing, been through some awful storm, whole ship's totally stressed, and every potential problem that was there before breaks out all at once. All kinds of things come up. And we get in there and do what we can."

". . . Actually, *we're* supposed to use the term *seafarer*. Well, some of the reverends decided, you know how things are now, sea*man* just doesn't cut it like it used to."

"Uh-huh. People *do* always think you're saying semen. On the phone you're always having to go, sea*man*—you know, as in sailor? *Ha-ha*."

"Johnny gets invited into the galley to taste every kind of food," Ariadne will say.

"Well no, usually it's not very good. But you do get to taste a lot of different foods."

"Sometimes I'll drive a bunch of them back to the institute so they can phone home from there. A simple thing like that means a ton. Though, of course, so many of them don't have phones at home, not where they come from."

"A ship is a ship is a ship? Not at all. Soviet ship's a whole different world from, say, a Korean one. Russian captains almost always invite you up to their cabin for a vodka; they like to shoot the shit. There's this one container ship comes in about three times a year, flies a Maltese flag, captained and crewed entirely by women, women from everywhere, a very well run ship—"

"No, not especially good looking. Some are. The most striking is the chief engineer, oddly enough. There's this other ship crewed by criminal fugitives. And another entirely by Portuguese monks, though

I've never seen it, was home with the flu when it came in last winter, Reverend Roundtree went—"

"Johnny and his colleagues make sure that every seafarer on every ship that comes into New Jersey and New York around this time of year gets a Christmas present," Ariadne will interrupt. "Even Islamic ships and Israeli ships."

". . . Hah! They *wish*. No. Socks, slippers, gloves, wool caps, mainly stuff like that."

"No, I don't have to wrap the presents myself. Volunteers from local churches—"

"Dress up like Santa Claus? . . . No."

"What I like about the job is getting to make a difference in the lives of people that hardly anyone ever even thinks about. We're doing important things, we're organizing a center for seafarers' legal rights that, well, if we get the right kind of international cooperation, can become a world center and advocate for a new, and we hope more enforceable, international maritime labor code. We organize conferences, forums. But what I like is being out in the van, out on the docks, boarding ships. The detective part of it, you might even say. Kind of like being a cop without having to deal with other cops, or having to shoot anybody. The freedom of it. This sense that you're getting to deal with the whole rest of the world, that in a hands-on way you're experiencing something about the way the rest of the world is now. It's a great job. Sometimes I really think I have one of the best damned jobs in the world . . ."

He'll feel, God, frustrated. How can he make them see? A thousand stories and images moiling inside him, and they want to giggle snootily over Christmas presents. Will have met a pair of stowaways from Hong Kong just last week, an old man and his eleven-year-old granddaughter, they'll have been traveling the world on this ship nearly two years already, at every port the authorities will have turned them away, and the Moroccan crew and Turkish officers, they'll have practically adopted the pair, the old man helping in the galley, the little girl becoming fluent in Arabic, she had a pet pigeon, fattest pigeon he'll have ever seen, nearly as big as a turkey, kept it in a cage one of the crew will have made for her from tar-stiffened rope. But the captain will have wanted it resolved, getting worried for the girl, her effect on the crew, this no environment for a little girl on the cusp of puberty: why tempt fate? Will have almost felt like a betrayal but it had to be done, getting in touch with people from UNESCO, convincing them to get the paperwork done and foot the bill for their repatriation without port authorities fining the ship for bringing in stowaways, no one else was going to do it. Captain Kemal will have even let himself be held over in port six extra hours to see it all through, invited him to the going-away dinner, broke out some not at all bad Moroccan claret. During the dinner the little girl will have stood on her chair and made a deft speech in Arabic and then sung a song in Cantonese . . . See what he gets to see? The girl took the obese pigeon with her, all the way back to Hong Kong.

Something will feel wrong. He'll have noticed it even in the bar, but later, alone with her on the sidewalk, he'll feel sure of it. As if the air has been let out of the complicity that usually binds them, that lets their inner gravity swagger elbow to elbow. She'll be walking slowly, hands in the pockets of her leather coat, brooding down at the shadow-strewn sidewalk. And when he'll say, "Ariadne?" she'll glance up at him as if surprised to see him there, her eyebrows slightly raised, and then she'll look away and keep walking. A typhoon of temper could be coming any second now. "You want to get a cab?" he'll ask. She'll say nothing, keep walking. Finally, two blocks later, she'll suddenly step off the curb and put her arm up for a cab, and he'll get into it beside her but she'll slide to the far side of the seat and look out the window. This distance between them like an unraveling. Caused, he'll anxiously decide, by his having blabbed on too long about his job, having carelessly let them in on something that Ariadne—unreasonably, of course—thinks of as solely their own. Well, he won't have told them much about the *Urus,* her abandoned crew and all the stories he heard from them today. Maybe that'll make it better, when he tells her . . .

She'll turn her head and look at him coldly as the cab hurtles and rocks over the West Side Highway, along the blackened river.

"Boy," she'll say. "We let them make a couple of bores out of us, didn't we?"

"You think?" He'll force a smile. Come on, Ariadne, it's no big deal. "Ariadne, if anyone was boring, it was them. Santa Claus? Gimme a break."

And she'll laugh softly, gloved hands folded on her lap, staring out the window again. "That Roberto," she'll say quietly. "He is such an *imp*."

For the rest of his life, the Ship Visitor will remember this moment as the one that foretold the end of their relationship—the dreary, heavy shock in his chest of a door kicked open and tabloid photographers in grungy black coats storming in to expose his hopeful, self-deluding heart mired in bed with a doomed love.

Though in the taxi the Ship Visitor's first response will be defiant—four generations of Staten Island men who've made their living, in one way or another, from ships and the sea, speaking inside him, with the usual family metaphors. He'll think, Stop loving my job, Ariadne, and you stop loving me. Because love comes and goes, Ariadne, just like ships do, coming and going over the horizon with all their secrets, and sometimes you don't find out what a fucked up ship it is until you're onboard and way into the voyage.

And he'll think, But I have a will too. I refuse to dread spirit-hollowing loss. Try to manage only the present. Let love do its supernatural work.

"Ariadne, you wouldn't believe this ship I found today, all covered in leaves . . . The crew came to New York six months ago, the very week we met, Ariadne, and they haven't budged an inch since. It's a fucking shipwreck, right here in Brooklyn harbor."

The next afternoon, after visiting the *Urus* with Reverend Roundtree, he'll take four of the *Urus*'s crew into Manhattan by subway to meet with a lawyer: when he returns to the Seafarers' Institute in the evening, the Reverend will be waiting for him with the news that the *Urus* has recently, in the last few weeks, become a stateless vessel.

"The ownership didn't pay the next round of fees and taxes, John," she'll say, "and claimed the ship wasn't ready for a new inspection. So they were taken off the Panamanian registry. That's why they painted off the name and home port. It's a brass plate ownership. Listed as Achuar L.T.D. of Panama, no idea who or what's behind it. And the ship's agent, of last known record anyway, is Miracle Shipping, office at 19 Rector Street, lower Manhattan. Never more than an answering machine in a rented or borrowed cubicle, I bet. Telephone no longer in service."

He'll remain silent—it's nothing he'll not have expected.

"And another thing," she'll say. "The crew was never Panama's responsibility anyway. They're unlicensed seafarers, John. Apparently they never signed shipping articles."

"Well, that complicates things."

"Oh, John"—Reverend Roundtree will sigh—"what are we doing in this business?"

"The Lord's work, I thought it was, Kathy," he'll say, more sympathetically, really, than glibly.

"Sure. Except nowadays any scum can hide from God. All you need is, whatever, a flag of convenience, brass plate incorporation. You don't even have to be rich anymore."

A HAIRCUT

(OCTOBER 15—OCTOBER 25)

1

GRIEF STAYS HIDDEN LIKE AN ALARM CLOCK WITH NO HANDS SET to go off at the bottom of sleep. But desire lies awake next to boredom, doing everything it can to keep depression and deepest worry out of bed, pleading, Don't fade, do that again, just like I first imagined it, Japonesa bella y sucia. For a while, after Capitán Elias told his story back in July, pilot boats plied darkened, rough seas to the *Urus* every night, on any given night as many as a dozen drop ladders lowered from the edge of sleep so that the provocative harbor pilot could climb up into a dozen separate insomnias and wriggle out of her jeans. It was el Capitán's mention of holing up with her and Japanese porno that had really done it, incited this florescence of Yorikos. Japanese porno, what's that like? And so they imagined . . . as much as they could. Well, they really hadn't been introduced to anyone else. (As El Tinieblas often reminds them, even in prison there were women: conjugal visits, administration workers, smuggled in whores pimped by guards, and even other prisoners. But here, the closest thing to a live woman to look at are the few images of sexy women tattooed here and there on El Tinieblas's body . . .) But that was three months ago. If you have hardly any idea of Japan, such dreams turn into Central American porno pretty quickly once the kimonos crumble, to universal porno, hard to keep even that going with someone you've never actually met. So tonight only four Yorikos visit the ship, two claimed by the same frenetic insomnia. The one being most patient and chaste in the production of his scenario is having the most success bringing her to life: he's escorted Yoriko home to Puerto Cortés, he's showing her around, introducing her to friends and relatives, he's put her in a pretty dress that bares her shoulders and long, beautiful neck, hombre, she loves Puerto Cortés, loves El Faro for bringing her there!

Elsewhere onboard that night as every night, in every dark and silent cabin, desire rummages obsessively through the same old trunk, digs at memory with a dog's frantic claws. Roving hands and minds grope behind, between, above, below, coming up with mute dolls missing faces and limbs, handfuls of air, until all that's left is the empty bottom of this trunk where you get to see yourself coming home after your glorious time at sea, penniless, still in debt, and will she still be waiting and what will she think of me then? The dog digs deeper, more and more frantically . . . what were you doing out there at that hour, Ana María, with your sister and our hijita, so far from your mother's house? (Roque Balboa asks Ana María that almost every night, lying awake on his belly, eyes shut, keeping as still as he can, even modulating his breathing, all his concentration focused on his memory tunneling towards her.) Standing on the small dirt hill on the other side of that drainage ditch in the dark, with a diaper in your hands, letting the wind play with it. There was a warm, steady wind blowing off the lake that night, I was walking to Lino's cantina and suddenly saw you standing there just up ahead on the hill, on the other side of the drainage ditch running along the road, you, our daughter, and your little sister. And I went a little closer. You dancing the diaper from pecking fingers, the diaper stiffening, fluttering, stiffening, and little Norma watching and laughing, her curly hair floating up in the wind. And the wind blowing your soft hair across your face, tugging your yellow dress across your body so that hip and thigh glowed through. Ay no, muchacha, it hurts. It hurts just to remember that, just my hand touching your warm skin through a dress. You didn't see me at first. La nena did, though she didn't recognize me, in her smudged white smock, two years old now. A tightening in my throat, va, pues. When you saw me standing there in the road, you froze with the wind pulling the diaper out sideways from your hands like it was trying to fly away with you, your eyes widening as they took me in, filling with, carajo, I know, every sadness, every reproach. I stood in the road and wanted to jump over the reeking ditch and take that rag from your hands, pull you into my arms and kiss you, tell you I was going to spend the rest of my life apologizing and making things good for us and kissing your monkey ears through your hair, but I was afraid I was going to cry, Ana María, I was about to cry so I just turned and walked off, and then the way you called out in the dark through the wind, with hate in your voice, "Qué poco hombre eres, Chávez!"—and I kept walking to Lino's—"Chávez Roque, eres un hijo de la gran puta!" And now, on this jodido ship I signed on to soon after, telling myself I'd come home in a year with enough money to win your love and respect back, I do it, I leap the drainage ditch and climb the muddy hill and snatch the diaper out of your hands, and every time I do this, you vanish, all three of you vanish, and I'm standing there all by myself holding this fucking diaper . . .

. . . In love as in war, every hole is a trench. A memorable joke, though not El Peperami's, or mine, but yours, La Tusa, no doubt taught to you, puta madre, so you could parrot it to drunken seamen. Because you had breasts just like a woman and smooth sweat-perfume-moist skin and a lustily heaving female ocean swell of a belly and a plush, lipsticked mouth, and you'd even perfumed your lacy panties like a woman though underneath you were a macho. Even your big, purple pene reeked of whore's perfume and like a wrestler's armpit when I finally put it in my mouth knowing that from now on I wasn't the same anymore, drunk as I was I've always been able to bring back the dizzying shocks and helpless degradation of that night, but now you don't want to anymore, cabrón, it's like trying to let a dusty old maid give you a hand job, I can't even get hard, I don't smell or feel anything, no surprise or even bleak humiliation, nothing, just me, I see my own face grotesquely straining in the dark to remember something, anything . . .

. . . You will be my wife, Natalia, my wife, forever and forever, we'll have a big, sunny bedroom with a big bed because I'll be rich—The Pink Horse will be just the first step; because I can fix anything, I'll have my own shop and scrap yard too, buy busted old machinery, fix it and sell it to factories—but we'll love each other just like we did when we were poor, so please let me feel that way now, the electric and slippery touch of our bodies together and your cool toes wiggling against mine, your nakedness against mine, which I'd never believed would actually happen and then finally it did, the warm, rubbery scent of your skin filling my nostrils like no other skin since that so long ago young tía who became a nun held me in her arms at the beach and I fell asleep inside her hug with my nose stuck into the soft, sticky, vein-pulsed warmth, why have I lost you, Natalita? Why can I barely remember your face? I used to feel my love like an inflamed organ inside, and now it's like someone operated on me in my sleep, took it out and sewed me back up and sold it to somebody else, probably to Hércules Molina, who was always trying to peel you with his eyes though I never really cared because I knew it was only me you loved . . .

. . . She was eleven, a virgin, her mother said. Bueno, she spoke no Spanish of course and about as much English as I, but I understood these words: *girl*, *eleven*, *virgin*, and that she was signaling with her fingers in the charcoal-smoky, howling dark full of strange music and smells that she was lowering her price, the most criminal act of my whole life. And now I drag this up, why now? The next morning I couldn't even bring myself to meet Capitán J. P. Osbourne's eyes, so deep was my shame. I punished myself by staying out of burdels for nearly a year and never told anyone and never will, there are some secrets you take alone to the final reckoning, no? And there it will make no difference that she wasn't a virgin after all and at least fifteen and that shriveled witch probably wasn't even her mother, because I hadn't been able to resist, led in as meekly as a depraved lamb. Vos, I was young, freer than I knew how to be, with an unloved wife, reckless and lonely and craving and protected by the anonymity of a poor young man beguiled by the magic of money in his pocket in an even poorer port city on the other side of the world where everyone thought even I was gringo, europeo—*Hey! Sir? You Eenglish man? Eenglish? Greek? Eleven! Virgin! Sir?* And look, there she is, her brown face and eyes full of a little girl's innocent terror (I thought), waiting for me in bed again, and when I pull back the sheet it's as if her skinny little chameleon's body has evaporated into it like an image on a shroud, there's nothing but an empty bed, so even the shame you've earned comes back like a ghost now . . .

There's another onboard who grieves for a dead lover: Caratumba, the Guatemalan electrician, keeps it to himself like Esteban does but harasses himself in a different way because he witnessed it, ran away to save himself and forget, but finds himself with nothing to do but remember the day, after lunch, when they left the oil exploration camp on the Río Usamacinta in a little launch he'd been lent the use of, headed for their favorite spot, on the Río Pucté. She worked as a laundress, one of the only females in camp, where the workers lived in tents and the gringo geologists and technicians in their own screened wooden cabins and big platform tents; she'd go up and down the rowed tents collecting laundry at dawn, bringing it back in the evenings, her face and loose, tendrily hair ducking in through the tent flaps in the gray, humid, bird-singing dawn for a quick kiss, a nibble at her thick, smooth lips. Lips that, even when closed tight, always looked as if they were gently smiling, and eyes so fiery she always looked angry at the same time. A pooled tributary covered with hyacinths, the water sweet and crystal clear, the bottom's white sand rising in sugary clouds around their feet, they'd made love and were now swimming around naked when the first shot shattered their shimmering delight, fired from the tall reeds, and then another shot; he ducked under the water and saw her sinking with blood billowing from her head like a magenta flare and knew she was dead and swam away as far as he could, came up quickly for air and swam some more and heard another shot, couldn't even risk going back to the launch for his clothes, knew who it had to be, he'd somehow followed them there, that soldier he'd taken her from, always bothering and threatening her ever since, one of the soldiers dispatched to guard the camp after that guerrilla raid when they made off with some of the oil company dynamite and burned their helicopter; he struck out naked into the rain forest, fled. It's almost like watching a scene from another man's life now. He shares that man's horror and grief, but numbly, almost resentfully. Knows he's doing penance for a crime he didn't actually commit but that he'll just have to keep on doing so, that's all, until his time is up . . .

Esteban is alone in the room watching in horror as la Marta's name writes itself in bright red paint on the wall. No brush or spray-paint can or hand, just paint slowly spelling out M A R T A in big, dripping letters on the gray-painted, insect-splattered plank walls, droplets of paint dribbling from MARTA to the floor . . . Wakes panting in the dark, heart pounding, the rest of himself flooded with terror around it.

"Qué haces?" rasps Bernardo softly.

His rib cage heaving, as if he wants to sob but can't, his almost-sobs like the last, slow-burning log impatient for the peace of cold ash around it.

"Nada. Una pesadilla," he manages. Sí pues, just a nightmare . . .

"I'm not hungry," Bernardo mumbles. Qué?

"Me voy!" he says. Springs from the bed as if it's on fire.

"Don't come back," and then in a louder, awakened voice, the viejo cries out, "Vos, Estabanito? Vete!"

Descending the mooring line, still trembling, he feels the cable-splicing knife sliding out of his pocket yet doesn't dare or can't let go of the rope to catch it, the tool falls away like a fatal mistake, hears the splash in the water below alerting the enemy, now they'd grab their weapons and fire blindly into the dark.

What an awful dream. Can't remember ever having a more upsetting dream. He feels cold and weak limbed, dazed and taunted. Marta's name writing itself on a wall. Why was that so terrifying and sad? Wishes he could just take off running. Run where? Into the city! She's never once, not once, come to me in a dream, staying away as if out of some mistaken desire to protect me. And, chocho, now she comes and writes her name on the wall.

A row of three-story, old brick warehouses, windows sealed with newer brick, rows of star-shaped floor-support caps protruding. Dove cooing resonates inside this darkness too, coming from inside the warehouses: like giant brick birdcages, warehouses full of pitch black nothing and doves. A pair of rats slinking along the bottom of a warehouse wall like the shoes of an otherwise invisible prowler. His own invisible shadow wearing shoes. Except some of these warehouses seem to be still in use, some of the ground-level iron doors in brick arches padlocked. He finds one door left slightly ajar, padlock uselessly closed over an unfastened door hinge. And he pushes the heavy door open, stares into the musty dark, and steps inside.

His lungs feel as if they should give off cold, dusty light of their own, but the darkness is absolute. This place must be full of rats. He takes one careful step forward and then another and another, walks right into something neither soft or hard, a cold crunch of plastic against his leg. Prods it with his foot, feels it with his hands, a pliant plastic covering and a packed looseness inside. Crackers? Cereal? Something like that. Something edible? Groping around, he finds that the darkness is full of these. Hoists one up, it's not so heavy. Carries it outside, where he can see it better by the weak glow of the city-suffused sky. Milky plastic, folded and stapled across the top. Carefully he pries the stapled seam open and reaches inside . . .

Wood chips. Holds a handful to his nose, breathes in the tangy fragrance, reminiscent of paint solvent. Cedar? A warehouse full of wood chips. These get shipped somewhere? Won't it make excellent tinder for their fires? It always takes a long time to get their fires going, the broken boards they collect from the rubble of the old terminals around the cove so heavy with ocean damp and air. Though when that old paint-and-creosote-scabbed wood does finally get going, it goes up like a whole tiny wharf-side warehouse jammed with barrels of flammable chemicals, fish meal, the ancient dust of Arabian spices and suddenly combusting, century-old stevedores' spit.

He walks back through the alley, carrying the sack of wood chips in his arms. What will they say in the morning, when they learn he's been leaving the ship, see what he's brought back? Why keep it a secret that he leaves the ship? Now they're going to see who he is. So they should.

He sits in the sand of the old terminal, listening to the buoy bells out in the harbor, the doves in the dark, clutching the plastic sack of wood chips to his side. Hates this taste and texture in his mouth, like the inside of a rotted aguacate shell, the itch in his crotch and ass, along his scalp, this passive filth caking him. Faint, chilly shudders—must be related, somehow, to the cold in his lungs—drift up and down through the skin of his legs, light as cobwebs, somehow inside his very skin, not over or under. Yet for the first time in months, he thinks, he's done something that lets him feel like he's slipped back into himself. If she could see him now she'd be less disillusioned with him than she would have seeing him yesterday, no? So he lies back in the sand clutching the plastic bag tightly against himself as if he loves it.

In a pasture just outside the town he sat with la Marta in his arms under a fruitless papaya tree, leaves like big, green, floppy ox ears. Rotting jocotes fermented in the grass under other trees, drawing wasps. Now and then an aguacate leadenly plummeted from a high branch in its towering tree, crashing through lower ones with almost the same sound a falling mortar shell can make before it hits and explodes: when she jumped inside his embrace, turning to clutch at him, he saw the sweaty strand of hair stuck to her cheek under her panicked wild stallion's eye and he felt so in love.

There were some cattle in the pasture, and that night his battalion was going to eat one of those oxen. The campesino who owned this small herd would be paid for his ox, though not enough to make him very happy about it. They'd roast it in big slabs over an open pit, long ribs standing up in the flames like the walls of a fortress in an infernal siege. Though he didn't know that yet, if he had he would have ogled the herd, wondering which one, perhaps marveling that that very night a chunk of that sinewy ox over there was going to be in his belly mixing and fermenting with whatever he could drink of Marta. She and Amalia and some of the other survivors of her Nightmare BON were going to be invited to dine with their heroes of the BLI, and there she was going to learn that everyone was calling him Squirrel now.

He held her under the tree with his arms wrapped around her soft, warm waist, under her breasts and the squirrel. The first few times he'd licked and kissed la Marta's chichis, sturdy, ash brown nipples in big, soft globes, he'd worried about getting rabies or something, because she said the squirrel was always peeing, though its pee was like a few droplets from an eyedropper and hardly smelled and dried so quickly you barely noticed. Now he'd just told Marta that as an infant Rubén Darío had wandered off from his house one day and his family had run around in a panic looking for him and finally found him in a pasture just like this one, sitting underneath a cow drinking milk right from its udder. Was she surprised he knew stories like that? About the great poet, eh? No, she knew that story too, of course she did, hadn't Darío spent much of his childhood in León and then come back after all his years of glory in Europe just to die there?

"I dare you to do that," Marta said. "Get under one of those cows and drink milk from it."

"Those are not cows. They're oxen."

"Ah sí? What about that one there?"

The cow's ribs pushed against its hide as if about to rip it open, and its flaccid udder was mottled with mud and bits of straw, dotted with tics and flies. But he thought about it anyway.

"I don't want to," he said finally, letting himself sound too sleepy to move. "Darío was an infant when he did that."

"Ve?" She grinned. "You don't love me so much anymore."

He said he didn't like milk that much anyway, which was true. She reached her arm back, around his neck, turned towards him, and they began to kiss. Both their hands were always grimy and smelling of gasoline and gun grease from the daily task of weapons cleaning.

Yesterday, when he'd unbuttoned her shirt in this same pasture, he'd said, Breasts like anvils and garlic. Told her that was from another poet, puta, forget his name. That made her laugh. La Marta didn't laugh much, but when she did, her laughter was like a gleeful child hiding inside her. She said she'd never suspected that being in a BLI was like taking a poetry class! Bueno, jah! not exactly, but his company's political officer was obsessed with reciting poetry.

Her eyes were like buzzing honey hives whenever they looked into his. She was already in love with him, he felt sure of it, if he'd ever been sure of anything in his life he was sure of that. Impossible to believe that in another few days he'd be back in the war. Amalia had rebuffed Esteban's friend Arturo and was appalled that her sister could lose herself in love so quickly amidst all their death, but Amalia had a novio back in León. La Marta looked up to him. Up to *him*. It was as if she needed his breath, sometimes they'd put their mouths together and just breathe air in and out of each other's lungs, hot air in and out, in and out, in and out of each other's mouths and lungs. No time to lose: the seconds and touches bearing them away nibble by nibble like the sail-shaped shards of leaves carried aloft by long caravans of leaf-cutting ants. Twice they'd fucked outdoors already, not daring to get fully naked, and each time they'd been spotted by little brats, campesino cipotes who weren't content just to spy but finally had to announce their presence, throwing clumps of dirt and rotted jocotes at them from their hiding places behind the brush-covered small hills at the edge of the pasture, one hit him with a wet *splat* right on his bared nalgas just as they were doing it. They had to find someplace else to go. He'd heard about two brothers whose parents had left them in charge of their two-pump gasoline station when they went to live in los Estados Unidos and who ran that small Red Cross station on the hill too; the brothers supposedly liked to seduce their own muchachas in the ambulance, and some in the battalion had already found out that they'd lend compas the use of the ambulance for that too. He lifted her arm, pushed back her sleeve to look at the red plastic Mickey Mouse watch: he was almost due back. And began undoing her shirt. Tomorrow, the ambulance. The faint baked, fecal scent of mud, sweat, and fear that never seems to wash out of military fatigues, that smell always stronger in the heat. The tangy, salty taste of her neck. Kissing her cheeks, he'd think that in fifty years he'd still be kissing these cheeks, they'd tell their grandchildren how they met in the war—the famous war for the future of their country, for the future of the world, for the future of Esteban and Marta!—in Quilalí, when she went around with a wild squirrel tucked between her breasts and came so much closer to death than even he.

* * *

A dentist's and a finquero's daughter. Who loved la Revolución. Because la Revolución helps those with money too, no? Maybe more than it helps the poor who, ni modo, usually want most from la Revolución the very things it can't seem to grant: more to eat, more to buy and sell, peace. But those who already have money want something else, things that can be named but not really touched and certainly not eaten, and these la Revolución does seem able to provide, especially if you're lucky enough to have been drafted and put in a BLI. And so she looked up to him. So she should have, because without the BLI, he would have been no one. Someone else entirely, whom she would never have looked twice at, and would have had no reason to.

Bueno, her family wasn't rich anyway, they were cómodo, and now barely that. Though as children, Marta and Amalia had even been taken to visit Disney World, in Florida, and another time to Miami, and once to Philadelphia, where they'd stayed for a whole year. La Marta lived with her family in an old colonial house with mildewed pink walls taking up half a block in León. Marta's mother was the dentist, working in a state clinic, still treating former and wealthier patients on the side: she was the ardent revolutionary, the Sandinista. Her mother took Marta and Amalia three times to see that movie *Apocalipsis Ya* to learn about the yanquis, except it backfired when both sisters developed a crush on the blond young soldier who water-skis and ends up, pobrecito, going crazy. Esteban had seen it too, in Corinto, that scene when the yanqui helicopters come flying in over the ocean with symphony music blaring from speakers and incinerate that Vietnamese village, the whole packed movie theater suddenly airless from everybody gasping and holding his breath, everybody thinking the same thing: chocho, the yanquis might come and do that to us any day now. They'd already mined the harbor, blown up the oil storage tanks, and every day the news brought more threats. How could anyone not feel a sickening terror just thinking about it? Marta's father had had two fincas where he grew cotton and raised cattle, but the government had expropriated the larger one, turned it into a farming collective; both farms were unproductive now. Her father had let the smaller one lapse in his disgust over the pointless prices the war-bled revolutionary government was paying for cotton and beef. Last year, when her father refused to hire extra workers to harvest the remnant of the cotton crop, Marta and Amalia's Juventud Sandinista group had gone out and camped on the finca for two weeks, armed with just a few old AKs and FALs against the plausible danger of contra raids, to finish the harvest themselves—so la Revolución would have a little more cotton to sell or to trade for weapons and oil and Polish potatoes. Yet her father was working as a warehouse inspector for the Agricultural Ministry because they'd asked him to and he hadn't dared say no—which made him a contra target too, he might be ambushed in his jeep on any lonely rural road. He wanted to move the family to Philadelphia, in los Estados Unidos, where his sister lived, married to a psychiatrist, also a Nica. Amalia and Marta had spent a whole year in Philadelphia, living with their aunt and uncle and attending a Catholic primary school so that they could learn English, spending part of the summer at a camp in the woods with other little yanqui children, the rest with their relatives in a big, airy wooden house on a beautiful beach somewhere, mother and father and baby Camilo having flown up to join them there. Her father even had some money in the bank in Philadelphia, waiting for them. He was always threatening to go ahead and move there by himself—but he loved his wife and daughters and little son, couldn't abandon them (anyway, what would he do in Philadelphia? his wife was the one with a profession), couldn't stop them from living the way they wanted, couldn't even stop two teenage daughters from going to war in a volunteer Juventud Sandinista battalion!

So Marta loved la Revolución—and Esteban loved his battalion: his BLI, conceived to operate not like a regular army unit but like guerrillas living off the land, always moving, relentlessly hunting the enemy, hounding them and sometimes fighting them every day for weeks until they'd finally driven them back across the border (the invaders, traitors, bestias, the dictator's old torturers and poor dumb rural lumpen turned yanqui mercenaries, no?). Even in his battalion, it seemed that everyone understood that when they talked about la Revolución they were really talking about the BLI—because outside the BLI there was so little else to go by, almost nothing else but jungle and mountains and what only warring armies can bring to these. The BLI was everything: fighting, staying alive. Con mucho *arte militar,* as their commander liked to say. A coherent and necessary concept once you saw what happened to those without it. So in this harrowing landscape they were elegant, did everything as they were supposed to, had never been routed in combat or blundered into an ambush . . . until that dog joined them, and then on the Zompopera Road, but that was after Quilalí.

Their battalion commander, Milton, one of the original members of El Coro de Ángeles, the very first BLI, formed at the start of the war, came from a campesino background. But his company's jefe, Noél, came from a burgesa family that was much richer than Marta's; they'd left for Miami just before the Triumph in '79, and Noél lived there four years, having a beach-cars-sex adolescence like in the movies until he turned eighteen, when instead of entering some university there he came back to Nicaragua on his own, enlisted in the Ejército Popular Sandinista, and had been at war against los yanquis ever since—Noél's older brother had been in la guerrilla, killed in combat in Matagalpa all the way back in '75. Noél died in the ambush on the Zompopera Road, after Marta, after Milton had been stripped of his command, even after the dog, all during that last furious contra offensive. Another officer, Jacinto, had spent two years studying in Bulgaria. Another compa, Guillermo, spent his childhood in exile with his family in Paris, his parents were intellectuals—Guillermo died in the Zompopera ambush too. Their medic, Nelson, though only twenty-four, was already a doctor, he'd studied in Cuba. Their best marksman and sniper, Frank, was a moreno from Bluefields who'd been to Angola with the Cubans, where he'd perfected his craft. A platoon leader, Aldo, who was also a circus clown, who gave clown classes through the Cultural Workers' Union, died because of that dog. Like Marta and Amalia, a few of the compas in his BLI had had parents wealthy enough to have taken them to Disney World. Some had parents and siblings living there now, in los Estados Unidos. Everyone else, of course, almost everybody in the battalion, was just a draftee like Esteban, poor people who'd never been anywhere. Poor people who'd been rounded up before they could run away from the draft, to Honduras or Costa Rica or elsewhere; and others, like him, who hadn't wanted to run. Many, especially among the campesino compas, had relatives and old friends fighting on the other side. Nobody wanted to have to kill his brother or cousin in battle, though everyone knew of others this had happened to and knew that if they had to do it they would and then carry the regret, though not the blame, forever. It was often talked about. His company had a political officer, Rodolfo—a professor before the army, what else?—who was supposed to help them think clearly about such matters; and who taught them about the Law of True Value, proletarians, lumpen, democracy, perestroika—words handed to them like extra bullet clips—tried to explain the changing world and the upheavals of history which they found themselves at the ferocious forefront of, their battalion's exploits already adding little daubs of wet ink to the great histories of the bloody century and the whole world that would one day be written! who tried to teach them about the sort of men they were supposed to be from now on, revolutionaries, and the ideal revolution versus the achievable one (for now, the BLI was the achievable one); and who loved to recite poetry from memory, political poems, love poems, poems about common things and about chichis, and poems so strange that in the silence after they were spoken the whole jungle seemed to tense around them, become even more ominous, their elusive meaning echoed in the throbbing uproar of tree frogs. Your breasts are anvils and garlic. At least that wasn't a lie, could never be a lie if it was also poetry, once spoken it became a thing in the world as real as any other thing—a hat, a rifle, an ox—that was Rodolfo's point about poetry. So he even learned to think of love in a new way. You were supposed to make something of it, not just let it happen. And if you couldn't make something of it, compa, then it couldn't be love. Somehow that went for everything, from killing to love. Knowing you had to kill and why, you were supposed to find a way to speak of love. What was it you were supposed to love? Claro, la Revolución, which was like a poem you were supposed to be writing in your head; and, most important, the BLI, which was real, and which had only one soldier in it whom la Marta loved.

Ve? He'd never be ignorant again. He'd never go back to being just this port town lumpen, a seaside peasant, a market cook's bastard, with an idea of the world that went little further than the tales of drunken seamen and whores. It had all sifted into him: everyone in his BLI, everything they talked and knew about. Then before you ever got the chance to understand what it was you'd actually learned, you could take a sliver of shrapnel in the head and all that new knowledge would rush out of you, compa, colder and remoter than the stars.

Or you lived. And then what good did it all do you? And what was it all for? Where's their political officer, that fucking Rodolfo, now? Whose ears is he filling with words about poetry and killing and revolution and love and heroes and martyrs now? Hijueputa, somewhere, right now, far away in Nicaragua, Rodolfo's mouth is still going. Vos, while here you are in los Estados Unidos, trying to work up the courage and resolve to disappear into it, puta, trying to find a reason to. Thinking you've done some grand thing sneaking off a ship that doesn't move to lie down with your stolen sack of wood chips in the sand in the dark that brings her as close as lovers' breath . . .

La Marta and her sister both wanted to be economists or accountants. Because la Revolución needed people who could manage money. Chocho, did it ever. They liked mathematics. La Revolución's accountants, that's what Marta and Amalia wanted to be.

The year before the sisters had applied for summer jobs in a branch of the Trade Ministry. They went for separate interviews with a tall, bulky, middle-aged man who kept his sunglasses on indoors, balding, a little mustache, always dressed in a spotless white guayabera and creased black trousers. He gave them each a psychological test and then had them come back to his office, separately, for another interview to talk about the test results:

"He said the strangest things," Marta told him under the papayaless papaya tree, with that startled, wide-eyed stillness she had whenever she was thinking of something serious. "He said my psychological profile showed I had a great capacity for love and that I was going to be a wonderful wife and mother. And then you know what he asked me? He asked me if I'd ever had anal sex." She rocked her head back to meet his eye.

"Pendejo," said Esteban. "What, he thought you were going to end up doing it up the culo with him right there on that couch?"

"Vos, it *was* disillusioning," Marta said, and smiled. "I asked him what he meant, because he'd taken off his glasses and was looking at me so sternly I felt nervous. He said, You know what that is, don't you? And I sort of shook my head yes and no at the same time and he said, You're not a virgin, are you? And I said, That's none of your business and yes, I know what it is. And he said, with much arrogance"—Marta made her voice go low and pompous—"Señorita compita, I have asked you a very direct question, the answer to which can help me finish your psychological profile. I asked if you've ever had anal sex. I've asked you this because according to what I'm able to deduce about you, the first time you have anal sex it will be out of true love, and that is the man you will marry. Your test suggests that you're that kind of female. It's important to know yourself. Such is the profound benefit of these psychological tests."

"I'll kill that hijueputa!" exclaimed Esteban. "Wanted to trick you into doing it with him because he thought you wanted to marry him or what?" He went on yelling vehement threats and curses against the psychologist for a while, while Marta slumped back against his chest and stared off across the pasture until he was finished and then she said, "Vos, Esteban, this is the strangest part. When I got home, I found out he'd asked Amalia the very same questions. He'd told her the very same things. Word for word! Bueno, qué onda? Was he a pervert, or a serious psychologist, or both?"

"A total pervert, Marta. You didn't work there—"

"Vos, had to. They gave us the jobs. But he never mentioned it again. Always polite and everything. Maintained a distance. It was rewarding work too, very educational, and they were very happy with our work, especially Amalia's. Vos, Esteban, have you ever done it that way?"

He almost lied. "No," he admitted, trying to sound indifferent. Putas do it all the time, he knew, and chavalas who don't want to get pregnant.

"Ve?" she said. "Because I think that what he said is true. Because otherwise, I'd never do it."

Which is how la Marta proposed marriage to him, if you chose to think of it that way. When he went to the brothers' gasoline station the next morning, there was a hand-lettered cardboard sign saying they were out of gasoline, no one there. He went up to the Red Cross station on the hill, and there was no one there either. The station was just one nearly bare room affixed to a shuttered garage. The door was unlocked, and he went in and looked into the garage at the ambulance: it was at least thirty years old but in spotless condition, long and cream colored, a red cross on the paneled side in back, a bulbous hood and bumper. The ambulance was slightly bouncing, shocks squeaking like quiet mice. He went back outside and waited. Finally a teenager, one of the brothers, came out buttoning his shirt, followed by a plump, pretty-faced muchacha combing out humid hair with her fingers, a blouse knotted over her rippled brown belly. "Claro, compa," said the brother after Esteban had explained what he wanted to borrow the ambulance for. "That's what it's there for."

The rear of the ambulance had a beige, stain-mottled, padded-cloth blanket spread over the hard floor, pillows propped against the back of the front seat, stretchers rolled up against the sides. Some light penetrated from the room off the garage, through the windshield. They spent nearly four hours there, drenched in sweat, loving each other in the heat of a bread oven. Even the squirrel looked soaking wet, paralyzed in a corner though temporarily freed from its umbilical of thread.

La Marta's caresses, the way she reached for him and so easily nestled herself against him, her utter lack of nervousness, confirmed what he'd already suspected, that she was more experienced in love than he. Hairy as a newborn monkey in places, and in others as glossily smooth and brown as chocolate toffee for all the insect bites and scratches and rashes strewn across her skin as if she'd been rolling in thorns and wet rose petals. Skinny arms, ankles, tapering shins, but other parts of her gorgeously round, with a soft plushness it was astonishing the war hadn't worn away. Hair like a submerged, softened spray of porcupine quills ran from her pubis to her navel. He felt all fumbling hands and hunger, confused by this intoxicating variety of places for his mouth and touch to go, his swollen pene flopping like a netted fish. Her chunchita, wildly hairy, its texture and taste, made him think of the earthy, mossy underside of some overturned jungle log; he snuffled into it like an anteater, swirled his tongue deep into the tart, pink buttermilk wet, her inner thighs shivering and quaking around his head. And when they fucked, such mute, earnest pushing, trying to pour all of himself, all of his emotion, into her, they both came quickly, flutteringly—he'd never fucked like that before, so solemnly and purely, almost religiously. Like a woman, he'd thought, he'd just made love the way a woman in love makes love. "Mi rey," she called him. Scar tissue like a tiny centipede from a childhood injury high on her hairy shin, now he thinks of it as the mark the infiltrator clawed into her skin to show death the way in. He was covered in insect bites too, and tiny bumps hard as pebbles. She spent a long time going over his body, popping the little infestations between her nails while he winced from the searing nips of pain and kicked his feet. Their fungused and rotted feet, inflamed, vinegar-reeking toes. Ay, Esteban, will she ever get to feel clean and smooth all over again? (Never.) A bubble bath! Or a manicure and pedicure—I've never wanted one but I'd take one now, I think I'd even let them use that hairy wax. Mami still gets her nails done and legs waxed, Papi likes her that way, she goes to a woman who runs a little salon out of her house in León. I went with Mami once, and, Esteban, it was so gross, this big bowl full of hard, yellow, hairy wax, all this hair from who knows how many women's legs all mixed in, from her using that wax over and over again.

I said, Puta, qué asco, Mami! You get smeared with that if you want, but not me! They made love again, nearly as earnestly as the first time. A while later she looked back at him with her serious owl eyes over her shoulder and said she wanted to do it, vos sabes, Esteban, the true love way. The little brown eye staring out of a tuft of mossy black. They weren't sure how to proceed. It took a while, but finally he put himself in, maybe not gently and slowly enough, but he'd tried, she moaned and flailed her arms around so much she batted the squirrel, sent it flying like a limp glove against the wall, and then he had to stop moving inside her while she reached for it, cupped it in her hands, murmured apologetically into its fur, set it back down. "Mi rey, te gusta?" she quietly screamed. "Te gusta, mi rey?" They both gaped with embarrassed delight at the glossy little gobs of her shit clinging to his pene when he pulled out, and looked around, stumped, for something to wipe it off with. Finally he reached for his pants, cleaned himself against the inside of the mud-caked cuffs, grinned. Monumental, together they'd both been someplace they'd never been before, bodies manifesting blossoming trust. He fell back into her sweat-slicked arms, said, "So this means we're getting married?" and she said, "Sí, mi amor, claro que sí. As soon as this fucking war ends." They spent the rest of the time fondling and making plans for the future, fondling the future. Two days later he went back to the war with her Mickey Mouse watch in his pocket and the raunchy smudge of their engagement vow mud-camouflaged on the inside of his pant cuff, marched out of Quilalí and almost immediately into the deadliest months of the whole war. A young man in love, with a future. They were always telling you that the war was over the future, no? But it was really always about the present, a world spiked and shadowed with portents that looked ahead to the next second, minute, hour, day, and no further. And now the future is here and, hijueputa, look at it: a ship that doesn't move.

A few weeks ago, on deck, by the light of their hissing-popping-cracking-pungently-fuming fire, El Tinieblas had taken off his shirt and then pulled down his pants to tell them his life story: that was the first time he'd ever told them what he'd gone to prison for, and how long he'd stayed. Some of his tattoos are just for decoration, or they're symbols: the scorpion over each forearm, Superwoman in a G-string, La Santa Muerte in hooded cloak. But others depict key moments and turning points in his life story: those banana trees, that's the coastal banana plantation where he was born, and, claro, that's Chiquita Banana, but it's also his mamita, and this is the cemetery she's buried in, and that weeping full moon over the cemetery wall, that's him. This is the Kentucky Fried Chicken in Tegucigalpa he robbed, though he fucked it up—two years he got, he went in when he was sixteen. And that's his novia, Leticia. She's sitting like that, so modestly—with her knees drawn up over her chest and her arms clasped around her shins—because he didn't want to commit a falta de respeto, couldn't have everyone staring at Leticia's secrets all the time, after all she used to come twice a week for a conjugal visit. Until she stopped coming. And this, here on his thigh, those are prison guards beating him because in the middle of another surprise search of the prisoners' barracks, he'd vomited up the plastic-wrapped mota and pills he'd hastily swallowed—another year added to his sentence, because of that. And here on his shin, this date, 5/13/86, wrapped in a snake chopped in pieces, that's the day Leticia came to the prison to tell him she was pregnant, maybe or maybe not his child, but she was getting married to another . . .

The tattoos were always done by another prisoner using a guitar string connected to wires and radio batteries rolled up in a magazine, the guitar string's filed point dipped in precious ink carefully doled into the indented top of a toothpaste tube cap. So that when the guards searched, they found nothing: batteries inside the radio, toothpaste capped, guitar string back on the guitar. Tattooing was against the prison rules, but every day prisoners had new tattoos as if images from their dreams at night revealed themselves on their skin by day.

"When this is over, you're not going to have enough room for a ship tattoo," said El Faro.

"No," said El Tinieblas. "Well, maybe a tiny ship."

"It would be a lie to get a ship tattoo anyway," said Esteban. "Because if you put a ship on your skin, people will think you went somewhere in it."

"That's true," said El Tinieblas. "Everyone would think I'd been a marinero, and they'd all ask, Where'd you go? And I'd have to explain over and over and over how I was on this ship that didn't go anywhere. Puta."

"You *are* a marinero," said Tomaso Tostado. "You just haven't gone anywhere."

"You know what maybe I'll do?" said El Tinieblas. "The day this is over, however it ends, I'm going to choose a symbol of what I feel then. Just for me. Like this one here, ve? Only I know the meaning of this one." And he lifted up his shirt again and tapped the small, inky image of a spoon on his chest. "That's a spoon," he said. "And I'll never tell anyone why."

"Puta vos, don't tattoo anything then," said El Barbie. "Sink the fucking ship. Sink it so no one can ever see it again. Don't tattoo anything, and then you can say, Ve? Underneath here?"—and he tapped his own chest—"there's a sunken ship."

"Tattooed on your heart," said Panzón.

"Sí pues, tattooed on your heart," said El Faro, nodding and squinting.

"Tattooed up my culo," said El Barbie.

In another seven days Esteban will meet Joaquina Martínez. In ten days, Bernardo will have his accident. In another six weeks, the Ship Visitor will finally find them. But for the next seven consecutive nights, beginning with this one, Esteban will prowl the waterfront neighborhoods looking for useful things to steal . . . Much later he'll remember what El Tinieblas said about the tattoo he was going to get when the *Urus* was finally over and he'll wonder how you tattoo a sack of wood chips.

"I don't understand why you don't leave, patroncito. It's a city full of opportunities. There must be thousands out there from countries like ours, young like you but less prepared, maybe less lucky. I promise you, this ship is going nowhere."

The viejo is going crazy, hyper and jittery. Why does he keep smelling his blanket? Suddenly obsessed with sniffing at his blanket. And always asking if I smell anything strange.

"Vos, qué te pasa? Why do you keep smelling your blanket?"

Bernardo looks at him like some sheepish little cipote, and then he asks, uncertainly, "Do you smell cat pee?"

"No."

The viejo drops the blanket back down onto his lap. "Bueno," he says. "Me neither."

Crazy viejo!

"I brought back wood chips."

"Wood chips?"

He explains. Tells him how he hid the sack behind the grain elevator and then climbed back up the mooring line.

"It will be good for lighting fires." And he pulls the blanket over him and turns towards the bulkhead and instantly falls asleep.

The day is partly overcast, sun fighting through clouds; a sporadic, chilling, mid-October wind, bringing the first sharp nips of winter, tatters the air, flickering uncomfortably up pant legs, under sleeves, through rips in their clothes, leaving a faint burning sensation against skin. The wind hums around the masts and stays, through the derricks and rigging; slides water in smooth, metallic, gull-skimmed sheets across the cove. Sunlight catches a swooping gull's chest, makes it arc radiantly-whitely through the air.

They haven't been abandoned, not yet: Mark comes to the ship that day in the Honda, with Miracle and groceries. Neither of their officers has been out in three days, but Mark's arrival—great relief that it is—is unceremoniously observed by both sides. He greets no one, and none of the crew allows himself much more than a glance at him.

El Primero stands on deck and says, in English, "Brought some food and stuff," gesturing down at the pier. He turns back to the gangway, and Roque Balboa and Cebo follow, to carry the groceries up from the car. Moments later they come back up, Roque carrying a bulky paper bag, Cebo a large sack of potatoes, into the mess. Mark and the dog go up to the bridge.

So capitán and primero haven't given up on the *Urus*. And if their officers haven't given up, that means there's still something . . . to wait for. As soon as they heard the car arriving on the pier, all the ordinary seamen but Esteban—still sleeping in his cabin—immediately resumed working, prying open paint cans, priming brushes, there was always something to be done. El Primero's arrival, rather than merely activating an innate obedience, has provided an excuse, and a context, to exchange a completely lethargic tedium for a somewhat more active one. Only the mechanics and electricians keep busy when neither capitán nor primero is there: they were already down in the two-level pit of the engine plant when Mark arrived, reengaged in the task of disassembling parts, cleaning, lubricating, tightening, reassembling, endlessly theorizing about how it all might work if only it all worked. The illusory satisfactions of studying and tinkering with dead engines, generators, and pumps, so complicated, mysterious, and inert, demands and compels an unreciprocated love. Last week el Capitán put some of the ordinary seamen to work welding fissures in the ballast tanks in the bottom deck under the hold—serious and dangerous work, without goggles, rags tied across their noses and mouths, the concentration it took burned up the day. But they haven't been able to finish the job with no one coming out to turn the generator and compressor on. Nor does Mark turn them on today.

When an appropriate amount of time has passed, some put down their paintbrushes and tools and go into the mess to look at the groceries, which José Mateo and Bernardo have already unpacked. Potatoes, cooking oil, chicken livers, six cans of peas, a plastic bag full of waxy pink apples, soap, five tubes of toothpaste, toilet paper. But el Primero forgot to bring razors again.

The crates of rusted sardine cans, paper labels rotted away, they found left behind in a deep corner of the hold back in June have been a salvation, but also a curse. There are still more than three hundred cans left—keys uselessly rusted to the sides, but José Mateo and Bernardo tear them open with can opener, hammered tools—so their officers know they can neglect to bring them groceries and at least they won't starve. But the rice is running low, down to five sacks.

Later they see Mark out on the wing having a smoke, leaning on his arms, staring out over wasteland, port and harbor. Too bad he didn't bring them cigarettes, not that they ever do. Wouldn't it be great to have a cigarette? Soothing, hot smoke bathing and cleaning your lungs. El Primero stays out there a long time. As if he's come just to show himself, as if to say, Don't worry, Capitán Elias and I are still here, responsible for all of you, little lambs. He looks calm and dreamy up there, as if the ship is already far out to sea and he's flicking cigarette butts in high arcs out into the middle of the ocean, into the wind. Doesn't seem to have noticed that Esteban is shirking his work today. Or maybe doesn't care. Wouldn't be likely to say anything about it anyway, since what's he ever say? Hi guys! Qué pasa! and today not even that. The viejo says Esteban isn't feeling well, to just let the chavalo be. Panzón will mark him down for a full workday with overtime anyway.

After the relief of just seeing el Primero there, what riled emotions and moods! Anger, humiliation, frustration, self-pitying sulks. Like a callously disregarded and tormented lover whose lover finally calls. That their most basic sense of security actually depends on one or the other of these two huevones coming to the ship! Relief to feel secure again, then fury over this deception camouflaged as security: just because what they most fear hasn't yet come to pass. El Barbie forgets what he's doing and paces up and down, paintbrush in his hand, dripping paint all over, fuming: he more than anyone else trusted and even loved his capitán, has behaved deferentially even to this maricón primero out of respect for his capitán. He lets them call him El Barbie, but he hasn't forgotten who Omar Usareli is, nor should they. It's Omar Usareli who allowed himself to accept the honor of being promoted to contramaestre, to dignify that honor with his own dignity, because let me tell you, cabrón, when you call on the dignity and honor of Omar Usareli, you're asking him to put the very best of himself on the line for you, to return respect with respect, and it isn't very often that Omar Usareli finds someone he respects enough to do that, but that's what he tried to do, and, look, they made a fool out of him! Let's get that pendejo primero, let's strip him and paint him, hold him down while I paint his pija bright red, see if he wants to have another game of Break the Cookie then, maricón jodido!

What will happen if capitán and primero never come out to the ship again? If they give up, quit, won't they at least come and tell them, ready them for whatever comes next? That's the question that crashes into thoughts at night like a sudden mud slide. How many days will pass without their officers coming to the ship before they'll have to accept that they've been abandoned once and for all? How will they know when they've been abandoned and what will they do then?

Abandoned ships and crews, José Mateo says it happens, pues. An abandoned crew can end up stuck on a ship forever while all the legal pendejadas get resolved, until they figure out who's responsible, who owes what to whom, who finally gets paid what. Sometimes, he says, they end up auctioning the ship off for scrap to pay everybody off, melt a ship like this down to make razor blades, beer cans, refrigerators . . .

Bernardo pictures gringos shaving with his tears, pulling cold cans of his bile from gleaming white refrigerators made of his hatred. A perfect immortality.

Three hours after they arrived, without once coming down from wing and bridge, Mark and Miracle leave without even saying good-bye.

Esteban comes out on deck, promptly descends the ladder, and comes back up carrying a large plastic sack in his arms, which he sets down at his feet.

"What's that?" Everyone is eating apples as they gather around Esteban and the mysterious sack. The cold crunch of teeth biting into apples. He tells them what it is and what he thinks it will be good for.

"Where'd you get it?"

"In a warehouse." He lifts his arm. "Way over there. I stole it, pues."

El Barbie's lips and nose are curled with dumbstruck, willed disbelief and automatic envy; he's speechless with confusion. The others look at Esteban with worried expressions, absorbing this surprising new development and its meaning.

"I've been going off the ship at night," he says, unable to repress a slightly boasting and defiant tone. "This is the first useful thing I found."

So, while they've all been sleeping or trying to sleep, the sulky thumb chewer, the old man's nieto, the reticent soldier boy, has been leaving the ship, prowling the waterfront.

"Just this? Wood chips?" says El Barbie.

"Y vos qué?" says Esteban. "What have *you* brought back?" Someone has handed him an apple, and he takes a bite out of it—the fruit tastes grainy, almost dry, weak in flavor for an apple though sweet, delicious.

Nobody bathes on the pier that evening; despite the new soap, it's too cold. They do enjoy the explosive sensation of toothpaste in their mouths. Night comes earlier now, swiftly erasing the peaceful pink and blue sky and its tamed, sinking sun, the yellowing tops of trees; the gulls go away to sleep somewhere, and the cats—Desastres's family—raise their usual incestuous racket. After they've gathered wood, they pull up the ladder, three grunting crewmen hauling it up by pulleys and rope, jerk by jerk.

On deck, Esteban lays wood chips as tinder under the piled planks. The wood chips ignite into small, prismatic flames, bubbling chemical colors, quickly combust into ephemeral puffs like marshmallows, and burn down to pungent nothing, barely singeing the wood laid over them. Wood-and-chemical marshmallows. So then what's this shit for? As tinder, it's useless.

But not even El Barbie wants to mock Esteban over the failure of the wood chips. They haven't dared to leave the ship and he has. Suddenly Esteban's stature is even greater than that of Tomaso Tostado, who is merely smart, quick, and decisive.

"Ni modo." Esteban shrugs. "I'll find something else tonight."

Pretty-boy Pínpoyo and El Tinieblas ask if they can come with him. He refuses. On his own, he'll be able to sneak around and steal better, he says. El Tinieblas feels hurt, after all, stealing is what he used to do, though not very successfully. They offer to lower the ladder for him, stand watch for his return. He refuses. No need. Doesn't know how long he'll be.

Now he loads his pockets with wire cutter, knife, short marline-spike, pliers. Should he bring the watch, in case he decides not to come back? But what if he gets robbed? He doesn't realize yet that when, in a few nights, he finds the more commercial-residential streets, even the few people out at those hours will eye him warily, or look right through him, or direct penetrating gazes of furious pity or disgust his way, but no one will think to rob him, filthy, dressed in rags.

2

HE HAS THESE REMOTER WATERFRONT STREETS ALMOST ENTIRELY TO himself at night. Hardly ever sees anyone out walking, and, when he does, they pass like shadows. The waterfront runs for miles and miles on both sides of where the *Urus* is berthed, ruins and weedy barrens mixed in with areas still functioning, warehouse and industrial zones, block after block after block. Walking, ve? with purpose. In his shredded, paint-grease-rust-stained jeans, wearing three T-shirts for a little warmth, boots laced with orange-insulated electrical wire. Past walled-in warehouses and truck lots surrounded by fences topped with concertina wire; the occasional walled-in, still-working shipping terminal; paved drives blocked by lowered crossing bars or locked gates and security booths and the harbor glittering beyond. Now and then he glimpses a berthed ship, lights on in the superstructure, the humming vibration of its auxiliary engine, iron nests of life tucked into this vast, slowly decipherable waterfront maze. He hears far-off whooping sirens; he hears gunshots, a brief burst of rapid fire, hardly notices these sounds anymore. A ship's horn bellowing far out in the harbor. He hears the muffled, irked shriek of a rooster, and this does surprise him; he's not sure, but yes, he hears it again, coming from somewhere amidst these tunnels of brick and concrete. It must be about 3:00 A.M. He spots a cat slinking through the dark at the base of a wall, and he hurries his steps to see if it's Desastres; it isn't. There's little traffic. Mostly multiwheeled trucks drive past, engines growling like the serious business of war, like dangerous nighttime maneuvers too noisy to be kept secret.

And now he looks up and sees this one place still open, at the back of a corner lot, silvery cutouts of naked women like shimmering angel apparitions embedded in the pink stucco facade, music pounding like a terrified heart inside, shiny, money-macho vehicles parked outside: Jeeps, pickups, motorcycles. The red door slams open, and a giant of a man wearing only a black leather vest over a short-sleeved T-shirt on top despite the cold is crossing the lot with a heavy-footed, steady gait. He's even bigger and possibly even hairier than El Pelos, with a short, red beard and massive forearms furry as a bear's. He's smoking a cigarette. He walks to the door of the Jeep Cherokee parked in front of where Esteban is standing and pulls out his keys. Esteban impulsively makes up his mind to ask the man for a cigarette, por qué no?

"*Hi!* eh . . . *Cigarro?* Please, *meester*?" Puta, hates the squealing sound of this stranger's voice that has just come from him—

The bearded man, his unruly hair taking on a frilly glow from the pinkish glare of the lot's sodium vapor lamps, scowls up at him; his drunken blue eyes have the cold sheen of jellyfish.

"Fuck you," says the man, and his eyes widen as if he's just startled himself.

Esteban walks off.

"Hey!" the man calls after him. "Hey you, *c'mere*."

Esteban turns and looks at him. The man is holding the pack of cigarettes out to him. Then he lowers the pack and draws out a cigarette like a tiny sword and holds that out to him. He's saying something in English.

Esteban feels a nervy flutter of fear in his chest. He turns and walks off again. The man says something, he hears another *fuck you,* but this one in an almost plaintive tone; hears the door shut, the engine start up. Then the Jeep is beside him on the street, and the man, a lit cigarette in his hand on the wheel, looks at him with that scowling, pop-eyed curiosity, and tosses the pack of cigarettes out the window; it lands at Esteban's feet.

"You don' say thank-you?" asks the man.

Esteban nods. "Thenk you," he says softly.

"You *hom-les*?" something like that, asks the man.

The man stares at him a moment longer, shrugs, and drives off. Vos, Nicas don't accept handouts from yanquis who say fuck you to them. Pues, I don't. But now these cigarettes are just lying there, the brand with a camel on the pack. He picks it up, the pack feels warm in his chilled hands. There are matches shoved down inside the cellophane—only four matches left. He pulls out a cigarette, it has a filter. He smells it, running it up and down under his nose; lights it inside cupped hands. The first inhalation makes him cough. He puts the pack in his back pocket and walks down the street, gingerly inhaling. Everything is quiet again. He thinks, I'm no one anymore. Puta, I've vanished. I wonder where I'll be a year from now? Ten years from now? Who knows, maybe in two years I'll be in Italy. I'll find work on another ship, get off and stay in Italy. Bernardo says Italy is estupendo. Once he met a woman there, a waitress in a tavern in the port, who took him to see that leaning tower; they went by train and drank a bottle of wine on the way. He has the impression, when he listens to Bernardo, that back then the world was more hospitable. Nothing like that could ever happen around here. One second anything seems possible, and the next, almost nothing does.

He tries to picture himself home in Corinto. Listening to the gray rain clattering off the corrugated zinc roof, splattering-simmering against the mud outside, lying on his bed with nothing to do, a war and la Marta to forget, or to remember, whichever, memory does whatever the fuck it wants. Plastic bags nailed to the planked wall instead of a wardrobe trunk, his belongings stuffed inside. His mamá and Tío Nelson sitting for hours in front of the rusted stove on the little concrete patio out back, rain overflowing the bent-up gutters of the zinc sheet over their heads, some of it flowing loudly through the aluminum trough aimed down at the water barrel. The stench of the outhouse, of low-tide beach rot. Tío Nelson weaving a casting net with his butterfingers. Tío Nelson used to work as a shipping clerk, but nearly everyone is out of work now that so few ships call at Corinto. While the putas languish in a perpetual distemper waiting for the stingy Russians to arrive on ships from Vladivostok, or for the Russians posted at the big tent hospital in Chinandega. Mamá fanning herself with a woven-frond fan, fanning the dying coals in the stove, trying to interest her languid brother in the latest market women gossip, her soft, sagging, patient face of an aging Chinese sage with amnesia. Esteban doesn't have the remotest idea, not even a fantasy, of who his father might be. Claro, that's not unusual in Corinto, though he was never able to claim anything as distinguishing as the green eyes of a Danish marinero, the flaxen hair of an Australian, the temptress gaze and falcon features of an Egyptian. His tíos like to joke that the new generation will be marked by the abundant nose hairs and six toes on each foot of the Basque priest, and by the three-nippled chests of pallid Russians.

Walking the waterfront streets at night, Esteban often passes fenced-off alleys or lots, and behind the padlocked gates, towards the rear of the alley or lot, he sometimes sees light over a loading dock and a truck backed up, men pushing hand trucks, tracing and retracing their own paths in and out of the light, or driving forklifts. There are lots of signs around warning against trespassers, or about dogs, in English and Spanish. Sometimes dogs run barking to these fences as he passes, stand like forlorn prisoners with forepaws resting on braided wire, barking—like these dogs now. There are five of them, running to the fence, barking.

He's astonished when he sees one of the dogs wriggling through a rip in the fence about two feet over the pavement, followed by the other four—like a nightmare suddenly real, like wolves diving off a movie screen down into the audience. The dogs pour through the fence like a five-headed snake and charge him, barking and snarling, backing him onto the sidewalk and against the wall of a building across the street, bristling, crouching, lunging, nipping at air, click of snapping jaws, baring their fangs like El Barbie. He stands there shocked, helpless before this uproar. Why, everywhere on earth, these crazed, vicious dogs? Has to do something, take a chance, now—so he just turns and walks off, his body cringing against the first bite as the barking grows louder and more frenzied, but it doesn't come. He just keeps walking with his heart pounding and blood flashing cold until the dogs, still barking but with less zeal, begin dropping away behind, pacing threatening little circles as if about to charge again, one pausing to lift a leg to urinate against a lamp pole before stepping forward to let out a few last desultory barks. Unlike any other domesticated animal or even wild one, not even enraged monkeys—bueno, poisonous snakes in another way—only dogs seem to hate the way some humans do: eyes flashing, sneering, screaming, cowardly, stupidly boasting, threatening and sometimes even deadly, like Ana. Dogs and men. Cobardes, hijos de puta. The way Ana ran down that wounded contra and tore out his throat, led a platoon right into an ambush. That bald Capitán Elias with his sad-eyed face of a mangy bitch, and Mark and Miracle, the bitch's two sons. So if monkeys are the most like humans, how come you never see a monkey pissing against the trunk of a tree?

He turns down an alley leading through buildings with smashed-windowed fronts to another long ago collapsed pier, no need to fence this off. And steps down onto the rubbled shore and begins making his way back along the edge of swift, choppy water towards that illuminated loading dock. Scaling a geometric tumble of smashed concrete slabs and gigantic pier splinters, the harbor night opening out to his right like a windy, sparkling void he might fall away into. Lifts himself up onto a concrete ledge over the seawall at the back of a warehouse and walks a short distance along it before he reaches a high, new-looking wire fence blocking his path, the fence extended well out over the water, the waves slapping heavily at the concrete seawall beneath—put there to prevent just this kind of prowling. But he easily makes his way around it, groping along the wire with soon-aching fingers and the pressure of boot tips, out along one side, over the foaming water, around and back along the other side; farther down, he makes his way around the barrier's twin. Then onto a narrow, weedy path behind the rear of the next building. Finally he slips under pliant, rusted chicken wire and crouches behind the corner of the warehouse in the dark at the back of the truck drive, looking into the light and the cardboard cartons piled onto the loading dock twenty or so yards ahead, two men wheeling hand trucks stacked with cartons out of the warehouse, into the trailer, in and out. No dogs, so far. The viejo likes to say that it isn't only when you gamble that you lose—but, viejo, when you gamble? Timing the workers' movements as they go in and out of the light and slowly edging forward tight against the wall. He just has to reach up, grab one carton, *uff,* fade backwards into the night, ni verga, and head up the shore the other way to avoid the chochada of those fences . . .

El Tinieblas, Canario, Caratumba, Tomaso Tostado, and even El Barbie have waited up for him anyway. As if too excited to sleep over the possibility of his bringing something back, something good to eat. They see Esteban coming around the grain elevator in the dark, his frame slanted under the weight of a large cardboard box on his shoulder. And they clamber out onto the ladder all together, clattering down it like bucking cattle spilling down a chute as they sink it towards him—Esteban on the pier, stabbing the box open with a knife.

Esteban remembers this when he sees what's inside: a time of hunger, no food, but Tío Beny had gone fishing, rowing far out to sea in his wooden launch because it was impossible even to get petrol for the little motor. The morning after his second night at sea he was spotted on the horizon, rowing through the blanching sun, stopping to bail; finally they were able to make out the shape of what had to be a shark roped to the side of the tilting launch. It seemed to take forever for Tío Beny to reach the beach, haul the shark onto the hot, black sand, a sawbill shark that would provide enough meat and bone for caldo to feed hundreds. His hands were swollen and blistered from rowing, his nose so sun-charred it looked like a moldy beet. Everyone crowded around. Tío Beny called out for a knife. Someone handed him a knife, and he stuck it in under the fin, pulled it out, and sniffed at the blood-browned blade. "Podrido," said Tío Beny, and he dropped the knife in the sand, turned, and trudged off the beach with just that one word, rotted, leaving the inedible shark just lying there.

The case is packed with long, rectangular boxes, almost weightless, wrapped in cellophane, covered with a colorful design, the most prominent word printed on them PARCHEESI. He shakes one of the boxes in both hands, nearly hollow, a few loose pieces sliding around. Not even edible. Some kind of toy. He drops the box onto the pier and starts up the ladder while the others delve in.

Midway up the ladder Esteban pauses, shouts "Oye," and they look up at him from around the carton on the pier, all of them holding Parcheesi boxes in their hands. He pulls the cigarettes from his back pocket—he's used up his four matches anyway—and flings it down to them; then instantly regrets it, should've at least given them to Bernardo. He shouts, "Share them with everybody else. And don't let anyone wake me tomorrow." Then he turns and walks up onto the deck.

Esteban doesn't make the same mistake the next night: he sees clouds of white vapor billowing through the light of a loading dock, and thinks, It's something frozen. White vapor pouring from the rear of the truck parked against the dock and out of the warehouse, and the workers are as bundled up as Russian seal hunters. In fact, they may be Russian. The snatches of conversation he overhears as he creeps towards them aren't in English, sound like Russian. One worker looks just like the Pope, much younger though, wearing a fur hat, clear blue eyes like a young girl's . . .

He walks back to the ship with the case of frozen shrimp burning his arms. On the lid, the words "Producto de Honduras." The first light of dawn is seeping into the dark, slowly dissolving it. Long rows of rooftop water tanks stand out against the paling sky like bleak guard towers. He finds the ship's ladder down and climbs it, steps onto the deck and sees that no one has waited up for him. He carries the case of shrimp into his cabin and lays it down at the foot of Bernardo's mattress without disturbing his blankly staring sleep, then gets into his own bed and lies there rubbing numbed, cold, soaked arms with his hands, an itchy horniness warming his groin and exhaustion warming everything else. He falls asleep thinking of putas in flimsy, satiny dresses carrying their high heels in their hands, walking home barefoot through warm mud at dawn, hips swaying, heads down, they sleep through the day too, hide themselves from the day, replenishing and storing up the bitter honey they sell all night long to men fleeing the day.

Esteban sleeps through the day and no one disturbs him, not even when Capitán Elias and Mark both come to the ship in separate cars. Later the crew hear capitán and primero heatedly shouting at each other up on the bridge, though no one can understand the words of their argument.

José Mateo boils the shrimp that night. Look, the case's lid says, "Producto de Honduras," the catrachos' native dish. Claro, many along the coast get work on those ships that stay out on the ocean for months, collecting shrimp from trawlers and deep-freezing them in their holds. And others, like Cebo used to, free-dive for lobster—so many of the divers ending up crippled, feebleminded, and sometimes drowned, from the bends—lobsters that go to the big freezer ships too. But how many ever get to actually eat them, brother? Bueno, never a feast like this, not even on the most special occasions! There's enough shrimp for every member of the crew to have thirty-three or thirty-four. Este Esteban, que cabrón! Tomaso Tostado leads a round of whistling cheers for Esteban, and he sits there nodding, feeling filled with a happy glow, thinking, Yes, this is a special night!

They have a chance to regain their appetite midway through the feast when the butane container under the stove runs out of fuel. Then a wood fire has to be hastily built on deck, the water boiled again.

This abundance of shrimp, it reminds Caratumba of another time he got to gorge himself like this, not with shrimp but with river fish, mainly perch. La guerrilla had attacked the oil exploration camp he was working in, in El Petén, on the Río Usamacinta—

"It's a long story," he says, dismissively waving the shrimp tail pinched between two fingers, "but el ejerci," and he pauses to suck on it, pushes it into his slotlike mouth, thin, straight lips pursed as he seems to knead the shrimp tail between his front teeth. Ejerci is what he calls the army. No longer chewing, Caratumba sits on the coaming with his hands on his knees, ignoring the pink-shrimp-heaped plate on his lap, his expression stilled. Coarse, straight, black hair dangles over his forehead like one ragged crow's wing, partially hiding piercing eyes deeply embedded in prominently hollowed sockets.

"Y los soldados, qué?" asks Pínpoyo.

"Nobody wanted them there." Caratumba grimaces, as if he'd just been asked his opinion of the army rather than to continue his story.

"Sí pues, 'mano. But what did they have to do with stuffing yourself with fish?"

"They came to guard the camp against another raid because they were afraid la guerrilla would steal the rest of our dynamite, use it against *them*." Caratumba shrugs. Half the workers in the camp informed for la guerrilla anyway, he explains, and half informed for el ejerci, and some for both. The gringos suspected that, but what could they do? La guerrilla had really only attacked the camp to destroy the helicopter, so that they could extort money from the oil company in exchange for a promise never to attack again. But the gringos were especially preoccupied because although la guerrilla had promised not to attack the oil camp anymore, they hadn't promised not to attack the soldiers now guarding it.

"One evening these two soldaditos get into the dynamite anyway, vos," says Caratumba. "Steal three sticks, cabrones wanted to use them to go fishing, vos. And they go a little distance from the camp, along the riverbank. They light the dynamite. Hijos de puta throw the dynamite upstream instead of down."

Caratumba smiles, just a tight spreading of his lips that shows his crooked teeth. He lifts another shrimp to his mouth.

Esteban giggles deeply; others smile, as if not sure . . .

"And then what?" asks Pínpoyo. "Hombre, no jodas!"

"Bueno, it worked," says Caratumba, chewing. "Fish everywhere. Looked like it had been raining fish."

And Esteban, laughing through his words, "Y esos hijos de puta . . ."

"Wasn't our problem, the soldiers had to pick up their pieces. And we gathered up the fish. Why waste all that fish?"

"Ahhhhhhh!" exclaims El Faro.

"And they didn't run, seeing the dynamite floating towards them?" asks Bernardo, looking horrified. "Pobres."

"Wouldn't have made any difference, the current was fast," says Caratumba, "and there they were, right down on the riverbank. Must have exploded right in front of them. They were so ignorant, vos, they'd tossed in three sticks of dynamite when even one would have been too much. *Pum Pum Pum*—three explosions, shaking the earth. Everyone thought it must be la guerrilla attacking. The gringos were all running around screaming, Get down! Get down! crawling under their platform tents and cabins. This was very powerful dynamite; they'd drill these deep holes and drop the dynamite down and set it off, take sonic soundings, and the gringo geologists would study the results on their computers, to see what kind of layers of rock were down there. Once they found a very ancient Maya pyramid buried deep under the earth, there it was, perfectly outlined on a computer screen. I saw it, qué maravilla, no? So you can imagine, vos. Fish everywhere, all over the banks and floating away belly up down the river. Those hijos de puta del ejerci, perdóneme Dios, but I wish they'd *all* gone down there to the river with those two clowns."

"Comunista," says El Barbie, chuckling.

"Not just because of that," says Caratumba coolly, and he eats another shrimp. "No tanto, vos."

"Vos, Piri," says El Barbie later. "Why don't you find beef next? Some big, fat cuts of steak."

And Tomaso Tostado says, "And those chunches, those Parcheesi. Don't you think we can sell them?"

The next night's booty is a carton packed full of men's underpants folded in plastic bags, three to a bag. All size extra large, though, they don't come close to fitting anybody, not even Panzón. But they put them on anyway. They joke that the underpants feel like diapers under their pants. But at least they're clean! And the next night, carajo, Esteban brings back a carton of swimming goggles. Why is it so hard to find food?

Every night he walks, not knowing the names of the neighborhoods he walks through, though that week he ranges as far as Sunset Park and Owl Point in one direction, through Red Hook to the petering waterfront edge of Cobble Hill in the other. But street names quickly become familiar enough to orient himself by: Columbia, Halleck, Coffee, Lorraine, Pilgrim, Bush, Second and Third Avenues. The elevated expressway and the avenue underneath enclose a long stretch of the waterfront, marking a kind of border: on the other side numbered streets ascend into hilled Brooklyn.

Los proyectos don't frighten him anymore. Coming and going that week, he walks right past them, on all sides, though never cuts through. During the hours he's out, los proyectos seem quieter and darker than the night the crew tried to cross; hefts of wind fill the gaps between buildings with the sparks of yellow leaves. He cuts across the park, the withered futbol and baseball fields, a few men even more ragged than he is sleeping on benches under tattered blankets and flattened cardboard boxes; when they call out to him in harsh or rumbling voices, breath steams up over their faces.

Sometimes he passes an all-night tiendita locked away behind dark, greasy glass, the rare customer doing business from the sidewalk, paying and retrieving his goods through a small, sliding window. Sometimes the tiendas' signs are in Spanish—what does *Quisqueya* mean? A crowd of men standing in front of a lit-up tienda far up a darkened street, he hears their urgent clamor, watches people drifting back and forth across the street as if disoriented by some great calamity as he cautiously walks towards them, half-expecting to see someone just murdered on the sidewalk, the crowd waiting for police, agitated and excited by the crime. But as he draws even with the tienda he realizes that nothing has happened there; the crowd is just milling out front, shouting and arguing, though dawn is only an hour or two away. Now there's a messy, gray-haired man reeling after him with his hands held out, calling, "Papi! Papi! Un peso para algo a comer, Papi, por favor! Just for something to eat," and Esteban says he doesn't have any money and keeps walking as if he knows where he's going, and turns the corner . . . On the horizon, behind the expressway, there's another bridge, and sometimes he sees long trains sliding across it like liquid light through a clear tube.

Truck-loading docks are most vulnerable when there's a way in from the harbor shore. He wends up and down the streets, back to the harbor, probing for weak points. Using wire cutters, Esteban snips two cases loose from a packed pallet on a loading dock before he knows what they hold. But he figures it must be food. There are piled cartons marked "tomatoes" too close to the back of the truck to risk trying to steal. He's already slipping away into the dark when he hears the first shout of a man who's just come out of the trailer, the man shouts, "Hey! Hey you! What the fuck—" and Esteban dashes into the wooded wastes behind the warehouse lot. Hearing haranguing voices somewhere behind, he runs, following a skinny, winding path up and down mud-slippery rises through pitch dark trees and slapping branches, past piled garbage, the skeletons of wrecked cars, feeling the ridiculous underpants sliding down over his nalgas and thighs, bunching loosely under his crotch. He follows the path all the way to the shore of the harbor and stands there listening for voices, but the crackling surf drowns everything out. Are they following? Will they have guns? He waits and listens, crouching in the brush with the two cases on his lap, staring into the darkened woods . . . Finally, he stands and looks around. From the shore, a narrow spit of mounded dirt, stone, rubble, and brush extends far out into the water. What's in this case? He wrenches the lid open, finds it packed with square little boxes, cellophane tops secured with rubber bands. Tears one open, scoops a handful of plump, surprisingly weighty little berries into his hand, then into his mouth. Hmmmm, rico. Tangy, juicy, sweet. Studies the lid, where the key word seems to be BLUEBERRIES. Saber. Sucking on weedy little bits stuck to the back of his teeth. Sets the case down and lifts out the little box he's been eating from. Carrying it in one hand, he picks his way along the debris-strewn peninsula, through high, wheatlike weeds and brush and chunks of concrete piling, hopping and stepping out among detached boulders and concrete to the very tip. Long, cresting combers roll in around him like real ocean here. He stands atop a concrete slab slanting down, surf breaking against it, flinging water up, spattering him; wind pushes against him. He eats another handful of berries; he can taste briny ocean mixing with the berry juice. But, chocho, these are good: The harbor looks wider here. The night an immense sticky-windy blackness, hollow at the core, that's been rolled around in multicolored spangles of light. The illuminated stanchions of the immense bridge. When he's eaten all the berries he tosses the empty little box up into the wind and turns back.

He feels a little nauseous. The next day several of the crew come down with diarrhea from stuffing themselves with berries.

That next night, underneath the expressway overpass, he suddenly hears the rising jabbering of ducks and smells a putrid stench. He turns and sees a truck moving slowly through the intersection, headed into the dark streets of the waterfront, its long flatbed neatly stacked with hundreds of square, wire cages holding yellow-beaked white ducks. He jumps up onto the tailgate just as the truck, gears grinding, straightens out of its turn, stays calm despite the duck nipping at his fingers as he clasps a wire cage with one hand, fumbling in his pocket for the wire cutters, nearly gagging from the duck-shit smell. He cuts the wire open quickly, reaches in, and grabs one duck, clutches it tightly to his chest while it flails, squawks, and bites at his head and ear, and makes a grab for the other, catches it by the neck and pulls it from the cage just as he's jumping backwards off the truck—and he lands hard, feet and legs buckling under, falling on his thigh, ribs, and elbow, still holding on to the ducks amidst a tumult of frantic wings, quacks, and snapping bills as the clamorous truck rolls off into the dark. He snaps one duck's neck between his hands while the other waddles away, flapping useless wings, drops the dead duck and chases the other down, snaps its neck against kicked-up knee except it's still alive, kicks his knee up again, slamming the neck down between both fists, feels it break like a stick, the duck instantly limp, like a heavy sack in his hand. Stands there panting. His fingers are bleeding; blood warmly trickles down his neck from a bite on his ear rim, his elbow bloody, his thigh throbbing.

Two moreno men have stepped out of the dark, suddenly they're out in the street, in long coats and wool caps, laughing and excitedly shouting at him in English. He stands there studying them, wiping his ear with the short sleeve of his outer T-shirt, his elbow with the shirt, wiping his stinging, bleeding, duck-bitten fingers against his pants. Decides they look harmless, happy drunks. Carrying one duck, he walks back up the street, looking for the dropped wire cutters, finds them and puts them in his pocket, and goes back for the other duck. The two morenos are standing over it now. The duck prostrate on its belly, soft and white, crooked neck and head on its side, big, rubbery feet heels up, like the elephantiasis-swollen feet of a beggar. The men are laughing, boisterously joking. He looks into their yellowed, brimming eyes, smells stale liquor. Deep creases in their faces, skin scarred and bumpy, one with a short, ragged beard, one with huge lips and missing teeth. "Yo," they say, "yo," some "fucks" and "ducks" and mainly words he doesn't understand. It turns into a little English lesson. "Duck. Duck. Yo, it's a duck, man . . ." Booming voices, laughter like jets taking off in their phlegmy throats. "Duck's fucked."

Esteban repeats, "Duck . . . Ajá. Sí. Duck. En español, *pato*." Prods the duck on the pavement with his foot. "Duck. Gracias."

"You too, brother, grass-yas . . . ," and more words he doesn't understand, but now it seems they are mirthfully redescribing his duck-stealing exploit to each other, one of them flapping his arms and hands as if drowning and rasping, "*Quack! Quack!*" The one missing teeth lightly plucks his blood-streaked T-shirt between his fingers, gravely asks him something, must be about the way he's dressed. The man says, "Ragmffn," something like that, and crosses his arms, mimes shivering with cold, shaking his head to flutter lips and cheeks while he groans. Esteban shrugs helplessly, smiles. And the other, the one with the beard and a long, ash dark, lusterless face, asks, "You Rican?"

"Qué?"

"You *Porta* Rican?"

"Ah. No. Nicaragüense."

"Mexican?"

"Nicaragua."

"Yeah? Sandin*ee*st*ee*s, right? Watch out! Watch out! Sandinistis be comin. Presdent say the Sandinistis be comin right up through Texas! *Ahwuuuu!* Kill us all!"

This Esteban has more or less followed—they laugh. Sandinista, sí pues, he nods. Touches his own chest. "Soy Sandinista." Used to be, anyway. That makes them laugh too. They put out their hands, wrinkled palms up, they coax him into slapping their large, soft hands with his own.

". . . duck? C'mon brothuh, jes one." Are they asking him for one of the ducks? He's sure they're hungry too, but the ducks are for the crew. He picks up the other duck. He's not wrong to keep both ducks.

"Bueno. Adios. Gracias." Puta, qué locura, what else is he supposed to say? Lifts one duck in a gesture of good-bye. "Duck," he says firmly, and they laugh some more, swiping hands down at him. He tucks one duck under each arm, says good-bye again, turns and walks off, grinning. These ducks are fat and heavy, not scrawny like chickens. Blocks later, he's still chuckling to himself.

He sits in the terminal with the ducks beside him in the sand, his thigh aching, skinned elbow burning. Hugs himself against the damp cold. Wings thumping air up there, and sobbed cooing. He runs a finger up and down over a duck's cracked neck, prodding for the fatal injury, over its hard skull, along its cold bill, touches an eye, it feels like a slimy snail's shell, smooths his hand over a wing and presses down on the feathers, the resilient meat underneath. Remembers once holding a sick garza in his hands, up near the Río Coco, its feathers this white, how light that bird was, as weightless and hollow seeming as a feather hat, flurried heartbeats inside the frail cage of bones. La Marta wants to talk about when and how she died tonight, but he doesn't want to talk about it. Really, he only spent that one week with her in Quilalí. But she always gets her way. As she should. Whatever you want, Martita. Since she died he feels he hasn't really talked to anyone. Not the way he talked to her. Not even to his compas. Not with Bernardo. He's lived closed up inside himself in a way he never even knew about until after he met her and lost her, no? He discovered loneliness, which somehow he'd never really even known about until the day he found out la Marta was dead. He discovered a fear different from the fear of dying, a fear of what life looked like now, stretching out before him like harshest sunlight steaming down on a long, ugly, mud street. So it was a good decision, no matter what, to hire out on a ship. The way la Marta made him feel all that week—he did everything he could to preserve that inside him during the months after; he carried his love inside him like a cupped handful of springwater, which, miraculously, hardly leaks. He carried her voice like a cupped handful of water inside of him. She could make him suddenly break out laughing or smiling during the worst of it. He carried, inside of himself, la Marta saying, "Fíjate, Flaquito. Last night I dreamt I was back in León and a polar bear was loose in our house."

He knew that modest mailman, new commander of hers, was keeping her alive. The Nightmare BON was just going to be stationed in Quilalí from now on—find something for them to do, plant an orchard, lay down pipes for potable water, build rabbit hutches, pull tics from donkeys' ears for la Revolución. The little cardboard sign her new jefe put up promised: The greatest victory is the battle we avoid having to fight. And even the yanqui priest had promised to use his influence with the Comandancia in Wiwilí. He felt swept with superstitious relief and tenderness every time he saw a red squirrel in a tree, darting across a path. From a high ridge one night he watched a meteor streak through the star-bristling sky, suspensefully watched it fall all the way behind the hills of Honduras without going out—which meant she was alive, still loving him, thinking about him. Then his battalion came trudging through Quilalí again nearly three months later, and the converted stables where Marta and Amalia had made their beds in the old hay, sleeping there terrified of rats and snakes, were deserted. And their jefe's sign was a rain-washed flap of cardboard still hanging outside.

The yanqui padre was in his little office at the front of the church when Esteban burst in on him, sitting with a withered old campesino who held his straw hat between his knees. The padre was expressionlessly listening while the campesino complained that someone had stolen his only macho, how was he going to survive? Could the padre lend him the money to buy a new horse, or even a mule? "Where's Marta?" interrupted Esteban. "Where's the BON from León?"

The padre recognized him but had to ask his name, and already, from the tone of his voice, the sudden expression of sorrowful alarm in his blue eyes, Esteban knew . . . The padre stood, and the campesino looked up, following him with his frightened eyes.

"Esteban," said the yanqui padre, his face burning bright pink, his blue eyes wet and magnified behind the lenses of his steel-rimmed glasses. "Your friend Marta . . ." The padre took a step closer and held his hands out. "They were caught in a terrible combate. Amalia was very seriously wounded, but Marta did not make it, Esteban, her spirit is with God."

Esteban stood in silence a moment. "But you promised them," he finally stammered. Hadn't he promised to talk the command in Wiwilí, urge that the Nightmare BON be kept in Quilalí? Then he started to sob.

"I did, Esteban," said the padre, his hand on Esteban's shaking shoulder now. "But there were so many combates to the north all at once, and they sent in everybody, Esteban, the local militias too, as reinforcement. They sent everybody. Everyone in the town is still angry about it, or still grieving, Esteban. There was nothing I could do."

The campesino, barefoot, his pants looking stitched together out of sugar sacks, his shirt frayed and missing most of its buttons, wrinkled face the color of an old cigar, just sat there holding his hat between his knees, mouth open, looking like he was about to wretch, his frightened little eyes focused on the paneled wall in front.

"Reinforcements? Hijueputa! They couldn't have reinforced a rabbit hutch!"

"This war, Esteban," said the padre almost indignantly, wet stare boring into his. "I pray for almost nothing else but for it to stop."

"Sí pues," rasped the campesino, not taking his eyes from the wall, briefly running his twiggy, viejo fingers through his gray, matted hair. "Si Dios quiere. Padre Guillermo es un buen padre. He helps the poor. He loves the young people."

He wanted to hit the campesino. Wanted to take his AK and smash his head in with its butt.

"But what happened?" he asked. "Where is she?"

"It was one of those LAU bazookas, Esteban," said the padre. "They fired it into her camp, and Marta was standing closest. They . . . I'm afraid they were under fire, so when the helicopters came, they only took away the wounded, and some of the dead. Marta was buried there. I'm sure they'll be going back for her."

"She was standing closest?" he said.

"Yes," said the padre. "So she couldn't have known, or felt anything. She didn't have to suffer."

He turned away without saying good-bye or thank you, and walked out of the office and into the sun and the dirt street. An LAU bazooka. He knew the craters they left in the earth, the shards of steel propelled deep into the trunks of trees. She was standing closest. He had seen what that could do to a body. Sometimes you found them torn to bits, sprayed into the brush, up in the branches of trees . . .

Later, the morning after the ambush on the Zompopera Road, he saw the IFA truck that had been carrying the muchachas of the quartermaster corps that had taken a direct hit from an RPG. He saw a severed head with long, black hair, the skull so deflated that the scorched face was barely recognizable as a face, it looked like a flounder, hollow eye sockets staring up. And then he knew, and he lost the whole Marta he'd, until then, been able to keep inside. (But here, in this empty terminal, la Marta comes back to him whole.)

Much later he learned that Amalia stayed in her coma for three days after she was helicoptered out, so many broken bones, and severe neurological damage and memory loss . . . He did not go to see her in the military hospital, in Managua. He told himself that she would not remember him and that even if she did, she would not want to see him. But he should probably have gone anyway. He hadn't been able bring himself to.

That little cardboard sign read: The greatest victory is the battle we avoid having to fight. The mailman-jefe wasn't asking them to be cowards. He was just offering another idea of victory. One perfectly suited to a Juventud Sandinista volunteer Nightmare BON, totally lacking in *arte militar*. But he's never been able to figure out what those words really mean. Claro, avoid *having* to fight. It's a victory because those who force us to fight have resolved their differences in a different way, decided that peace is better all around, which takes a different kind of human being from the humans who actually exist, which is why it's too easy, a completely ignorant fantasy, and not the mailman's fault or responsibility anyway. So what did he mean? A victory just to stay in Quilalí? If only.

Now Esteban sits up straighter in the sand. Has he been a coward? It's just another word sometimes, no? Sometimes people forget they're not supposed to be cowards, they live in a cowardly way without even realizing. You don't have to fight all the time, just don't shame yourself. On our ship we're sick with shame, because our situation has become shameful. If I desert the ship like the viejo is always telling me to—will that be brave or cowardly?

Arte militar. Here you are going to learn to live and fight *con mucho arte militar,* Milton had told them, his very first day in the BLI. And they all had, because they had to. But when Milton was stripped of his command of the BLI, finally, it was for having too much arte militar. Milton, with his pocked, hard Indian face and granite build, his big, effusive personality, always going on about arte militar and amor, the love he wanted (ordered) everyone in the BLI to feel for one another; he didn't need all the words their political officers used to be more convincing. Milton was full of amor, always bedding the compitas in the BLI's quartermaster corps who trailed them into battles and waited for them at their bivouac points. A member of El Coro de Ángeles, the very first BLI, who lost nearly half their battalion back in '83 at the legendary battle of Jalapa and Teotecacinte, when they turned back the first big yanqui-contra invasion almost single-handedly, fighting across a flat, wide plain jutting into the triangle of Honduran hills the contras were attacking from, keeping up a constant hail of machine-gun fire and mortars, most of the fighting at night. Milton's problems started during that last contra offensive, when he refused the orders to make them all carry three hundred extra rounds in clips in their packs instead of the usual hundred. Along with the extra bullets, the Comandancia's

Grupo Operativo wanted all BLI troops to carry 82-mm mortars, extra grenades, and mines from now on, instead of just the usual AK, Tokarev pistol, and knife. Milton, explaining his vehement refusal of the orders to the BLI, said, If all of you carried just one bullet apiece, I guarantee you every one of those bullets would kill a contra. Because when soldiers have too many bullets, they shoot wildly, loose their concentration and focused fear, turn back into just a bunch of undisciplined draftee cipotes, firing off into the trees and all over the place, never hitting anything or anybody, and war turns into a fucking children's game. And with their packs so heavy, by the time they encounter the enemy, they're too exhausted from the march to fight well anyway. But the Comandancia was panicking, the yanquis had loaded up la contra with so much new firepower! Good, said Milton, let them be the tired and wasteful ones. Esteban's BLI kept on fighting just as they had before, light on their feet, stinging everywhere, from one cachimbeo to another, always in hot pursuit (their only calamity that one with the dog near Wamblán).

But two thousand contra were pouring down through the Cerro Chachawáy and Wina, where the Coco and the Río Bocáy meet. Milton was put in charge of the counteroffensive: three entire BLIs subordinated to his command converged on the front. And when everyone was in place Milton directed a triangulated attack, and within a week had the enemy pushed back against the border and fenced in on three sides. Over the radio the Grupo Operativo said it wanted Milton to go in and finish the attack. But Milton thought too many compas would die if they went in: the contras were well dug in, had laid mines everywhere, they had riverbanks under control and reinforced hills at their backs, it reminded him too much of what El Coro de Ángeles had faced at Jalapa and Teotecacinte. He wanted to bring in the helicopters, rocket the territory from the fearsome Soviet M-27 transport-attack helicopters first. But the Grupo Operativo only gave him permission to use the helicopters to ferry soldiers to the edge of battle, they were afraid of more helicopters being shot down by the contras' new Redeye missiles. They were afraid of provoking the yanquis. They were worried that there were too many civilians in that zone the contras were trapped in. Milton was infuriated: why should his soldiers die instead of contras? Why should they die instead of civilian contra supporters, because of course they're contra, because if they're not, then what the fuck are they doing there? Degenerate satraps, that's how Milton was beginning to refer to the officers in the Comandancia and Grupo Operativo, the new breed of subcomandantes rising up through the army, puteros, drunks, enjoying the perks of war in their headquarters and in Managua, always worrying about pissing off the yanquis, taking too much advice from the fucking Cubans. Milton ordered Esteban's company to lead the attack, to ride the helicopters into battle. Ten came, huge, black and green, armored, bristling with rocket launchers and machine guns, petrol reeking, their whirring blades working up a hurricane gale of hot wind. But Milton had changed their orders at the last minute: the pilots were under his command, he'd been put in charge of this offensive, he ordered them to arrive ready and loaded to go in and attack . . . Milton climbed into the lead helicopter himself, and Esteban's company stayed behind. They flew in high, firing off magnesium flares to divert the Redeyes, flew right at the hills, rocketing and strafing with high-caliber machine guns, and returned to their base to reload and then came back and did it again; the operation went on all day. While the BLIs on the ground and the artillery units aimed a steady fire of Katyusha rockets and shells into the zone. Not a single helicopter went down. It wasn't until the next day that Esteban's company boarded them and flew in, the helicopters firing off more rockets: Rigoberto Mazariego briefly held his novia's doll out the bay so that she could watch the dirty, smoky explosions in the landscape below, the wind pulling out some of her hair. They were landed near now-empty trenches outside an abandoned hamlet that had been taken over by la contra. There was not that much resistance. And many contra dead, often found in clusters. The dead like the dead always, their deaths so poorly disguised by their grimacing and flinching and astonished and sometimes peaceful expressions, some already bloating, stinking. Vultures everywhere. And dead mules and horses. Milton claimed four hundred contra had died, but that must have been an exaggeration, there weren't that many bodies; but who knew how many dead they'd carried back across the border? They recovered at least that many weapons, and radios, all kinds of yanqui equipment, left behind when they'd fled. Milton wanted to cross the border and wipe them out, but the Comandancia forbade it. Esteban's entire BLI lost five compas, three to mines, and nine wounded, several by cazabobos, those mines that blow off a foot. But the problem was, supposedly there were a number of dead civilians—women, children—too. Though he, personally, saw only a few, a family sprawled along a riverbank, a mother and three children, two of them chavalitas, their shredded dresses dark brown with blood, their bodies already dissolving into the warm mud. It wasn't the first time he'd seen such an obscene sight: more than a few times they'd come upon the still-smoking rubble of farming collectives and hamlets razed a day or two before. Supposedly there was a too high number of dead civilians. Supposedly the yanquis were already complaining about their counteroffensive. Milton was summoned to the Comandancia in Wiwilí by helicopter, and as soon as he stepped out he was stripped of his command and publicly humiliated by the jefe of the Grupo Operativo for having disobeyed orders and acted irresponsibly, and transferred to the draftees' training camp at Mulukuku to wait for the results of the investigation into the civilian casualties at Wina. And the BLI was ordered to stay where they were, in that landscape of silent death, to await their new comandante.

His name was Eliseo. He was buena onda. Though they weren't the same BLI anymore, they were more like the other BLIs for a while, carrying the extra weight in their packs, fighting fewer combates, which was fine, though everyone remembered what it had been like before, and that was confusing, to feel proud of your past while you still had to keep on fighting. What happened later on the Zompopera Road wasn't really Eliseo's fault. That was after they'd returned to Quilalí and Esteban had learned la Marta's fate, so by then the extra weight he carried on his back was nothing compared with the weight of grief and dread in his chest. Though maybe what some said was true, that Milton would have checked over and over to be sure that the Comandancia had executed and confirmed and reconfirmed the order he'd requested for army regulars to secure the road against ambush before the BLI's convoy traveled down it. It turned out that the officer in the Comandancia who'd received the order from Eliseo had been drunk.

Later they heard Milton had left the country and was living in Miami, working as a nighttime security guard in a perfume warehouse. A perfume warehouse? That's where arte militar finally got Milton. Pues, at least it isn't a Parcheesi warehouse. Wonder if he's still there. Maybe he should go to Miami and look for Milton . . .

José Mateo has cooked duck before. Once, when his ship docked in Shanghai, they went to the market and bought half a dozen. But then he had an oven. He says it's too bad they ate all those berries, he could have made a nice sauce. But how was anyone supposed to know Esteban would bring back duck? Boiled duck, in a fatty broth filled with peas, potatoes, and rice. The broth poured into their plastic drinking glasses, layer of smoky, golden fat on top. Delicioso.

Esteban says, "Vos, you know what that truck sounded like? Like hundreds of honking little Cuban patos in cages all going *coño coño coño coño*!"

3

HE'S CROSSED UNDER THE EXPRESSWAY, CLIMBED INTO BROOKLYN. IN THIS neighborhood, there are many signs in Spanish. *Paco Naco's Tacos*. A place that arranges money transfers and telephone calls to Mexico and the Caribbean and all the Central American countries. There are people out on the streets, lots of men, many mestizo looking, wearing baseball hats, bulky, plastic-looking jackets of different colors, who seem to be in a hurry to get wherever they're going, to work probably. Many descend stairs that lead beneath the sidewalk to the underground trains—he can feel and hear the pavement thundering under his feet. Nobody looks at him in a friendly way. It's nearly dawn, but he finds a little corner restaurant that is open, drab blue walls, steam tables in the window, some of the dishes he recognizes—arroz con pollo, looking like it's been sitting there all night—and others he doesn't. He wishes he had some money so he could go in, order a cup of coffee, get out of the cold. The greasy smell of food, a smell of sauce-saturated chicken, fish, and overripe fruit, makes his stomach rumble; mixing with bus exhaust and the chilly, faintly briny breeze channeling up the long street from the harbor.

He's never stayed out this long. By now, they must be waking up on the ship, wondering where he is. On a side street he finds a puzzling sign, a white sheet of paper covered with photocopied handwriting taped to the glass behind the bars of a lowered shutter: someone has lost a cat named Dolores and is offering a fifty-dollar reward. There is a photocopied picture of Dolores, too smudgy and gray to help you distinguish this cat from most others. But here is the rare thing: the cat's color is listed as "aceituna." But olives can be black or green. If black olive, why list the cat's color as olive and not black? And who's ever heard of an olive green cat?

"Tu, güey!"

He turns and sees this golden-curly-haired muchacha glaring at him, slight and pretty, holding keys to the lock in the door to this place that has lost its cat. She has a soft, almost nougat-hued face, her eyes big, stormy pools framed by blue eyeliner and long, black lashes. Small, puffy nose. Pert, lipsticked mouth, pouting angrily at him. "You're the güey that's been urinating in this doorway, no? Pinche asqueroso!" And now her affronted brown eyes are *pulsing* at him.

"No!" exclaims Esteban. "I've never been here before!"

"Ah no?" accusingly.

"No!"

He can smell her perfume. How old is she? Young. About his own age, no? She's wearing a long, blue wool coat with a collar that looks made of coarse lamb's wool, skinny ankles in whitish tights descending from the coat, into glossy black, sturdy high heels. Now she's looking him up and down.

"Qué triste, güey," she says, with impassioned mockery. "Letting yourself go around looking like that. Güey, you're too young to be homeless. Any güey can find *some* type of job. Bueno. What can you do? Otro desgraciado sinvergüenza." She shrugs, looks at him with exaggerated pity, shakes her head. "En fin."

He gapes at her. Her lips look blistered, chapped, through her lipstick—and the way she talks, hombre, it's no wonder!

And she turns back towards the door, and stops, and then she starts up again, mouth working like an agitated choir singer's, keeping her own temperamental rhythm with the keys in her hand, flopped up and down: ". . . Hijos de la chingada, patanes, come and stand in the doorway all night pissing, drinking beer, smoking marijuana, leaving their piggishness all over. Y la policia, qué hacen? Cabrones de mie*rrr*da. Absolutamente nada! No, no, I can't take this anymore. It's too much to ask. Starting your day having to step through *this* porquería. No! Pinche degenarados . . ."

She's stepped backwards, for a moment isn't even facing him anymore as she orates at the doorway, and then she spins around, glaring at him again. He laughs, he can't help it, and she says, "Ah, sí, güey? Go ahead and laugh. Laugh all the way to the homeless shelter, ándale."

"Chocho," he blurts, "Qué agresiva!"

"*Qué!* Vulgarote!"

"Bueno. *OK!*"—flinging his arms out. Amazed at himself, standing on a sidewalk in Brooklyn, arguing with this loca! A corner of her lower lip tucked between her teeth while she glares at him like some infuriated abuela again. But what eyes!

Finally, seemingly calmed down a little, she says, "Don't you feel embarrassment, going around like that? Not to mention the cold. You're going to catch something. Bueno, what's it to me? . . . Except you could catch tuberculosis, güey, and give it to somebody else. That happens, you know. It's been on the news."

And he says, "I'm not a vago. I *have* a job. I'm a marinero. I've been stuck on this ship down in the harbor for almost four months now, with no pay, hardly anything to eat, working. The whole crew looks like this. Down there." And he gestures towards the harbor.

"That doesn't happen here," she says flatly. "Four months with no pay? Güey, that's not very intelligent. And I can tell you're not stupid. It's a story. I don't believe a word of it."

"Va, pues, don't believe me, what's it to me?" he says, suddenly angry. "We thought we were going to be paid. Vos, we thought we'd be sailing in a few days. And instead they put us to work repairing this old, broken ship. They keep telling us that when the ship is fixed, we'll sail and we'll get paid. Puta, what were we supposed to do? No one has the money even to go home. We hardly even know where we are." Suddenly he pulls some of the tools from his pocket, holds a wire-splicing pin and the wire cutters out to her. "What do you think these are?"

"Qué sé yo? Burglars' tools. You break into parked cars, no? Police catch you with those, you'll see what happens to you, güey"—and she shakes her head. "Just the pretext they'll need to leave you in a bloody pulp."

"These are mariners' tools," he says, thinking, Puta, I guess they *are* burglars' tools.

She looks at the tools, and then up at him. "You have a funny accent," she finally says. "What's all that with the *vos*?"

"Soy de Nicaragua," he answers. "Esteban Gaitán. Mucho gusto. Y usted?"

"Joaquina," she says warily. "Encantado," she says with a certain sarcasm and a slight smile. "Bueno. En fin," she says sternly, and lifts the keys towards the door again, grimacing as she steps towards it. "Hasta luego, marinero."

"How can a cat be olive colored?" Esteban points at the sign in the window. "Why doesn't it just say black?"

She steps back from the door again, smiling quizzically, a little slice of a smile that suddenly widens: her smile so lights up her face that suddenly she looks about eight years old.

"I've never thought of that," she says. "Gonzalo thinks Dolores is olive green. Claro, she isn't. More like muddy gray. Maybe he's color blind and hides it. But imagine. You think women are going to come here to get their hair dyed if they know he's color blind? But my jefe, bueno, that's what he's like, full of inventions." She chuckles softly. "Like you, verdad?"

"This is where you work?"

"Pues, claro," she says, as if suddenly annoyed by him again. "I'm the one who has to come and open it up in the morning. Can't you read?" and she points at the sign over the door: *Salón de Belleza Tropicana—Unisex.*

"I can read," he says.

She's looking at him thoughtfully now, not angrily like before. "You're really a marinero?"

"Sí pues."

"Then you must be good with a mop, no? Isn't that what marineros are always doing, mopping the deck?"

"Sometimes."

"Bueno, te propongo algo. If you mop and sweep the doorway here, I'll make you a cup of coffee. Órale?" Her eyebrows go up.

He smiles. Doesn't understand that word. "Órale?" he repeats.

"Papas!" she says. Potatoes? And she steps forward and opens the door, turning various keys in various locks. As she's going inside, she looks at him standing dumbly on the sidewalk. "Ven!"

He follows Joaquina inside, into the almost noxiously sweet-smelling salon, the gray glow of mirrors in the dark; he stands inside the door while she crosses the room to the light switches. The light comes on, and she disappears behind a red-yellow printed curtain into the back. He hears water pouring against metal, filling a pail. He gapes at himself in the mirror, appalled at his beggar aspect of long, dirty hair and light beard, his hollowed face and frightened eyes: he looks like one of those boys raised by wolves. The water stops; she steps back out through the curtain, she's taken off her coat and is wearing a pleated gray-black wool skirt, a pink cardigan sweater over a white blouse with a lacy collar. She gestures to him. "Ven," she says. "*You* carry it out, güey."

He follows her through the curtain, into a corridor with three closed doors, a coat rack hung with her coat and blue smocks, supplies arrayed along shelves, an industrial sink. Joaquina is pouring ammonia from a plastic bottle into the metal pail, and when she's done, she carefully twists the cap back on, holding the bottle away from herself. He notices an earring, a small, glassy-purple star, on her lobe. She hands him a mop and a broom, steps out through the curtain; he follows her out, carrying the broom between biceps and rib, the mop in one hand and the sloshing pail in the other.

"I could use a haircut," he says, wanting to make a kind of self-dignifying joke. "And a shave, pues."

"Pinche güey!" she exclaims, darting her eyes at him. "You're out of luck. I'm just the manicurist."

He's walking to the door when he hears her say, "Bueno, I can also wax your legs. Even your bikini line, güey. Ja!"

He turns to look at her, her back to him as she fumbles with the coffee maker on a side table against the wall. She says, "Gonzalo will cut your hair for ten dollars." The hem of her sweater falls like a soft bell over her slender rear. "Clean everything well, güey, and I'll let you have a pastelito too."

The reek of urine is strong in front of the door. He thinks, Bocona, mandona. He really doesn't like the way she speaks to him, mouthy, bossy, patronizing, eh? He picks up two empty quart bottles of beer standing in paper bags between the salon's door and another door with affixed buzzers and scrawled numbers on a battered metal sheet, carries the bottles to the trash cans on the curb, and laying them in, prods open the tear in a plastic bag, sees it full of hair, mainly dark hues of hair. Hairy wax, he remembers, la Marta. Sweeps cigarette butts, a few tiny marijuana butts in pinched pink paper, all the way across the sidewalk—people hurry around and past him on the sidewalk. He stares down at his boots with the broom in his hands. Thinks, This is totally strange, no? His scuffed, grease-stained black boots, made in the Soviet Union, laced with electrical wire, which accompanied him all the way through the war, which la Marta unlaced and tugged off his feet more than once, which that German tracking dog sniffed with its nose of sorrow, boots that stood in a pile of tumbling bullet cartridges as he returned blistering fire through truck planks during the Zompopera ambush and got soaked with the blood of compas while somehow he wasn't killed; and then went home to Corinto with him and walked through the shitty, steaming, salty mud of its streets and which, oddly yet typically, his Tío Nelson and not his mamá used to like to clean and polish for him; boots which watched his pathetic freak-out with that puta in the burdel, standing empty by her bed, stinking up the already smelly little room and filling it with silent howls of fucked up grief, and then a week later went away to sea with him: and now, vos, here they are, while he sweeps up outside a beauty salon in Brooklyn, these boots like a last living witness to his life, like the only proof he has of the life of Esteban Gaitán . . . He gazes up the ramshackle row house–lined street—brick, wood, concrete, and aluminum-sided facades, some with tiny, littered gardens out front behind corroded gates—past trash cans and parked cars, at the avenue flashing busily with traffic and pedestrians now. These people passing, they're probably thinking, Look at that dirty beggar, sweeping up in front of a salon, he must be mentally retarded or a drunk, working for just a few pennies. Puta. Y qué? He finishes sweeping, nudges the small pile between two trash cans. Then he mops vigorously and thoroughly, wringing the mop out with his hands, breathing in the strong scent of ammonia, slapping water all over the place, from the door all the way out to the curb—

"Oye, chamaco," Joaquina says, standing in the door. "Did I ask you to mop all of Brooklyn?"

Inside, they sit on folding chairs against the wall, a white cardboard box holding a few pastries on the chair between them, sipping their coffee. So how should he to talk to her? Like she's his boss?

"Y usted, where are you from?"

"México," she says, yawning, lifting the back of her hand to her mouth. "And you don't have to say *usted*." She gestures at the box. "These are left from yesterday, so they're a little stale."

She's already explained to him about how she made the coffee in that machine over there, told him it's real coffee. Sí pues, like the coffee he had on the airplane. The first of any kind in months, since their officers stopped bringing them jars of instant coffee, which apparently isn't real coffee. He savors the strong, muddy taste, feels the warmth and caffeine hitting inside, feels his intestines cringe. He looks around at the salon, the glossy color photographs of men and women with different hairdos; a framed picture of La Virgen del Cobre against a red backdrop with lighthouse and palms painted in, seashells glued to it; and another framed photograph of a man dressed like Pedro Picapiedra, in a tunic that looks made of leopard skin, holding a spread-eagled, platinum blonde woman in a silvery leotard over his head in muscular arms.

"I don't usually have to come in this early," Joaquina is saying, "but I have a customer coming in for a special appointment."

"Ajá," he says softly, not looking at her. He reaches for one of the pastelitos, crescent shaped, glazed, and sugar sprinkled, bites into the chewy crust, jam squirts into his mouth. Dismally, he watches himself chewing in the mirrors.

"So you're a náufrago, güey," she says. "De veras?"

A shipwrecked sailor—that's true enough. "Sí pues," he says, "it's true. But my name isn't güey, it's Esteban. Our capitán always calls us güey."

"He's a chilango?"

He asks what a chilango is, and she tells him it's someone from México, el Distrito Federal. "*May-ksee-koh Ceetee,*" she says, trying to imitate a gringo accent.

"No, I don't think so. Bueno, he's a pendejo, wherever he's from. Americano. Inglés. Griego. Las Amazonas. I guess he's from all those places." He shrugs. "Is that where you're from in Mexico?"

"Sí. No. Zacatecas. But I lived there for a few years, that's where I went to beautician school, and worked awhile, before I came up here to live with my brothers. We all lived there, for a while."

"It's a big city, no?"

"Sí güey, it's a big city. Much bigger than this one, they say, though it doesn't seem like it."

"Is it difficult to live here as an immigrant?"

For some reason this makes her laugh, a brief, airy giggle. "Más o menos. Bueno, es bonito . . . *Esteban*." She sips her coffee, eyes beaming as if she's said something funny; holding her cup with her little finger out, chin up, gazing off with a tight-lipped little smirk, as if she's savoring the taste of whatever it is she thinks is so funny and not just the coffee.

They fall into a silence while she holds the cup up to her lips in both hands, taking steady little sips. Her fingernails cut short, neat, glossy. She sits, bent over her coffee, with her legs straight out and a little apart, her feet pointed up in her high heels and gently rocking, the fabric of her tights wrinkled around the straps over the ankles. He lets his eyes coast quickly over her slender, curving calves. He inhales with his mouth closed, slowly drawing in her perfume and faint soapy scent, along with the coffee, all the salon smells. In a nose full of *Urus,* no? Corroded nostrils that by now must be like portable bits of the *Urus:* rust and paint, old diesel oil from the depths of the ship, his unwashed compañeros. No wonder he's a little dizzy, perspiring from the cold, frothy ache in his bowels. And her perfume is beginning to affect his breathing, making his breathing passages feel wooly.

He's finished his coffee, sees that there's more in the pot. Should he ask for more? Doesn't think he wants any more. Can't think of anything to say. Shouldn't he ask to use the toilet? Doesn't dare, what if he stinks the place up. Golden curls partly tucked behind her ears, falling down around her thin neck and lacy collar, a fine silver chain dangling over her small chest, disappearing under the sweater; she has one of those little stars on both lobes. She has a surprisingly low, chesty, womanly voice that goes shrill when she's excited. Kind of a baby face, for all her haughtiness and mouthiness. How old is she? Maybe even younger than he, because all that makeup must make her look older than she is. Hair must be dyed. Decides not to like her, much. Compared with la Marta, he decides, she seems stuck-up and artificial.

"So you like it here," he says.

"Siií. 'sta padre, 'sta chingón."

Uses too much strange slang.

"So what are you going to do?" she asks.

"When?"

"On your *boat,* güey."

"Maybe I'll leave," he says. "Try to get a job here in the city. Of course, I'll need a haircut first. Some clothes." Wonders if he can find some way to sell all those Parcheesis, and the swimming goggles too.

"Claro," she says.

"But I think I should try to find the United Nations first. See if they can do something to resolve our situation. Do you know how to get there?"

"I think it's somewhere in Manhattan," she says, seemingly unimpressed by this bold, new plan. "I'm sure you can get there by subway. Claro, you can't go there looking like that, though, they'll think you're a terrorist. I'd lend you some clothes, but— My brothers have clothes, but they're shorter than you, and wider, and I don't think they'd like me to be giving away their clothes."

"Bueno," he says. "Thanks for thinking of it."

"Por nada," she says. "Anyway, there are places that sell very inexpensive clothing, secondhand, sometimes you find some nice things . . . Ah! Here's my customer! Esteban, you have to go now."

He looks up and sees a broad-shouldered, tall, yet squarely built man in a bright red, white-trimmed jogging suit outside the door; ebony hair slickly smoothed back over a broad, sharp-featured indio face. Joaquina opens the door for him, and he bends down to embrace her, they give each other kisses on the cheek, she says, "Chucho, corazón, cómo te va, eh?"

"Joaquina, ángel de mi alma," his voice a gruff singsong. "I haven't made you get up too early, I hope. In this pinche cold."

"Sí, 'sta friolín, no?"

Chucho looks down at Esteban, his briefly puzzled glance resolving into an unfriendly stare through narrowing eyes, his chin seeming to pull back into his brawny neck. He is wearing shiny black ankle boots tucked up into his sweatpants; three gem-studded gold rings on one hand, a big, gold-banded gold watch peeking out from under a red sleeve.

"This is Esteban," says Joaquina, glancing over at him and scoldingly widening her eyes. "He's a shipwrecked marinero. Imagine."

"Ah," says Chucho. "Don't tell me."

"Mucho gusto," says Esteban, rising from his seat.

"Sí pues," says Chucho, and he looks over at Joaquina.

"Really, it's true," says Joaquina, flustered, taking Chucho's arm in two hands and tugging him lightly across the room—she walks, thinks Esteban, as if her shoes are both too heavy and loose fitting for her, yet with a certain elastic rhythm and grace—and starting to explain how she found Esteban outside. ". . . He wanted to know how a cat could be green like an olive. Isn't that cute? When he said that I knew I didn't have to be afraid of him. He cleaned the doorway"—laughing, guiding Chucho to a leather-backed metal chair with leather armrests, next to a footstool, and a small, wheeled cart loaded with bottles of nail polish and other potions, delicate, silvery tools laid out across it, and a cup holding emery board files that remind Esteban of tongue depressors in a doctor's office. And when she has him seated she breathlessly says, "Chucho, un momentito y ya," and Chucho says he's in a hurry, guerita, and she says, "Sí, sí, corazón, I just have to let Esteban out," and she glares at Esteban and walks towards the door and he turns and says good-bye to Chucho and follows her out the door, which she holds open with her shoulder. She gives Esteban her hand.

"Oye, gracias por todo," she says. "And good luck with everything, eh? If there's anything I can do to help? Órale?"

"Gracias a vos!"

"Por nada, güey. Órale?"

"Órale."

"Papas!" a quick smile, and then she's already turned back into the salon. He watches her hurry back to Chucho, pulling the little stool in front of him, sitting down on it as she smooths her skirt around her, pulling the little trolley cart to her side while Chucho lifts his hand, extends it towards her; he can see them talking as she takes his hand in both of hers. Chucho glances over at him. He'd better go; he goes. Thinking, Qué cosa, qué cosa. That macho prepotente getting a manicure first thing in the morning!

Feeling elated and then bewildered and then a little less elated as he strides down the sidewalk. Wishes he'd asked to use the toilet. Total mandona, though. Mouthy! She and Chucho, y qué? What's so great about how *Chucho* was dressed? She's one of those chicas plásticas. Not the type that sees into your heart, your values, sees who you really are.

4

CEBO, THE SWEET-NATURED ADONIS, THE FORMER LOBSTER DIVER, SWEARS he once saw a golden-haired mermaid at the bottom of the ocean, beckoning to him just as, already out of breath, lungs aching, he was about to push down through the water to pluck a lobster from between the rocks the mermaid hovered over. But Cebo knew from other divers that the blonde mermaid only appears when she wants to draw you down a bit farther, just far enough to give you a possibly fatal attack of the bends. So he resisted, and swam up, and up, so far up that he was almost unconscious and feeling torn apart by invisible sharks when his head finally popped above the surface. That's how close he came to the bends. He quit lobster diving after that. He never wanted to see that beautiful blonde mermaid again. That's why he started looking for a job on a ship. Though it does seem, Bernardo has often reflected, that all that deep-sea diving must have affected Cebo's brain anyway. Not that Cebo seems feebleminded. It's just that someone always so sweet natured and uncomplaining, even in a situation like this one, has to be a little *slow* in the coco.

So Cebo—of all people!—punched Canario in the mouth early this morning, before dawn, in their cabin, bloodied his lip, woke everyone with their shouts, and now neither of them is saying why. Only Bernardo knows, because Cebo came to speak to him alone, and they've agreed to keep it a secret. Cebo told him that Canario came stumbling in from sniffing rags soaked in paint solvent with Pínpoyo and El Tinieblas in their cabin, out of his head and giggling like a ghoul, so disoriented that he even tried to get into bed with him. Cebo has promised Canario he won't tell anyone why as long as Canario never sniffs paint solvent again. This is bad news, claro. Santísima Virgen, that's all they need now, a ship full of paint solvent sniffers. Bernardo has agreed to have a private conversation with the pretty boy and the tattooed former prisoner about it if they keep it up. But he feels reluctant. He's afraid he won't have any influence. Somehow, he lacks the energy, the *ganas*. A part of him thinks, Let them get high if they want, destroy their own brains if they want. El Tinieblas probably already has, long before he ended up here. But he will, Bernardo decides, he'll try to talk to them. Especially if they keep it up, if the disgusting habit starts to spread.

Then Capitán Elias came out to the ship and called them together for a meeting. Several of the crew were still asleep, including Canario, Pínpoyo, and El Tinieblas; they had to be roused from their cabins and staggered out like drunks. Bernardo noted José Mateo suspiciously watching, as if wondering how they'd gotten their hands on alcohol and why they hadn't shared it. Esteban wasn't there either: he left last night—and still hasn't returned. But el Capitán didn't seem to notice that he was missing.

El Capitán made another of his speeches. Said it was time to start working long and hard hours again. Canario listened with his hands over his face, and Pínpoyo sat on the deck cross-legged, his head nodding downwards, downwards, and then he slumped over sideways. Though El Tinieblas seemed his usual opaque self, his small-featured face expressionless as a snail's. Apparently, the circuit breaker problem will soon be resolved. And next week there's to be an inspection. Then el Capitán turned on the generator and compressor and the ordinary seamen went back to work welding the ballast tanks in the hold; el Capitán went down into the engine room. Later he came up, fuming about the engine crew, mocking Pínpoyo and Canario as a pair of drooling idiots. Then he descended the steel ladder into the hold and saw the muchachos welding ballast tanks in swimming goggles. What could he say? After all, he'd neglected to bring them goggles. Where did you get those? el Capitán asked. Bought them, said Tomaso Tostado. And what could el Capitán say to that?

But *then* he noticed Esteban was missing. Where's Esteban? el Capitán asked. And supposedly everyone just said, No sé, mi Capi. Saber, mi Capi. Don't know where he went. Not here today, mi Capi. Claro, el Capitán seemed angered over the insolence of everyone's tone.

But what could he say, that they're all slaves? That Esteban's fired? Instead he said to Panzón, If Esteban doesn't want to be paid for today, it's his problem, no? And soon after, el Capitán left. He didn't bring food today.

Then Tomaso Tostado and El Buzo brought the carton of Parcheesis out of Tomaso's cabin, where he'd been storing them, carried them all the way to los proyectos. They came back about an hour later, without the carton. Told how they'd just put the carton down on a sidewalk in front of los proyectos and started yelling in English, "*Wan dólar! Wan dólar!*" They sold eight very quickly. But then a group of those delinquents came and chased Tostado and Buzo away, and kept the rest of the Parcheesis, though they didn't do them any physical harm this time, nor did they take away the eight dollars.

Of course everyone was worried about Esteban, wondering why he hasn't come back, hoping he's all right, wondering what he might bring.

Sí pues, an eventful day. There are changes in the air, some ambiguous, others ominous, muses Bernardo, mopping in the darkened steel corridor outside the cabins on the second story of the deckhouse. But then he smells cat urine again. He goes out on deck and sits against the base of the deckhouse, near the gangway, feeling hollowed out by apathy.

He's still sitting there, with his knees up and his hands on his knees, when Esteban comes back. The crew gathers. Of course everyone is happy to see him safe and well, but their expressions can't hide their disappointment that he hasn't brought back anything to eat. After shrimp, blueberries, and duck, it's hard not to get carried away with expectations, harder still to go back to sardines. Even Bernardo has let himself hungrily fantasize about what Esteban might bring back.

About this, Esteban is tersely unapologetic. Why should he apologize? He's been away all night, well into the day. Knowing Esteban, he tried hard to find something, and simply had no luck, and is feeling tired and frustrated now.

So, claro, El Barbie has to open his bocón and say, "Nada? Gone all this time, y nada?"

Esteban scowls at him, as if to say, You again?

And Bernardo thinks, Esteban doesn't realize this is just El Barbie's way, that actually Barbie really wants Esteban's friendship now, but it's just his way.

"Why don't you bring something back, fucking huevón," says Esteban. "I'm not doing that anymore, güey. So far, I've been lucky. What if the police catch me, eh? They'll beat me to a pulp."

Güey? And before El Barbie can answer, though he's glowering and puffing himself up and trying to think of something that will no doubt be provocative, just then El Faro excitedly says: "El Buzo and Tostado brought something back. Eight dollars! They sold the Parcheesi!"

Esteban's face falls. "Qué?" he says. And honestly, the chavalito looks like he doesn't know whether to cry or just go ahead and punch Tomaso Tostado, who has already started telling about his and El Buzo's adventure today—

"Those weren't yours to sell," says Esteban.

And now Tostado looks upset, and it's his turn to exclaim, "Qué? What in putas are you saying, 'mano."

And El Barbie laughingly mutters, "Dé a verga. What a piri."

"Those were mine," says Esteban.

And Bernardo cringes with dismay.

Tomaso Tostado puts out his hands, looks around at the others, and says, "Esteban, qué le pasa? We're all in this together—"

"Together! But I'm the one who does everything."

"Sos un comemierda, de veras." El Barbie sneers. "One week of activity after sucking your thumb for four months. And who covers for you when you sleep all day while we work, eh, Piri?"

"You ever call me that again, I'll kill you, I swear it—"

"Come mierda, Piri." After all, what does El Barbie have to fear? He's bigger, physically stronger—

But Esteban charges him, and El Barbie is up; there is a flurry of punches and kicks while everybody else except Bernardo jumps in shouting, wrestling the two fighters apart, while Bernardo just sits there feeling helplessly dismayed. But no one gets hurt very badly, there's no blood this time, they're pulled apart, both of them panting heavily. But,

Dios mío, look at that!—that chavalote El Barbie has tears in his reddening eyes, tears running down his grimy cheeks. He can't even talk, he's trying to say something but he can't even get out the words. And Esteban is glaring around at everyone, making those sniffling, angry otter sounds through his nose. And El Barbie, his voice quavering, choking on emotion and rage, his massive chest heaving up and down, finally begins to speak:

"Piri, sos un hijueputa, sos un cabrón. And I am too, I know. Basically, I respect you. But the differences between you and me are many. And these are the differences. *One,* I'm not stuck-up. Two, I believe in God. Three, I can take a joke. Vos, you can't!" and El Barbie is overwhelmed with emotion, he can't speak, he looks down at his shoes while everyone looks at him with bewilderment, except for Esteban, standing there looking as blank as if he hasn't heard any of it anyway. El Tinieblas mutters some words of encouragement, lays his hand on El Barbie's shoulder, and Barbie shrugs it off.

"Four," says El Barbie, "vos, number four is Tostadito's been saying for days that he thinks we should sell those chunches, and you were just ignoring him, which is what I meant by stuck-up. And number five, vos, piri hijo de puta—"

"Ya, Barbie, that's enough," says Bernardo, slowly getting to his feet. "Carajo! Stop all this craziness!"

"Vos, what's number five?" says Esteban calmly, staring sadly at Barbie. "I want to hear this."

"The fifth way we're different, vos, is I didn't break the hand off the clock."

Panzón says, "Vos, Barbie, Esteban didn't break the clock."

"Who'll ever know, hombre? But I think he did." Now El Barbie grins. "Oiga, Estebanito. Let's make a pact. You treat me with respect from now on, I'll do the same to you. But don't ever tell me I can't say something, because you can fucking be sure that then I will. And the next time we fight, I'll kick your fucking culo in."

"Bueno," says Esteban indifferently. He steps forward and shakes El Barbie's hand.

It doesn't seem that El Barbie's speech has had quite the effect he intended; he seems instantly plunged into a brooding gloom.

Bernardo says, "Chavalos, we can't have these kinds of disagreements. You were wrong, Esteban, to react that way about Tomaso and Buzo selling those things."

Esteban nods. "I'm sorry," he says. "So how much money did we get?"

"Eight dollars," says Tomaso Tostado.

"Está bien." He shrugs. "Excuse me. I'm tired." And he turns and walks off to his cabin.

And before El Barbie can say anything, Bernardo says, "Of course he's tired. He's been up all night. And he feels bad, because he didn't find anything to bring back. It's time to start the dinner fire."

"The menu tonight, gallos," croaks José Mateo, "is sardines and rice."

When Bernardo comes into the cabin, he's surprised to see Esteban wide awake, lying in bed with his hands clasped behind his head, smiling at the ceiling.

"Un centavito for your thoughts."

Esteban glancingly grimaces and looks back up at the ceiling, his smile gone. "I was thinking what a good thing it would be to put rat poison in everyone's sardines."

"I'd rather use it on the rats, if we had such poison."

"Then you and I could live here, fix it up, move upstairs, take steam baths, it would be like having our own mansion de Playboy, no?"

"El Capitán and the owner might have something to say about that."

"Poison them too. Malditos."

"De veras, chico. People who know what it's like to kill shouldn't joke about it. Somehow it never sounds funny."

Esteban says, *tch,* with his tongue.

Claro, Bernardo knows he sentimentalizes Esteban, thinks of him as youthfully pure hearted, even innocent, always forgetting that not so long ago he was a baby-breathed military killer. Isn't it true that those who kill, even in war, become dead inside too, at least in certain ways? Maybe that's why the chavalo has so little fear, has revealed himself to be such a blithely intrepid felon, because he feels dead already. Though he never talks about it; just once, when he told that barbaric story about the German dog. He's never even been in love, thinks Bernardo. That's the saddest thing. Has never even alluded to ever having felt the elation or sorrow or rage of love—

"I know I acted like a pendejo out there," Esteban is saying. "But I was planning to sell those things, those Parcheesi, myself, to get the money for a haircut."

"Ah."

Bernardo goes to the porthole and pulls it shut, a rather pointless gesture, given its broken pane.

"We should find a way to fix this," he says, "now that the nights are getting cold."

"I met somebody today who works in a beauty salon," says Esteban. "It's unisex."

"Unisex?"

"That means it doesn't matter what sex you are, they still cut your hair."

"Where was this place?"

"In a part of Brooklyn where all the signs are in Spanish. I think a lot of Mexicanos live there."

"Pues, you see? Didn't I tell you? I bet you can find a job there just like that—" He snaps his fingers.

"Maybe. But not looking like this. That's the point. She said a haircut would cost me ten dollars."

"She's trying to rob you. Was she pretty?"

"No. Pues, maybe. Y qué?"

"Young?"

"She looks young."

"Vos, then it shouldn't be a problem. Ahhh, Esteban." He sighs. "I think you've missed all the lessons about how to get your way in life. Be audacious, muchacho, charm her, flatter her, seduce her into cutting your hair for free. When you're all cleaned up, she'll see how handsome you are and fall in love. And that will be your entrance to Nueva York. It'll be good for you, anyway. You're in no position to be choosy."

"She doesn't cut hair," Esteban says heatedly. "She's the manicurist. Her boss does. His name is Gonzalo. I suppose you think I should try to seduce him? Hijueputa, güey! The things you say!"

"Why are you saying *güey?*"

Esteban laughs up at the ceiling. "De veras? I caught it from her, I guess. She never shuts up and uses it twice in every sentence. Güey, you're the one who's been urinating in this door, güey."

"You urinated in her door?"

"No! But that's the first thing she said to me, I was just standing there. She's completely horrible, a total agresiva. From then on, everything she said was a provocation." Esteban tells Bernardo all about his encounter with Joaquina.

"Something was going on between her and that Chucho. I was supposed to believe this macho pato was there to have his hands manicured at eight in the morning? Please!"

So, this pistolito has a trigger after all! Bernardo has listened in growing astonishment.

"Chavalo, bossy, difficult women are the greatest thing on earth!" he exclaims. "Bueno, as long as they don't overdo it. My Clarita was like that. I tell you, they only do it out of love, and they never let you fall asleep at the wheel. And after, docile women seem tepid forever. Why should it bother you that she has a lover? It's good that she's not a prude. You'll have him out of the way pretty fast, if she's already talking to you like that, already trying to take control of your life, eh?"

"Qué? She's not trying to—puta!"

Bernardo cackles with excitement. "You don't know what you're in for, muchacho! Let a woman like that down, she'll have you burning in hell. You'll have no choice but to be a success in life. Get used to the idea, chigüín: I'd say she already owns your salary."

Esteban is sitting up now, glaring furiously at him. "Salary? You're really losing your mind, viejo. Chocho! And she *does* overdo it! Who wants to burn in hell?"

"Ya, ya, ándale." Bernardo nods. "If you're so sure. Just stay here on our barquito. Eventually, I suppose, they'll have to deport us. Sí pues, that's what I would do if I were your age, just wait here until somehow we get sent back. Our country has a wonderful future, sí pues. What is it your family does for money? Pilfer cargo from ships that don't come anymore? That's a good life."

He lies back on the bed and listens with guarded happiness to Esteban's infuriated breathing, his angry sputtering.

"Clara was the love of my life. But she used to overdo it too," he says finally. "But that's because I let her down so often. Maybe you won't."

"Ya! I just want a haircut! . . . What a pest!"

"A haircut would be good, claro."

He lies listening to Esteban ventilating his fury.

". . . Bueno. OK," the chavalo finally mutters. "How did you let her down?"

"I was a marinero. I'd promised her when we married that I wouldn't be anymore, but there was no other way of escaping being even poorer. The same story as always."

"She should have understood that."

"She was twenty years younger than me, and I only saw her once or twice a year. And gradually I became old and she, when still young—" He sighs. "Pues, you know what happened."

"Bueno," he says after a long while. "The sardine cans are waiting for me."

The mood at supper is dismal. Esteban has stayed in his cabin. The crew seems to take his absence as an unjustified rebuke, sullenly chewing as if being forced to eat oily beach sand. Bernardo thinks, They have every reason to be sick of sardines and rancid rice. But it's sustaining enough, they're lucky to have it, often it's the only meal of the day and usually they eat like the nearly starving men they are. In the past, whenever Bernardo's felt too tired or apathetic—or whenever los blacks were already on the pier—to wash the plates after supper, he's always let it go until morning with a clear conscience, knowing he'd be leaving the rats nothing but plates licked clean. But tonight, several set their plates down on the deck still loaded with food. He stares wearily at those plates, waiting for a surge of temper to bring a stinging reproach to his lips; it doesn't come.

"Not hungry?" he says with an arid sigh. "Then you can eat it tomorrow."

Nobody replies.

"You don't think I'm going to throw all that out, do you?"

"I'm saving mine for the piricuaco," snaps El Barbie.

When Esteban comes out of the cabin, Pínpoyo has already started in on dessert, though without any sugar to sprinkle over it: scraping and peeling up pieces of el raspado with his fingers, the rice scorched to the bottom of the pot. Usually the pot is passed around, everyone gets a few pieces of crunchy, oily, charred rice. Pínpoyo looks up as Esteban approaches, smiling as he holds the smoke-blackened pot out to him. Esteban takes it and carries it to the starboard rail, sets the pot on top, and eats from it while looking out over the breakwater and the harbor night beyond; after a while, he turns and sits against the gunwale with the pot between his knees, tilting the pot towards him with one hand and reaching in with the other, scraping up raspado, licking and sucking on his fingertips. The crews listens with averted eyes to Esteban's fingers scratching inside the pot, the sound mixed with the clack of dominoes and the rhetorical retorts of the domino players, the cracking and wheezing of the fire, the rustling of water in the cove. Finally Esteban lets the pot clang down on the deck. He mutters buenas noches and heads back towards his cabin.

Four of the crew lying in a circle on the deck, stretched out on their sides with arms curled protectively around their dominoes:

"I'm out of the shoe!" and the clack of a domino slapped down.

"Hair oil!" Clack!

"Yo no me meto con nadie!" and El Buzo slaps down a double six. "Make the soup, cabrón!"

Bernardo gets to his feet. He picks up the rice pot and looks inside, the bottom gleaming as if scoured with a wire brush. Then he starts collecting the plates. He can't stack them, because of the uneaten food. He picks up two, and in the darkness just beyond where one of the plates has been set down he sees a large rat wriggling up through one of the still unplated holes in the deck, watches the rat waddle up to the plate, attacking a sardine with starved frenzy. Only then does his anger finally flare; he hurls a plate towards the rat and misses it wildly, sardines and rice sliding in one clump to the deck while the plate shatters near the rail and someone shouts, "Not again with the bottles!" and the rat with sardine scurries back down through the hole. Bernardo turns, sees their astonished faces. But he doesn't say anything, just goes back to collecting the plates, carrying those with food one at a time to the rail, using a fork to push the wasted food off, down into the water.

When he returns to the cabin, Esteban is asleep. He steps through the pitch dark, sits on the mattress, takes off his shoes, and gets under the blanket fully clothed, oblivious to the sour reek of the bedding. The cabin smells cleaner from the briny autumn air streaming in through the portal. He lies listening to faint tickings and scrapings in the ship's iron canyon of silence, and to Esteban breathing through his mouth and snorting runnily through his nostrils. The chavalo sounds like he's coming down with another cold, he thinks.

He decides to fall asleep thinking about Clara. He wants to try to remember that long and tortured courtship: waiting for her every day, at siesta and in the evening, in the little park full of flame trees by the lake, outside the telephone building where she worked as a teller, twenty-five years ago. That's nearly the age Clara was when he set out to convince her that what she really needed in her life, rather than the treacherous muchachitos endlessly pursuing her for the ephemeral prize of her yellow hair and German surname despite her bulk and frankly plain features, was an ardent ship's waiter three years older than her late father would have been, who could give her the security and adoration a grown dama deserved, one who'd saved nearly enough money to buy a nice little house, with plumbing. One sultry evening, as he was walking her from teléfonos to her mother's house as usual, their lips stained purple from the pitaya juice they drank through the torn corner of a plastic bag, holding it to each other's mouths like a translucent udder and squeezing, she finally relented: they shared their first triumphant, lingering kiss, hidden in the shadows of trees and wall. But now, somehow, it's like watching his own dulled nostalgia disguised in Clara's chubby features and clothes, waving good-bye to him from a receding pier. Her love turned out to be a sharp-tongued, needy demon, which he learned to satisfy with joy in his heart. She always hated him for going away to sea again, but whenever he returned they ended up holding hands everywhere they went, behaving in public like teenage lovers—until he had to go away again, spattered by the abuse provoked by her already missing him. He tried to save every cent of his wages, and his daughters were always so well fed and neatly dressed that their schoolmates believed he was either a ship's capitán or a smuggler. They were one day out from Port Suez the evening Capitán J. P. Osbourne quietly called him out from the crew's mess where he'd been playing dominoes, saying, Sorry to bother you, Bernardo, but I'm afraid I need a button sewn onto my shirt for when we berth tomorrow. That was ominous, because the portly English capitán usually called him either Bernie or Old Bean. Capitán Osbourne led him up the switchback stairs to his quarters, stepping gingerly from the gout in his left toe and making light conversation about the button popped off his shirt: I suppose I really shouldn't drink so much beer and try to do some sit-ups, but really, what a bore! In his quarters he shut the door, said, Have a seat, would you, Bernardo? and then sat himself in the armchair on the other side of the desk while Bernardo anxiously wondered what he'd done to merit being fired with such English politeness. Capitán Osbourne told him that he'd received notification over the radio two days earlier that his wife, Clara, was in the hospital in Managua and that it was apparently serious and that he and the radio operator had agreed not to say anything until now to spare him the anguish of feeling trapped onboard with land still so far off. The company was paying for his flight from Egypt to Nicaragua. Oh yes, and a neighbor was taking care of his daughters. And then Capitán Osbourne gently said, As for that button, Old Bean, I'm afraid that wasn't only a ruse.

He notices the chill in the air somehow touching the tears in his eyes like a searing light, making them burn even hotter against his cheeks. He begins to fade into sleep with his mouth open and tilted towards the porthole, already dreaming that this invigorating air he's so hungrily gulping down is really Esteban exhaling the cool, moist air of a new love. It seems to fill the cabin with the most perplexing smell, autumnal and tropical at the same time, as if cold northern weather had suddenly descended on a port town that has been rotting in steaming weather since the beginning of time.

5

ESTEBAN HAD MADE UP HIS MIND WHILE EATING RASPADO AT THE RAIL, staring out the harbor: he'd accept the challenge of, at least, the viejo's more practical advice. He'd gone to bed feeling impatient for morning, wrapped tightly in his blanket, belching from the nervous fluttering of his stomach around a slag heap of greasy, charred rice. Turning over in bed, restless with excitement, he gulped down cold air as if to douse the oily flames rising in his esophagus. On top of everything, his nose felt runny and stuffed from the cold air; this was just how that terrible grippe and cough the month before had started, it had come on this swiftly. This is going to be one of those nights, he thought, when every minute passes like a drop of dripped water. But then his ingrained soldier's habit of answering nerves and fear with sleep took over, and he didn't even hear Bernardo come in.

When he wakes the next morning Capitán Elias is already onboard, so he can't leave. His cold is worse, and he spends the day lost in a solitary storm of impatience, applying a new coat of paint in a corner of the deck that had been too hastily painted three months before and is already flaking with rust and salt. In faraway Brooklyn, he can hear church bells tolling.

"Are you trying to dig a hole with that paintbrush?"

Esteban looks up and sees the viejo standing over him with raised eyebrows and a silly expression on his face.

"Dreams of who have you flying so low, eh, chavalo?" Bernardo winks. "Una cierta manicurista?"

Esteban glares at him with a horrified expression, shakes his head, snorts, "Puta!" and returns his attention to his work. But he feels a pang of guilty affection when he looks up again and sees Bernardo shuffling away with slumped shoulders.

By the time Capitán Elias finally leaves the ship that afternoon, Esteban has resolved never to set foot on the *Urus* again. He puts Marta's watch in his pocket and takes three dollars of the Parcheesi money from Tomaso Tostado. "Tell Panzón he can deduct it from what I'm owed."

"Where are you going?" asks Tostado.

He can't resist. "To get a haircut and a real job." And he leaves the ship without saying good-bye to anyone else.

It is already dusk when he reaches the neighborhood of the unisex salon. On every side street, golden leaves drift down through the yellowish blue air behind the glare of the streetlamps. Now a pale, full moon hangs low in an unusually clear indigo sky, over the street, over the distant harbor. It's probably an auspiciously beautiful night, he thinks, though he can't smell or taste it because of his stuffed nose and cold. And this chilly air would probably feel good too, if only he were warmly dressed. The more he ponders his strategy, the more impossible it seems, and he finds himself just walking around, evading the street the salon is on: Silly viejo, he thinks, you just can't walk in and talk someone into giving you a haircut for three dollars. He stands shivering from the cold on the avenue at the top of her street, looking down it at the light radiating over the sidewalk from the salon. The sight of that illuminated patch of sidewalk and the trash cans on the curb fills him with a confused emotion, both proprietary and foreboding.

Maybe if he just makes a sincere speech, appealing to her sense of solidarity with a potential new immigrant, she'll convince her boss to cut his hair in exchange for sweeping up in front of the salon every day. Or he'll promise to pay in full later when he has a job. He feels a tightening of his stomach just at the thought that Joaquina might step out of the salon any moment and come up this sidewalk with her determined stride of a doe trapped in big wooden shoes. Hola, he'll say. Qué tal. Here I am, just walking around, looking for a job. How's that Chucho?

He retreats down the avenue and stops in front of a tienda with flowers set out in plastic buckets on the sidewalk, some of them holding bouquets already wrapped in paper. A muchacho in a black jacket and baseball cap is sitting on a crate amidst the flowers and Esteban asks him the price of a dozen roses in Spanish without even wondering if it's the right language to use. The muchacho answers, "Ten dollars, jefe."

"Puta. How many can I get for three dollars?"

"Three."

"Give me one," he says. "A red one." One seems as meaningful as two or three, if he's just trying to make her feel well disposed towards him. The muchacho shows him the sharp red rosebud he's picked, and Esteban says, "No, that one." He points down at a big, purplish red rose drooping on the end of its stem, wet and flagrant looking as a still-beating ox heart.

"Whatever you want, maestro." The muchacho shrugs. "But this one is younger; it will start to open tomorrow and by then, yours will already be dead."

Esteban tries to find the trick in this proposal. "Bueno," he says finally with a relenting smile. "Can you wrap it in paper?"

The muchacho tears a sheet of silvery paper from a roll, spreads it on the table, and lays the budding rose on top. Then he pulls a handful of ferns from another bucket and starts arranging them around it—

"I didn't ask for those!" blurts Esteban.

"Cálmate, güey." The muchacho grins. "They're free. It makes it classier. You want a ribbon?"

"Gracias." His hand in his pocket has already peeled one dollar away from the other two and holds it ready in perspiring fingers; he wonders if he has a fever. The muchacho hands him the ribbon-tied paper cone with a single rose buried in ferns, and Esteban thanks him and pulls out the dollar.

"Good luck, maestro," says the muchacho.

He turns down the street carrying the bouquet, infuriated over his thudding heart, scolding himself. Qué te pasa, güey? He stops in front of the salon's lit-up window, the sign about the olive cat still taped inside the glass. He looks in but doesn't see Joaquina. Mierda. Where is she? His heart stops its pounding like a suddenly switched-off engine; it's as if he can feel quieted motor oil draining through his body into his boots. Maybe she's in the back. There's a man—Gonzalo, her boss, he has to be—cutting a woman's hair, tufts sprouting from clips all over her head. Gonzalo has shoulders as broad as an Olympic weight lifter's under his white sweater, a waist as thin as a schoolgirl's, and legs and nalgas so muscular they ripple and stretch his jeans while swaying back and forth to the music, a brassy salsa Esteban can hear playing inside. The back of his head is covered by flowing, wavy, black hair tied into a rough little ponytail. So, he thinks, Joaquina works in there with this cabrón, superwomanizer written all over him, eh? And what about that Chucho? Why doesn't she step out through the curtain in back? Maybe she went out to get more pastelitos. His fingers tighten around the wrapped rose and fern stems; he can feel the paper dissolving in his sweaty grip. Gonzalo steps around the woman to start in on the other side of her head and looks right at him, scissors poised in the air. The hijueputa even has emeralds for eyes! Straight, noble nose, lips ripe with self-love, no? His face reddens as Gonzalo aims his green, curious stare right at him. Suddenly he sees himself as Gonzalo must see him, pathetic and scrawny as a street orphan. He turns and walks down the sidewalk. Chocho, now what? He wishes it was still seconds ago and instead of sealing his fate by walking away he'd just stayed there waiting, or stepped through the door and asked for Joaquina. But how can he do that now without looking ridiculous? He stops and looks back up the street at the light from the salon over the sidewalk. He feels like whipping the rose against a lamppost but stops himself. Idiot, he seethes, now what are you going to do?

He'd imagined that this Gonzalo was going to be old and lethargic like most barbers, full of heavy sighs and the usual listless complaints about the world, too bored by everything but his own fantasies about olive green cats to resist his and Joaquina's arguments. That's what he'd imagined, pues. But that vain human statue with a movie star face is never going to cut his hair for free. He walks all the way around the block and then down the salon's street on the opposite sidewalk. Hurrying his steps as he draws even with the window, he looks over and sees Gonzalo still working on the woman's hair and no Joaquina. He decides to use the rose's paper wrapping to blow his stuffed nose and then decides not to.

This time he goes a long way down the avenue, until the commercial district is past and he's walking along a low wall with a darkened, hilly park, vividly shadowed from moonlight, rising behind. And then he's in another neighborhood, less lively with people and business. He turns back, and when he returns to the salon, the window is dark, the gate pulled down. He crosses the street and looks into the darkened salon through the gate and his image reflected in the glass. He takes out la Marta's watch, tilts it in his palm to catch some of the street light. It's nearly eight. He's chilly and sweaty, his head aches, and his throat is starting to feel sore. He decides, I'm not going back to the ship no matter what.

Bernardo is heating cooking oil in the bottom of the pot for the rice. The stove's butane canister ran out during the shrimp feast, eight nights ago now, but their officers haven't replaced it: ever since, they've been cooking all their meals out on deck over a wood fire, a few iron bars laid over the flames, supported by bricks. He's felt happy all day, knowing that Esteban has gone into Brooklyn again to see the manicurist, but inwardly disquieted too. He thinks, It's like two parallel disappearances, the chavalo disappearing off the ship, into life and maybe even love, into his youth, and himself left behind, disappearing into, pues, into the other. Claro, an old man can't help but be reminded of himself at a time like this.

When the oil is spitting and smoking, he bends to take the pot off the fire, holding it by rags. And just as he's turning towards José Mateo so that he can pour in the rice he feels something brush with soft static against his calf and the soft, solid thump of the cat's tail, and he turns with a breathless shout of "Desastres!" and his heels slide out on something slippery underneath and he lands sitting on the deck holding the pot tilted over his leg, the oil burning through a pant leg, through his skin, sizzling right down to the bone.

He smells burnt cloth and his own flesh frying. His whole leg is on fire but he can't feel anything or see any flames—that's the last thought he has before he passes out.

Bernardo is carried into his darkened cabin and laid out on his bed. Some of the crew try to pull off his pants, but the fabric is burnt into his flesh, it resists coming loose as if barbed right into his wounds. Finally they just yank the pants off. Cebo comes into the cabin carrying a pail filled with water. Tomaso Tostado, using the cleanest rag he can find, mops Bernardo's wounds with soap and water in the dark. The crew members take turns sitting by the bed, coming and going from the cabin, having whispered arguments over what should be done, which always end in the decision just to wait for el Capitán. The full moon outside dissolves the cabin's darkness enough so when Bernardo opens his eyes, they can see the whites murkily shining, and then they ask him if it hurts, and try to speak consoling words. They hold a cup of water to his lips. He's in shock, they think. His eyes are open but he doesn't seem to hear anything they say. He curses Desastres. Desastres? Esteban should be here—the viejo would feel better if Esteban were here.

Hours later, only Panzón is still in the cabin, dozing off on Esteban's bed. When he hears Bernardo calling to Esteban in a quiet, lucid voice, he wakes up and sees the viejo sitting up in bed in the dark.

"Chavalo," says Bernardo, whispering excitedly. "Listen! You've heard this before, haven't you? This old sea chantey?" And the viejo begins to sing in a low, rasping voice,

Quiero morir cuando decline el día
Con la cara al sol
y la mirada al cielo . . .

And when he's finished singing the song about a marinero's wish for an honorable death at sea, he cackles. "I was just remembering a story my old friend Gustavo Robles told me, muchacho, when I visited him in Panamá. We'd worked together on a few ships, over the years. Everyone used to call him El Domino because he had three moles in a slanted line on his cheek . . ."

Gustavo Robles, an able-bodied seaman, had a little daughter, his only child so far, living at home with his wife in Panama City. Claro, she was the light of his life, chavalo. Still, whenever he was home, Gustavo used to sing her the chantey about wanting to die at the end of the day with your face to the sun and sky and so on, and it always made her cry. Don't sing that song, Papi. It makes me sad, because if you die, I'll never see you again! Please don't sing that song, Papi. But men are perverse, no? He always sang it to make her cry so that he could feel how much she loved him before he went away to sea. Gustavo shipped out again, on *La Reina de Guayaquil.* The ship hit a hurricane in the Gulf of México, and some poorly battened hatch covers were swept away by waves breaking over the deck. The hold filled with water when the ship rolled, and she sank quickly, taking most of her crew down with her. They never had a chance, chavalo. Thirty-two dead! But Gustavo had managed to grab a life raft and was swept overboard holding on to it. He inflated it in the wild waves and crawled in and somehow survived the storm. He floated for days, while the sun came out to cook him alive. And he kept thinking of his daughter, and of that song. And he cursed himself: So you got your wish, hijo de la gran puta! But I don't want to die with my face to the sun and the sky! I don't want to die. No quiero! Carajo, I just want to see my daughter again! So he prayed not to God but to his daughter, promising her that if he somehow survived he'd never, ever sing that song again, and that he'd never go to sea again either. When a Pemex tanker picked him up two days later, he was delirious, raving, and still praying to his daughter.

"My daughter saved my life, she kept me alive! That's what Gustavo told me, with total conviction, chavalo, when I visited him in Panamá," says Bernardo in the dark. "And he kept his promise."

And then Panzón hears Bernardo softly chuckling to himself, and a moment later sees the viejo's silhouette sinking back down onto the bed.

And then he hears the viejo mutter, "That fucking cat."

6

ESTEBAN DECIDES TO GO INTO THE LITTLE RESTAURANT HE NOTICED THE first time he happened on this neighborhood. There's a hand-printed cardboard sign on the door saying it stays open twenty-four hours. Steam tables in the window and platters under heat lamps in glass shelves behind the counter. Three men eating at the counter, sitting with empty stools between them. A few tables, one with a young couple and a little boy seated around it. Two tourist posters from the Swiss Alps on the blue walls. A merengue is playing on a radio. He walks to the end of the counter, sits on the last stool, setting his wrapped rose down in front of him. He looks at all the dishes and prices printed with red crayon on sheets of paper taped to the wall. He can't smell anything through his nose, but he's glad to be inside someplace warm.

"Qué te puedo servir, Papi?" says the waitress, a fortyish, dark-skinned mulata with freckled cheeks and tired smudges under her liquid eyes, coarsely straight, reddish hair pulled into a braid at the back of her head. She is long limbed and slender, wearing jeans and a tight, long-sleeved navy top with white stripes, scattered white threads frayed out from the stripes.

He thinks it over a moment. "Agua," he says. "Gracias." He blows his nose in a napkin and then holds it in his hand, not sure where to dispose of it.

The waitress comes back with a glass of water, setting it down in front of him so noisily he jumps.

"Estás listo a ordernar?" It sounds like a command.

He nods. "Bueno. Un café con leche."

"Nada más?" she asks, and he nods again.

He drinks the water down in fast gulps, then stuffs the crumpled napkin inside the glass.

She brings him his coffee, and he asks how much and she says fifty centavos. She looks expressionlessly at his bouquet, the paper raggedly melting around the stems, while he wriggles his hand into his pocket to pull out the two wadded dollars and hands her one. She takes the napkin-stuffed glass away with her. He pulls another napkin from the dispenser and blows his nose again. The little bit of breathing he can manage through his nostrils now feels hot. He takes a sip of coffee, hiding the soaked napkin in his other hand. The coffee stings scratchily in his throat, warms his feverishly swarming insides. His eyeballs ache; de veras, he feels like shit. The waitress comes back with his change, two large silver coins. Fifty centavos this must add up to. Then he must have enough for three more coffees, which he's going to need if he's going to sit here all night. The waitress is still standing in front of him. He looks up at her stern yet attentive face and asks for a glass of water.

He slowly sips his coffee, and drinks down his new glass of water and puts the used napkin inside it, which eventually she clears away too. A while later, when he asks for another glass of water, she looks at him with a skeptical smile, reaches under the counter for a large plastic ashtray, sets it down in front of him, and says, "I'm not getting you a new glass of water every time you need to blow your nose, muchacho."

She comes back again with another glass of water anyway.

"That's no way to cure a grippe," she says. "Mixing hot and cold. You should be drinking tea."

"Bueno." He pulls la Marta's watch from his pocket; it's nine-thirty. He should order one hot drink every three hours. "Does it cost the same as the coffee?"

"Claro."

He says he'll have one a little later.

"Are you a mechanic?"

"No. Why?"

"Your clothes, muchacho," she says, touching her own shirt, wiping her hand down her ribs. She has long, slender fingers and fingernails painted a shade of green that looks pretty against her chocolate skin. "How else do you get so dirty?"

"I'm a marinero."

"No! De veras?" Her voice squawks with enthusiasm.

"Ajá." Seamen sure seem to be a novelty in Brooklyn, he thinks.

"One of those with a woman in every port, eh?" She presses his wrapped rose with her finger, and he grins reflexively. A customer calls to her by name, Marilú, and she says, "Qué quieres, Papito?"

Marilú goes from that customer to another and then to a group of people sitting at a table, and seemingly forgets all about him in her journey through their orders and chatter, back behind the counter and to the kitchen window, to the steam tables, back to her customers. But the light makes him happy. It's dark outside, and here he is sitting inside, in the light, and when was the last time he experienced that? He savors a yawn, and wishes a good deep yawn could last as long as a cup of coffee. He thinks that at least he should say good-bye to Bernardo and everyone else. He even feels a stab of pity for El Barbie, but then he thinks, Qué se jode, that ridiculous huevón.

The music on the radio fades and, for the first time since the night of their shipboard barbecue in July, he finds himself listening to the news. The news announcer speaks as rapidly as a Cuban; when Esteban finally understands that while he's been locked up on the *Urus* the world has changed, the announcer has moved on to the fatal shooting in Brooklyn by police of an elderly black woman who'd brandished a steak knife at them. Several of the customers explode into expletives over this last bit of news while Esteban gapes around in confusion.

Finally, when Marilú approaches again, Esteban leans forward on the counter and asks, "Oye. Are the Sandinistas still in power in Nicaragua?"

She seems almost frightened by him. "I think so." Then she repeats his question, shouting it at the men along the counter, who instantly answer with another storm of ambiguous expletives, and she looks back at Esteban and says, "Parece que sí. But not for long, eh? The way things are going. Bueno, qué sé yo?"

"Honecker resigned in the German Democratic Republic," says Esteban. "At least that's what it said on the radio. And that the days of communism in Germany are numbered, that it's total chaos and the

Soviets are doing nothing." The radio said that in Poland they were already gone, and in Czechoslovakia all but gone, and on their way out nearly everywhere else too.

"Así es, Papito," she says wearily. "Los comunistas are going. But Balaguer stays forever."

She answers his blank expression with a more explicit reference to the ancient and decrepit perpetual political boss of the Dominican Republic.

"And in Cuba?" he asks.

"Ja! That cabrón stays forever too. What, you don't get any news at sea? Here, every time you turn on the tele they're knocking over those big statues and running crazy in the streets."

"And the war in Nicaragua?" he asks, and she says, "Que vaina, muchacho, you think I work for telemundo?" But she shouts his question down the counter again and again is answered by a brief bombardment of conflicting opinions and obscure expletives, from which he's able to deduce that the peace seems to be holding.

He blows his nose again. He must sit that way for a long time, lost in thought with the napkin held over his nose and his elbows on the counter, because Marilú taps his shoulder and says, "*Ahlo?* That's the first time I've ever seen someone fall asleep in the middle of blowing his nose."

He drops his hands, sees Marilú's bemused smile.

"I'll have a tea," he says.

"Con limón?"

"Ajá. Gracias."

"You want me to put these in water?" She gestures at his bouquet. He thanks her and she picks up the cone, looks inside, and laughs. "All this for one rose? Muy elegante. Did someone give them to you, or are you the giver?"

"Neither," he says placidly.

She carefully peels back the ruined paper around the stems and stands the bouquet slantingly in a glass of water. When she brings him his tea, she asks if he's from Nicaragua. There are a few Nicas who regularly came into the restaurant, she says, including a pair of married butchers. Then she goes away to tend customers just coming in or leaving.

He's hungry, but he can hardly keep his eyes open from the pressure inside his head. He sips at his tea and wonders, Y nosotros? Are we communists? Bueno, many say we aren't and many, like my tíos, say we are. But, chocho, even in his BLI there was always some confusion about this, some said no and some said yes and many didn't give a shit. Though without their weapons and money, we wouldn't have stood a chance. Rodolfo and all the political officers must be talking and talking and talking now, trying to put the world back together, no? And here I am in Brooklyn, where I'm nothing. Do East Bloc ships still come to Corinto? Will the other ships come back? The world changes, and Capitán Elias never even mentions it. And here in this restaurant, it's a little spurt of news between music, and good for a few jokes. And la Marta lies buried. A commemorative rock planted near her house. Amalia ruined, a vegetable in the military hospital. A hundred and forty-seven compas killed on the Zompopera Road, nearly a third of his BLI. Among how many tens of thousands more? And the world changes. Like a wind that drowns out voices and when the wind stops, you don't hear the voices anymore. And I'm here, with la Marta's watch—he takes it out of his pocket. It's just past eleven.

"Papito," says Marilú. He's resting his head on folded arms now, and looks up.

"Your boat, Papito," she says. "Don't you have a boat to go to? Or somewhere?"

"Not anymore," he says. She looks worried, so he says, "I don't have to be anywhere until the morning."

She gives him a don't-lie-to-me look. "Are you really a marinero?"

"Ajá."

"OK," she says. "I mind my own business. But you're planning to sit here all night?"

He shrugs. "Más o menos." He looks at her green nails and a thought occurs to him: "Do you go to a manicurist for your nails?"

She smiles quizzically. "Cómo?"

"Your nails are pretty." He feels flustered. "I have a friend, a manicurist, just around the corner. Joaquina."

"Where does she work?"

"In that salon, El Salon Tropicana."

"Claro, Gonzalo's place. That little rubia, verdad? I've seen her. If she's the same one who comes in here with Gonzalo now and then."

"They come in here together?"

What is he, made of glass? Her laugh is a raucous blast, and then she says, "No te preocupas, amorcito. Gonzalo's not more homosexual than he already is because you can't be. That's why he was thrown out of Cuba with all the Marielitos, tu sabes? They just came to his door one day and told him he had to go. A dancer at La Tropicana, and they still made him leave. Him and as many of los*gays* as they could get their hands on. Caráy, que bárbaro."

Now Esteban remembers the framed photograph on the wall of the salon: the strong man in a leopard-skin tunic holding a woman over his head is Gonzalo. So, the stud is a pato—

Suddenly Marilú's eyes widen. "Don't tell me this is a get-lost rose. Ay no, pero que dramática!"

He laughs. "It's nothing like that. No sé, I wanted a haircut . . ."

"Ajá?"

"Bueno, I went by, and she wasn't there."

"Maybe she doesn't work on Sundays, muchacho."

"Ah, sí pues . . . I'll have another tea."

He feels almost wide awake now. For a long time the restaurant stays empty, and he and Marilú sit at the counter. Despite his cold and her scolding, she even shares her cigarettes with him, and when he's finished telling her the story of the *Urus,* she immediately gets up and brings him a bowl of rice and red beans and two pieces of chicken and a cola. Marilú tells him about her life too: she lives with her three children and sister on Smith Street, a street he knows from his nocturnal prowling; her husband left her for a boricua and is living with her in another neighborhood that's mostly Dominican; he works as a doorman. This neighborhood is mainly Mexican now, but it has people from all over Latin America. It's true, you can live in Nueva York, says Marilú, and never have to speak English to anyone but telephone operators and bill collectors. Later two men come out from the kitchen, Melgar and Juvenal, the former the cook, from Barranquilla, Colombia, the other an Indian-featured dishwasher from Ecuador. Marilú says she doesn't have enough room in her apartment to offer him more than a few chair cushions on the floor to sleep on, but he's welcome to it in an emergency, and she writes her telephone number and address down on a napkin for him, and Juvenal does the same. Melgar says there isn't a phone where he lives, nor even any spare cushions, but he can have a piece of the floor should he find himself in need.

He falls asleep with his head in his arms at a table, and when he stirs and wakes later, the restaurant is empty, Marilú has gone home, and the cook is sitting at the counter, staring out at the avenue and smoking. He looks at his watch, it's twenty-three past four. His throat aches. He feels heavy with sorrow; it must have something to do with whatever he's dreamed, but he can't remember any of it. He lowers his head to the table again. The communists are going, he thinks, and la Marta is gone forever. She's gone. It's too horrible to think about where she's gone, and suddenly he feels his whole body stiffen and cringe as it always does when the Zompopera Road comes back like a sudden bout of clairvoyant madness: remembering drowsing in the back of the truck one second and the next machine-gun fire tearing into the truck's cab like rocket-propelled sledgehammers and the truck rocking and wooden planks in back rattling and splintering in the firestorm of tracer bullets coming out of the darkness on both sides of the road, the screams and shrieks of compas around him and all up and down the road; all up and down the road that resounding leaden rain of metal tearing open metal and explosions and flames and voices calling from the darkness taunting them with death to all piri comunista hijueputas. Crouching near the back of the burning cab aiming his fire back at death through planks, the AK jumping and shell casings tumbling around him and jamming in another clip and firing wildly into the dark and a shattered plank smashing him in the face, knocking him back and stunning him and he was sure that his life was flowing out through his face. And he lay there on top of someone who was wet for seconds that passed like hours, clutching a wrist that turned out to be not his own until he felt someone pulling him back up and he was still holding his AK and he saw Rigoberto Mazariego's novia's doll's red hair, and following this small torch he crawled over the bodies in the truck with his nostrils and face full of blood and he fell and felt his teeth gnashing against wet hair on the back of someone's head; and then he spilled down onto the road and rolled behind the tires softly hissing air and seconds or hours later followed Rigoberto Mazariego's howl and his novia's doll out from behind the truck, sprinting straight ahead into the dark, began the long night of holding off the enemy until the helicopters and reinforcements came. In the morning they saw the long line of East German IFA trucks haphazardly skidded to stops up and down the road and off of it, the green steel of the cab hoods and doors ripped apart as if by the iron claws and beaks of giant iron birds of prey, bullet holes glinting like small stars cut from tin, shell casings spread thickly on the ground around splattered tires. And they heard the moaning and weeping of the wounded and saw uniformed bodies sprawled over the rears of the trucks and on the ground amidst wet gore and drying pools of blood and insects everywhere and some started firing off their remaining rounds at the vultures, and then he saw the truck that had been carrying the compitas in the quartermaster corps . . .

He sits slumped with his head in his arms for a long time, staring blankly, breathing through his mouth. He must have drifted back to sleep, because when he looks up again the light outside is gray and there are a few customers at the counter and a new waitress and his wrapped rose has been moved to his table, still propped inside the glass of greening water. The new waitress brings him a cup of café con leche, gives him a pat on the shoulder, and tells him that he's been snoring. He blows his nose and drinks the coffee, thanks her, thanks everyone though there's nobody there now from the night before, picks up his rose, and goes out the door into the chilly air.

7

WHEN BERNARDO HEARS CAPITÁN J. P. OSBOURNE APOLOGETICALLY speaking his name as if he's about to say he's sorry to bother him but he just needs this button sewn again, he thinks it's just one more of his nightlong hauntings. But then he opens his eyes from the bottom of his well of pain and meets Capitán Elias's sad sheep eyes. El Capitán is squatting by the mattress, wearing an unzipped black leather jacket, a hand on each black-jeaned knee. He lifts a hand and places it on Bernardo's forehead, holds it there awhile, his hand feels like a cold sponge. He takes Bernardo's wrists in his hands, puts his fingers over his pulse.

Bernardo is lying on top of the mattress with the blanket flung off him, naked from the waist down, shivering with cold.

Capitán Elias gestures with a nod of his head towards the leg. "That's a nasty burn," he says. "Nastier than it looks, I'm sure. You're probably still in shock, a little bit."

Bernardo grunts, forces himself up on his elbows, and takes his first look at the leg in the light; his shin looks splattered with wet, pink blisters, some of them fringed with blackened shreds of cloth. His head feels heavy. He lies back down.

". . . Bernardo?" He opens his eyes and sees Capitán Elias still kneeling beside him, slowly rubbing the side of his close-shaven head with his hand while staring across the bed at the three dusty, plastic-wrapped snapshots arrayed along the floor. El Capitán says, "Bernardo?" again, looks at him, and realizes.

"I have medical training," he says, along with something else which Bernardo doesn't grasp, complicated words and something about plants. ". . . That's what I used to do. Before I decided that my heart was really with the sea and ships."

"I'm glad to hear that," says Bernardo, surprised at his own angry tone. "But it's just a burn. Shouldn't we have first aid equipment onboard?"

"But we do," el Capitán says, and he taps a greenish metal box on the floor by his side. "It was up on the bridge. Of course, you're right, it should have been where you could get at it. We've had such complex problems, I guess we often overlook the obvious things."

Now el Capitán slides down the mattress and with one finger lightly touches one of the liquid wounds.

"Does that hurt?"

"I didn't feel anything. But the pain seems to come from the whole leg."

"I'm going to ask you a few standard questions, Bernardo. They may sound a little odd to you, but it's an important part of the homeopathic method."

"Bueno," says Bernardo listlessly.

He feels Capitán Elias shaking him awake again.

"Have you been having any unusual food cravings?"

"Cómo?"

"Before the accident and since?"

"Eh?"

El Capitán smiles wanly. "Is there any one food you can't stop thinking about because you want it so much? Or is there any food that, whenever you think of it, disgusts you?"

Cool leche agria, with a little salt. A whole pitcher of pitaya juice. Ice cream. A big, steaming bowl of mondongo—no.

"Those little blue berries, what are they called?"

"Bueno, blueberries."

"They're cool and wet and sweet in your mouth, and that would be good now. As for the other thing, I could easily never eat another sardine."

"Is there any time of day during which you usually feel especially happy or melancholy?" el Capitán asks expressionlessly, squatting on his heels.

"Melancholy in the evenings, Capitán. Like most people, no?"

"And where do you feel happiest, in the mountains or by the sea?"

"I've never actually been up in the mountains. I've seen them many times, of course, on horizons, along certain coasts."

"I guess that's the wrong question to ask an old lobo de mar like yourself. Your element is definitely water."

"Maybe it would make me happy to be in the mountains, but I doubt it."

"Bernardo?"

He opens his eyes again.

"Are you afraid of death?" asks Capitán Elias. "What I mean is, when you find yourself thinking of death, do you feel afraid?"

Fear and sadness grip his heart at these words.

"Afraid? No tanto. But a man my age, claro, he thinks about it."

"Angry towards death?"

Right now I'm angrier at that hija de la gran puta cat.

"It would make me angry never to see my daughters again."

"You'll be seeing them very soon, I'm sure." For a moment Capitán Elias looks as if he's contemplating his face without really seeing him. Then he glances across the bed and, propping himself with one hand on the mattress, he pushes himself up, over, and across Bernardo to pluck one of the plastic-wrapped photographs; he pushes himself back into his squat with a grunt and looks at the picture, and then hands it to Bernardo. "Your daughters."

"Sí pues." Bernardo looks at his daughters and grandson through the fogged plastic, gathered on the little front porch.

"You're a lucky man. I'm going to be a father soon too."

Suddenly Capitán Elias's long, black-clad body is spanning him again; back again, he studies Esmeralda the beauty queen through plastic.

El Capitán smiles slightly. "An old love?"

"No, another daughter," says Bernardo, surprised again by his own angry tone.

"Muy bonita."

"The other picture. That's Clara, my wife, the mother of my daughters."

"Ah." El Capitán reaches across the bed again, and then he's looking at blurred Clarita and Bernardo standing in front of the *Mitzi* in Veracruz; he glances at Esmeralda in his other hand with a briefly puzzled expression. "Lovely," he says. "You look very happy."

Bernardo lifts his hand from his belly to hold out the picture of his daughters. It takes a few seconds for el Capitán to react, but then he takes the picture from him, and this time pushes himself up onto his feet and walks to the other side of the bed, where he sets the three snapshots back more or less as they were.

El Capitán stands over him, looking around the cabin, at Esteban's empty bed, at the two open suitcases filled with neatly folded, tattered, filth-darkened clothes at the foot of each mattress. And then he's scrutinizing him again.

"You're an *Arsenicum* type, I think," he finally says.

"Cómo?"

"I can't be sure, but I think I know you well enough to say that." El Capitán smiles. "An *Arsenicum* is the type of person who decides to commit suicide by putting his head in the oven, because that seems the least messy way of doing it. But when he sticks his head in, he sees that the oven needs cleaning. And while he's cleaning it, he forgets all about committing suicide."

"Sí pues . . . It's just a burn, no?"

And then el Capitán squats by the bed again and rummages through the metal box.

"Just a burn, of course. It's not a complex case. But I'm going to mix a constitutional treatment with a fundamental one just to be sure. Have you been drinking much coffee?"

They haven't had coffee in weeks. "None," says Bernardo.

"Good, because coffee interferes with the effectiveness of these medicines," says el Capitán, moving down the bed to Bernardo's leg again, pulling the metal box after him. "You really shouldn't have any until you're healed. Let's try to clean you up a little."

With tweezers, el Capitán plucks at the bits of cloth scorched into his leg.

"Feel anything?" he asks.

"Nada."

El Capitán sprays his leg with water from a plastic water bottle and dabs his numb wounds with cotton balls.

"This is going to sting," he says.

El Capitán is soaking cotton balls with liquid from another bottle and dabbing his wounds again, but he feels nothing, but then in that spot he does, fiery needles of pain that suddenly explode through his leg—

"I'll be back in an hour or two," he hears el Capitán saying through a roaring bonfire.

When he opens his eyes again, Tomaso Tostado is cleaning up the litter of cotton balls by Bernardo's mattress. Standing inside the doorway Panzón says, "El Capitán says he's a— A licensed qué?"

"A master herbalist," says Tomaso. "And something called a—no sé. Un médico homeopático. No?"

"Así dijo"—Bernardo turns his head towards the voice and sees José Mateo looking up from the picture of Esme in his hand. José Mateo says, "El Buzo, that cabrón, told el Capi that it sounded like witch stuff to him, told him to just take you to the hospital instead. And el Capi said no, this is the medicine the king and queen of England use. It's the new medicine, the most modern. Better than or just as good as what they'd give you in the hospital. Isn't that what he said?"

"Sí pues," says Panzón. "Your whole body is a vibration. Qué sé yo?"

"A vital force," says Tomaso Tostado.

"It's just a burn," says Bernardo. "Put that picture back."

"Sí pues, compadre," says José Mateo. "He knows what he's doing. Puta, it's not surgery."

"Qué loco, ese capitán, no?" says Panzón.

"But he's educated," says Tomaso Tostado.

"What was that story about the rat?"

"With this kind of medicine," says Tomaso, "to cure a burn, you give a medicine that burns a little less, and then the body knows what to do. Like cures like, that's what he said. Scientists gave this medicine to a rat and put it on the stove and it could stay there without burning up and the other rats that didn't have it couldn't."

Bernardo grunts. "He was going on about putting my head in an oven."

"So you're telling me, to cure a burn, he's going to have to burn Bernardo?" says Panzón.

And then Capitán Elias is waking him up again. Now only el Capitán and Tomaso Tostado are in the cabin.

El Capitán is holding a red plastic jug with a white cap, smaller than the jug he brought the medicine in when they were all sick from drinking rat water. He's explaining to Tomaso Tostado that Bernardo has to drink some every half hour.

"It's a combination of cantharis and arnica, diluted," says el Capitán. "You might know it as Spanish fly and leopard's-bane."

El Capitán pours some into the plastic cap. Bernardo takes a drink; it tastes like rust-silted water. There's something else for them to wash his burns with, a tincture, it's called, made from calendula and Saint-John's-wort. And gauzy bandages to lay over his leg.

Just before leaving the cabin, Capitán Elias says, "Try to think of happy things, Bernardo, it helps the healing process."

"Gracias, Capitán," says Bernardo. "I feel a little better."

"This medicine works fast. The *Urus*'s segundo oficial will be back on his feet in a few days, eh, güey?" Then el Capitán frowns, as if chagrined with himself over that tasteless remark. He lingers a moment, his hands thrust deep in his pockets. "Don't forget, Bernardo," he finally says, forcing a smile. "It's impious for a good man to be sad."

And Capitán Elias leaves the cabin. Bernardo never sees el Capitán again.

8

ESTEBAN HAS ALREADY CARRIED THE BEER BOTTLES FROM THE SALON doorway to the trash cans and kicked cigarette butts all the way over to the curb when, after he's been standing there nearly three hours, he finally sees la Joaquina coming down the sidewalk in her coat, with her limber, scuffing, shoes-too-big gait. Her tights are black. When she notices him waiting, her eyes widen into dark disks and she briefly stops, but she doesn't smile. She's already holding her keys when she reaches him. He watches her eyes glide from the bouquet in his hand and, suspiciously, up to his face.

"Buen día, Joaquina," he says, so out of breath and with his head so clogged he can barely hear his own voice.

"El marinero," she says, in her deep-toned voice. "Esteban, no? Qué paso?"

"Joaquina . . ." Her controlled, almost subdued manner, confuses him. She seems an opposite person from the volatile tyrant he met the other day. He says there's something he wants to talk to her about.

"Bueno. De qué?" Her mild interest dismays him.

"I cleaned up around the door," he says nervously. "I'll mop it if you want."

"Oiga, güey, you're not trying to take my job, are you? There's more to it than that, you know." She smiles.

He's so relieved to see her personality flaring back that he blurts, "I know that. You'd have to pay me a million dollars to get me to hold hands with that Chucho." He cringes inside over having betrayed himself.

But she laughs and puts the key in the door. "And how much would you charge to do his feet?"

He thinks, Chucho gets his toenails done? But he doesn't let himself say anything about it and follows Joaquina into the salon and says,

"I brought you this," holding out the bouquet so that when she turns around she only has to reach up her hands to take it. She says, "Ay, Esteban, por qué?" looks down into the cone at the single rose, smiles thinly, and thanks him. She turns and walks swiftly to the back of the salon to turn on the lights. Then she steps through the curtain, and he hears water running, briefly, but when she comes out she isn't carrying anything. She's wearing a smocklike, velvety crimson dress with two rows of brass buttons down the front, and a black ribbon falling from the collar. She starts making the coffee.

He sits in a chair against the wall looking at himself in the mirrors and then at Gonzalo dressed like Pedro Picapiedra holding the woman dancer over his head. He feels drugged from his cold and sleeplessness, his skin caked with dried perspiration and grime. He's furious at himself for having brought her the rose, and then he's furious at Bernardo for having heated up his head with his preposterous notions. Joaquina is embarrassed that he's there. Pues, who wouldn't be? But then he remembers how kindly Marilú treated him, and he resents Joaquina for misinterpreting the gesture of the flower.

Joaquina brings him a cup of coffee and sits with a chair between them sipping hers, her legs straight out and her feet apart just like the last time. She asks him what it is he wants to talk about.

"I've decided to leave the ship," he says, and waits for her to finish her yawn. She drops the back of her hand from her mouth and looks at him.

"Perdón," she says with a sleepy smile. "Entonces?"

He notices that her earrings are different today. Instead of tiny glass stars, these are tiny glass triangles, yellow.

"I've left—"

"I told you you were going to catch a cold going around like that, didn't I?" And she gets to her feet and quickly crosses the salon and comes back with a box of tissues, setting it down on the chair between them. "Güey, you have to take better care of yourself."

He repeats that he's decided to leave the ship, and she nods, and he says, "I was wondering if there was anything I could do, maybe clean up the doorway, and here inside too, for as many days as you want, in exchange for a haircut."

She seems to be giving his proposal serious thought. "We'll have to ask Gonzalo," she finally says. "He should be here any minute."

And they sit in absolute silence until finally she asks if he'd like some aspirin. She goes in back again and comes out with a glass of water and two aspirin.

When he can't stand the silence anymore he almost asks if that's Gonzalo in that photograph, dressed like the cartoon caveman, but he realizes that could expose what he did and learned about Gonzalo last night, and with a surge of embarrassed apprehension, he realizes that Gonzalo might recognize *him*.

"Do men really get their toes painted?" he finally asks.

"Some," she says. "But not Chucho." And then she looks directly at him and says, "Por qué, güey? You think there's something wrong with men having pedicures?"

"No," he says. Though of course he does. "I'd never do it."

"Some men like it." And she smiles strangely, as if that puzzles even her. "My novio likes it when I do his feet, but I guess that's different. He doesn't put any polish on, claro, but for anyone it feels nice to have your feet pampered, no? Nails trimmed, cuticles cut away, your feet scrubbed y todo."

"You have a novio?" Ve? It doesn't bother him. She isn't his type anyway, a manicurist. A chica plástica, hair dyed, probably fake curls too—

"Bueno . . . Sí," she says. "But he's in México, in the D.F. He's a lawyer."

His heart leaps at the hint of hesitation in her voice.

A moment later Joaquina says, "There's a nightmare I've been having for years. A fat man in a business suit comes in for a manicure, and I say, Take a seat, momentito. And when I come back out he's sitting there, but he's taken his shoes and socks off. And he has horrible, dirty, smelly, hairy feet. I say, Ah, you want your feet done too? And he looks at me and says, No." She pauses. "Then I always wake up."

When Gonzalo comes in, he's wearing a long, black wool coat, a newspaper folded under his arm; he stands inside the door pulling off a leather glove and then pauses in the middle of taking off the other to look down at Esteban with a delighted grin.

"This is the marinero I told you about," says Joaquina, with a disconcerted expression. "Esteban."

Gonzalo finishes pulling off his glove, as if only to free his index finger so that he can dangle and circle it while he says, "He went around the block at least twice, and kept looking in the window, holding flowers. At first I thought it was someone sending *me* flowers." And he laughs, showing perfect white teeth, his emerald eyes and ruddy cheeks radiating good humor. Then he says, "Coño, qué genial! You know, later, going home on the subway, still trying to solve the mystery of this wild boy too shy to deliver his flowers, it suddenly occurred to me that you might have been that shipwrecked sailor Joaquina told me about."

Esteban sits rigid in his seat, frantic with humiliation, his face hot as red steel.

"It was Joaquina's day off. You should have come in anyway." But the cheerfulness drops out of his voice when he looks back at Joaquina. "Oye, niña, don't get angry. I was just—"

Esteban glances over and sees that Joaquina's eyes are stormy pools again, seething furiously at Gonzalo just as they had at him the morning they met.

"You just can't control your mouth, Gonzalo, not ever! Bocón!"

"Bocón? Yo? Look who says so!"

She gets up and walks through the curtain in back, and when she comes out she's carrying a skinny vase holding the rose and ferns. She slams it down on the counter with so much force Esteban is surprised it doesn't break.

"Elegante," says Gonzalo.

"Sí pues," she says. "And he brought it for me, not you, güey. Órale?"

"Claro," he says. "OK." He smiles furtively at Esteban, and then looks at Joaquina again. "Did you have a good day off?"

Joaquina is still glowering at him while she nervously fidgets with her hair, winding and unwinding one golden curl around her finger. "Ajá," she says.

"You went on one of your shopping trips, no?"

"Y qué?"

"You bought another colander, no? Or a tea strainer or something like that?" He looks like he's trying to hold in his laughter.

"Don't start," she says.

"This is one of the most eccentric women in the whole world," he says to Esteban. "Any kitchen thing with holes in it, she has to have it. What do you think a psychologist would say about that? She doesn't even cook!"

"Ay no. Tus obsesiones!"

"Mis obsesiones? I don't collect colanders and strainers!"

"It's not an obsession, it's a collection! I like colanders. But it's your obsession that I like them! I'm not obsessed with *anything* you do, güey." She covers her eyes with her hand. "No, I just can't take this man. Chiiín."

And Gonzalo chuckles richly again, and takes off his coat, and carries it into the back. He's dressed the same as the day before, only now his sweater is gray, and close up he seems even more herculean and graceful.

Joaquina sits in the chair next to Esteban, who must look as if he's in a state of shock, because she speaks in such a grave and soothing tone: "Esteban, I'm sorry if Gonzalo embarrassed you. He's completely insensitive."

"Embarrassed me? No. Claro que no."

She giggles. "You kept going around the block?"

He sighs. "No sé," he says. "I didn't have anyplace to go."

When Gonzalo comes out he pours himself a cup of coffee and then sits down on the other side of Esteban.

"Joaquina and I," he says cheerfully, "we're like a bad marriage. We despise each other, but we would wander the streets howling in grief and tearing out our hair should either of us ever leave the other."

"You wish, güey," she says. "You used to say that about Dolores."

"That was our cat," he says to Esteban. "We hired her to conquer our mice, and one day she went out that door and has never returned. Maybe she went to work for somebody willing to pay her more. Or maybe la migra got her."

"Oiga, Gonzalo, Esteban needs a haircut," says Joaquina bluntly. "But he doesn't have any money." And she explains his situation and his offer to mop the doorway and sweep out the salon until he's paid it back, though she doesn't think Esteban should mop outside until he's over his cold.

"But that's your job," says Gonzalo when she's done. "That's part of what I pay you to do." And then he collapses into laughter over Joaquina's stricken expression and stands up and says it's fine with him. "Wash his hair," he says to Joaquina. "And check for lice. No offense, Esteban."

Joaquina had grown up in a tiny poblado near a lightly traveled highway at the desertlike edge of the Western Sierra Madre, in the Mexican heartland state of Zacatecas. Her father worked as an auto mechanic out of a junk-filled one-room workshop right on the highway, depending mainly on the occasional nearby breakdown or blown-out tire for business. Their poblado was so remote that Joaquina and her siblings—there were eight, five brothers—had no way of getting to and from school unless her father drove them in his ancient car. Often the car broke down—despite her father's occupation, none of the car's doors opened from the outside and only one could be opened from the inside—and Joaquina and her siblings would find themselves stranded, having to disperse among various homes in the poblado the school was in to sleep. Joaquina's mother was an austere rural woman with no room in her life for any feminine luxuries whatsoever. So Joaquina had never even seen a nail file until she was seven, when her tía Hermalina came all the way from the Distrito Federal to visit her brother and his family. Joaquina was transfixed by her tía's shapely, lustrously polished red nails, and by the way she would sit idly filing them while ignoring almost everything else around her, eating up the hours of a visit she seemed to find interminable. Joaquina coveted the nail file as the magical object it actually was to her, and sat in the school yard filing her own nails with a Popsicle stick in imitation. Right before Tía Hermalina was leaving to go back to the city, Joaquina stealthily opened her purse and stole the file. It was one of those old-fashioned metal nail files. But nail polish remained a mystery. She tried the colored Chinese paper at school, wetting and rubbing it against her fingernails to see if any would come off. She tried crayons. Once, when she'd walked down to her father's workshop, she discovered that he had some paint for touching up cars that looked as glossy as nail polish even when it dried. When her father caught her dabbing her nails with the paint, he hid his paint cans somewhere amidst the clutter of the workshop, and she never found them again no matter how thoroughly she searched when he wasn't there. Meanwhile Joaquina was already filing everyone's nails with the durable metal file—her schoolmates' nails, her mother's, sisters', even her younger brothers' and their few neighbors'—until there wasn't a woman or girl in sight without perpetually shapely, unpainted talons. She didn't get to wear real nail polish until, two years later, she was sent to visit Tía Hermalina in the biggest, most polluted city on earth. (Also, in Joaquina's opinion, the craziest, the most surreal, the most full of music, the saddest, the most fun.) When she was fifteen she finally realized her dream of going to live there with her tía, and enrolled in beauticians' school. She was indifferent towards the courses in hair-styling. Really, it seemed her special destiny to become a manicurist . . .

Some of this Esteban learns while sitting in a padded chair with his head over the sink in back, behind the curtain, wearing a blue cotton apron, while Joaquina washes his hair; and some of it he'll learn later. Joaquina keeps her own nails short for her work, and prefers painting them in what she calls the French style, with a clear, glossy polish, sliver-thin white stripes along the tops. She does them herself, of course. Before she'd started shampooing him, she'd held out her hands so that he could see her nails, and then she'd pulled on a pair of translucent rubber gloves. Here at the salon Joaquina has to do all kinds of things besides manicures and pedicures, everything from leg waxing to running errands for Gonzalo. But she can't get a job in a nail parlor—one of those places always up-to-date on every new fashion and breakthrough in the science and art of beautifying hands and feet, and where she's heard they give you the title "nail technician" instead of manicurist—while she's illegal and speaks so little English. So many of the new nail parlors are Coreano anyway, owned and staffed completely by Coreanos. She likes to stand outside those nail parlors sometimes, watching through the window. But Gonzalo is an honest and fair boss, muy padre, they have fun together most of the time.

Esteban's hair is so dirty and tangled she decides that it needs three washings. But he doesn't have lice, she announces cheerfully. The feminine fragrance of the shampoo she's using is so strong he thinks he must be smelling it through his eyeballs, since his nose is too blocked to absorb anything. On the floor, against the wall, he sees a white enamel pot full of clean, yellowish brown wax, free of hair, and he feels a moment of sad wonder over being able to identify this substance, which la Marta first described for him as leg wax. In the middle of the second washing Joaquina pulls off her rubber gloves and he feels her fingertips sliding through his hair, massaging him until his entire scalp is full of exploding stars, their pleasant itchiness traveling down his spine and making him shudder. He opens his eyes and tilts his head back even farther so that he can see her, looking up past her chapped lips and nostrils at the faraway expression in her eyes.

"Why did Chucho need a manicure so early in the morning?"

"He gives cooking classes on television. Canal Sixty-seven, something like that, it's in Nueva Jersey. But I've never seen it."

"Does your novio visit you?"

"He's coming soon." Her fingers stop moving in his hair—it's as if she's about to say something earthshaking, but then she starts up again. A thought comes to him unbidden: he doesn't care who Joaquina's novio is, or if her novio really is visiting soon or not, because eventually he and Joaquina are going to be together no matter what. Chocho, he whispers silently to himself: He wonders if that was just his pride speaking, or if he's too soothed by this comfortable chair and the visceral pleasure of being shampooed by her to worry about a rival. Let the lawyer come.

He shuts his eyes and settles into himself to better enjoy the massaging of his scalp, and concentrates on trying to use the power of thought to tell her fingertips about his new resolve.

He feels himself being shaken awake to the sound of her voice: "Marinero. Despiértate."

He grins dumbly at Joaquina, feeling surprised to find himself here and not in his cabin waking up next to Bernardo.

"Were you just snoring because of your cold?" she asks. "Or do you always snore?"

"Because of my cold," he says, though he isn't sure.

She isn't washing his hair anymore. She sits on a stool beside him, letting the conditioner work into his hair.

"That happened to me the other day in the middle of a pedicure," she says. "You know how it is, the women who come in, they talk, talk, talk, and talk. And some of them have voices, I don't what it is, it's like they hypnotize you. You feel yourself nodding off and nodding off and trying to keep your eyes open and taking drinks from a coke to stay awake and worrying about your hand slipping and cutting their skin. Pues, the other day? It happened, güey. There I was, chin down on my chest, fast asleep, I even dropped the tijeritas onto the floor. But you know how she woke me? With her big toe. Chiiín, she put it on my nose and gave a little push and stood up making a coraje. But I got angry too. Her toe on my nose? I sent her to la chingada, güey."

She rinses his hair. He follows her out through the curtain wearing a towel turbaned over his head. Gonzalo is already at work on another woman's hair. And there's a heavyset, Spanish-speaking moreno man in a black-and-white pin-striped suit with a red vest waiting for a manicure. How come every time he's here, only men come in for manicures? And why are the men who come for manicures always so burly?

Joaquina stands looking at Gonzalo's back, twisting a curl on top of her head around her finger again. Esteban smiles to himself, recognizing the gesture as her anxiety's signature.

"Gonzalo," she says. "Esteban can't sit here with wet hair, not with the cold he has."

"Then put him under the dryer," says Gonzalo. "What were you two doing back there that took so long? No. I don't want to know. I have one appointment after another now."

It isn't until six-thirty in the evening that Esteban is finally summoned to Gonzalo's barber's chair. By then the light outside is murky gray and sad under the street lighting, and a steady parade of people headed home from work are passing by the salon's window, wisps of vaporized breath around their mouths. Esteban has spent most of the day feeling forgotten by both Gonzalo and Joaquina: they've tended to one customer after another until both seemed as drained of their usual humor and emotion as outside is now of midday's autumn sunshine. Esteban has already begun to learn some of the lyrics of the more popular songs played over the radio on the Spanish-language station. He's listened to more snatches of news about the changes in the world without having anyone to share his astonishment with. He's read through every page of Gonzalo's Spanish-language New York newspaper, and the international page and the section called "Nuestros Países" several times: in the latter he learned that the wars in El Salvador and Guatemala continue, but there's no news at all of Nicaragua in the paper that day, which gave him the eerie sensation again that everything and everyone he used to know have disappeared forever while he's been stuck on the *Urus*. Yet his horoscope advised him it was a good day for patching up relations with estranged relatives and old loves. He's leafed through half a dozen back issues of *Vanidades* and *Hola,* catching up on the real-life love dramas of telenovela stars and other apparently famous people, few of whom he's ever heard of. He's used up a whole box of tissues and spent hours fighting off sleep, sitting there in a soporific stupor, building and rebuilding scaffoldings of air in his eyes to hold them open so that he can watch Joaquina bent over customer's hands and feet, working like a meticulous surgeon. He's fascinated by the variety and delicateness of the instruments she uses—she seems to have almost as many tools at her disposal as they have on the *Urus,* all in miniature—and by the aura of fastidious concentration and stillness that envelops her, whether she's snipping at cuticles, or filing, or sanding with a little pumice stone, or applying lotions, or using a hand towel to dry feet lifted from a bowl of hot water, or massaging, or painting nails, or squeezing glue from a tiny tube to attach synthetic nails, then having the women put their fingers and new nails inside a little machine whose coils glow purple. Most of her customers are women after all, and they do tend to talk so much that Joaquina has seemed transformed into someone who hardly ever opens her mouth. Esteban has eavesdropped on all kinds of amorous, familial, and neighborhood gossip. A woman with a droning voice and feathery lisp soon had both him and Joaquina nodding off towards sleep in unison.

At lunchtime Gonzalo had opened the drawer in which he keeps the money and given Joaquina a twenty-dollar bill, telling her to go for sandwiches and to stop in quickly at the Salvation Army store to buy Esteban a sweater and whatever else with the change left over. In the grocery store Esteban ordered a ham and cheese sandwich like Gonzalo's, and Joaquina bought herself a plastic-wrapped cardboard tray of raw chícharos. That was her lunch; she said it was one of her favorite foods. Outside on the sidewalk she peeled back the wrapping and began popping raw, green chícharos into her mouth one at a time.

"Híjue," he said. "You eat like a pavo real."

"It's funny you say that," she said. "Because in English these are called *green peas.* And that bird is called a *peacock.* See how clever you are?"

She told him she studies English two nights a week at a church in the neighborhood and that the lessons are free, and that he should sign up too.

"And you live around here?"

"Not far."

Then she led him into the Salvation Army store, up a narrow flight of stairs into a room with ill-sorted secondhand clothing spread out on long tables, crammed into boxes, hung on racks. When she saw the look of disappointment on his face she said that she only liked new clothes too, and apologized for taking him to this place. But the little money they had would go further here than even at the most inexpensive stores along the avenue. But he said he was just surprised, not disappointed, because he couldn't remember ever having been in a real clothing store before. In Corinto he'd always bought contraband clothing in the market, or directly from thieves' middlemen like his tíos, all of it brand new, fresh from ships' cargo holds or smuggled across borders. He tried on at least a dozen sweaters and didn't even have a chance to see himself in the mirror until she'd chosen the one she wanted. It was a thick, green wool sweater with a black stripe around the collar, only slightly fraying at the ends of the sleeves and hem, and it smelled pleasantly of old mothballs and boiled milk.

"Chamaco, sabes qué?" she said while he stood looking at himself in the mirror, glowing with gratitude but still thinking that he looked as if he'd been raised by wolves. "I like you with your hair long, now that it's so clean." She reached up and briskly smoothed hair out of his face, and combed it out with her fingers. "A trim, maybe, is all you need. And, claro, a shave."

"I want a haircut. This hair has been unlucky. Bueno, vos, until the other day, because that's when I met you."

"Ay no, qué cursi!" But she smiled, shyly he thought, and even blushed a bit, and then turned her attention to a rack of dresses, rapidly thumbing through them with her back to him. And he knew his comment, even if it *was* corny, had hit its mark, awakening her to his sudden existence in her life in a way that so far nothing else had, not even the rose.

There was enough money left over for a red T-shirt without any advertising on it and a pair of thick socks. He kept his new sweater on for the walk back to the salon, during which he kept looking for himself and Joaquina reflected together in the windows of the stores they passed, though all he saw were fleeting, translucent shadows barely denting the midday glare. Joaquina was eating peas again, telling him about how she'd been setting money aside for a José José concert in Manhattan, in a huge arena there, it wasn't going to happen for another six weeks, but just the other day she'd been shattered to learn it was already sold out. Her friend Rebecca had two tickets, but she was going to invite some galán, that traitor. He felt flushed with pleasure over how natural it suddenly felt and must have looked to others, he and Joaquina on the sidewalk together, she so absorbed in eating peas and telling her story and walking so close to him that he felt the constant pressure of her shoulder tucked against his biceps, shifting without breaking contact whenever she brought another pea up to her mouth. Yet he sensed that if he were to call her attention to this proof of what seemed an instinctual intimacy between them, or try to press it further by putting his hand on her back or by turning his head to lower his nose into the golden clover of her hair, which he was dying to do, she'd instantly pull away. Love hasn't caught up to us yet, he thought, but it's following a trail of dropped peas down the sidewalk. He wanted to impress her with another clever remark but couldn't think of a way to make this one sound less presumptuous or more believable. She'd only dropped a few peas anyway, and every time she did, she said, "Chiiín," or "Mierda."

When Esteban is finally seated in the barber's chair, he profusely thanks Gonzalo for the haircut and promises to pay him back as soon as he can for the clothes and the sandwich.

"Coño, don't even think of it," says Gonzalo. "We refugees from the communist countries have to look out for each other, no?"

He feels his face turning hot again. He doesn't know what to say, but he knows he has to say something if he doesn't want to end up losing himself in the maze of a prolonged lie. Gonzalo is fastening a scratchy paper collar around his neck.

"The truth is I'm a refugee from a ship," says Esteban.

Joaquina is standing beside them, sipping at a can of coke through a straw and watching in the mirror.

"Pues, sí," says Gonzalo. "But you're from Nicaragua and I'm from Cuba. *Same boat,* as they say here, no?" Gonzalo is misting his hair with water from a plastic bottle. "The same rapidly sinking boat, I hope. Why did you leave? Did they want to take you and put you in that horrible war?"

"I *was* in the war," he says. Joaquina looks up from her can of coke in the mirror. "In el Ejército Popular Sandinista," he says, holding her gaze in the mirror until she glances away. "I served in an irregular warfare battalion for two years. And that's all I'm going to say about it. Bueno, if that means you don't want to do me the great favor of cutting my hair, I understand, I—"

"Niño, shut up," says Gonzalo. "We do not discriminate against nice people here. Bad people, I snip off their earlobes. But it will be much easier for you to get legal status here when you tell them you're fleeing those maldito Sandinistas. If you say the opposite, chico, you won't stand a chance."

"You know, earlier I was thinking that with long hair you looked something like that famous güey revolucionario," says Joaquina, sitting in one of the chairs against the wall now. "That güey, tu sabes, in the Zocalo they sell T-shirts with his face."

"That famous homophobic-assassin-psychopath, you mean," says Gonzalo. "That's another reason to cut off all this hair." He pulls on Esteban's earlobe and lightly closes his scissors around it. "Do you agree? You have three seconds to answer, Che Güey."

"Gonzalo, putísima madre!" Joaquina laughs.

Esteban, still reeling with confusion over what Gonzalo said about legal status, says nothing: It's as if he's completely overlooked all the implications of being in the United States. What, he's going to have to betray old War Gods to stay in this country with Joaquina? Vos, now that the world is changing, he's going to have to figure out on his own what should stay the same, no?

Gonzalo has resumed cutting his hair. Joaquina goes into the back and comes out with her coat on, holding a spiral notebook with a glossy yellow cardboard cover. Esteban is stunned that she's leaving.

"I have to go," says Joaquina. "Or I'll be late for my class." But she's doing that thing with her hair again.

"You don't want to see what this niño marinero looks like under all this hair?"

She laughs. "Marinero or soldier boy. Who knows what he'll claim to be next? I think Esteban is as full of fantasies as you are, corazón."

"No one is as full of fantasies as I am, corazón," he says, and he gives Esteban a firm tap on the top of his head with the flat side of his scissors. Esteban stiffens with alarm.

"Ah sí?" she says. Joaquina seems on the verge of saying something else, but then she simply says, *"Bye."* And she's out the door. It's night out now. She looks in through the window as she hurries up the sidewalk, carrying her yellow notebook, giving Esteban a quick wave and a smile, and then she's gone.

Esteban stares at the empty window.

"Sí, mi reina, vete," says Gonzalo under his breath, as if insulted that Joaquina hasn't stayed to see the haircut. "Que Dios te acompañe."

Esteban has never before in his life been aware of being in such intimate proximity to a homosexual, nor, certainly, has he ever felt so beholden to one. Claro, in Corinto there were plenty of patos, but most depended on foreign seamen for their kind of love, just the way the putas did, and were forced to seek it much more furtively. But because of what Gonzalo said just before Joaquina left, he feels pushed overboard into a sea of suspicion and unease.

Gonzalo must sense it, because after a few moments of cutting his hair in silence, he releases Esteban from his guilty misery and hostility with what seems a studied observation:

"Why do you heterosexuals always play such games? You two have been steaming up the mirrors in here all day, and look, you barely say good-bye to each other. I suppose she wants you to think that maybe you'll never see her again." He laughs. "She wants you to *suffer* for her. And she wants to *suffer* over you."

Esteban is too surprised to refute him. It occurs to him that, in a way, his first impression of Gonzalo was correct, he's the same as any inveterate womanizer: his attitude is so simplistic because, with his physical beauty and self-confidence, he's used to getting his way, and quickly.

"She told me she has a novio," he finally says.

"Who? That little lawyer? Don't worry about him." Gonzalo works silently awhile. "You know what everybody says, Amor de lejos, amor de pendejos."

The world's most famous love slogan. Even la Marta teased him with it, when he had to go back into the war. And he'd answered, But I'm not going to be that far away. Then they'd both felt shaken by the unavoidable mine lying at the heart of what he'd said, because of course where he was going it was easy to end up in the infinite far away. And then la Marta had—

"Vos, Gonzalo. Does Joaquina dye her hair?"

"She's as blonde as a truck tire. Curls it too. Needless to say, I'm the one responsible for that. I tried to talk her into going platinum, but she wouldn't have it."

He tries to imagine Joaquina with straight, black hair and finds the image so adorable, so strangely sexual and private—as if he's undressed her and is seeing her naked for the first time, which is what he finds himself trying to imagine next—that his pija begins to stiffen and he wants to shout out in surprise from the vibrant warmth flooding through him.

"Chocho!" He grins like a fiendish monkey in the mirror.

"Eso qué?"

"We use it the same way you do coño. I guess they're both words for vagina too, no?"

"Coño," says Gonzalo. "If you two ever have children they're going to have filthy mouths."

Then the haircut is done. But Esteban feels disillusioned: he looks like a crazy monk, short hair on top and almost as bald as Capitán Elias on the sides, ears sticking out and the bottom of his face full of soft, messy hair. Impossible that Joaquina could have felt anything for that goatish gnome in the mirror! But Gonzalo comes out from the back with a hot, wet towel to put over his face, and uses a short, stubby brush to lather his face with the shaving cream he's mixed in a small bowl, and strops a razor against a leather strap attached to the chair, then slowly and carefully shaves him. He fills his hands with talc from a green tin container with an elegant man in a top hat depicted on it, claps it around his neck, and then frees him from the hair-covered apron and paper bib. Gonzalo holds an oval mirror up so Esteban can see the back of his head, rounded and black as an overripe plum, with a mouse tail hanging out of it.

"I left a little in back, you can grow it out, even braid it if you want. It's the fashion with all you young machos."

Esteban is so disturbed by this notion that he has trouble appreciating the shock of how clean and neat and changed he looks, with his haircut and new sweater. He remembers a teacher he had in Corinto, Compañera Silvia, who painted her nails bright purple, wore specially made maternity militia fatigues through the last months of her pregnancy, and let the hair grow out from the mole under a corner of her lips until she was able to twirl a fine, thin, braid that hung down like one of Ho Chi Minh's whiskers.

"Mira qué guapito," says Gonzalo. "Do you like it? You'd better!"

"Claro," he says. "Gonzalo, I don't know how to show my gratitude."

"A week of sweeping and mopping should do it. Now that you're in New York, chico, you have to learn: nothing is for free. *Nothing.*"

Gonzalo opens a cabinet under the mirrors and brings out a dark green bottle, which he uncorks, pouring dark red liquid into two glasses. "It's good for your cold," he says.

"It's wine?" asks Esteban, uselessly trying to sniff it.

"Pues, claro." Gonzalo touches his glass to his. "Salud."

Gonzalo sits in the other barber chair, sighing over his exhausted feet, and sips his wine.

Esteban sits up in his chair and takes a slow drink. At first it doesn't taste like much, a bit sour, but it doesn't taste like anything else either. But even with his cold, he feels his mouth pucker and decides that he likes the sensation.

"Where are you going to sleep?" asks Gonzalo.

"No sé." Hijueputa, one thing after another! He has nowhere to sleep. "On the ship," he says, finally.

"But you can't go back there after you've come all this way, chico."

They sit in silence a moment.

"Where I live, the bed barely fits in the one room we have," says Gonzalo. "Maybe one night on the floor, but I'd have to ask Marco."

Esteban says nothing. There's nowhere else but the ship. At least there's a mattress there—

"Oye," says Gonzalo. "Why don't you just stay here for the night? I can lower your chair all the way. It will be like sleeping on an airplane, no? There's a blanket in back." Gonzalo stands up from his chair, gives him a light tap on the arm. "And then, first thing in the morning, you can see her."

BUT LUCK IS NOT
FOR EVERYBODY . . .

1

ELIAS HAD FOUND THE SHIP THE PREVIOUS APRIL, IN ST. JOHN harbour, New Brunswick, in a little shipyard there, in unseaworthy condition, declared a total constructive loss by her insurers and waiting to be sold as scrap. In February the ship, then called the *Seal Queen,* port of registry Monrovia, had been disabled by an engine plant fire that broke out during a heavy storm while she was en route from Yarmouth, Nova Scotia, to Sydney Harbour, N.B., to load a cargo of wood pulp; the *Seal Queen,* dark and without power, was stranded outside St. John Harbour with the crew still onboard, including two who'd been badly scalded by sprayed diesel fuel and steam and urgently needed to be evacuated, and the body of one dead engineer—rescue helicopters weren't able to reach the ship until the blizzard began to calm.

Elias had read about the *Seal Queen* in a Lloyd's casualty report and made a few phone calls. The ship's owner, listed as Gemco Corporation of Monrovia, had apparently decided that it wasn't worth the bother or expense to repair her at shipyard prices. Gemco was probably a single-vessel owner, eager to get out of shipping now; so Elias had deduced in a telephone conversation with the ship's operator, Corfian Ship Management, out of Staten Island, a Greek guy. Elias flew up to St. John, changing planes in Montreal. When he arrived at the shipyard, workers had already begun removing everything of salable value from the ship, the galley equipment, all the furniture and light fixtures, paneling from the bulkheads, even some of the porthole covers and watertight doors.

That night Elias phoned Mark in New York.

"This is the one, I think," Elias said. "Maybe just a little older than what we wanted, built in Japan in nineteen seventy-one. Overall length four hundred thirty-six feet, seven inches. A converted dry cargo ship, tonnages four thousand, eight hundred eighty-eight gross and three thousand six hundred thirty-eight net—"

"Yeah, I get it," said Mark, impatient as always with such details. "Big."

"Well, medium. Mitsubishi engine in very good shape, thank God they haven't started pulling that apart yet. Janmar generators somewhat *scorched;* we'll need some new parts. But mainly it's a wiring problem. I can fix that, and with a little luck, we'll get it right the first time. Cargo gear, all fine. Would have been nice to have hydraulic hatches. And for all the pounding she took, hull's OK too, just scraped up, rusted. They agreed to put most of the navigation equipment back."

"How much?"

"I talked to the operator—"

"C'mon, how much, Elias?"

"Mark, *chill,* fuck's sake. I said, How much do you expect to get selling her for scrap? and he said, Fifty thousand. I offered him five thousand more and said we'd take over the maintenance expenses from day one."

Mark felt his spirits plummet. He was expecting a bargain? "That's in the ballpark of what we were aiming for," he acknowledged.

"I'm happy," said Elias. And Elias did sound about as giddy as he ever does. "Upstairs in the officers' quarters? It has these wonderful tiled Japanese steam closets. They're practically worth the price all by themselves."

Get one of those cheap flag of convenience registries and incorporations. Import the cheapest possible crew, even have them pay their own airfare. Work night and day, repair the ship fast, in a month to six weeks. Keep expenses to a minimum, pile up debts. And then decide if they want to sell her: should be able to get half a million dollars, *at least,* for a decent working ship like this. *Then* pay off the crew, the port fees, the equipment rentals and materials and everything else, shouldn't come to more than fifty grand if they work fast. Or maybe even keep the ship and go into business, see how they feel about it. Lure in some investors, and really fix her up and modernize her. Not as much money up front of course, but a ship like the *Urus,* in good working condition, should bring in five thousand in charters a day, before operating expenses.

Maybe go into the Amazonian timber trade, with all Elias's connections down in South America, they'll be able to get something going pretty fast. Eventually branch out, build an eco lodge in the rain forest, charge rock stars and such a ton to stay there. Hey, a fun life, Mark. Just the sort of thing we used to dream about back in college. A guy Elias had gone to the Nautical Academy in Mexico with had been working the scam for years, out of Panama and Venezuela, had sold some ships off and kept some, steadily building up a small fleet. Just a little bit illegal at the start-up end, like so many other risky businesses that, in the end, become legitimate and profitable. Elias liked to use a homeopathic metaphor for this: the Law of Similars. Just a little bit of evil to defend against the inner rot of a greater one, leading to buoyant good health.

Such were the arguments Elias Tureen used to persuade Mark Baker, his best and nearly oldest friend, into investing the insurance money he'd collected after his father's death. Elias was going to be a father soon, and as much as Kate loved him, he worried over his kid having a loser for a dad. A man of adventure, of jungle and sea, a risk taker, a shipping and timber magnate, an eco lodge owner with his own medicinal plant business down in the Amazon—Elias's holistically interrelated dreams—there'd be nothing wrong with all that. It really anguished Elias, Mark knew, the thought of his kid having a father he or she couldn't look up to, a clever, dabbling-in-this-and-that, philandering, deeply insecure, do-nothing dad; and Mom with all the prestige and money and always bringing in more. Kate's love for Elias certainly seemed unconditional, but would it always be?

Mark, it's not like you have anything else going right now, Elias would say with the bluntness of an oldest pal. True, Mark's video rental shop had gone bust. Blockbuster came to the neighborhood and took him right down, though of course like an idiot he'd tried to hang in too long; had to go back to waiting tables, until his father's heart attack (the life insurance policy had originally been taken out in both his and his younger sister Linda's name, but last year, with uncharacteristic intuition and . . . pity? . . . his father had changed it so that Mark would get most of the money, because Linda was already rich). Then Sue, a graphic designer with her own small company, left Mark after six years of their living together. She kept the apartment. So she really didn't leave, she booted him, and Miracle. And so there he was, *suddenly* pushing forty, living with his dog in a tiny, thousand-dollar-a-month Upper West Side studio, nothing hopeful going on except for this stressfully provocative amount of money in the bank. What if one day he had to go back to New Hampshire, go into the dry-cleaning business with his mother, just not to fucking starve? So worried was Mark about his future, so certain was he that his father's bequeathed treasure represented a final opportunity to make something of himself on his own, that during the week he spent pondering Elias's proposition he kept waking up in the middle of the night to rush into the bathroom and vomit, once tripping over Miracle and not making it in time.

It never even occurred to Elias that it would turn out to be nearly impossible to find replacement circuit breakers for a circa 1970 made-in-Japan generator. Just the other afternoon he and Mark argued about it up on the bridge, shouting. Elias started talking about buying a whole new generator switchboard, said it would cost about thirty thousand dollars. That was just a bit less than what Mark had left in the bank, and he was resolved not to put in another cent. And Elias couldn't go back to Kate for more. What do they owe already? Including the crew's wages, about a hundred and fifty grand.

Elias is flying out to Los Angeles today. Because of the much heavier Asian trade in the West Coast ports, the scrap yards out there are more likely to turn up the circuit breakers. This is probably their last chance. Elias could hardly have asked Mark to go. Elias can hardly get him out to the ship. Mark can't bear the sight of the *Urus* anymore. He can't bear the sight of *them* anymore, useless nitwits.

Last night, after Kate and Elias's pathetically pretentious dinner party, where at least he got to sit next to Moira Meer, he and Elias dismissed themselves to go to a bar for a nightcap and a little business chat. Kate and a friend were doing dishes in the kitchen down at one end of the Imperial Loft, Kate wearing some probably Soho designer maternity apron and looking gorgeous, bathed in muted industrial lighting amidst all the restored old metal shapes of a turn-of-the-century rum still Elias had found in the Amazon and brought back in crates, with Kate's money —huge kettles converted to cabinets, condensation tubes hung with utensils, smokestack-steam-whistle-looking things fitted with lights.

"Now, Mark," Kate sweetly thundered across that vast interior tundra, "you leave my savings alone! It's expensive having a kid!"

At the bar Elias wasted no time. He said, "We might have a bit of a problem."

"No kidding." Mark was already drunk but feeling elated about Moira Meer, one more bourbon he was going to be all over the place, but he ordered one anyway.

Elias clutched a pint of beer without even drinking from it. He said, "This is serious, Mark."

"Moira's a wonderful—"

"Mark, shut up. Bernardo had an accident. He burnt himself."

"The old guy?"

"Bernardo. The waiter."

"I kinda like that guy." Just that night, he'd told Moira about the pistachios and pink-lipped sailors and she'd giggled.

"I treated him this morning—"

"Oh, come on, Elias!"

"It's just a burn. Second degree, mainly."

"Elias—"

"Mark, for fuck's sake, I studied for two years, I've always kept it up, I was practically licensed in London, I—"

"I know, Doc, I know, the shamans," said Mark. Elias's high-tech greenhouse and herb garden on the roof of the loft, his little alchemist's laboratory. Even Kate lets him give her stuff for her pregnancy and something made from pineapple extract for her tennis elbow.

"He goes to the hospital we could end up sued for everything we've got and will ever have. We could even end up in jail, do you realize that? Do you know the Jones Act?"

"All right," said Mark.

"Not to mention," said Elias, "that we'd be responsible for the medical bills."

"John Paul Jones, it's named for?"

Elias shut his eyes. "No." He opened them, coldly glaring. "You catch my drift, don't you? We cannot risk taking him to the hospital."

"So how bad is it?"

"It's just a burn. He's healing. I'm fairly sure I prevented an infection. Those idiots tried cleaning him up with a dirty rag."

"So what do I do?"

"Just leave him be. He's being looked after now. Tomaso Tostado—"

"Jesus, their names. Which one's he?"

"The one with a gold tooth. He and Panzón are changing his dressings, giving him his medication. I showed them what to do."

"You gotta admit, Barbie's a pretty hilarious name for a guy looks like that."

"Hmn."

Mark ordered another bourbon.

And then he said, "Elias. That Moira Meer. I mean, what a really wonderful, remarkable girl."

"You can't have her," Elias petulantly snapped, eyes flashing. "She's mine. And if she's not mine, she's Phil's."

"She's—*what* did you say? *Phil's?*" Phil the Landfill?

"Moira would be good for Phil."

"Elias, she'd be good for *me.* Anyway, who the hell are you to—What the fuck you mean, she's yours!"

"You think you're God's gift to women, Mark," said Elias. "I've got news for you. You're not."

"*Me? I'm* God's gift to women? Wow, Elias."

God's gift to women! If he were feeling any more demoralized, he'd fuck Miracle.

* * *

Mark Baker and Elias Tureen had met sixteen years before, at Bley College, a venerably dilapidated and sufficiently ivy-covered, little coed private college that lured most of its students from prep schools and affluent northeastern suburbs: kids who hadn't been accepted to the better schools but whose parents still wanted to pay that level of tuition and board. Bley College was situated in upstate New York's snow belt, amidst frozen Finger Lakes. Every November psychologists were sent into the old steam-heated dorms, where no one who'd ever grown up to be famously eminent had ever scratched initials into an old wooden sill or door, to counsel the students against the suicidal depressions inevitably brought on by the long, brutal winters. Elias was a transfer student living on Mark's floor. It was unusual for anyone to transfer to Bley; the most exalted idea about the place was that it was a good school to transfer out of if you had the grades, a second-chance sort of place during an era when second chances were, perhaps, especially prized (they all had been taking drugs since they were about fourteen and spent their freshman year realizing they weren't going to be poets after all). Most upperclassmen lived in fraternities or off campus, so the transfers were sifted in among the freshmen. In Mark's dorm there were three, two Vietnam vets from nearby farming towns, there on the G.I. Bill, one of whom looked nearly forty and kept a pet lizard under his bed and who dropped out after just a few weeks; and Elias Tureen, who'd grown up in Mexico City, where his father, British, was a former journalist turned investment analyst, and his mother, Greek-American, ran a small art gallery. He'd gone to private schools in Mexico City, where he'd been precocious but wild, already full of romantic ideas about an adventurous life out in the world like his own father had, covering wars and revolutions during the fifties and into the sixties. At the age of sixteen Elias had entered Mexico's most prestigious nautical academy, La Escuela Náutica at Veracruz, where he'd chosen to major in mechanical engineering and engine plant studies rather than in navigation and deck officer training because that seemed the most practical, and also more romantically rugged. The training and education there were excellent, but the discipline was severe. After a year spent circling the world in the engine room of the academy's training ship, back in Veracruz, at the beginning of his fourth year and already confined to his quarters for curfew violations, he'd been caught with marijuana and expelled. Bley College had accepted Elias as a junior engineering major. Several Ivy League schools, according to Elias, had accepted him as a sophomore, so he'd chosen Bley. That was Elias's résumé as he described it, then.

Mark was not a freshman, he was a junior, and the resident adviser on Elias's floor of their coed dormitory. He probably didn't have the grades to transfer out and up. No, he definitely didn't have the grades. But he loved Bley. In his own way, he'd shined there. At Bley he'd found an acceptance that he'd never known before, an outer peace that soon became almost an inner one. Mark's wholesome, cheerful demeanor—the wholesomely cheerful one he had back then—came partly from his shyness, partly from his having grown up in suburban Peterborough, New Hampshire, and partly from his joy in being away from a father, mother, and sister who lived as if they violently despised one another, and him. Mark was the quiet one, whom his father was given to beating on with a belt and open-handed wallops and knee kicks to the back, often saying, I'll wipe that silly grin off your face. His parents owned a chain of dry cleaners, one in every thriving New Hampshire ski resort. In his hometown, where he was not especially good at any sport—terrible at hockey, an acceptable skier, bored by fishing, hunting, "Funny Car" races—his brilliant, year-younger sister, Linda, had gained a notoriety that had oppressed and depressed Mark for years. She was a miraculous girl, really, one leg shrunken by polio beneath the knee but a busty, high-spirited and defiant beauty, a straight-A student who hung with the baddest girls and greaser boys, who by the ninth grade was already known as the *very* loosest girl in town, affectionately nicknamed Lousy Linda (she was destined to go on to Stanford; despite the peg shin she swaggered along on like a pirate, unverified rumors of summer vacations spent as an exotic stripper in San Francisco circulated among enviously left-behind former classmates for years; Linda was now a heart surgeon in her second year of residency at San Francisco General Hospital, living in Berkeley with her husband, a musician and record producer, and their two children). So Mark hadn't had an especially happy adolescence and had arrived at Bley College a virgin. At Bley the girls found Mark naive, cute, and sweetly, fashionably neurotic: New York City Jewish girls who dressed like rich gypsies and whose fathers were psychiatrists; extravagantly spoiled yet doting Long Island girls; California hippie girls; arty girls from everywhere. Only the WASP prep school girls were indifferent to Mark's newfound charm, but they were like a separate species, seemingly indifferent to anybody who didn't give off the same pheromones. During his freshman year a famous mystical poet had come all the way to Bley to give a reading, and when he spotted Mark sitting eagerly in the second row of the auditorium, he turned to the student girl charged with tending to his needs during his visit, and said, Who's that angelic cherub? I bet the girls love to mother him. He has Federico García Lorca's light in his eyes.

Lorca's light. Yeah, right. Mark's newly discovered inner sensitivity had not revealed him to be a poet after all, but the girl was in his creative writing class and was a total Lorca freak; she was so struck by what the visiting poet said that she led Mark back to her dorm from the postreading party that night, ordered her roommate to go sleep somewhere else, and fucked him. Honest to goodness, that's how he lost his virginity. Lorca's light, can you believe it!

And now Bley College had even made him a resident adviser. It was like a reward for the cultivated but not dishonest, quietly cheerful sensitivity that Mark had discovered inside himself at Bley. His parents were certainly happy that his room and board were free now, one less thing to torment him about during school breaks. As an RA, he had his own room. Up and down the long hallway on his floor rooms shared by freshman girls alternated with those shared by freshman boys. And all the way down at one end of the hall lived Elias Tureen, the crew-cut transfer student who'd grown up in Mexico but spoke with a British accent, who'd spent three years enduring the military discipline of a nautical academy and a year at sea, and who immediately began to terrorize his freshman roommate, a premed student from New Rochelle who had styled, feathery hair in the manner of Jane Fonda in *Klute* and who played Bread on his stereo all day. Davey was his name. Not David or Dave. Davey had a girlfriend at nearby Cornell, they'd been going steady since junior high. He was going to be on the golf team. He had excellent study habits, which meant he was at Bley because he wasn't very bright, yet he always found time to tie up the phone talking to his girlfriend, or spent hours primping his hair with a portable hand dryer and eating the grilled cheese sandwiches he made in his portable oven, listening to Bread. Soon, every time Davey played Bread, Elias put some raw-throated Mexican bolero chanteuse on his own stereo, or some howling mariachi band, and turned the volume all the way up, sat at the edge of his bed facing his stereo with a bottle of cheap tequila in his hand screaming and howling along.

When students had problems with their roommates, or any other problems they felt like talking about, they were supposed to come to Mark, their resident adviser. And they often did. The boys especially knocked softly at the door during the late hours of the night, with their eyes red from marijuana or crying or both, slipped in to sit on his little couch and spill their troubles. The girls could go upstairs to talk to Tish Carter, the female RA on that floor; but sometimes they came to Mark, and sometimes he slept with them. It was easy, because often that was why they'd come. When they lay on his bed in the deepest hours of the night, the conversation having switched from the usual problems with parents or friends or boyfriends, and suddenly started talking about sex in the way that girl from California had, talking about her summer passion with a surfer who was now in jail or something, meticulously and longingly describing their fires on the beach and how happy she'd been lying there naked and stoned on her back in the sand looking up at the stars and listening to the waves while he ate her out for hours, for hours, ate her out for hours, Bro. They'd get themselves and Mark so turned on, well, what were you supposed to do?

Davey had come several times to complain about his roommate. At first, Mark advised that Davey and Elias come to some agreement about taking turns enduring each other's music taste. He was reluctant to impose on Elias, who seemed so aloof and mocking and *foreign*. Mark was afraid of Elias. With his crew cut and tall, lean build, his dark, narrow face like the imprint of a forearm smash in wet sand, his unnervingly somber eyes. Conflicts over music tastes, those were the sorts of problems roommates should be mature and socialized enough to solve themselves. Whenever he passed Elias in the hall or ran into him in the showers, Elias seemed to scoff at him silently. Or he would put on a garishly whinnying voice and say, "How do you do, Mr. Adviser?" One night Mark was walking down the hall and Elias and two freshman football scholarship guys and a couple of girls in nighties were sitting in the hallway together drinking tequila and beer and smoking pot—it was against the rules to do that, in the hallway—and Elias shouted at his back, "What fucking advice do *you* have to give, *motherfucker*!"

Soon Elias was sleeping with Tish, the resident adviser upstairs. She fell so desperately in love with Elias that she started coming to Mark for advice, and when Elias dropped her later, she was so overwrought she flunked all her finals and had to leave Bley for a term. Soon Elias was sleeping with some of the girls Mark used to sleep with, and often locked Davey out; Mark let Davey crash on his own floor a number of nights. And now, when girls came to his door late at night, often they wanted to talk about Elias, the hold he had over their hearts, this Mexicanized English seaman seducer or whatever the hell he was, this "man"—the girls often said so—among "boys." Then one day Davey came to Mark's door in tears because his girlfriend Elaine had come to visit him from Cornell and he'd had a three-hour lab class that day and now Elias was in there fucking Elaine with both Bread and Chavela Vargas turned up full volume.

That was a problem. That was terrible. Mark was ready to take a fire ax to the door, if that was what it took. He promised Davey he'd have a new roommate next term, no matter what. They went down the hall, and Mark rapped on the door, ready to give this arrogant son of a bitch hell. Davey sat on the floor with his hands over his face and then suddenly sprang to his feet and kicked at the door, cursing Elaine savagely and loudly.

Finally Elias opened the door, both stereos still pouring forth their ludicrous music. He yawned sleepily. "I was just having a nap," Elias said calmly. "What's the racket?"

Davey charged into the room and began looking in closets, calling Elaine as if he expected her to appear out of some fabulous hiding place, like genie smoke from under his putting pad.

"I thought Elaine left," said Elias. "Didn't she say good-bye?" He made a little smile at Mark and shrugged.

"He heard her in there with you," said Mark.

"Bollocks, cabrón," said Elias—Mark was familiar with neither word and must have looked puzzled. "She wasn't," said Elias. "Maybe you should advise him a little before I break his face."

Now Davey was screaming hideously at Elias; even students from the floors downstairs and above were coming to see what it was all about.

"Do get a hold of yourself," said Elias, putting a hand on Davey's shoulder. Davey punched Elias; it connected and looked as if it hurt. After all, Davey, an empassioned golfer, was no weakling. To Mark's amazement, Elias did not hit him back; he simply stood there glowering thoughtfully, rubbing his cheek as if he had a toothache.

"Where's Elaine?" bawled Davey. "I heard her in there with you, I know I did. You fucking degenerate Mexican piece of dog shit." In a tone of voice that made him sound like a strangling Holy Roller duck possessed by tongues, Davey was jabbering incoherently—this turned out to be his fed-up imitation of all the Mexican slang Elias had been insulting him with for months.

Again, Elias did not even bother to reply; he simply watched Davey's performance with a saddened expression, then looked at Mark.

"Come with me," said Mark. Elias followed Mark to his room, through the crowd in the hallway, their grinning or horrified expressions.

"She left through the window," said Elias, with a thin, wry smile, seated on Mark's couch. "A game girl, I'll give her that. Chíngale. Tied sheets and T-shirts together, seaman's knots, you know, tied it around her waist and lowered her down, while you all were trying to kick down my door. And then I lowered her suitcase down. Funny thing is, I don't think anybody even saw." The rear of the dorm faced a paddleball court and woods. "She's had it with that twot. He'll never see her again. He's all wrong for her. She's mine now."

Mark laughed, he couldn't help it, Elias's composure and self-possession struck him as hilarious. Elias's winning heartlessness suddenly reminded him of his little sister, Linda.

"I suppose she's on the bus to Ithaca now," said Elias. "I'll go see her in a few days. Funny, I almost went to school there myself, but they wanted me to start as a sophomore. Don't have the time, güey."

"*Way* what?"

Elias spelled *güey* and shrugged. "Mexican word. Obviously, you weren't paying attention to Davey's Spanish lesson out there."

"I think you should have a new roommate," said Mark. "Actually, you should probably live alone."

"Maybe I could take Tish's room. I think I'd make a good resident adviser, don't you?"

They stayed in Mark's room talking and smoking pot until they heard Davey knocking at the door and Mark realized he'd forgotten all about him. God, he felt terrible, but Elias's weed was really strong.

Mark stumbled out into the hallway. Davey's eyes were puffy and red from weeping.

"You're in there getting stoned with *him*?"

"I'm finding you a new roommate," said Mark.

"Yeah, I know. But where's Elaine?"

"I don't know. Davey, are you sure you weren't just hearing things? That would have been unbelievably cruel of her."

Later that night he and Elias walked into town together for some beer and pizza at Onondaga Tavern, went there and a few other places together, trying to pick up town girls.

Streaking was in fashion, and in the middle of the long, terrible winters, especially during blizzards at night, Elias liked to sprint naked across the quad, screaming at the top of his lungs into the wind and snow. Stranger, he became somewhat obsessed with the preppies, who held themselves aloof from the rest of the student body. He began adopting their words, especially when he addressed other preppies, calling them Ace and Sport. He began to dress like them too, in tweed jackets and pastel button-down shirts, baggy chinos or jeans, wore those clothes and nothing else when he went outside in winter, with the added embellishment of going barefoot. Elias went barefoot in winter, said it was good for the whole spirit, somewhat like walking on hot coals. Despite these peculiarities, the preppies even tried to rush him for their fraternity, inviting him to cocktails in their pillared southern, antebellum-style mansion with maid service, all those Benzes and BMWs parked out front. Soon, of course, Elias was seducing the preppie girls too. Mark was often at his side now during those and all other outings, though the preppies still wanted nothing to do with him. No matter how hard and sweetly he tried to charm, they were barely polite, and soon Mark often felt as unhappy as he had in high school.

That summer, while Mark went home to New Hampshire and worked as a waiter in a tourist hotel, Elias went to the Amazon, found work as an assistant river guide for an adventure tourist operation, and contrived to get full course credits for all of it. He came back for the winter term, to graduate. Now Elias was full of stories about shamans and taking a drug called ayahuasca that made you vomit and shit all over the place before taking you off on incredible twenty-four-hour trips during which your spirit merged with those of jungle and river animals; he'd turned into a jaguar and a pink river dolphin. The notion of such a drug did not appeal to Mark, but he pretended he couldn't wait to return to the Amazon with Elias and try it himself. Someday, yeah, man, maybe they'd go into business there: have their own adventure expedition company, find ways to market the medicinal marvels of the shamans, buy one of those old-fashioned steam-paddle riverboats and turn it into a floating, very hip hotel, open a beach bar in Rio. Great life, Mark. You want to spend the rest of your life in a suit, in some bleak little office? It's not like you're getting into Harvard Law, is it?

Immediately after graduating from Bley, Mark moved to New York City with his new girlfriend, Mindy Olin, who wanted to be an actress; they both waited tables. Mark and Mindy broke up, and he moved to the Lower East Side. He went on waiting tables, and lost himself in the rocker night life, CBGB, Barnabas Rex, Mudd Club, the years plowing by through a sludge of stuporous late nights, drugs and alcohol, minor fashion adjustments, and downtown women variously tuned to a muffled key of desperation, Mark harmonizing with them well enough. Elias often wrote, and visited at least once a year, sometimes staying with Mark in one dingy apartment after another for as long as six months. For a while Elias was making good money trapping baby spider monkeys in the jungle, selling them to the pet trade. He assured Mark that he did this as humanely as possible, employing Amazon Indians who used blowguns to incapacitate the mother monkeys, the darts coated with nonlethal doses of *curare,* just enough to knock them out awhile, the dart points left sharp and smooth so that they'd be easy for the mother monkeys to pull out, and then Elias and his "boys" would climb up into the trees to go after the baby monkeys with nets. (Elias told that story in CBGB's one night and a German punk girl spit in his face and started to cry.) He attached himself to one Amazon adventure travel outfit after another, keeping up his interest in medicinal plants and natural hallucinogens; once, Elias was hired to serve as guide for a group of physicians and medical specialists from the United States who wanted to witness firsthand the way Amazon shamans treated people's health deep in the rain forest. One was a young woman physician who was also a licensed naturopath and had incorporated herbal and homeopathic treatments into her practice. She and Elias almost married; she spent months at a time with him in the apartment he kept in Iquitos, Peru, studying medicinal plants and trees with the licensed shamans who ran their own clinics there almost like Western doctors, buying their cuttings, bark, and roots from the river and forest people who journeyed to Iquitos to sell them. After they broke up, Elias went to sea again, signing onto a freighter as third engineer out of Santos, Brazil. (Peru's Sendero Luminoso rebels were then a furtive presence in the Upper Amazon, ruining the adventure tourist trade for years.) He lived in London for two years and enrolled in a homeopathic medicine institute there. He returned, briefly, to the Amazon. He spent a year in Mexico as first mate on a yacht that took tourists deep-sea fishing out of Isla Mujeres, owned and captained by an old schoolmate from La Escuela Náutica. Back in the Amazon, he worked the specialty timber trade as the front man for a Swedish investor he'd met in Mexico City, procuring cargoes of a relatively rare deep-forest tree whose wood is naturally blue for export to fashionable furniture makers in Europe. On vacation in Rio he met the young conceptualist photographer Kate Puerifoy, who was having a show at a gallery there, her famous series of gigantic photographic flip books illustrating midwestern recipes. They fell torridly in love, and Elias followed her up to New York, staying in the apartment where Mark had been living with Sue for two years already, and with Miracle—Miracle had been a birthday present, a puppy waiting for him inside a cardboard box at the breakfast table—until finally Kate decided she was ready to let Elias move into her newly purchased loft. Elias and Kate were married a year later. That was three years ago.

In all the years that Elias was in and out of the Amazon, Mark only visited him there once. In Iquitos's floating slum of Belém, amidst the river traffic of long dugout canoes and barges bringing in all the nibbled wealth of the Amazon forests and rivers, he and Elias drank a liquor made from fermented monkey testicles that was supposed to increase your sexual potency, though there was no way he was having sex with one of those painted up, sweaty little Iquitos whores, attractive as their sprightly, small-breasted bodies were. And no, he didn't want to try ayahuasca, he already had diarrhea, thanks. But Elias really put himself out to give his friend a true Amazon experience; they boarded some kind of long, narrow, screened-in riverboat-bus called the Worm and slowly chugged downriver in nonstop rain for two days, struggling with the passengers—mainly people from little river towns who'd come to Iquitos to sell one thing or another—for places to hang their hammocks. Many traveled with live chickens roped together by the claws into giant, multieyed dusters. They got off in a desolate little river village where everyone lived in wooden huts elevated on palm-trunk stilts over a sopping, muddy marsh. There they borrowed a dugout canoe and Mark sat in the bow under his poncho, already out of cigarettes, miserably steaming, his skin colandered with insect bites, shining a flashlight ahead, while Elias paddled them up a tributary at night, making his way around and under fallen trees so expertly that Mark was not once smashed in the face by a looming branch, though there were some close calls. Fish kept jumping into their canoe, thudding around on the floor, some of them as dangerously horned and plated as miniature rhinos; some flopped back into the water, and one, leaping out of the dark, crashed into Mark's chest with the force of a flying wet dog. Some of the fish were piranha, chuckled Elias. Now and then Elias stopped paddling and swept his own flashlight's beam along the banks, looking for the red eyes of crocodiles. Mark made sure he kept his hands inside the canoe. Or Elias stopped and stood up in the canoe with his hands cupped around his nose and mouth, making strange snorting and grunting sounds, claiming that he could hear wild boar stampeding through the forest and that he was calling to them. Elias stopped the canoe midstream, and Mark sat face to face with a poisonous, lime green frog the size of a basketball, perched in a crook of a tree fallen into the river. Finally they reached their destination, a river hamlet even smaller and more ramshackle than the last one. Here lived Elias's great shaman buddy, Cumpashín, with his family: apparently everyone in the village was his relative, and they'd followed him here out of some even more remote, dark place in the forest, a place so wet and mushy, said Elias, that they thought stones were magical objects because the only stones they ever saw there had been brought from far away.

Oh well. Something to tell your grandkids about. Cumpashín *was* a riot. Mark hardly grasped a thing that went down for the next three days. Cumpashín and his, Mark guessed, *immediate* family lived in one of those elevated huts, a big one, with no walls, a floor made of thin, springy slats cut from a bamboolike palm that somehow you didn't fall through, which also supported a sandbox for cooking fires; a thatched roof, with an attic, which Cumpashín was always climbing up into, bringing down jaguar skulls and pelts, long blowguns and a double-barreled shotgun, all his stuff. There were animals and kids and mothers and wives all over the place. Cumpashín had named one of his sons Elias, another Thriller, and he had a little daughter named Elvis. (The more intrepid adventure travel outfits had been coming through the area for years.) All of them, including some of the animals, slept in hammocks; Elias and Mark hung their own hammocks in Cumpashín's big, happy "house." Cumpashín changed his headdress, made from the feathers of all different birds, about three times a day; he wore necklaces made out of jaguar teeth. The women wore loose, ragged T-shirts like dresses, and intricate necklaces and bracelets made of porcupine quills and colored seeds. Cumpashín had hardly any teeth, a smooth, brown jack-o'-lantern of a face, and always went shirtless, wearing frayed black jeans. He had the build and muscle tone of a lightweight boxer.

"Guess how old he is," said Elias.

"As old as the father of all the great waters," guessed Mark.

"At least fifty. Can you believe it?"

"Well, this is a pretty good health club." He just couldn't stop being the lame New Yorker.

Mark felt nervous around Cumpashín. Whenever the shaman stared at him for such a goddamned long time, Mark sensed that somehow his *aura* and ineffable *core* were on display—quills of tainted spirit radiating out through all his mosquito bites—and tried to summon Lorca's long-lost light to his eyes.

Cumpashín and Elias would talk baby talk all day, a mixture of the little Spanish Cumpashín knew and the little bit of the shaman's Amazonian language that Elias had picked up; except Cumpashín spoke in a whirring, nearly whispered way that sounded as free of consonants as his home terrain had been of rocks, Mark didn't see how Elias could understand any of it. But they'd roar with laughter, and stamp their feet, and call *each other* Cumpashín, which Mark didn't get at all. The first morning that Mark woke up in Cumpashín's palatial hut, he looked out from his hammock and saw a wild boar's head in one plastic tub on the floor, and another tub filled with a boar's entrails, and boar's meat hung in red, ropy clumps all over the place, all of it clouded with flies. Cumpashín hunted with blowguns and only sometimes used the shotgun, ammunition being hard to get. He fished using just a sapling trunk, string, and a hook with no bait, dancing the hook over the water, and somehow caught thirteen fish in half an hour and put them whole into his fire to cook like baked potatoes. When Mark had used up all the mosquito repellent they'd brought, Elias taught him to rub red ants into a rudimentary paste between his palms and smear it on his skin to keep mosquitoes away.

The next night Mark watched Cumpashín cure a patient who seemed to be suffering from, Mark would have guessed, a gallbladder attack, he so painfully writhed and groaned on his palm-sapling floor, clutching himself above the groin. The whole thing was crazy: Cumpashín drank from gourd bowls filled with wild garlic root shavings and aguardiente, and smoked wild tobacco while Mark quaked with nicotine fits. And then Cumpashín pulled a little stone out of a leather pouch, a smooth little egg-shaped stone, cupped it in his palms, and spoke conversationally and sweetly to the stone for about an hour, going, Sí . . . No . . . Ahá . . . Sí . . . No, no. Sí! Looks like a gallbladder problem to me too!—who knew what he was saying? It was his magic stone, Elias solemnly whispered. He'd found it as a boy apprentice shaman: the stone had been hopping around on a jungle path. Through it Cumpashín was consulting with the spirits of all the medicinal plants in the forest. These spirits told the shaman what to do: apparently they told Cumpashín to suck the illness out of his patient's body. The shaman placed his mouth against the guy's belly and made loud sucking noises, got to his feet holding his hands over his mouth and making horrible retching sounds, staggered over to the side of the hut, and then theatrically spat the illness out into the darkness of the forest. (Every time Mark gets up in the middle of the night needing to vomit, staggering to the bathroom with his mouth already filling, he remembers that.) And then Cumpashín went away and came back about an hour later, gave the guy something to drink brewed from a tree bark.

Later that night Cumpashín offered to treat Mark for whatever was ailing him. He tapped his temple in such a way as to indicate that he'd cure Mark of mental illness; Elias and the shaman had a good laugh over that.

Mark said, "He's not sucking on me no matter what." And then he said, "I don't know. I'd like to quit smoking, I guess."

Cumpashín asked if Mark had a photograph of himself. A photograph? Well, yeah, he did, an extra passport picture in his wallet. Cumpashín put Mark's picture into his little leather pouch with the magic stone and looked at Elias and said something like "Done."

Mark had been out of cigarettes for days, and the one puff he'd tried of Cumpashín's wild, leaf-rolled tobacco had him practically coughing his brains out through his ears. By the time he and Elias were back in Iquitos, Mark had already been more than a week without smoking, and the cravings had passed. Mark hadn't smoked another cigarette since, not one—until just about a month ago. Now he's up to two packs a day. At dinner parties like the one last night, Elias used to enjoy telling people about how Cumpashín cured Mark of smoking.

Parties like the one last night used to seem like the most interesting thing Elias had been doing during his three plus years as kept husband of the Imperial Loft: posturingly reliving his Amazon exploits for a very captive audience. There was something poignant about Elias; there was a restless greatness of spirit in his friend, Mark began to believe during those years, that was slowly being laid waste. Who knew what Elias would have talked about instead, if all that rain forest stuff hadn't become so trendy? Well, perhaps not the *most* interesting thing Elias had been doing: all his secret women. He kept saying he was going to go back to school to become licensed as a master herbalist, naturopath, or homeopath or some combination of all three, then open up a practice. But, really, back to school, at his age?

Then Elias found their ship. Three weeks later, and sixteen years after he and Elias had first imagined sharing in such adventures, Mark put Miracle in the kennel and flew to St. John, took a taxi to the shipyard, and climbed the ship's ladder onto the iron-and-rust manifestation of a dream finally made real. A ship, and he was part owner. Mark had never even owned a car. A dead ship, dumped by an owner too impatient and cheap and unimaginative and law-abiding to know how to make her seaworthy again; a ship that was only acting dead, just waiting for someone to come along, recognize her true worth, and rescue her from scrap. Haley, Elias's big, hairy ex-soldier friend—he'd been attached to a U.S. Marine and DEA outfit based in Iquitos that monitored Sendero Luminoso's narcotics trafficking in the Upper Amazon basin—and Yoriko, dressed in black, a pretty, willowy, twenty-something Japanese girl Elias had been secretly seeing, were already onboard. Haley was a nightclub bouncer now; Mark and Elias had hired him to help out in getting things under way.

"Nice rust bucket." Haley sneered-smiled, putting out his hand.

"Watch out for the holes in the deck, Mark," said Elias. "Wouldn't want you falling through, all the way down to where we won't be able to hear you calling for help."

"I didn't think it would be so rusted," said Mark.

"They were really running this thing on the cheap," said Elias. "Mainly just the coastal trade up here, working her like a truck, running cargo to and from Halifax. There was money even in that. But she used to sail all the way from Japan, through the Panama, believe it or not. Found the manifest of the last crew up on the bridge. Polish officers, mainly Chinese crew."

Everything had been arranged for towing the ship to New York. The only problem was that the ship's classification society, Nippon Kaiji Kyokia, upon being informed of the sale, was refusing to declare the ship seaworthy even to be towed until an inspector could come from Halifax to conduct the required survey. Elias's attitude was, Fuck that, they were going anyway. He'd foreseen the problem and knew they could get away with it. The tug company was charging two thousand dollars a day for the slow three-day voyage to New York. Setting his checkbook on the rail, Mark wrote out his share of the payment. He looked out at the placid harbor and the Bay of Fundy, the spread, shimmering tautness of the outgoing tide. It was late afternoon. He'd never been so far north and told himself that he'd never breathed air so fresh and clean. Wooden fishing boats were chugging into the harbor, trailed by thick flocks of gulls, and the moon was out, pale as a smudge of soap against a mirror in the limpid blue sky.

While the tug's deckhands prepared the towlines, Mark, Elias, and Yoriko climbed dark stairs to the wheelhouse. Mark grasped the spoked ship's wheel mounted on the Gyropilot and gazed out over the long, cluttered deck and complicated masts to sea. Elias briefly explained the radar equipment—fairly primitive, he said—the loran and echo sounder, the VHF radio, all of it needing electrical power to run. This button sets off the ship's horn, dead right now too, of course. There was a charts table, narrow drawers still filled with nautical charts. On the wall, a windup chronometer set to Greenwich mean time, a barometer, and a yellowing poster illustrating the Beaufort wind-force scale.

Elias and Yoriko had already gone out and procured mattresses and bedding for the voyage, two mattresses in two of the stripped officers' cabins and one in the two-room suite of the captain's quarters, which Elias had of course taken for himself and Yoriko. In St. John, Elias, with their new corporate credit cards—Achuar Corp. of Panama City (named for Cumpashín's tribe)—had bought Coleman lamps, plenty of spare batteries and cassette tapes for the boom box, coolers stuffed with food and beer, bottles of liquor, barrels of drinking water, a small barbecue grill, and a two-burner gas grill, which they'd transfer later down to the galley for their eventual repair crew to cook on. He'd even bought a little camping toilet. It was like they were going on a three-day camping trip in a floating mountain cave.

They went and looked at the individual steam baths behind their newly polished mahogany, brass-handled doors, the only remaining touch of luxury onboard. The baths' black-and-white tiles gleamed.

"Someday soon," said Elias, "these will be working. We'll take herbal steam baths." He squeezed his arms tighter around Yoriko's waist and smiled dryly. "Oh Yoriko, my love, what emotion."

Yoriko, nestled into Elias's frame, said, "They are beautiful. I can see that this is going to be a beautiful ship." She smiled up at Elias.

"Though it's pretty squalid now." Then she looked at Mark, shut her eyes, and said, "This macho thug had me cleaning up here all day."

The Canadian tugboat men did them the favor of pulling up the accommodation ladder—winches would raise the ladder automatically when they had electrical power again—and then climbed over the side, down to the pier, on a Jacob's ladder. Then Elias, Haley, and Mark hauled in the mooring lines—like real sailors, thought Mark, laughing from the excitement of it, pulling with all his strength on the fat, slimy, kerosene-smelling rope, while Yoriko snapped photographs.

With a big tug—4,300 horsepower, said Elias—called the *Lilly* leading the way, pulling the two thick cables of the towlines, wrapped around bitts on the prow and faked down through the bulwark, and two smaller tugs bumped up alongside, one at the stern and another out of sight under the flare of the bow, the ship began to move, slowly maneuvered out of her berth and into the Bay of Fundy, the water dappled with the soft pastels of sunset, stars already coming out in the clear, deep blue of the sky. The *Lilly,* captained by a middle-aged Scotsman with a walrus mustache named Maurice, who liked to be called Captain Mo, blasted her horn. Elias gave Yoriko the honor of smashing a bottle of champagne against the gunwale on the foredeck, and then he brought out four glass goblets and two more bottles of Moët & Chandon and popped the corks. They sat on the black iron bitts and leaned against the rail, sipping champagne, making toasts.

"To my first mate," said Elias, tapping Mark's glass.

"Oh yeah? Let me guess who the captain is."

And Elias, in his best attempt at a thick Long Island accent said, "I bet you wish *youu* could be the *cap-tinnn* of *some-thinnggg.*"

Mark cracked up, and Elias explained the old joke: back in college there'd been this guy, captain of the golf team or *some-thinnggg,* and once, when Elias was dumping on him, this girl had gotten pissed and said that, and he and Mark had picked it up as a goofy refrain—

"Oh boy," said Yoriko. "I'd say you guys have known each other *too long.*"

And then they were out in open ocean, peacefully wavelet rippled and moonlit under the night sky, and the two smaller tugs fell away hooting their whistles, and the tug up ahead—the Little Tug That Could, they called her, though she was the big one—headed south beneath Nova Scotia, the tug's wake foaming back towards the ship like a luminous, lacy bridal train trailed all the way from New York.

They barbecued hamburgers outside on a bridge wing. And Elias told stories about ways of making money through shipping fraud:

"Say someone in Brazil has ordered a cargo of, say, vacuum cleaners through a West German dealer . . ." That fellow in Brazil pays his money for the sale to a bank, said Elias. And the dealer arranges the transaction, insures the vacuum cleaners, gets the proper invoices, sees that it's all loaded onto a ship, then takes the shipping documents to an appropriate bank, and is paid. Everything hunky-dory. But what none of them suspects is that the captain of the ship is also her owner, and the name of this ship is just one in a series of names he's been sailing her under over the last few months. He sets off for Brazil, with more than a million dollars' worth of cargo in the holds, and hits a storm, a storm which doesn't show up on any weather satellite photo or anything, but what the hell, it's far out to sea, they can't track every little sudden typhoon, can they? The ship sinks to the bottom of the ocean. But most of the crew survive. They're picked up in a well-provisioned lifeboat and tell their terrible tale of the storm and sinking and the tragic fate of their captain, chief engineer, and a few others, who'd set out in the *other* lifeboat. But they'd lost sight of that lifeboat in the storm, and then that other lifeboat's radio suddenly went dead, and now they hadn't seen or heard a peep from them in days. Oh well, the vacuum cleaner buyer in Brazil, he just collects on his insurance, as does everyone else who had cargo on that ship. While that ship, already under a new name, slips quietly into a small Guyanese port, manned by its anonymous skeleton crew, takes on more crew, and sets off to, say, Cuba or Mexico, or maybe all the way to the Middle East, where the captain sells off everything he was carrying in the ship's holds, pocketing all the money, dividing it, unequally, among his loyal coconspirators.

Elias told a few more stories like that. Easiest way to make money with a ship like this one, he said, was to fix her up cheap, insure her for much more than you'd paid, and sink her. Easy to get rich, all you need is the imagination and cojones. Cheerfully, playfully, they all drank to that.

Later Mark leaned on the ledge beneath the wheelhouse windows, staring ahead through the tinted glass, sipping a scotch. Already, after a few hours, darkened ocean seemed a pretty monotonous sight. Wasn't like they were going to see any whales. Elias and Yoriko were out on a bridge wing now, chatting and laughing away. Elias was entertaining her with a sextant and his knowledge of the stars. Haley had drunk too much and was sitting at the charts table with his head rested on folded arms. The ship's progress felt steady and sturdy through the tranquil ocean, so why did he feel nauseous? He was jealous of Elias and Yoriko, not of their affair per se, perhaps, but of Elias's easy way with women. Mark was a little obsessed with Elias and Kate's marriage, was always studying it for edification about what had gone wrong between himself and Sue. Elias and Kate just got along so damned well. Elias was never too lazy or self-preoccupied or overtly egotistical to be inattentive to Kate, and he seemed always to get a great kick just out of amusing her. It was always almost as if they'd both just met and wanted to present each other with their best sides—well, what Elias and Kate thought of as their best sides. Elias was Kate's best friend, and though Elias knew how to act like almost any woman's best friend, with Kate it really seemed believable. Since Sue had left him, and even before, Elias was always saying, Mark, don't do *this* with women, Mark, try to do *that* next time you're hooked up to a woman. Elias said once, Mark, you made a common but stupid mistake with Sue, thinking that just because you'd been living together for so long, that meant you could be as nakedly *yourself* as you were as a little boy in the bosom of your psychotic family. That you could whine and emotionally overindulge yourself. That you didn't have to try to pull yourself up for her. So Sue had to suffer through your every little trauma about your video store. But, Mark, if you were just starting to go out with Sue, would you let yourself sit there all night in a depressed gloom about your video store? Would you try to make her want to share a life with you by telling her how hopeless you felt about your situation? Mark, mommies, not even yours, don't throw you out when they've had enough of you, they don't banish you from the family when you get boring, but women certainly do. Especially when they're still fairly young and attractive and justifiably dying to be appreciated and have some fun, like Sue. (Had Elias slept with Sue too?) Elias said that the thing about women was that you had to win them over to your side every day. You have to be *gallant,* Mark. And even kind of formal. He said the nice thing about that was that it didn't preclude sincerity, and actually got easier, not harder, as time went by. He said to save that sorry-ass, sad-sack stuff for a real crisis, when you'll really need her—whoever she'll be, Mark. I'm sure there'll be someone coming along soon.

One day not long after Sue left, when Mark felt like he was *really* falling apart, he said to Elias: I feel like I'm lugging a thousand-pound lead weight around in my chest, Doc. That Cumpashín, does he have a shaman cure for heartbreak?

Absolutely, Mark, said Elias. You take a stone and boil it. And when the water cools, you drink it. Makes your heart hard.

Mark went out onto the other wing, the one Elias and Yoriko weren't on, to get some air. He stayed out there for a long time with the cold ocean wind in his face, blaring in his ears, filling his lungs. He looked up at the thickly blazing stars, and down at the churned water fanning away from the ship, the swells slightly flecked with glowing foam now, and then at the warm light of the Little Tug That Could way up ahead, like a solitary cabin in the middle of a great wilderness.

When he went back inside Haley was snoring on the charts table and the door to the other wing had been slid shut and he thought Yoriko and Elias must have gone to bed, until he heard a muffled, sharp yelp of laughter out there, Yoriko's. He took a flashlight and went to explore the pitch dark ship. Elias had advised against such wandering at night; it was dark and there were lots of carelessly fastened objects around, the ship might suddenly pitch and roll and you could break a leg. With one hand on the stair rail, he went down past the floor their cabins were on, then pushed the door open into a corridor on the floor below. He found himself swaying unsteadily as he made his way down it, shining his flashlight into the bare, scarred little cabins where their crew was going to sleep—on this floor and the one below—the ocean murkily framed in the portholes. Down here, he could hear the hollow ship sighing and creaking like a haunted house from the strain of its pulled-along forward motion. He heard the faraway clangs of metallic objects falling as if to the bottom of a deep iron well. He went down another floor, following his flashlight through the dark, feeling fascinated by his own uneasy sensation of being all alone in an utterly alien and spooky environment—one that was half *his* now, after all. Recently, a man had died on this ship. He felt drawn towards the engine room, where it had happened. He found the handle to the steel door leading into it at the end of the corridor, cranked it down and pushed the door open, and made his way down a steel stairway and through another door into the control room and stood there bouncing his flashlight beam around the catwalk-hemmed, two-level steel box of the engine plant. The reek of diesel oil, machine grease, and doused burning was strong. He shined his flashlight on a grease-blackened metal table covered with tools and old papers, at the smoke-smudged control panel and breaker boxes, at the boiler forward, at thick pipes, scorched cables, and stems of packed wiring. He edged out onto the catwalk, holding tightly to the rail, shining his light on enginery whose purpose was a mystery to him, then aimed it down into the bottom level, at the immense engine in the middle, with its six faintly glowing turbine cylinders, and the machinery and pumps arrayed around it. He sat on the catwalk in the dark with his legs dangling, thinking that just a few months ago someone had died somewhere down there. He switched off his light and sat in the absolute darkness. He thought he could hear wind moaning in the cavernous, empty holds on the other side of the engine room, the deep, muffled roar of ocean parting heavily around the hull. He sat swaying side to side, his unsettled stomach making him feel a little dizzy again. He felt sad. He really wasn't used to hope. He'd had a mistrustful relationship with hope for years now. He thought, Please let this work out. Please let this lead to something good.

He woke in his cabin the next morning, pitched off his mattress and onto the floor. He got to his feet, and the floor receded under him again, his feet stepping backwards like falling dominoes until his back thudded against bulkhead. He danced forward across the floor and landed with his hands on the porthole, and he looked out at gray fog and slate gray swells, rising and sluggishly collapsing under crests of sprayed foam. The wind sounded desolate, an unwavering, low howl through an endless iron tunnel. He got back onto his mattress and clasped both sides, just lay there hanging on for who knew how long. He heard the clatter of unfastened objects falling and colliding everywhere.

Later, when he went down onto the deck to throw up, it was raining hard. He saw a cargo hook swinging wildly back and forth at the end of its loosened whip. He clutched the rail and vomited over the side, letting the wind carry it away, watching the waves rising against the side of the ship and breaking in broad swaths of hissing foam, rocking the ship and him backwards.

Soaking wet, he went back inside, and holding on to the stair rail with both hands, slowly made his way all the way up to the wheelhouse. Yoriko and Haley were sitting side by side on the floor against the bulkhead under the rain-lashed forward windows, swaying to and fro. Haley smiled weakly. Elias stood near them, one hand clasping the rail under the windows, and even he looked paler than usual. "Of course if we were under our own propulsion, it wouldn't be so bad," Elias said, as if mitigating his own responsibility for the weather. "It's at most a five on the wind-force scale. Nothing."

Mark stood beside him, looking ahead through the rain at the tug pounding through and over the swells.

"Go, Little Tug That Could," he said listlessly. Talking incited another wave of nausea. He sat next to Yoriko.

Only Elias ate that day. Once he called them to the portside windows and they watched another ship, its long deck stacked with containers, bucking past on the fuming horizon. They could see the ship's forward weight rocking her downwards, waves breaking over her prow and onto her deck in great bursts of water and spray.

The rain and winds, the ceaseless pitching and rolling, went on with stupefying monotony all that day and night and into the next morning. It was the longest day and night Mark had ever known, time turned into a sluggish element you were dunked in and out of, in and out of, light and darkness an irrelevancy. And then the weather began to calm.

By nightfall they were approaching New York, the outer waters off Sandy Hook and the Ambrose Channel running into Lower New York Bay. Already they could see faraway, thin stripes of light along Staten Island's shores, and the faint lights of ships up ahead, waiting for passage into the harbor, for the tide to rise high enough to allow their drafts to clear the mud-shoaled channels.

Empty of cargo and riding high, pulled along behind the Little Tug That Could like an immense iron box kite, and without power of her own, the *Urus* would be allowed directly into the harbor. They stood out on the starboard wing, the night air warmer now, the humid, heavy breeze like a premonition of the stagnant summer lying just ahead. They cheered when the pilot boat came out and the pilot stepped across bumping bulwarks to board the *Lilly*.

Soon they could see the lights off Coney Island and the blue lights of the Verrazano Narrows Bridge. They passed an immense tanker, lit up like a power facility at night, off-loading oil onto a barge. Pulled along against the slack tide, the *Urus* slid under the bridge, through the narrows, and into the Upper Bay between Staten Island and the Bay Ridge Anchorage Flats. Now the lights of the harbor simmered all around them. Haley poured scotch into their cups. At the mouth of the Kill van Kull, where most merchant ships turn off to run between Staten Island and Bayonne to the terminals and tank farms of Newark Bay and the Arthur Kill, two tugs came out to meet them, bumping up on either side of the hull, gently jolting the whole ship; up ahead they saw the pilot stepping off the heroic *Lilly,* reboarding the pilot boat, which sped off towards his next assignment. They cheered, touched their glasses, and hugged like old-fashioned immigrants when the illuminated Statue of Liberty came into view, the narrow cluster of gold-lit skyscrapers at the tip of Manhattan behind.

They proceeded past the long, darkened shores of Sunset Park's dead piers and into Gowanus Bay and down a nearly darkened channel past a tank farm and a barge port, through the mouth of an enclosed basin; the tugs danced around the hull, ruddering and propelling her almost like a weather vane against the tide, finally pinning her by stern and bow against a long finger pier overlooked by a tall, concrete, rectangular structure, surrounded by darkened terminal ruins and collapsed piers.

"Cheapest berth in the whole damned port," said Elias, while Mark, Haley, and Yoriko gaped at the silhouettes of the ruins.

There were two parked vans on the paved pier, and union dockworkers spread out along the wooden stringpiece, standing by the bitts (they'd be *billed* for that). Elias led them down to the deck and said, "I have to toss them the hawsers. Haven't had any practice in years."

He held a coil of thick mooring line over his thighs, then whirled almost like an Olympic hammer thrower and released it, the rope's monkey fist sailing out into the air and plummeting down to the pier. Elias did it again, and again, and again, and then let Haley have a go, the four of them marching down the length of the ship.

And then Elias showed them how to lower the accommodation ladder by walking out along it, and Mark's first and last ocean voyage came to an end.

Now Mark's the Little Tug That Couldn't, turned into a slug. Lying in bed with a hangover, ashtray on the night table overflowing with filthy butts. Little Tug better get up and move his car if he doesn't want it towed. Walk his dog. Go grocery shopping for his "crew." Little Tug went to Kate and Elias's dinner party last night, and what a night he had. But at least he got to sit next to Moira Meer—who's Elias's, and if not Elias's, Phil's. Uh-huh. So here's an amusing little riff he thinks he'll sit down and compose over breakfast (coffee, two-day-old refrigerated fried rice from a carton), send it in to "Talk of the Fucking Toy Town": How to comport your soul at a dinner party with wealthy young artistes, liberal do-nothings and the really wonderful, remarkable girl innocently seated next to you, when you happen to own a secret slave ship in New York Harbor. Hire the Little Tug to drag that soul and dump it with all the other garbage, right?

First draft needs work, but he better get going, Little Tug has to bring food to his *crew,* check on the injured old guy. Our little brown guys, property of Capitán Elias Cortés and First Mate Mark Pizarro. When he says that, Your Honor, he's not being racist, naw, he's using self-mocking irony to serve honesty, bitter humor to get to the heart of what he acknowledges is a horrible situation now and his own culpable but initially well-meaning—well, at least not slave owner–meaning—position vis-à-vis. Not all of them are little anyway, they're not *all* even brown. He's sick of being reminded, of feeling angry and guilty everywhere he goes, that's all, because everywhere he goes he sees them: busboys, McDonald's, even working in pizza parlors now instead of Italians and Greeks, lined up outside that taco truck on the corner of Ninety-fourth and Broadway, in the subways, working in delis, the Koreans always sending them down into basement to bring up your bag of ice and they come up holding it, dark eyes anxiously scanning customers for someone who *looks* like he's just standing around waiting for his bag of ice because they don't even know enough English to ask, Who's waiting for ice?—little brown guys but hardly ever any little brown females, yackety-yacking in Spanish, dark glare of their eyes, squat Napoleon builds and proud, serious Aztec (whatever) faces. By now there's not a Korean Deli owner in New York who doesn't know how to say, at least, *Qué pasa?* (Mark has noticed.) Which is about all the Spanish *he* knows . . . All those rich babes at the dinner party so entertained by Elias's magic shamans of the rain forest stories: why no magic Central American seamen-slave stories, eh, Elias? You don't see these guys levitating or vomiting butterflies or doing voodoo or communing with ghosts and spirits, just a bunch of fucked-over guys like fucked-over guys anywhere and they know it. (With, for a while, that Cat That Sat.)

Never talks to them anyway, makes it a point to keep his distance, doesn't try to bullshit them the way Elias does and laugh about it later. Well, not speaking Spanish, he couldn't even if he wanted to. Elias thinks these guys'll put up with anything from him cause he's such a regular dude. Thinks he's fucking Indiana Jones (a jungle explorer! born in the wrong century, he likes to say), Señor Regular Dude of the equatorial regions (wrong century for slaves, he means), knows how to get down with jungle thugs and shamans and smugglers and monkey hunters and whores and seamen, Elias could have ridden with the Wild Bunch, could have been Bart Oates! Know what paradise is, Mark? (was quoting someone, forget who). Paradise is a cantina in the tropics full of *machos y putas* . . . What's a puta again? A whore, Mark, Christ! Hey, least I know macho. Likes to say that at heart he isn't, isn't really a . . . *white boy*. Not like *you,* Mark. Yeah, right, Doc, OK.

His best friend since college, best man at his and Kate's wedding, definitely going to be the brat's godfather, covered up for him and lied for him in front of Kate for how many years now? All Elias's *womenz*. And what's Elias say last night when he hints at an interest in Moira Meer? Not that Elias has any say in the matter, but that he *thinks* he does! They've never gone after the same woman before. Had always expected if such a thing came up, though, that Elias would stand aside. Being married and all. Is he that competitive? that sick? Phil? Helpless rich-kid geek! Phil the Landfill, about as lively and full of it. Can't have her she's mine and if she's not mine, she's Phil's, Elias said after Kate's—really, it was Kate's—cleverly themed dinner party where totally unpretentious people had to pretend to be totally pompous posers, only el primero Mark wasn't really clever enough. But at least el Primero got to sit next to Moira Meer, whose occasional velvety gray sighs and smoky stares (one of the dinner guests was saying, "Yes, they're evil, sick photographs, but then, if you can . . . *cure* them—" and another said, "In the act of *looking,* you mean?" "Absolutely.") soon enough established that she found the whole subtle scene as enchanting as he did. Kate's prize student three or four years ago, they've always kept in touch—despite insinuations that Moira, while most talented, hasn't seized her opportunities, output too small, straying from conceptualist integrity into sadly bourgeois subjectivity—they let Moira loft-sit when they went to Thailand last winter. Elias always kisses and tells, because Elias *needs* to brag to Mark about his conquests and patiently cultivated harvests. So because Elias had told him so, he'd believed that as far as Moira was concerned, Elias had settled for a chaste, sort of paternal friendship despite feelings of deep esteem for this really adorable but vulnerable young woman. Mark had first begun hearing about her two summers ago, when Kate rented that place on Shelter Island and invited Moira out for a week (he was the next week's guest, their love boat–ferries may even have passed each other). There, Elias and Moira's always playful and affectionate acquaintanceship became a true friendship between mentor's student and mentor's hubby. Great girl, rather insecure but very sweet, needs a ton of love and devotion, needs her Tin Man, unfortunately her boyfriend's a *cunt,* he remembers Elias telling. Moira adores Kate! Her brilliance and self-confidence and beauty and accomplishment. (Mark admits he's not qualified to judge all those theoretical essays Kate writes, though he can't help but notice an aroma of industriously recycled bullshit: only an Inca can photograph other Incas and so forth, otherwise it's racist and imperialist and not *true,* which is why she photographs recipes, her own body, and whatever.) Mark had met, seen, talked a few times to Moira over the last few years, while he was still living with Sue and Miracle, and Moira had that boyfriend, that's finally over now too.

So last night, they kind of clicked, didn't they? So last night he said, Wow, that Moira, what a really wonderful, remarkable girl! That's all he said. A really wonderful, remarkable girl! Not babe, et cetera. You can't have her, she's mine. What a dumb thing to say to your old pal, Elias. Married, with your beautiful, classy, pregnant wife who supports you, who has to give you *lunch money* and, let's face it, loves the very ground you slime on. Who hell he? So he has something going with Moira, does he? Does he? In the bar he asked, Elias, you have something going with Moira? No, said Elias. We're in love with each other, but she knows there's nothing I can offer her. In love with each other! he said. So tender eyed and solemnly. *But there's nothing I can offer her. Because I'm still in love with Kate, of course. And there is the baby to consider, after all.* Nor is Moira rich. But why Phil? Wouldn't it have been not just decent but merely the expected thing for Elias to have said, I'll do what I can to help, Mark, put in a word. Or at least encourage. At least not say that. You know, just say nothing. Nope. She's his, and if not his, Phil's. What, he wants to use Phil as his smoke screen, knows Phil's so vague and geeky and egotistical that he just won't notice Father Elias poking around? Or is he really just being a responsible surrogate pop, wants to hook her up with Phil because Phil is just about the wealthiest guy he and Kate know. But Moira didn't even talk to Phil all night, didn't even seem to notice him. But Mark did, over predinner cocktails. Tall, blond, icky, aristocratically emaciated Phil, in his bright yellow sweater, looks like Big Bird in the end stage of that fucking disease. I'm planning a documentary on the rise of the Christian right, Phil smugly-morosely said. Well, whoop-de-do. Always planning something and never doing. When did it start, the rise of the Christian right? You starting in B.C. or A.D.? What's the sequel, the Christian wrong? You going to pay someone to do it for you, huh, Phil? You know what Christ said to the Puerto Ricans as he ascended to heaven? Don't do a *thing* until I get back! Put that in your doc, Phil, that's a rise that'll get a rise—

How's the shipping business, Mark? dryly asked Phil.

Rather depressed at the moment, Phil, said Mark.

Let me tell you about depression: weird urges on the subway to pull out your cigarette lighter and set the guy sitting next to you's newspaper on fire, or to lick the floor, what's to stop you? Man, really disgusting stuff goes through your head. At dinner, it was me Moira sat next to, me who basked in her smoky gray gaze—something about her eyes, they match her smoky, low voice, like the soft glare of stage lights behind dense clouds of cigarette smoke in some very dark basement cabaret. She loved that story about the crew hooked on pistachios. That old waiter's a nice guy, hope he's not hurt too badly. The rest of 'em . . . well, I don't really know them. Zombies. Look, they think I'm pretty weird too, I know, ever since that night I—ouch. You could barely hear her giggle, but she put down her wineglass and leaned into me, her whole body shaking with one long giggle, over that story about the pistachios. That's the silliest story I've heard in ages, I love it, she said. Leaning right into me, I could smell her shampooed hair, the faint, wet mushroom scent of her skin, her damp, wine-sweetened breath, a touch of salty garlic. Then she told me a joke about the Lunchbag of Notre Dame. She giggles through her teeth, beautiful white teeth, eyes squeezed shut, deep dimples you want to bury your nose in. Makes you feel like the only guy on earth ever shared her weird sense of humor. Silly jokes a way into her heart, and isn't that gosh darned wonderful! Meanwhile all that lah-di-dah talk, him and Elias, shipping magnates, dining with the artistes. Capitán and turned on primero. And Elias doing his smooth-superior-negative-cool-worldly-vaguely-Brit thing like always. Elias said: In the Amazon there's a tribe, the most paranoid tribe on earth, of which I met the remnants. You see, they have this belief that any bad thing that happens, from a stuffed nose to a broken fishing line to an old man dying in his sleep, was caused by someone else's malevolence, a spell, or maybe just a malevolent thought. And that it has to be appropriately avenged. So that there's no death, however natural its cause, you see, that doesn't have to be avenged by another death. Small wonder there aren't many of them left. Not your usual Amazonian rain forest UNICEF poster tribe, is it? Sounds just like the art world, someone said. Art world? scoffed Elias. Bollocks. Art world? How? Paranoids and people wishing ill on others, definitely. But how many have the cojones to exact even, or especially I might say, a *deserved* revenge. Why, you might offend somebody *important*! Hey, I interrupted, Hey, Elias, how do you appropriately avenge a stuffed nose? With insects, Mark, he coolly replied.

That really got Moira giggling too, until she seemed practically out of breath. Insects up your nose? Felt like he was watching his love boat sail away without him while she giggled over Elias's juvenile, deadpan retort like that, eyes mirthfully brimming down the table at Elias with a generous modesty that pierced Mark's heart. I'm phoning her anyway. She said, Sure, Mark, give me a call, and smiled . . .

Lugging three bags of groceries for his *crew,* Mark is walking to his car, Miracle already locked and waiting inside it, when he sees that Latino boy waiting to cross Broadway with a wrapped and ribboned bouquet in his hands. A flower seller, or a delivery boy. Send Moira flowers! Maybe he should just buy this kid's bouquet and tell him where to bring it, scribble a *gallant* note. But then he realizes that the kid probably isn't a flower seller, because usually they push shopping carts full of flowers; he probably isn't even a delivery boy. He's holding his bouquet so carefully in both hands, and was just fidgeting with the ribboned bow, making a tiny, finicky adjustment. And he's with a friend. He's crossing Broadway now with his friend beside him, talking and laughing. He's bringing those flowers to someone *he* loves.

Mark feels terrible. What if he'd stopped the kid and offered to buy the bouquet, said, How much? in the usual brusquely commanding way. How embarrassing! But that's what he almost did. He doesn't even step off the curb to cross Broadway, he just watches the two friends reach the other side and go ambling up Ninety-fourth Street. Elias is fucking Moira. Of course he is. And Moira's in love with Elias. Well, he *told* you, didn't he?

2

LATER, AFTER GONZALO HAD GONE HOME, ESTEBAN PACED THE DARKENED, shuttered, locked-up salon, sipping at his refilled glass of wine, letting the radio play very low. Gonzalo had said he could finish the bottle, that it wasn't very expensive wine. And before leaving and locking him in, Gonzalo had told him to keep the lights off after he swept up so as not to draw attention to his sleeping there, and showed him how to go out the back way into an asphalt alley in case of, God forbid, a fire. Gonzalo is the only Cuban Esteban has ever met who doesn't smoke.

The barber chair had been cranked back, and the blanket lay folded on top of it. Esteban paced through a dark foliage of shadows thrown by the bit of street light penetrating through the window and barred gates. He assessed his situation: a haircut, a new sweater, and he was wearing new socks—the old, rotted ones lay knotted inside a plastic grocery bag, stuffed inside the plastic garbage bag along with his own and everyone else's swept up hair. He had no place to live, no money, no job, and no legal right to be here (though apparently that doesn't stop anyone). He thought about everyone else left behind on the *Urus,* and wondered why it felt so easy to forget them now that he was here. Pues, they'd never left the ship and he had, they could have done the same. But it made him feel guilty, this realization of how easy they all were to forget. He should have at least said good-bye to Bernardo. He told himself not to think about the ship anymore, to concentrate only on the present and future. But this new existence of sleeping in chairs in strange places, depending on luck and generosity, felt as furtive as a rodent's, and couldn't last anyway. And with every passing moment the confounding reality of his situation eroded his delusion of being well on his way to love and a new life a little bit more.

But look, here he was drinking wine right from the bottle! Almost five months ago he'd reclined in a chair something like this one—as

Gonzalo said, it was like sitting on an airplane—on his providential flight to Nueva York to meet the *Urus,* and he'd wanted to celebrate the occasion with wine but hadn't dared to because of Bernardo's adamant abstinence. The strange thing was that he'd felt no less on the verge of a new life then than he did now. And though of course he'd let himself feel more optimistic that day, he felt a little more at home in himself now. Now that he had no home at all. More frightened of the world, and less frightened of himself. And puta, who could make sense of that? Maybe it was just the wine fortifying him.

He went into the back, took off all his clothes, and stood over the industrial sink washing himself in the dark with soap and water. And then he decided to clean his hands with the stiff-bristled brush over the sink, and to clip his nails. He stepped naked through the curtain to Joaquina's manicure trolley and groped among her instruments in the darkness. Chocho, wouldn't you know it? The one thing she doesn't have is a common nail clipper. He chose a pointed little tool for cleaning under his nails, and small scissors, and then went into the bathroom, closed the door, and turned on the light. It seemed to take at least an hour of scrubbing to get all the old paint and grease out of his hands, until his fingers were raw and pink. He did the same with his feet, sitting on the toilet, and then stood in front of the little sink, awkwardly hoisting and holding his foot with both hands under the faucet. With the scissors, he cut all his nails slowly and carefully, and then cleaned underneath them. After he'd put Joaquina's instruments back exactly as he'd found them, he pulled the clean T-shirt on, and the sweater over it, and then his big underpants, pants, and socks, though not his boots. He folded the three tattered, filthy T-shirts neatly, and set them on a chair.

And then he corked what was left of the wine, got into the barber chair, and arranged the blanket over himself. He fell asleep thinking about the story Gonzalo had told him about his days as a Tropicana dancer, which had made the world sound more unstable than ever. Gonzalo and a legendary dancer named Lisette used to star together in a number where she played a woman fleeing her savage jungle tribe because they wanted to punish her for loving someone from another tribe, climbing up onto a catwalk high above the stage, and hurling herself to her death, except her lover surprises her by catching her in his arms: that's the image in the photograph, Gonzalo just after he's caught her. She'd performed her famous swan-diving leap into Gonzalo's arms from balconies and rigging high above stages all over the world and always to thundering ovations, though the one Gonzalo would never forget happened one night in La Habana, when El Líder himself shocked them by leaving his table full of visiting dignitaries and government officials and climbing up onstage, in his pressed military uniform, to deliver an armful of white roses to Lisette and embrace the two stars. Gonzalo was surprised by the feminine softness of his hand when he shook it, and when he was embraced to receive a kiss on the cheek, Gonzalo said he almost swooned from the silkiness of his beard, the pampered satin of El Líder's cheek against his, and the overwhelming scent of baby powder and cologne that wafted off his skin. Es tan regia! Gonzalo had exclaimed to Esteban. That fat jota queen! He's as regia as any of us! Yet *he'd* thrown him out of Cuba for being homosexual and for no other reason, sent him to Florida in a boat crammed with lunatics, criminals, and all the pajaritos they'd been able to round up. And what do you think happened, chico? The first time Lisette had to perform her leap with a new partner he mishandled the catch and she cracked her skull on the stage and fractured her neck and spent a year in the hospital and never danced again. Gonzalo said that whenever he meets someone who's traveling to Cuba, usually a European or rich South American, he sends Lisette a present: the expensive chocolates she'd become addicted to during the long run their Tropicana traveling troupe had in Rome, and once, though this had cost him a fortune, the very latest in lifelike falsies built into a fancy brassiere. Pues Lisette has the tiniest tetitas, he said, and likes to wear them.

The voices of the drunken revelers outside briefly woke him—the infamous urinators. Through the lowered gates he could see the shadows of men huddled together, hear their boisterous laughter; voices in English, and then someone asking in Spanish about what had just been said, and then someone else translating, "He said he stabbed the fucking Jew!" And more laughter. Puta, like any bunch of friends reminiscing about some old prank, except they were reminiscing about murder!

When he wakes again it's morning, and the lights are on in the salon, and for a moment he doesn't know where he is except he's still frightened and depressed by the voices and he sits up in the barber chair and sees Joaquina in the mirror sitting in a chair along the wall, drinking coffee. Their eyes meet in the mirror a moment, and then she says, Buenos días, and asks him if he wants a cup of coffee and he says yes and thanks her, his voice croaking. She's in another smocklike dress though this one has no sleeves, and underneath she's wearing the same white, lacy blouse she had on the morning he met her.

"I realized after I left that you probably didn't have anywhere to sleep," she says. "I was so worried about you. Ni modo, Gonzalo took care of it."

"Sí pues."

She comes over to him with a cup of coffee. She's wearing the same earrings as yesterday.

"You look a lot different." She smiles. "But I still think you should wear your hair long."

He frowns. "Vos, I don't like this tail in back. Can you cut it off?"

She stands there looking at him appraisingly. Finally she shrugs. "Ahorita?" And he nods. She puts down her coffee and opens a drawer and takes out a pair of scissors.

She stands close to him. His nose is still stuffed, and he wishes that he could smell her.

"Bueno, chamaco," she says. "Lean your head forward." He feels her warm hand on the back of his neck. "Don't move," she says, and for a moment she stands there shaking with silent giggles. "I don't know why I think this is so funny!" she says, barely able to get it out.

"Just cut it," he says. "I hate it!"

Hágalo! he tells himself. You have to do it. His heart pounds. Right now!

Then she's leaning against him, smiling and holding up the cut strands of hair, about five inches long. Hágalo! He reaches up and takes her pinkie between his thumb and finger and holds it. They look at each other, and her expression is suddenly serious.

"Esteban," she says, finally. "There's someone else, I told you. I don't want to lie to you. It's just that I don't know what's going to happen."

"I'm glad you told me. But to me, that has no importance."

Then he puts a hand on either side of her face and raises his head and kisses her and her eyes widen. Her lips are so chapped under her lipstick he almost pulls away, but soon they become wet and soft from kissing. They keep on kissing, and then he feels her tongue slip into his mouth against his. She lifts her arms around his neck.

And then they stop kissing and she rests against him, a hand on each of his shoulders, his snipped-off hair still sprouting between her fingers.

"Let's go in back and make love right now," he says. Though he begins to panic, because he remembers the last time, in the burdel in Corinto, when she took off her clothes and her damp nudity and fragile, childish skin made him think of what had happened to la Marta and she turned over on the bed and thrust her nalgas at him and grinned over her shoulder and told him to suck her there, amorcito. He hates himself! Don't think about it! No pasa nada. Except, puta, it's like having uncontrollable lunatic voices in your head! He's trembling.

"Estás loco, güey," she says. "With Gonzalo coming in any second? We shouldn't even be kissing, I don't want to catch your cold."

He feels relieved that they aren't going to do it right now.

"I want to make love right now," he insists.

They start to kiss again, and he feels momentarily swirled away from his panic by the caresses of her lips and tongue. He slides his hands inside her dress and feels her small breasts through her blouse.

"Esteban, qué haces?" she murmurs, slowly pulling herself back. "Don't be naco. There are people out on the sidewalk."

She takes a step back and looks at him a long time with a dark-eyed cat's mesmerized stare. "I feel good with you," she says. "But we can't do it now." Then she smiles. "When we do it, güey, it's not going to be in front of an audience."

"Bueno."

"Because I'm going to eat you alive," she says. "You'll see, guarrito."

His pija climbs even higher. He has to swallow just to say, "Ah sí?"

She grins and gives him a skeptical, sideways look. "The little soldier, no?" And then she takes his hand and slaps his hair into his palm. "I cut off your tail!"

She picks up her coffee and walks back to the chairs against the wall and primly sits herself down.

She sits in silence a moment while he tries to compose himself in the chair, and then she astonishes him again with her frankness: "The only question is where. We can't do it where I live, not with all my brothers around. Your ship?"

"Olvídalo. Here. In the middle of the night."

"Está bien." She shrugs. "If there's nowhere else."

"Vos, Joaquina," he says after a moment. "If you ever come here alone at night and those hijos de puta are out there, whatever you do, don't give them any of your mouthiness." He pauses, he was about to tell her they're murderers, but he doesn't want to terrify her. "I know how you are, Joaquina. But be careful with them. They're dangerous."

Esteban leaves the salon that morning before Gonzalo has arrived, but he's arranged to come back in the evening, so that he, Joaquina, and Gonzalo can make some plans, try to figure out where he can live, where he might look for work. Before leaving, he took off his new sweater and T-shirt, folded them, and put them on a shelf in back. He's wearing his old clothes. He doesn't want to get his sweater dirty: he's going back to the ship. In his elation, he's conceived a plan, not well thought out yet, of confronting Capitán Elias to try to collect his pay, formally quit even. With the more than a thousand dollars he's owed, Joaquina says he could easily rent a room and not even have to share it like she still shares hers with one of her brothers. If only he can think of some way of pressuring Capitán Hijueputa, something to threaten him with.

He's on his way back to the waterfront when he sees the truck parked on a side street, alongside a corner butcher shop. Its rear doors are open, and inside it's full of giant slabs of beef. Entire sides of beef, legs and thighs, marbled with fat, hang from the roof inside, and against the back are long racks of ribs that look like bloody, grotesquely wrenched piano keyboards. The only person he sees is a morena woman pushing a baby stroller on the opposite sidewalk, far down at the end of the street. An aluminum-sheeted side door in the butcher shop's concrete wall stands open a crack. Maybe they're inside lingering over coffee. He'd promised himself not to steal anymore but feels now as if he's soaring on spirit and luck towards an act of duty. If anyone comes out he'll just drop it and run like crazy: he leaps up into the back of the truck, positions himself under a hanging leg and thigh, pushing up against it with his back and hands until the wire comes unhooked and the side of beef falls down onto his back while he grabs and wrestles it onto his shoulder. He jumps down from the truck onto the pavement with the enormous slab of beef over his shoulder, both hands wrapped around the shank just over the hoof, and starts walking.

3

WHEN MARK BOARDS THE *URUS,* THE FIRST THING HE SEES IS A WHOLE SIDE of beef on the deck with seagulls all over it: red and fat-marbled, a wire hook over the hoof. Just lying there, like it fell out of the sky, and gulls stripping pieces of fat away in their beaks, stretching their black-tipped wings, pecking at one another and at the hunk of cow, screeching and laughing, flapping up into the sky, landing, spattering the beef with shit. Miracle is even more stunned by the sight than he is, barking, charging it, and dodging back, while the gulls shriek and flutter up, hovering over the dog and the beef, soaring and circling. And then some of the crew are standing around the side of beef, flapping their arms up at the gulls and shouting in Spanish and others pushing Miracle away and Mark's asking where it came from and "Qué pasa?" but they're pulling him towards the deckhouse and into the cabins, saying something about Bernardo.

They lead him into one of the dingy cabins where he never goes, and he sees the kid who supposedly fought in a war sitting cross-legged with his chin in his hands by the mattress the old man is stretched out on, the old man naked from the waist down, dirty gauze bandages heaped around his legs, one leg swollen and discolored and covered with oozing liquid sores. There's a putrid smell. The old man's eyes roll blankly, his lips look blistered and dry. He's shivering and shaking. And the kid is standing in front of him now, screaming something, screaming, *"Hospital."* Other words and that one word over and over, *"hospital!"* And something else is strange, so strange that he stands there pondering it a moment, as if he's wondering where he's seen the kid before, and then he realizes what it is, the kid has a new haircut.

"Sí!" says Mark. "Sí. OK!" And he walks out of the cabin and onto the deck. The side of beef isn't there anymore. They've carried it away somewhere, and Miracle is sniffing and licking at the spot where it had been lying. His hands are trembling and his heart is thudding with fear. What's he going to do? Well, he has to get the old man to a hospital. He has to, doesn't he? What, Elias would want to just leave him there? It's a burn, probably an infection, hospital can cure that, and then the old man'll talk, and they'll be in deepest shit. What's the alternative, wait for him to die and dump him in the harbor? Not even Elias— Elias is out in L.A., it's not his decision.

The big smiley guy, though he's not smiling now, has carried Bernardo out on deck in his arms, they've pulled these big, baggy underpants onto him. And the kid with the haircut is screaming at him again and shoves him up against the side of the deckhouse and Mark grabs the kid's hands off his chest and pushes them down and screams, "Get your fucking hands off of me! I'm taking him to the hospital. Carry him down to the car!" He points and shouts, "The car! We're going to the hospital!"

And Gold Tooth is trying to calm the kid with the haircut. And he sees that the kid's shoulder, his dirty outer T-shirt, is bloodstained and slicked down with grease, a few little bits of fat clinging to the fabric; the sight almost makes him retch.

Mark leads the way down the ladder, the big guy carrying the old man and all the others and Miracle following him to the pier and the car. He opens the door, pulls out the groceries, sets the bags down on the pier, and adjusts the passenger seat so it's all the way back.

"Put him in there!" The big guy and Barbie lay Bernardo into the front seat, and Mark goes around to the other door, calls, "Miracle, get in!" and the dog climbs into the back and Mark gets in behind the wheel. The kid with the haircut wants to go.

"No!" shouts Mark. "There's no room!" Well, there isn't. "I'm taking him right to the emergency room, they'll carry him in!" He looks up at the kid almost pleadingly. "We're going right to the emergency room. Everything's going to be OK!"

They seem to understand. They fall silent now, standing around the car, almost all of them, watching.

"I'm going to the hospital now, OK?" And he looks from face to face. "OK?" He shuts the door and starts the car and drives off with the old man prostrate and silent and his horrible stench; he rolls down his window, lights a cigarette.

Where to? Doesn't know any Brooklyn hospitals, doesn't have any idea where one is. A hospital that takes indigents. A Manhattan hospital. That's better, get him far away from the ship. As if then it will take longer for the shit to come down. As if the shit that comes down can get stuck in traffic trying to get across the Brooklyn Bridge too.

He finally gets across the bridge and turns up onto the FDR, traffic still slow and blaring. Bernardo doesn't even seem to stir, but he can hear his dry, rasped breathing. They'll cure him. And then maybe he'll just be deported, an illegal alien who somehow snuck into the country in just his underpants with a burnt and infected leg. Or maybe there'll be no one who cares enough to ask him anything, in New York you ought to be able to count on that.

He parks illegally, of course, and sees ambulances pulled up outside the emergency entrance, and people all over the place, some of them in medical uniforms. Someone should be able to help. And he decides, no. And begins wrestling the old man out of the front seat, into his arms, shouting, "Stay, Miracle!" Holding Bernardo like a fainted bride in his arms, he kicks the door shut, doesn't even lock it, anyone wants to steal the dog that badly they can fucking have him. And he carries Bernardo in his arms towards the emergency room entrance, cringing inwardly against his stink and infirmity and the intimacy of his flesh, astonished by how little the old man weighs.

He sets him down on the floor in front of the reception desk while the nurses, black and Asian, glare at him. Right down on the floor. And the words just come tumbling out, he hadn't even rehearsed them:

"Look, I just found this guy in my doorway. He's really in bad shape, look at his leg, I mean, I think it's infected. I don't know his name. I don't who he is—"

"You just can't bring him in here like that," the Asian nurse is waspishly saying. "You should have called an ambulance. This hospital is overcrowded as it is, sir—"

"I did the right thing," he yells, telling himself, Go ahead, lose it. "I'm helping the guy. I saved you the trouble, didn't I? What, he should die? I'm supposed to just leave him? Yeah, yeah, because this is New York, right?"

"We do not have the room. We cannot accept—"

"Look, I'm going. Take him somewhere else then. You're *sworn* to help him. Don't you take an *oath* or something?"

And he's turning to leave.

"You have to sign him in, sir. You can't just —"

Someone's waving a clipboard at him.

"I don't have time," he shouts. "My name's Mark Baker, OK?" Why'd he tell them that? He feels his chest heaving as if he wants to cry. "My address is 529 Grand Street!" That just popped out, Elias's address. Well, good. But he doesn't see any of the nurses writing it down, they're just glaring at him. And he's already walking out the door while a nurse yells for a guard, but Mark pushes through, shouting furiously about how he's done the right thing and leave him goddamned alone, and before he knows it he's outside in the cool autumn air again and jogging to his car; he looks back and sees a bunch of people standing outside the entrance just staring, and he gets in and drives off.

When he gets home, he leaves a message on Elias's answering machine: "Elias, I took the old guy to a hospital. He was in really bad shape. I guess it's over, Doc. Your medicine didn't work so well. Sorry, man." And he hangs up. Let Elias explain *that* to Kate.

That night Mark, with Miracle sedated in a portable kennel, his carry-on bag stuffed with traveler's checks, boards a flight out of Kennedy, to the Yucatán, via Cancún. He was smart, he's kept his personal credit cards out of all *Urus* transactions. He'll rent a little place on a beach. Chill until it's all in the past. Maybe even learn Spanish. Look, he can live with the lost investment, and feel lucky he got out without having to sink in another cent. Mark, you stood up. You're a hero, man. Wonder boy, kept your soul clean! Sort of. Sure, he'll take headphones, what's the movie? Already seen it, sucks, what the hell. And another double Jim Beam on the rocks, please. Did the right thing today. Probably saved the old guy's life. Elias was willing to just let the guy die. Elias can go to hell.

4

ELIAS ASSEMBLES THE CREW AS SOON AS HE COMES OUT OF THE ENGINE ROOM. They can't be too surprised that he went right down into the engine room carrying the two circuit breaker boxes as soon as he arrived, can't be surprised that he flipped out when they didn't fit. But now he has to pull himself together. Casual, he tells himself. Smooth, this is no big deal. Of course, you feel a little hurt, a little humiliated that your remedies didn't work, that the old man had to resort to the allopaths, and so, adopt an air of wounded but generous dignity, cabrón. Anyway, it was *their* fault . . . Some of these kids are starting to look pretty bad, completely spaced and lethargic.

"Bernardo is doing very well, and sends all of you his regards and an abrazo," Elias says. "He's cured of his infection. I'm afraid the infection was caused by those dirty rags you cleaned him with the night it happened, güeyes. But luckily, no lasting harm was done, aside, por supuesto, from the hospital bills. These are astronomical! The health system in this country is *mierda.* They didn't have to amputate, thank God, another day and they might have. But Bernardo is still quite weak, and we've decided that it's best that he go home to Nicaragua. He'll be flying home as soon as the doctors think he's well enough to, in another few days, hopefully. So, if some of you could collect and pack his things, including his passport, very important, and bring them to me, please."

Necessary touch, that—leave the possibility of a few days, in case the old man suddenly comes back to the ship. And then he'll have to make something else up.

Esteban says he wants to visit Bernardo in the hospital. Where did he get that haircut?

"Esteban, you can't, cabrón." He smiles. Keep it casual, Elias. Don't get uptight. Remember, this is *good* news: the old guy's OK. No big deal, an injured seaman going home, happens all the time. "I've told you over and over, you are an illegal alien whenever you set foot onshore. Bernardo has permission because of his injury. You want to go on and off the ship like you've been doing, Esteban, it's your risk. But if they catch you at the hospital, *I'll* be in trouble too. Nice haircut." He smiles. "Muy guapo!"

See? A few of them even grin. They seem relieved to hear that the old waiter is going to be OK, maybe even jealous that he gets to go home.

"What hospital is he in?" asks Esteban.

"New York Hospital. But you're not going there. That's an order from your capitán."

"Are you going to pay him before he goes home?" asks Esteban.

"I should think so," says Elias. "The owner will have to pay him, yes."

"He won't take the hospital expenses out of his pay?" asks Esteban.

"No. Look, I won't lie to you, I'm sure he'd like to! But I'll make sure that he doesn't. OK? Really, don't worry about it, Esteban," and he claps the kid on the shoulder.

"Maybe the hospital wouldn't have charged so much if you'd taken him there right away instead of trying to cure him yourself," says Esteban, eyes smoldering. "It should come out of *your* pay."

"I didn't clean his leg with a dirty rag! Maybe it should come out of *all* of your pay!" he says vehemently, trying to stare the kid down. Christ! Stay cool, Elias.

"We have an inspection in a few days . . . ," Elias continues, changing the subject. Which is true. The Panamanian Registry is sending someone by for the annual checkup, left a message on Miracle Shipping's answering machine, time to disconnect that thing. The guy at the shipyard thought the breaker boxes would probably match but he couldn't guarantee it. But they didn't fit. If it weren't for this other problem, he probably would have started weeping right there in the engine room. As it was, he practically kicked in the control panel. He'll tell the inspector the ship's still under repair, nowhere near ready to sail.

When he's finished telling them about the inspection and what needs to be done beforehand, Elias leans on the rail, stares out at the cove. Two black grebes have settled on the water, they dive under like seals, stay under for such a long time, bob back up fifty yards away. A smell of charred steak somehow lingering in the air. Where's it coming from? The swept, blackened circle of soot on the deck from their cooking fires seems to have widened.

Where the hell is Mark? Sue hasn't heard a thing from him, nor has Moira. Maybe he killed himself, the little wanker. *Which* fucking hospital, Mark, you *cunt*. After he got back from L.A. last night and heard the wanker's message, he phoned every hospital in Brooklyn to ask if they had a patient named Bernardo Puyano, in for a burn. Luckily he still had the crew list Constantine Malevante had faxed him (used a stationery store's fax), had all their last names and passport numbers (still owes Malevante the hiring fees). And then he started in on the Manhattan hospitals.

So what else to do but wait? A crisis. Separates the man from the boys. Rapid response. Deal with it, cabrón. Been in worse scrapes. Well, no, probably haven't. Police or harbor authorities might come driving onto the pier any moment. Maybe he should get to work on trying to sell the ship, as is, where is, whatever he can get. Maybe there's no time even for that. Tell Kate that Mark absconded with all the money. He can file for bankruptcy when the old man talks and sues. Oh, someone will tell him he can sue, someone *will*. Confess all to Kate, hire a good lawyer himself. Or take off too. Then, when the old man talks and sues, maybe they won't be able to find him, even if they want to. A lot depends on what Mark told at the hospital. But if he takes off too, he loses everything. Baby coming in December. Otherwise, he'd cut out. Maybe I should fly to Japan and scour scrap yards . . .

Driving home that night with Bernardo's suitcase on the seat beside him, he thinks of pulling over to throw it into the harbor, like he did with some of their mail, months ago now. But Bernardo will probably turn up back at the ship—unless he can find him first, send him home, bribe him, I don't know. Think! The prudent thing is to keep it. Yes, keep the suitcase. When he parks the car, he locks the battered cowhide suitcase in the trunk. But what if Kate looks inside? Better steal her copy of the trunk key.

Elias sits in his lab late into the night, phoning hospitals, looking for a patient with a burned leg named Bernardo Puyano. Finally he gives up and sits staring at the floor between his feet with his head cradled in his hands.

5

THE GERMAN TRACKING DOG IS LEADING THE LONG COLUMN OF TROOPS through the jungle. The chavalo is telling him about it: how they had to move along so slowly, how they were used to relying on their own senses and intuition but now they were dependent on this hija de puta dog named Ana, and so everyone was in a bad mood. Every half hour or so, and even more frequently when the compa holding Ana's leash said the enemy must be close, the entire column had to stop while soldiers fanned out into the dense jungle and crept ahead, searching for ambushers. So they moved through the jungle slowly, but la contra were moving slowly too, because they were carrying wounded. A campesino admitted to having seen them go by, and to having given them platanos. They found the scattered sticks of lean-tos they'd built the night before, a single, wet rolling paper draped over a weed. Then it rained, and they marched all day, grateful for the coolness of rain, and like always when it rained like that they marched along feeling made of jungle and rain, the rain vibrating off broad leaves, vibrating inside them too, following the dog that followed the scent. Up ahead in a small clearing, a wounded contra sat up on his dropped litter and Ana broke the boy's grip on her leash and charged the poor hijo de puta—those near the front of the column who survived said later they'd just had time to see the blood spurting from the contra's neck when the shooting broke out and the dog fell away dead from his neck.

And Bernardo is shouting, "Ya! Basta! Puta, qué bárbaro! Brother killing brother is bad enough! And now letting this foreign cannibal dog loose on your brothers—"

He wakes on his gurney, staring up at tubes of sizzling, grayish fluorescent lighting in a dark ceiling, barely radiating. He looks over at Esteban's bed and sees nothing but darkened wall painted a dull shade of yellow. Where is Esteban? And then remembers this: Esteban with a haircut leaning over him. And he raised his arms and clasped the chavalo's head in his hands, pulled him towards him and gave him a kiss on the cheek, and then everything went dark . . . Or was that just another delusion?

Now, with great effort, he lifts his head a little and sees gurneys like the one he's on lining both sides of the long corridor, some with IV bottles and rigging at their sides. He drops his head from the pain in his neck. Santísima Virgen, where am I? He hears screaming, the most horrible screams ever, and then scolding, angry voices answering the screamer in English.

He closes his eyes. He's never had such a headache. But his leg feels numb. He has no strength in his limbs. Pitaya juice cools his parched, caked mouth. He hears someone treading by softly like a walking breeze and tries to call out, but he can't, his throat feels full of hot sand. Clarita always merely said, "Qué tal, Bernardo," when he came home from the sea, as if he was a friend she hadn't seen for a few days instead of a husband away nearly a year; and then he'd have to ignite her love again. Qué tal! Ve? I've brought back two chicken incubators! From now on I'm just going to sit in this chair on my porch and be old. I made a friend, a good chavalo, he was my cabin mate on the *Urus,* you should try to get him to marry you, Freyda, bueno, he'll be by one of these days . . . Pues, qué tal, Clarita. He left the ship at Puerto Cabezas and boarded a bus, setting out on one of those journeys that lasted days, through stifling heat, by bus and then the Rama ferry and bus to Managua just to hear Clarita say, Qué tal, Bernardo. There was an old Indian woman on the bus, Miskito probably, and she stank so badly, like rotted cheese. The hijueputa cobrador wanted to eject her, and the passengers wanted him to, because of the way her smell filled the packed oven of the bus. The Indian woman didn't seem to speak Spanish, seemed unable to explain or defend herself. She was terrified. They were in the middle of nowhere, and this hijo de cien mil putas cobrador and the driver were going to throw her off the bus because she was just a poor indita who stank. He was gagging from the smell and airless heat too, felt nauseous from the smell and the bus's rattling over rutted dirt roads. But it was abominable to throw an old woman off a bus, he would not permit it, he'd get off here in the jungle with her if it came to that, though he was willing to come to blows first. He rose from his seat to defend her. First, he spoke gently to her, said, I'm not going to let them, mamita. That was all it took! The old Indian woman whisperingly confided that she smelled like that because that was what she did for money, she made cheese, pues. And he turned to the other passengers and shouted, She only smells like that because she makes cheese!

6

THE HOSPITAL IS SO OVERCROWDED THAT DR. OFORI, FROM GHANA, WITH A trim, black beard and a coppery, bald head, spends half his shift making his rounds in gurney-crowded corridors like this one. Now he stands over the blankly staring old man on the gurney—yet another anonymous indigent, dirty, with messy, sweat-matted hair and stubbled chin, well shaped though smudged and fungused bare feet, and a jungle tiger's long toenails. And he starts shouting in a commanding baritone that rises querulously with outraged emphasis, and brings exhausted nurses running, "How long has this patient been lying here? No one has even cleaned his leg! There is dead tissue here all the way down to the bone! Clearly an infection has formed, I see signs of gangrene, of clostridium! This man's leg is rotting, and he has just been left to lie here! The infection may have already entered his bloodstream! Is this a hospital or a charnel house!" And then he notices. He waves a hand over the staring eyes. He checks the pulse, and drops the cold hand. "Take this man down to the morgue," he says, his voice flat with drained fury. Another corpse destined for Potter's Field, the indigents' cemetery on Hart Island. God speed you, old man. And Dr. Ofori, trembling, moves on to the next gurney, thinking, Whichever God that might be.

SCRAP

1

WHEN THE NIGHTS BEGIN TO FALL BELOW FREEZING, THE CREW drag their mattresses and blankets into the iron cave of the galley and mess. Every night, in the mess, they light fires inside a rusted barrel sheared in half. The weathered scraps of wood gathered from the ruins, paint and creosote scabbed, burn slowly, smokily, spitting and popping: instead of flowing up and out through the open porthole the barrel sits under, the smoke often spreads over the sleeping and trying-to-sleep crew, causing coughing and cursing.

"Putísima madre, saca esa bestia jodida de aquí," Cabezón suddenly shouts out one night, as if it's just come to him in a dream, the revelation that they don't always have to put up with the barrel. From then on, almost nightly, after the fire has peaked, someone gets up and drags it spitting and fuming out on deck, burning his fingers, cursing, stamping back in through the cold. No one sleeps much, or well. No one really has for months.

Whenever Esteban comes back to the ship in the mornings, he changes into his old clothes, he doesn't want to get his few new ones dirty. Esteban now has a wool jacket, with red and black checks, bought secondhand, and a wool cap to pull over his head. He has a new blanket; he dragged his mattress into the mess too, but when he comes back to the ship, usually during the day, he still sleeps in his cabin, on the mattress that used to be Bernardo's. Esteban has a night-shift job in a small chair factory. And he has a novia, la Joaquina: he's saving his money to live with his novia. But he spends some of his money on the crew, bringing food, sacks of potatoes and rice and beans, and, claro, he spends some on his novia. He brought some old sweaters from a church charity to the ship for those without sweaters. And bought Vicks VapoRub and a bottle of aspirin for those with colds. Esteban spends too much of his money, he doesn't earn nearly enough to provide for a crew of fourteen. The chair fábrica is owned by a Colombian, and he makes a little more than two dollars an hour there. But it's risky, because if the immigration authorities ever find it, nearly everyone who works there will go to prison to wait to be deported. Esteban never brings la Joaquina to the ship.

Esteban has many nicknames now, a new one almost every day: El Patrón. El Millionario. El Capitán. Don Joaquina. El Manicurista. El Niño Mimado, the pampered kid, or just El Mimado. Cazapatos, duck hunter, especially whenever El Barbie wants to prove that he still can't take a little joke.

It's been eight days since Capitán Elias last came out to the ship. So, at last, it seems they've been abandoned once and for all. El Capitán has taken his defeat home to his wife and new baby. Pues, what now? They've been waiting to see what happens next. It seems unlikely that a ship can just sit there forever without somebody coming to assert some authority over the hulk. The generator and compressor are still down on the pier. They've been trying to come up with a plan. At least the ship is a place to sleep, Esteban has shown them that. Until yesterday morning, when John the Ship Visitor came, everyone but los drogados, the paint solvent sniffers—who can barely hold a coherent conversation anymore—has been talking about trying to find a job, the way Esteban has.

He never brings his novia to the ship, though one afternoon, a few weeks ago, he led everybody off the ship and everybody thought that at last they were going into Brooklyn to meet la Joaquina, get free haircuts and jobs. But they didn't go far, only to the futbol field near los proyectos, and she wasn't there. They stood on the sidelines watching a bunch of muchachos in uniforms playing futbol, and two referees running around in striped shirts. Most of them turned out to be guanacos, from El Salvador, though there were some catrachos and chapines too. Bueno, Centroamericanos, and Esteban was friendly with some of the players on one of the teams. There were some women there too, selling and cooking pupusas on a stove they'd set up, and some older men sitting there in chairs, drinking rum. The futbol field was lined with trees full of brown leaves, the trees looking like the withered remnants of a burnt forest against the emptiness of the harbor behind, and the sky was full of wind-swirled leaves and litter. The crew stood on the sidelines watching the game on that weedy, pocked dirt field with the wind blowing dirt in everyone's face, and cheered with so much passion for the team Esteban's friends were on that they all felt depressed when they lost. Then they shared some pupusas that the women donated, the tortilla dough around the filling not quite as chewy as at home, with cabbage and salsa picante on top. They felt a little embarrassed by the way the futbolistas in their satiny uniforms and fancy long haircuts and the women and especially the children stood around staring at them: as if they were monkeys in a zoo, fighting over a few pupusas. The men sitting in chairs apparently didn't want to share their rum, not even with José Mateo, the cook, who asked. One dollar, just for a little glass of rum, they told him. Stingy fucking guanacos. And Esteban said he wasn't going to spend half an hour gluing seats to chair frames just so José Mateo could have a few drops of rum. Then they all walked back to the ship, feeling glad to know there were so many Centroamericanos living in Brooklyn and to have met some of them, and to have been treated so kindly.

Sometimes Cebo, El Buzo, or Caratumba goes into Brooklyn with Esteban, usually to buy potatoes or beans at the supermercado. Esteban never lets El Barbie, strong as he is, come with him to buy and carry back potatoes and whatever else. Pues, they all take little walks off the ship now, never going very far, embarrassed by their appearance and having no money to spend, and still a bit frightened of the neighborhood. These brief sojourns have increased everyone's awe of Esteban's resourcefulness and luck, because none of them ever meets anyone who seems even remotely friendly.

Pínpoyo, El Tinieblas, Roque Balboa, and blind-without-his-glasses El Faro have been wasting away from sniffing paint solvent fumes. (After the night Cebo punched him in the mouth, Canario never sniffed paint solvent again.) They don't even try to hide it anymore. They walk around with their little soaked rags in their hands, holding them over their noses. They say it keeps them from feeling hunger and cold. It's best just to ignore them. Because if you try to talk to any of them now, they talk such crazy mierda, even poor little El Faro, and it just makes everyone feel angry and sad.

The other day the wind brought Cebo a woman's hair: one long, fine strand of blonde hair landed against his burly chest, he looked down and found it sleeping there. Before he became a pathetic ghost of his former self from paint solvent fumes, maybe that hair would have chosen Pínpoyo. Typical of a beautiful woman's hair, to choose the handsomest cabrón left!—that was the chiste. That Cebo refuses to lend the hair to anyone is another one. He calls the hair La Gringita. Cebo keeps his gringita inside a piece of plastic wrap in his pocket and is always taking her out and looking at her, running her through his fingers, putting her in his mouth, pinching La Gringita just below her end to tickle the inside of his nostril with her, trying to make himself sneeze. Who knows what he does with her at night, ties her around his pija no doubt.

Esteban has friends at a restaurant in Brooklyn who send food sometimes, mainly beans to put over the rice, sometimes a couple of roasted chickens, or some pork. And la Joaquina has a brother who tends the flowers, fruits, and vegetables outside an all-night grocery store owned by Coreanos. It seems they throw out food there as soon as it gets even a little bit old, and sometimes Esteban drops by at the right hour and, if his novia's brother can get away with it because the Coreanos aren't watching, he stuffs as much as he can into a large plastic bag and brings it back to the ship. On Panzón's birthday, Esteban even brought him wilting gardenias. Though nothing Esteban has brought back since, or even before, rivaled the feast of the cow. A whole leg and thigh of bloody beef, sawed and hacked apart by Cabezón the Butcher with engine room tools, roasted out on deck over a bonfire, puta, how they stuffed themselves that night, the very night of the day Mark took Bernardo to the hospital—which was the last time the crew saw either of them, el Primero or the old waiter, back in October, almost six weeks ago. El Capitán drove Bernardo directly from the hospital to the airport, pues, there wasn't even time to come and say good-bye.

They'd never realized how solely responsible Bernardo was for keeping order on the ship until he went home to Nicaragua. Bernardo used to sweep and mop everything. Now there's wind-borne litter and leaves and garbage all over the slippery deck, everything covered, especially in the mornings, with a skin of ice. Bernardo used to do their laundry, but lately nobody has the initiative or the energy to go down to the pier and wash clothes in ice water.

The gulls circle the ship laughing and shitting all over and landing on deck to fight over garbage, and once one even swooped down and grabbed a sardine right out of Panzón's fingers—one of the last sardines, from one of the last rusted cans.

But one night, about two weeks ago, Canario went out to piss at the rail and came running back into the mess, where everyone was trying to sleep without choking to death on the smoke from the fire in the barrel, shouting in his high, twittery voice, The rats are leaving! And everyone, even los drogados, staggered out on deck to watch the rats leaving the ship because finally the ship was too cold even for them. It was an unforgettable sight: so many rats swarming around the gunwales and mooring pipes, while over the side their black silhouettes emerged one by one from the mooring pipes and descended the mooring lines to the pier in such orderly progression they could have been tiny circus elephants on parade, holding each other's tails in their trunks. Watching the rats leave like that, they'd all felt filled with the same revulsion. Instead of a relieved sense of release from a plague, the spectacle of the rats departing the *Urus* left them nearly speechless with shame and fear. As if the rats had been *their* fault and now were escaping from inside of *them,* and not from the ship. So no one even cheered, or said very much at all.

Though el Capitán was happy to hear the news. He'd predicted, back in the summer, that the rats would leave once it got too cold. That was one of the last times el Capitán came to the ship, and he smiled and said, "Well, that saves us some money, eh, güeyes? At least we won't have to pay exterminators." But he must have known by then that he'd soon be abandoning the ship too, maldito hijo de puta.

Except some rats don't mind a refrigerated ship. Now and then, they still hear a rat scratching along behind a bulkhead, or spot one splashing through the bog at the bottom of the hold, or squirming through garbage; and you still can't leave food out. So there are still some rats, which is why every time they ask Esteban why he never brings his novia to the ship, he says, "Qué? With all these rats? What if she gets bitten?"

Esteban brought a pair of barber scissors to the ship. Everyone took turns sitting on a crate on deck, while José Mateo tried to cut their hair. José Mateo is not much of a barber, and they ended up looking not much better, though with their hair at least shorter. Everyone's hair was left lying there on the deck and the wind carried it away. The chiste was that maybe one of Cebo's hairs landed on La Gringita somewhere in Brooklyn. True love, eh?

Yesterday, early in the morning when most were still sleeping in the mess, after a night of icy rain and fanged winds, the coldest and wettest night yet, the few who were out on deck heard a voice calling up to them from the pier. And when they looked down over the rail, they saw a blue van parked there, and a tall gringo with reddish brown hair, wearing a pillowy green parka, standing there waving up at them.

They lowered the ladder, and he came up onto the icy deck: John, the Ship Visitor. He was clearly shocked by what he saw, by the condition of the ship and the crew. Esteban wasn't onboard, he must have gone right from work to see la Joaquina, as he often does; he must not have wanted to walk back to the ship in the icy rain. They didn't tell the Ship Visitor anything about Esteban and la Joaquina, or about Esteban's illegal job in a chair fábrica. The Ship Visitor says he is not a policeman or government official, or anything like that. But they should be careful what they tell him, especially if it involves breaking any laws. The Ship Visitor brought them food and socks and plastic sheeting to put over portholes and doors. He said he'd come to help them, that that's his job.

The Ship Visitor had a strange conversation with José Mateo: Wasn't he the older man a lady from Argentina had met down on the pier? Finally they realized, sí pues, that it must have been Bernardo the Ship Visitor was referring to. But Bernardo had never said anything about meeting anybody down on the pier, or anywhere else.

It wasn't that they'd forgotten about Bernardo, but suddenly it seemed as if it had been weeks since anyone had actually mentioned him in more than a passing way. Suddenly it seemed so long ago that the old waiter was there: cleaning everything, complaining, fussing over everybody but especially Esteban, telling his stories. So much has changed since the viejo went home! In the end, though, Bernardo was pretty lucky, no? Lucky viejo lobo de mar! He went home to his daughters with a scarred bump on his head, a scarred but healed leg, his old suitcase stuffed with rags, his photographs, and maybe even his pay—if el Capitán was telling the truth about that. Maybe by now Bernardo has even bought those chicken incubators and is selling chicken and eggs to his neighbors, and telling them horror stories about the *Urus*. Or maybe by now he's forgotten all about the *Urus,* feeling so happy to have gotten out alive, and with his pay, a little salvaged dignity.

The Ship Visitor has a potato nose, pale blue eyes, and hair falling over his forehead. He's a quiet and solid type. His Spanish isn't as good as el Capitán's, though, claro, a million times better than el Primero's. He likes to sit and smoke and listen to the crew's stories, except sometimes he doesn't seem to be really listening; that is to say, his attention comes and goes like a little light in his eyes. But, except for when he went away to buy the food, socks, and plastic sheeting, he sat with them all day, first in the mess, and later out on deck by the fire, listening and asking questions. He seemed a little disappointed that nobody could tell him much about the phantom owner. But then he wanted to know all about Capitán Elias and el primero Mark. He seemed disappointed that nobody knew either Capitán Elias's or Mark's last name. But they tried to give the Ship Visitor as clear a picture as they could of el Capitán and el Primero, and about everything that had happened since June, trying to get it all in order, interrupting each other, everyone wanting to give his own version of certain events so that the Ship Visitor sometimes had to hear the same story told over and over, which was when, claro, he would seem to be no longer listening. And los drogados kept interrupting with snarled curses: Fuck el Capitán! That primero, what a pato! and so on.

But it had been six weeks since they'd last seen Mark. They told the Ship Visitor they hadn't given it too much thought when, in the days after el Primero took Bernardo to the hospital, he didn't come back to the ship, because by then he was already coming much less frequently than Capitán Elias. Then el Capitán told them that Mark had found a new job. Not only one that was better paying, el Capitán joked in his dry, raised-eyebrows way, but one that actually paid. In a bank. El Capitán said that Mark was better suited for life in a bank, because he wasn't much of a ship's officer, no?

They worked hard those few days, getting ready for the inspection. Mainly, the ordinary seamen painted, as if they were trying to disguise the ship's infirmities under shiny paint; while Cabezón and the others in the engine room crew—minus Pínpoyo, already becoming useless from paint solvent fumes—kept up their ceaseless tinkering and maintenance. The inspection did seem like a definite sign that they weren't all trapped on an eternal ghost ship after all. El Capitán isn't a total lunatic, they told themselves. Why would he have us get ready for an inspection for no reason at all?

The strange thing is, now that they've been abandoned, it doesn't feel as terrible as they'd always imagined it would. Maybe the worst has passed. That is—they more or less admitted to the Ship Visitor—the crew has had a long time to get used to the idea of going home broke and in debt someday, total and humiliated failures. They've had a long time to get used to that.

Capitán Elias and the owner were having a grave problem with money, they'd understood that. Bueno, the phantom owner was obviously out of money. Especially now, according to el Capitán, that he's had to pay Bernardo's hospital bills. El Capitán said the owner had been so exasperated by those expenses, added on to everything else he already owes, that he'd even threatened to sign the *Urus* over to Bernardo.

When Esteban (he didn't have his job in the chair fábrica yet) demanded to be paid anyway, el Capitán said, No, Esteban, you cannot be paid, none of us can, the money simply isn't there. That's why this is our last chance. Because there's going to be an inspection. And I think it's probable that then the owner is going to want to sell the ship, just to be able to pay off some of his debts, including all of our wages.

And just like that, after so many months of trying to believe that when the ship is fixed she'll sail and we'll all be paid, the rosary changed. Now it was: When the ship is sold, we'll all have to be paid.

Capitán Elias had never seemed so serious, so grim and preoccupied as he did during those days when everyone was put to work preparing for the inspection, just after Bernardo went to the hospital and was sent home. That was another reason they believed in this last chance. As in their very first weeks onboard the *Urus,* el Capitán came to the ship every day, bringing them food; they sensed his urgency—as different, as changed as el Capitán and this new urgency now seemed. He stayed out of the engine room; it was as if he'd given up on the engine ever since the new circuit breakers hadn't fit. He tended to stay by the gangway, by the rail, for hours, often just staring out at the lot behind the grain elevator. He came and stayed all day and hardly talked to them at all, staring off as if he was waiting for somebody—as if he missed his old adjutant and friend, and was hoping to see Mark in his yellow Honda driving into the lot and onto the pier, Miracle sitting beside him.

The days went by, and el Capitán began to relax his remote and somewhat despondent mood. He was a little bit more his old self. Sometimes he asked the crew questions:

What made Mark decide to take Bernardo to the hospital?

Though he seemed to be asking just out of curiosity, the question confused them. Why was he asking? Did he and the owner still wish

Bernardo hadn't gone to the hospital so that they could have saved money? But then, puta, what would have happened to Bernardo? Did he think that, given more time, his medicine would have worked?

Tomaso Tostado answered that el Primero had taken Bernardo to the hospital because his leg was beginning to stink and rot and the viejo was delirious.

(El Capitán also asked, Where does Esteban go all the time? And they answered, No sé. Saber. Quién sabe, mi Capi? And when el Capitán asked Esteban directly where it was he was always going off to, Esteban just answered, Nowhere. Though none of this was part of the story they told the Ship Visitor.)

One day Capitán Elias took a long walk off the ship himself, into that empty field with that big old terminal at the end of it, and when he came back he was holding a bunch of gray weeds he'd pulled up by the roots. He said it was dogbane, one of the plants he'd used in the medicinal mix he'd brewed back at the end of their first week on the *Urus,* when everyone was sick from rat water, which had worked pretty well, no? He only wanted the roots, he cut the rest of the plants off with a little pocketknife and threw them overboard. And then he put the roots into both pockets of his leather jacket.

For all their sense of a resolution of this last hope approaching as tangibly as freezing weather, coming a little closer with each night's dropping temperatures, most of the crew were soon working lethargically and without commitment. Because they'd noticed that el Capitán didn't really seem concerned with how their work was going. José Mateo said, Maybe the ship is going to be sold, but sold for scrap after all. Bueno, in that case, they all thought, it won't make any difference what she looks like.

The inspection was surprisingly brief. A car drove up and parked on the pier, and a white-haired man got out wearing a thick, nylon-shelled blue parka and black trousers. Those who were by the rail saw him standing on the pier scrutinizing the hull for a long time. And then Capitán Elias hurried down the ladder to meet him, and when they both came back up onboard together, they heard Capitán Elias refer to this inspector as *Captain* something, they didn't catch the name. They noticed that Captain Something walked with a slight limp, and that his heavy cheeks looked scraped raw, and that he seemed to take an immediate liking to Capitán Elias. But they also noticed that Captain Something didn't call Elias Captain in return, he just called him Elias. This captain's accent was a lot like Elias's—an English accent, supposedly. *All right then, Elias,* they heard him say a few times, among other words they didn't understand. Tomaso Tostado is sure that he heard Capitán Elias say, *February,* and then the other repeating this, nodding. And he heard Capitán Elias say, *The Amazon*. The inspector didn't even bother going down into the engine room, or looking in the cabins or mess, nor did he seem at all interested in the crew. They could tell that he did say something about the missing lifeboat. He seemed most interested in the cargo rigging, looking up the masts at the booms, blocks, and derricks; down at the winches at the foot of the masts, now and then drawing Elias's attention to something or other. And then the inspector was shaking Elias's hand, and they heard him say, *Good luck, Old Boy*.

When the inspector was gone, El Barbie asked Capitán Elias how the inspection had gone. And Capitán Elias calmly said, Bien, Barbie. I told him we weren't ready for a full inspection because we're still under repair, that's all.

Capitán Elias didn't come to the ship quite as regularly after that. He said he had to stay home with his wife, because the baby was going to be born soon. But el Capitán also told them that soon he would begin bringing potential buyers out to look over the ship. And he warned the crew not to interfere or contradict anything he might say in front of those potential buyers, nor, if asked, should they say anything to these potential buyers that might damage their impression of the ship. El Capitán laughed a little when he said all that. He said, Let's face it, güeyes, this isn't a ship you can sell just by telling the truth.

They understood why he was worried about what the crew might say when he arrived at the ship with the first potential buyer: he spoke in Spanish to el Capitán. But he didn't talk to any of the crew. He was wearing a fur coat, a crimson beret, had a pencil mustache and a long nose like a tapir's. He just walked around the ship and went down into the engine room, where Cabezón, Caratumba, and Canario, though not Pínpoyo, were hard at work as always; they heard el Capitán telling the potential buyer that it wasn't hard to find replacement circuit breakers, but the owner had decided to sell the ship as she was, where she was, because he didn't want to put in any more money.

There were other potential buyers, gringos who spoke in English to el Capitán. But one was a robust and happy-seeming man with a roaring laugh, thick eyebrows, and thick hair sticking up through the open collar of his shirt and even out of his ears. El Pelos Segundo, they instantly nicknamed him. Capitán Elias called this man Captain too, and this man, José Mateo said, appeared to be Greek. Capitán Elias treated this Capitán Pelos Segundo with uneasy deference, seeming to sink into a gloomier mood the more the other walked around the ship inspecting and laughing. But this laughing capitán was the only one of any of the potential buyers to strike up a conversation with the crew: down in the engine room, he complimented Cabezón, Caratumba, and Canario on how well maintained the engine was, told them they all had the makings of a first-class engine crew.

Eight days ago el Capitán came to the ship and told everybody that his baby son, Hector, had been born two days before, and nearly everybody said, Congratulations, Capitán. And el Capitán rigged a bosun's chair and summoned El Barbie and Cebo to lower him over the side with a can of gray paint, and el Capitán himself painted over the name *Urus* on the prow; then he had them lower him over the stern, and he painted over *Urus* and *Panama City*. Why didn't El Barbie and Cebo just drop the hijo de puta *down* into the water? Because, they claim now, it had occurred to them that el Capitán was about to rename the ship in honor of his newborn son.

El Capitán called the crew together and told them about his baby again, and then he said, We have a buyer for the ship. That's why I've just painted over the name. In another day or two, caballeros, this will all be over.

Y ya. He said good-bye and left the ship, and hasn't come back since.

The Ship Visitor seemed disappointed that no one had ever thought to write down or memorize the license plate number on Capitán Elias's or el primero Mark's car.

But Esteban is there this morning when the Ship Visitor returns: he comes in a van, bringing cartons filled with old, warm clothes; and with him is another woman, in a small white car. The woman in the car is la Reverenda *Runtree*.

"Now what's all this about an old man?" she asks when she comes onboard. She speaks Spanish, a little bit, too. She has red hair, and blue eyes too, and everyone think's she beautiful, though she is not young, and, claro, she's a reverenda protestante, more like a priest than a nun. Though she barks questions at them, and sometimes seems impatient with the length of their answers, and interrupts to ask another question.

Later, after la Reverenda has gone and everyone (though not Esteban) has tried on the new warm coats and gloves and hats, the Ship Visitor tells them to choose four crew members for the trip to the lawyer's office. Then the Ship Visitor leans back against the rail and watches the crew hold their election. It seems obvious who the four will be—Esteban, Tomaso Tostado because he's the most intelligent, Panzón, because he keeps a record of what everyone is owed, and Cabezón, the highest ranking engine room "officer"—but everyone feels obligated to try to say something about the good qualities of each crew member, though not about los drogados. José Mateo, the cook, is the oldest, the most knowledgeable about maritime matters; Cebo is the kindest and strongest; Caratumba the most serious and also the hardest working after Cabezón. What about El Buzo? He's the best domino player and speaks a little English, even if it's just the words to that reggae fulano's songs. El Tinieblas, his paint-solvent-fumed voice more whispery than ever, argues that El Barbie deserves to go because Capitán Elias appointed him contramaestre back in July. And El Barbie says gracias, I was wondering which one of you pendejos was going to get around to mentioning it, though I was hoping to be nominated by Cazapatos.

Canario's chances are completely dashed when Cebo stupidly argues that his cabinmate Canario should be chosen because he had to stay behind to guard the ship the night they crossed los proyectos—that's the luckiest thing that's ever happened to the twittery cabrón! So they all, even los drogados, cast votes by raising their hands in the air, and José Mateo, Cabezón, and El Buzo tie for the final spot. After two more rounds, José Mateo says he can't go after all because he has dinner to prepare, and Cabezón finally wins the fourth spot.

The Ship Visitor takes them in by subway, so that they'll know how to make the journey alone later if they need to. It turns out that there's a subway stop only about a twenty-minute walk from the ship. And they're on a very crowded subway, speeding-screeching-rocking through a tunnel, when Esteban suddenly turns to Panzón and says, "Puta! I can't go to the lawyer!" By the time they get all the way in, meet with him, and come back, he'll be late for work! It's unfair that Esteban has only thought of this now, because El Buzo could have gone instead—pero bueno, that's Esteban. Probably he just wants to go and see la Joaquina. When the subway doors open at the next station, Esteban squeezes through the standing crowd and is gone and the train starts moving so suddenly that Panzón is thrown forward and lands against a pretty gringa's back with his nose in her hair and she spins around with a frightened shout and glares at Panzón with hate at first sight but Panzón doesn't notice because he's too busy regaining his balance, knocking into other passengers, clutching his ledger book, and trying to reach for the bar over his head at the same time.

They switch trains, crossing the platform in one of the underground stations, from the F to the A train. But the Ship Visitor hasn't even noticed that Esteban left when they were still on the F, because when they get off the A train in another station, he looks at them with an astonished expression and says, "Weren't there four of you?"

He frantically looks around at the people coming and going on the platform, at the A train disappearing into the tunnel, and then looks back at them wild eyed and says, "*Oh no!* Didn't he notice we were getting off? *Shit!* That kid's never going to find his way back! *Oh no!*"

And he gapes from one face to another, at Tomaso Tostado, at Panzón (still secretly overjoyed by the clean, flowery scent and silky touch of that gringa's hair), and at Cabezón, but all three are thinking the same thing: We're not supposed to tell the Ship Visitor about Esteban's illegal job.

The Ship Visitor seems to be trying to control his panic. He says, "You don't understand. That train is an express. Do you think he'll be able to find his way back?" Then he lifts his hand to his forehead, partly covering his eyes. "*Why?*" he nearly shouts in English. "Tell me *why*."

Another of the long, silvery trains rages into the station, startling them with its iron screeches, making them cringe. When the train is gone, Tomaso Tostado blurts, "He went to see his novia, pues."

"His novia!" exclaims the Ship Visitor. "He has a novia?"

"Sí, sí tiene."

And the Ship Visitor grins with surprised relief. "You muchachos have novias?"

"No, no, only Esteban. He met her around the time Bernardo was sent home, pues. He used to share a cabin with the viejo."

"Esteban? His name's Esteban?"

"Sí, Esteban."

"How did Esteban find a novia? Stuck on that ship, and he finds a novia?" Apparently the Ship Visitor hasn't realized that today is the first time he's seen Esteban, that he wasn't on board yesterday.

"No sé," says Tomaso Tostado. "He found one, pues."

They walk up the stairs and onto the sidewalk, and there they are, in the middle of the faraway island vision they've been watching for so many months from their ship: buildings climbing up all around them, steep, dirty walls soaring into the faraway looking sky; and down on the sidewalk, everything cold, heavy shadows, and lights in all the lobbies and store windows, and the street jammed with traffic; and everywhere, everywhere you look, people rushing, in warm, long coats, and so many pretty gringas. But in the lawyer's office, the secretary is an older, fat woman with glasses and orange hair and pink lipstick, she looks like a dowdy circus clown. The lawyer's office is cluttered and warm, but no one takes off his new coat, just his hat. The lawyer, Mr. Angus Moakly, is also fat, youngish but balding, wearing suspenders and a tie. He's eating chocolates from a white paper bag, which he passes around. There's a stationary bicycle for exercise near his desk. Licenciado Angus Moakly seems sleepy: he speaks in a groggy way for a long time, until everyone feels drowsy from the heat in the office and the droning of his voice and no one understands a thing that is said until the Ship Visitor explains some of it and then they sign some papers.

It seems to come down to this: the lawyer is going to have "a lien" taken out on the ship, which means that if the phantom owner doesn't pay them their wages and for their airfares home right away, the government is going to seize the ship and auction her off in court, and their wages will come out of that sale, and the lawyer is only going to take a little of the money.

On the subway back to the ship, Tomaso Tostado sits next to the Ship Visitor, who stifles a yawn, and then looks down at him and asks him his name for about the tenth time.

And Tomaso Tostado looks up at the Ship Visitor with what must seem like drenching adoration, he's feeling so happy and grateful inside, and says, "Tomaso Tostado. A sus órdenes."

The Ship Visitor says he guesses that's the last they've seen of Esteban, no? And he lifts his hands off his lap to mime flying away, and says, "Se voló, no? He ran away to live with his novia!" And then he grins.

And Tomaso Tostado answers the Ship Visitor with just a slight, uncomprehending smile, gold tooth glowing over the gap of missing teeth, because of course he knows Esteban will be back, and he wonders why the Ship Visitor seems so cheerfully taken by this idea of Esteban running away to live with his novia . . . Then he thinks to himself, Pues sí, it is an incredible thing, a novia. And he remembers Ramona Goyco, who's the closest he's ever had to a novia, until Ramona's husband threatened to shoot him on sight if he ever saw him again and he went away to sea, and it hits Tomaso Tostado that he has nothing to go home to and that if he does go home that crazy matón might still shoot him on sight anyway, and now he doesn't feel so elated . . . The train has stopped in the middle of a tunnel, but apparently that's normal, nobody seems disconcerted. He takes a long look around at the other passengers. Few people are talking, most look lost deep inside themselves, patiently waiting for the train to move again. So many look tired; white, black, brown, yellow, those who obviously have money and those who obviously do not, they look tired. An old morena woman slouched in her seat, a shopping bag between her legs, deep, unhappy creases around her mouth. People sitting with their heads tilted back against their seats and the walls, some with their eyes closed. He looks across the train at Cabezón and Panzón: Cabezón's big head tilted back too, he's staring up at the ceiling, and Panzón sits with his ledger on his lap, drumming his fingers against it, furtively watching a group of dark-skinned muchachos and muchachas, quietly talking and laughing, standing down at one end of the train. He looks around and sees a few young men who could be catrachos or from any of our countries sitting, alone with themselves, looking tired but calm. If Panzón and Cabezón were not so disheveled and dirty, wouldn't they'd fit right in among the passengers on this train? Tomaso Tostado looks at one of the other Latino-looking muchachos sitting and tries to imagine what and who he's going home to. He tries to imagine himself sitting here a year from now, and wonders what and who he'll be going home to, and from where. He imagines himself working in an office, wearing a tie, stamping sheets of paper with a rubber stamp, a pretty gringa in a dress walking by and saying . . . este . . . saying what? "It's cold out, Tomaso, better dress warm." But he'd already know that. He imagines himself going home . . . to a muchacha like that one sitting over there, leafing through *Vanidades*, wearing portable stereo headphones. She's pretty enough, no? A serious, pleasant face and demeanor, her delicate hands turning the pages of her magazine. He can picture that, going home to her. But where would they be living? The train starts to move again. People shift out of their dreamy attitudes just so, some look around, waking up. He meets Panzón's eye, and Panzón grins, showing all his yellowed, crooked teeth.

As soon as they've returned to the ship, the Ship Visitor tells the crew more about what to expect from the legal action, which is going to take a few more days, at least, to set in motion. He says, "I think you should have the clearest idea of what you're in for, because you've certainly all been lied to enough." It's not that the lawyer lied, but he may have painted a slightly too rosy picture. He says the lawyer is a good person and charging the lowest possible rate, but that he does like to hear himself talk. The Ship Visitor says that, first of all, he doubts the phantom owner is suddenly going to come forward and pay. And he says that if the ship is seized by the courts and auctioned off, most likely it will be for scrap, which brings in much less money than the sale of a working ship. Unfortunately, the crew will have to stay on the ship until that happens, and the Ship Visitor says he's sorry about that. Unfortunately, he says, when the ship is sold off, the harbor and court authorities will take what they're owed first, and that then there might not be enough money left over to cover all the wages they're owed, of which Panzón has kept an exact record, more than two thousand dollars each now. Still, he says, they should collect some portion of what they're owed, though it might take a while. Unfortunately, because Capitán Elias never gave them shipping articles to sign, they have never been a legally employed crew anyway, which makes their case less solid. In the Ship Visitor's opinion, Capitán Elias might not even be a true capitán.

The Ship Visitor really is muy buena onda, and so is la Reverenda, and so all this more or less unfortunate news is not their fault. And, claro, the news could be so much worse. So who can doubt the Ship Visitor's integrity, after all he's already done? But when the Ship Visitor is leaving the ship, Pínpoyo, stumbling forward with his blanket still wrapped around him despite the new clothes, blocks his way in front of the gangway. He's raving about gringo hijos de puta stealing his pay and calling the Ship Visitor a liar and a bunch of other babosadas. Hands still inside the pockets of his pillowy parka, the Ship Visitor looks around at the crew with a baffled expression, while Pínpoyo goes on raving. But then El Barbie steps forward and firmly pulls Pínpoyo out of the Ship Visitor's path and throws him down on the deck, and Pínpoyo lies there as if he's dead, though of course there's nothing the matter with him except for paint solvent fumes. The Ship Visitor, with an embarrassed smile, mumbles gracias to El Barbie. And then Tomaso Tostado remembers and announces another round of applause for the Ship Visitor, and everyone but Pínpoyo applauds and whistles like they do now whenever the Ship Visitor is about to leave the ship. The Ship Visitor stands there blushing, with an almost apologetic smile, until they're done, and then he thanks them, waves good-bye, and goes down the ladder to his van.

2

JOAQUINA REALLY DOES COLLECT COLANDERS, THOUGH SHE DOESN'T HAVE that many, and most of them are made of *peltre,* enamelware, because these are the most inexpensive, and she likes the bright colors; her mamá has always cooked with peltre at home in Mexico. The colander that Gonzalo gave her for Christmas is made of stainless steel, so silvery and shiny it looks made from a perforated mirror. She doesn't like anything made of plastic. She also collects steel balls full of pinprick holes that you fill with tea leaves and submerge in hot water. And spoons: big ones, with holes in them, and others that are like broad little shovels, also with holes in them, and that the Chinos, she says, use for lifting dumplings out of caldo; she has spoons that are not really spoons but coppery wire baskets at the ends of wooden handles. Joaquina can't explain her preference for perforated cooking utensils. Even when Esteban asked, Why do you like things with holes so much? she blushed and grinned ear to ear, as if she herself had only now recognized this, and found it embarrassingly odd herself. And then Joaquina looked at him with an almost hopeful expression, as if she wanted *him* to explain it to her, since he's supposedly the one with too much imagination.

At first Esteban thought that maybe it's just that more work has gone into making a spoon with holes than one without, and so Joaquina thinks she's getting more for her money. A plain metal bowl with holes looks more elaborate than one without. But once he discovered, as Esteban did on his shopping trips with Joaquina, the incredible variety of colanders and other perforated utensils for sale in this city, he began to understand how someone with a magpie's eye like Joaquina's might become fixated on this variety: the challenge of recognizing what makes one utensil more beautiful than the other, and the pleasure of orchestrating your own collection, one where all these utensils with holes in them, all different sizes and colors, become their own ordered little world, one without any other justification. But if you have to explain it, he thought, you might as well say that since Joaquina says she wants to have a fabulous kitchen of her own someday, it seems methodical enough to begin by collecting colanders. Otherwise you'd go shopping and want to buy everything and it would be chaos.

Joaquina also collects teas to put in the little steel balls, and tin containers to keep them in. And she collects spices, which she buys in little plastic bags at Indian, Arabian, and Oriental tiendas in far-flung corners of this city, and containers to keep these in. And she also collects slim, cardboard boxes of flavored rice that she buys in these tiendas too. These boxes of rice come in bright colors and are covered with exotic scripts—just like those still barely legible on the collapsed Wienstock Spice terminal on the cove—and evocative decorations such as elephants and tropical flowers. Most of these things she buys because she can afford them. Because Joaquina's English comes out sounding like halting, monosyllabic utterances in a rapidly fading radio transmission from Mars—provoking shopkeepers to patronizing grins that vanish from their faces as soon as her glaring eyes plunge them into the brimming caldrons in which she boils her frustration alive—she usually ends up having to point at whatever she wants to buy.

Esteban has traveled all over the city with Joaquina on her shopping trips, riding subways and buses for hours, to neighborhoods where he sees bearded Indian, Pakistani, and Sikh patriarchs in turbans strolling the sidewalks with their families, the women dressed in gaudy, flowing, silken robes; to Chinatown's reeking labyrinth, where Joaquina is capable of spending hours in a trance as still and focused as her manicuring one, trying to choose just one perforated, three-dollar ladling spoon. Having finally chosen, she tries to convince even Esteban of the utensil's perfect—though not yet practical, in the sense that, pues, Joaquina doesn't cook—beauty. They journey to a row of Arab tiendas in Brooklyn so that she can buy an ounce of black cumin there, or that jar of tamarind paste or concentrated pomegranate juice with the beautiful label that she wishes she'd bought the last time. In some of these tiendas the merchants are sometimes so hectoring, familiar, and infuriatingly flirtatious with Joaquina that she marvels that so many different languages can come out sounding just like a Mexican market vendor's Spanish.

Joaquina neatly displays her purchases along a wall of the single room she lives in with her brother, Martín, or crams them into a three-level wooden shelf in the corner, as if she's getting ready to open her own spare, highly specialized tiendita. She does like to dream about the kitchen she'll have someday, the cooking classes she's going to take to learn how to use all of these spices, oils, pastes, and perforated cooking utensils. But the kitchen where she lives is shared by too many people, most of them muchachos with sloppy habits and some of them with personalities she finds off-putting and even threatening. Mainly she uses the kitchen to brew her fragrant teas, which she carries back to her room in one of her peltre pots.

Along with her three brothers, she sends some of her earnings back to her parents and younger siblings in Mexico, though not as much as they do. She spends more than she should on clothes, and Martín has given up fighting with her for a share of their small plywood closet, keeping his things in a suitcase and folded in piles on the floor against a wall opposite the one along which she's arrayed her collection. The earrings she wears, and changes every few days, come stuck onto pieces of cardboard; she peels them off and sticks them on her earlobes. Joaquina has pierced earlobes, but she says she prefers these earrings, and they're very inexpensive, she buys them at a tienda on the avenue and in Chinatown.

Esteban thinks she lives in a wretched place, and wants nothing more than to free her from it: a three-story building where all the walls have been knocked down and replaced by warrens of plywood cubicles with padlocks on the doors, a kitchen and two bathrooms on each floor. It's mainly full of Mexicans, most from the states of Puebla and Guerrero, though there are people from other countries there too. Sometimes Joaquina and her brother have to sleep in the bed together, when Martín has day or evening instead of night shifts in the grocery store where he works. Down the hall, her brothers Abél and Juan, the oldest, share another. Each room rents for three hundred and fifty dollars a month. Once, when Esteban and Joaquina were making their way through the plywood-cubicle maze to one of the bathrooms, they came upon a masculine-looking muchacha with hair dyed an unnatural shade of red, dressed in black stretch shorts and a sleeveless T-shirt, brandishing a baseball bat embedded with nails at a gringo standing in the open doorway of one of the cubicles. The gringo was trying to talk in a reasonable voice, which was coming out tremulous with fear anyway. He was wearing just a white shirt and a suit jacket and no pants and holding a necktie in his hand, and the woman with the bat was threatening him in a fierce, low voice, telling him that she was going to smash his head in if he didn't shut up. The man said, OK, OK, and put up his hands. Down at the end of the corridor another muchacha, younger than the muchacha with the bat, an adolescent face and pert, butter-colored breasts, was sitting naked on the floor with the gringo's trousers, pockets turned out, across her lap, and she was pulling everything out of his wallet.

Joaquina immediately led Esteban back to her room. He was appalled that she could live in such a place, and infuriated with her for being so icily complacent about it. She answered, That's how that putita works, bringing gringos home and before she even fucks them that big macha bursts through the door. Pinche gringo, she said, it's his own fault for whoring around. When Esteban vehemently disagreed, her eyes turned to saber thrusts, and she asked if he had a better place for her to live. If she paid any more in rent, she'd have to live like a nun to afford it! Maybe she'll come and live on his ship? Órale, güey? Would he like that better?

They decided that as soon as they had the money, they'd find a place to live together, no matter what her brothers said. Of course it was a strange existence, with almost everything about it unsolved but for love and his tedious job at a chair fábrica on the other side of Brooklyn, still having to go back to the ship to sleep. Life went on aboard the *Urus* almost exactly as it had before, though Bernardo and el Primero and his dog weren't there anymore. Esteban ignored el Capitán in his comings and goings. He bought stamps and stationery for the crew so that everyone who wanted to could finally write home and tell his family and novia where he'd been all these months—only four chose to. Thanks to him, the crew is eating no worse now than before the sardines ran out, but over the last month the crew has been costing him almost as much money as renting a share of a plywood room would.

The night that el primero Mark took Bernardo to the hospital, the crew roasted the beef Esteban brought back over a roaring fire on deck, on spits fashioned from long steel pipes. Esteban had forgotten his morning's anger over Bernardo's neglected leg; he thought the viejo must be happy now, in a warm hospital bed, being treated by yanqui doctors. At least he's not here, he thought. Because if the viejo were here, he'd be jodiendo with his corny, insinuating remarks about Joaquina. Puta, the last thing he needed; he felt nervous and excited enough. Esteban intended to go back to the salon and make love to Joaquina there that very night. It was already growing dark, and he pulled out la Marta's watch. He had to go soon. Joaquina had said that Gonzalo usually closed the salon before eight. José Mateo was heating him a cup of pure beef blood and marrow, said it would be good for his cold. The fire was already going, but Cabezón was still busy hacking up beef. Esteban was hungry, but they hadn't started cooking yet. They didn't know he had to go, or where, or why, he hadn't told them anything. He chose a big hunk of beef out of the pile and impaled it on a wire splicing pin, then cooked it over the flames until it was seared on the outside, the fire's heat hurting his hands. He ate the cooked fat off the outside first. When he bit into the beef, holding it like a melon in both hands, the meat was still nearly raw on the inside; warmed blood filled his mouth. Then he drank down the plastic cup José Mateo had filled with a thick soup of simmered blood and marrow—marrow which the cook had scraped out of hacked bones. Bueno, this had to be fortifying, no? It probably wouldn't be very romantic, to bring Joaquina the gift of a big slab of raw beef. He said a quick good-bye and left the ship, still eating. He couldn't even finish it. He tossed the rest over a fence, let those crazy barking dogs fight over the bloody, rubbery scrap.

When he reached the salon he wanted to die: the shutter was lowered, it was dark. They were gone! But he went to the window and stood in front of the shutter's metal slats, and then he saw her getting up in the dark. Joaquina had been sitting there in the dark, waiting. She opened the door and he went in and she said, "Ven!" and took his hand and turned to walk him towards the back, but then she let go. "What's on your hand?" she asked. "It's sticky." And he resisted the urge to laugh, and said, "Blood." He could barely see her in the dark, but he could tell she was looking at him oddly. Suddenly he burped. She said, "Pig!" "Perdón." "What have you been eating, chamaco naco?" And he had to take a deep breath against the fear and excitement already rising from the sloshing sea of blood and raw beef in his belly, and he said, "Meat and blood, pues. Too much of both, I think." They kissed, and she said, "Your breath smells like a butcher shop." And he laughed. Joaquina pulled him through the curtain and said, "Wash your hands." When he came out of the bathroom, he saw that she'd lit a candle inside a red glass next to a blanket spread over the floor and then the way she was smiling at him. They kissed standing up for a long time.

Then she sat down, pulled the straps of her dress down over her shoulders, and began undoing the buttons of her blouse. He sat on the floor and untied his bootlaces. He had an erection and struggled getting his boots off, and then his socks, as if he was in a frantic hurry. He wanted to say something, something that might calm and anchor him, that would make clear why he was there. And when he stood up to take his pants off, he found himself silently speaking the words, Te quiero, wondering if it was time yet to speak out loud about love.

Then he heard Joaquina saying, "Sticky hands. Runny moco nose. Burping," and he looked over. "You're like a human swamp! Leaking and oozing all over! Whole cows vanish into your quicksand, verdad? Caráy! What am I getting myself into?"

She was smiling, and sitting there completely naked now, her legs crossed at the ankles under the chair, her hands holding on to each side of the seat. He stood there with his pants half-tugged down, bent over, looking at female nakedness for the first time since the burdel in Corinto six months before, when the sight of that puta's nakedness, her pretty young skin gleaming in the humidity and the harsh light of a bare bulb, had filled him with a sudden, vivid terror of what had happened to la Marta. Now he looked at Joaquina's chichis, small and upright, coppery pale in the wavering glow from the candle, the little cones of her hardened nipples, and he looked at her slender arms and shoulders, at her soft-looking belly and her long, skinny ribs as she pushed herself up from the chair and came towards him, at her lithe thighs and the triangle of black hair. He let go of his pants and stood up again, and they fell around his feet while he put his arms around her and ran his hands up and down her slender, hard back and down onto her smooth, rounded nalgas and felt her lips warmly touching him there, on his neck, on his cheeks, on his lips. And then she whispered into his ear, "Qué te pasa?" just as he was letting out a long sigh of bewilderment and relief, because she'd stayed whole, her body had stayed whole and he didn't know what to do now with so much sudden pleasure. And then she was undressing him, pulling his dirty T-shirts up over his head and then he felt her hand on his stiffness through his underpants and she laughed. "Ay no! Ve? Leaking!" His underpants were wet and sticky there. And when she pulled them off, a long spider's thread of jism flared silvery red in the candlelight as it dropped from his trompeta and they started to laugh. Too much! Qué ridículo. He couldn't stop laughing. They held each other laughing, each one's laughter inciting more laughter in the other and she squealed, "*Ujujuy!* Esteban the Swamp Monster!" with her arms around his neck, and they tumbled down onto the blanket. They were fucking before he knew it, and he came in about two seconds. It was an explosion—more so than even the abundant elephant's pee of his dreams on the *Urus,* when he was so dehydrated his bladder had turned to rust. He felt as if his whole insides were collapsing, leaving him so emptied he could hear his own heart pounding loudly in a void. Joaquina murmured, "What a mess, Esteban. Now I feel like a swamp too." They lay kissing, touching—he burped again—until he was ready for more.

Joaquina, as she'd vowed, ate him alive. Then they lay there a long time, holding each other tightly, his lungs feeling twitchy and gilded again, riled by the heavy, sweet fragrances of the salon . . .

During the three days in mid-November that Joaquina's other novio, the lawyer from México, visited, Esteban felt more trapped on the *Urus* than ever. The lawyer was staying in a hotel in Manhattan. He'd been a client of Joaquina's in México, when she'd worked as manicurist in a salon in the city's colonia of Polanco. Joaquina insisted that she had to see the lawyer, that she'd never lied to Esteban about the lawyer, and so he had no right to be angry. Esteban vowed to break with her forever if she went to see this little lawyer who paid to have his hands manicured. Joaquina sent both Esteban and his mother to la chingada on a blisteringly foulmouthed comet of insults and abuse, and promised *she'd* never set eyes on Esteban again.

And maybe she wouldn't have, if five days later, on his way to work, Esteban hadn't found himself standing outside the salon window with one wrapped rose in his hand and a suffocating head cold, in perfect imitation of his first attempt to win her. They completed the new ritual by coming back to the salon after Gonzalo had closed up to make love in the back again, on a blanket on the floor, only this time without a candle. Then Joaquina had him sit fully clothed with the blanket wrapped around his shoulders and his bare feet submerged in a pot of scalding water, and told him that he should never, but absolutely never, ask her what had transpired with the lawyer.

"It's finished between us," she said. "And if you ever bother me about it again, güey, you'll learn what it's like to believe in God in the land of *indios*!"

Joaquina's room is where they usually make love now, and only when she's sure none of her brothers is around. Joaquina has her brothers' constantly shifting work schedules constantly memorized. All three of her brothers have black hair, and two are darker complexioned than she is. But Abél has Joaquina's nutmeg-and-cream complexion, with more freckles. All three brothers are given to constant hard slaps on the back and bewilderingly slangy salutations, and they travel in packs whenever they go out, they and a bunch of other muchachos. They seem to neither like nor dislike Esteban, to neither approve nor disapprove of his seeing their sister, though Martín, whom he sees much more frequently, is the friendliest. Most of all their stance towards Esteban and their sister seems worn like a hard-faced mask, not out of personal meanness but out of an impersonal meanness they think enhances and protects their own and her stature—so his future brother-in-laws irritate him, he being accustomed to outwardly much easier-going tropical port town ways.

Whenever he and Joaquina manage to steal some time alone together, in the little plywood room, heated by a small electric heater with glowing orange coils, the air so spice scented that even his sluggish nose can smell it, Esteban is the one who sometimes still finds himself conquered by his secret inhibitions. While Joaquina sheds her outward restraints, takes control, does what she wants, until, with voracious hands and mouths and finally their whole bodies, they're eating each other alive. Sometimes she mounts him and goes away, far away inside herself, traveling the secret paths of her own pleasure, eyes closed, lips silently mouthing some lost language, until she cries out and quakes and her cheeks flush almost ashen blue and her eyes open as if waking from a hundred years' sleep to find him still there, still watching—a little unnerved over having been left so far behind, but glad to have been found again; then it's his turn to let go, if he hasn't already. She tells him it isn't always like this, that it has to be love and even then, it won't always be like this. What does he know? Chocho Joaquina, he lives now for their time together, in this little room. He thinks there's no better answer to life than this. She also cuts and files his toe- and fingernails, snips his cuticles, sands his soles with a pumice stone, rubs lotions all over his feet, and tells him that now he can never make fun of men who have manicures and pedicures ever again. Joaquina loves Esteban with a solicitous tenderness and exacting passion that dissolve his self-doubts and fears or startle them away like a flock of crows. Her love comes out of the same seemingly bottomless well of emotion that causes all her moods and outbursts, from rage to hilarity. When she's sullen her face seems to deflate, she turns into an abuela with enormous, blind person's eyes that accuse the world of a whole lifetime of unendurable grief. And when she's ebullient, her smile stretches ear to ear in the most deliriously childlike way, her eyes shining as if they're telling silent jokes only cats can hear. He sometimes feels frightened that so much emotion can dwell inside one slight frame: he's seen her topple in a split second from giddy affection to blaspheming, sobbing fury, sometimes with no provocation other than being overwhelmed by so much love that she can't control.

Esteban has told her everything about himself now—pues, almost everything. Joaquina knows about la Marta, even about her watch, which he still carries in his pocket. She leaves Esteban alone when he sinks into one of those faraway moods, gnawing at his thumb, sniffling and snorting. Joaquina broods over him, and has a talent for finding practical solutions to his most unnameable dilemmas. It was her idea to start going to the Friday night dances in a certain Salvadoran restaurant in another part of Brooklyn, which draws Centroamericanos from all over New York, and even, regularly, a pair of black ex-soldiers who'd been stationed at the U.S. military base at Palmerola, Honduras, where they'd picked up an honest enthusiasm for the local muchachas. A live band plays música tropical there on Friday nights, and he and Joaquina share a few beers and dance in that nalga-swinging Centroamericano way that at first she found tastelessly lascivious, and still has her doubts about. The restaurant is owned by a middle-aged woman, Doña Chilcha, who'd been a barracks chef in Salvador, and who, when she'd foreseen the way the war was going, had fled to Nueva York with her five children. On his very first Friday night there, Esteban met a fellow Nica who worked as foreman at a chair fábrica, and who wrote down its address and the name of the nearest subway stop and told him to come by on Monday morning. He's met refugees from the Salvadoran and Guatemalan wars and death squads there, including a doe-eyed, skinny chavala chapina who'd had sixteen members of her extended family disappear, and until recently had been living with a group of nuns in Coney Island, who'd helped her to get out of Guatemala and were extremely kind to her, though somehow that very kindness had made it impossible for her to cure herself of a paralyzing sorrow. But then, at a Friday night dance there last winter, she'd met the Salvadoran college student, and soon after had left the convent house and moved in with him. Their love struck Esteban as rapturous and mature, they both had night jobs, and she was still attending high school by day. One of the cooks in back, slapping out a perpetual train of pupusas, was from Nicaragua too: she had a son who'd died fighting in a BLI, another still living in the contra camps, and two more children with her in Brooklyn, and she'd wept and embraced Esteban when he was taken back into the kitchen to meet her, introduced as a survivor of the war, a former soldier in a BLI. Esteban sat at a table one night listening to Nicaraguans of three generations arguing about the Sandinista military draft with the same ardent vehemence they might have skewered each other with at home if they were all one family, until the muchacha named Barbara, who hadn't been saying anything, got up from the table in a flood of tears over her lost novio and fled the steamy-smoky, packed restaurant to collect herself out on the sidewalk in the cold air. Esteban saw her shadow through the fogged window and was about to get up and go outside and weep with her, but her older sister put a hand on his forearm and told him to just let her be, that this happened every time they came here. But many who come to that restaurant on Friday nights are so young and have already been here for so long that the wars that have been ravaging the isthmus for at least a decade are like a dark fairy tale to them, and they already consider themselves Nuyorquinos as much as anything else; they tower over their parents, growing up tall and radiantly chubby faced because here even the tap water is supposedly good for you—at times Esteban, who'll turn twenty in January (for five months he and Joaquina will be the same age), so burdened by the war that broke his heart, feels like an irrelevant abuelo around these jokey jovenazos, most of them actually a bit older than he.

Many people, there in the restaurant on Friday nights, and elsewhere in Brooklyn, when they learn of Estéban's ambiguous refugee status from a phantom ship on the Brooklyn waterfront, offer him a temporary place to stay, a couch or floor to sleep on until he and Joaquina can find their own apartment. He always writes their names, addresses, and telephone numbers into a little pocket-size notebook Joaquina gave him for just this purpose.

The night the Wall came down in Berlin, Joaquina bought a bottle of red wine and took Esteban back to her room to celebrate what she'd decided had to be his final liberation from an obsessive confusion she didn't pretend to understand, which included his obscure sense of loyalty to a certain make of military transport truck, and a constant outrage over a certain cannibalistic dog named Ana.

For over a month now, Esteban has timed his comings and going from the ship to meet la Joaquina—she is, of course, extremely punctual—by la Marta's watch. He still thinks of la Marta as being with him. Claro, he's corrected the watch so that it no longer just tells the time over her grave, which was one way of timidly saying good-bye. He is not so morbid as to think he has betrayed la Marta by falling in love with la Joaquina. He tells himself that he'll never love anyone the way he did la Marta, whom he knew for so short a time, and that because it was for such a short time, this love, on such intimate terms with her absence, can do nothing but endure. Even the war they shared, in comparison, won't last inside him in quite the same way. La Marta was just a chavala, one with a majestic, grave, and courageous woman growing up inside her. We even have children, he thinks one day, feeling stuck on the ship, leaning on the rail, waiting for it to be time to go and see Joaquina. So who are their children? And he thinks, They're orphans. They're everything that's invisible but still more enduring than a fucked up iron pirate ship that's made a bunch of poor men ever poorer. Everything that gets lost, that never gets a chance to learn what it was going to be.

"Joaquina? You know what happened? A gringo came to the ship. He's called a ship visitor."

"Un qué?" she answers drowsily.

"A ship visitor." He's taken a seat against the wall, near Joaquina, who is sitting on her stool, manicuring Chuchu's hands. He doesn't tell her now that he's just come from the subway stop after deciding not to go to the lawyer's office after all. He has to be at work in another two hours.

"Güera," interrupts Chucho, "Hueso is having a party Saturday night. It's going—"

"Chucho, shhh," she says. "Un momentito." And Gonzalo, working on another customer's hair, glances over sharply—

"Qué pasó, Esteban?" she asks.

And Esteban grins back with a bit of embarrassment at Gonzalo, because he knows why he's just looked at him that way. Before, when Esteban would sit in the salon for hours watching Joaquina do her manicures, he would sometimes get jealous when some of her male customers were too flirtatious with her. He'd sigh and glare and snort through his nose, until Gonzalo finally lost patience and began sending Esteban out for café con leche at Marilú's, or pastelitos, or to the post office or on some other insignificant errand. And then finally, after one of these episodes, Gonzalo exploded. What kind of men do you think come in here for manicures? he shouted at Esteban. Pues, claro, said Gonzalo, answering his own question before Esteban could, they're men who want to get to feel like a king for a little while, a pretty chica on a stool at their feet. The last thing they want is their manicurist's novio sitting beside them, pouting and staring daggers every time they flirt a little! Coño, Esteban! You're turning into a real pain in the culo!

But this is different, and Esteban ignores Chucho's grunt of impatience and says, "This Ship Visitor thinks there's a good chance we're all going to get paid, and he's taking Panzón, Tostado, and Cabezón to a lawyer this very minute to see about it. It's finally over, Joaquina. Chocho!"

Three days later it snows, fat flakes that have been falling all morning, the gray slush on the sidewalks slowly becoming covered with a soft white blanket. Esteban, who hasn't slept since leaving his night shift at the fábrica, stands on the sidewalk in front of the salon's steamed-up window adding snow to all the elements his indestructible boots, happy with their new laces, already know about. Then Joaquina comes out singing, "Friolín, friolín," because it's so cold, and she stands beside him with her pink tongue out.

And Esteban says, "Snow is just like what I've always imagined a rain of volcanic ash must be like, Joaquina. Only cold instead of hot." And then he tells her about a school outing he was taken on when he was eleven, to a volcano that was a historic sight because its eruption a century and a half before blew out the side of the crater with explosions so loud that supposedly military garrisons throughout Centroamerica and as far away as Jamaica were put on alert against British invasions. All along that part of the Pacific coast, the eruption turned day into night for a week, pouring down a rain of ash that ended up two feet deep on the ground, so coating everybody and everything with volcanic ash that not even mothers could recognize their own children or husbands in the streets. On the bus ride to the volcano, their teacher, Compañera Silvia, who he's already told Joaquina about, vos sabés, the one with braided mole hair, told them the history of the volcano, which most already knew anyway. But then she told them the part about how every domesticated animal that wasn't suffocated in the ash and even wild ones, even tigers and monkeys, had tried to find shelter from the raining ash under any roof they could find, crowding into churches, convents, and thatched huts, pushing nuns and children out of their beds. That Compañera Silvia, she was buena onda! Esteban laughs out loud at the memory. Bueno, when they reached the foot of the volcano, everyone rolled around in the ancient ash of the lava fields just for fun. And when he got home, all coated with whitish gray ash from head to toe, you know what he did? He sprang through the door waving his arms and howling, excited by the idea of frightening his mamá with this ghost-zombie disguise. His mamá put her hand to her chest and said, Dios mío, Estebanito, you look just like your papi!

". . . And that's the only time in my whole life that I ever heard Mamá make any reference at all to what my father looked like!"

Joaquina, with one of her ear-to-ear smiles, says, "Chamaquito, qué historias! That accelerated head of yours, full of nothing but stories, no?"

And then Joaquina tells him there's something she wishes she could take him to see that very minute, something she went to see last winter when it snowed. In the botanical garden in Brooklyn, she says, there's a glass house kept heated with steam, and it's full of tropical plants and palms and banana trees, and, pues, everything you find growing in the jungle, even live lizards running around and iguanas.

"So if you're inside and look out through the glass, Esteban, it's like it's snowing in the jungle. Chingón, no?"

And he barely has a chance to tell her how much he looks forward to seeing that, when he hears someone calling his name through the snow, and sees the Ship Visitor's blue van parked by the opposite curb, and then the Ship Visitor getting out and crossing the street in his pillowy parka and a black wool cap pulled down just over his eyes, wearing black boots with thick black rubber soles that crunch loudly against the snow.

Esteban shakes the Ship Visitor's hand and manages to introduce Joaquina, though he feels disturbed and confused that the Ship Visitor has been able to find him here; he counts on the protection of complete anonymity in his new, illegal existence off the ship. Now the Ship Visitor is explaining how he'd asked that gold-toothed marinero where it was that Esteban's novia worked, and that then he'd put two and two together and driven to this neighborhood and asked in a restaurant if anyone knew of a nearby beauty salon owned by a former Tropicana dancer. And Esteban thinks, Tomaso has a big mouth. That was stupid of me, telling Tomaso Tostado about Gonzalo. The day before yesterday, on one of his visits to the ship, the Ship Visitor had told Esteban that he'd really given him a fright, disappearing from the subway like that, and Esteban had laughed and shyly apologized. But then the Ship Visitor had asked Esteban about Joaquina, and though Esteban hadn't denied having a novia, he'd been careful not to really tell him anything. And then the Ship Visitor had asked him if he knew Bernardo's last name, and he hadn't.

The Ship Visitor says, "I just wanted to tell you, Esteban, that because of the snow, the Seafarers' Institute has decided to evacuate all of you from the ship. It's going to happen sometime tomorrow." The Seafarers' Institute's board had authorized the unprecedented step of taking the crew off the ship, putting them up at the institute for a few days, and flying them home, all at the institute's expense. "I have a feeling that you won't be coming, Esteban," the Ship Visitor says, with a smile at Joaquina, "though of course you're welcome to, if you want." And then he says the U.S. Marshals Service will be posting a lien on the ship and officially seizing her the same day.

"Ajá," says Esteban. Because the Ship Visitor seems perturbed . . .

And the Ship Visitor says, "But I wanted to talk to you about something else, Esteban. I know you were the closest to Bernardo."

Though he hadn't even remembered Bernardo's last name, which had made him feel bad . . .

"Ajá," says Esteban, noticing how the cold is beginning to make his ears hurt. "We shared a cabin, pues."

The Ship Visitor, towering over him and Joaquina, looks down at him through the snow with a worried look in his pale eyes, and then he shrugs and lifts his hands away from his sides. "Esteban," he says. "Bernardo's last name is Puyano. We finally got it from the U.S. Embassy in Managua, because they issued his visa back in June." And he said that he and la Reverenda had made a lot of phone calls and everyone was checking and they were going to check again, but so far there was no record of a Bernardo Puyano having left the United States in late October, or having come into Nicaragua. And someone from the embassy had done them the favor of going to Bernardo's address to see if he was there, and he wasn't.

"I told them about it, on the ship, before coming here," says the Ship Visitor. "You can imagine how everybody felt. After everything you've all been through, and now this."

"Sí pues," says Esteban. He feels Joaquina take his arm in both of her hands and stand closely against him. "I felt bad," he says flatly, "that I couldn't even tell you his last name." Then he begins to understand that this terrible though not unfamiliar sensation swelling inside him is terror. And he feels tears like tiny, hot beads rolling over the cold-numbed rims of his eyes.

Then Joaquina asks if they want to come inside. Gonzalo keeps the heat turned up all the way, she says. Inside, she brews a pot of coffee while Esteban sits in shocked silence next to the Ship Visitor. He hears a toilet flush in back, and a moment later Gonzalo steps out through the curtain.

Gonzalo says, in English, to the Ship Visitor, "Are you here for your nails or to have your hair cut?"

With her back to them at the coffee stand, Joaquina says in Spanish, "It's serious, Gonzalo, it's about the viejito who was on the ship with Esteban. They don't know what happened to him."

And the Ship Visitor turns to Esteban and says, "I wish I could even be sure Bernardo was taken to the hospital. None of the Brooklyn hospitals, anyway, has any record of a Bernardo Puyano having been a patient. We're going to keep looking, of course. There must be an explanation. I don't know, maybe, somehow, Bernardo is still here in New York."

Esteban covers his face with his hands and sits back in his chair. And he remembers the day he came back to the ship with his new haircut, soaring on love and carrying the side of beef over his shoulder, and suddenly found himself being hustled into his cabin, which stank of rotting cheese and an old man's illness. Bernardo was in delirium, eyes blindly rolling, but he'd reached up his arms and in an iron embrace had pulled Esteban's head towards him and kissed him with dry lips. But he'd been too wrapped up in his love even to realize how alarmed he was until he set on eyes on Mark, when suddenly he'd felt capable of murdering that useless hijueputa unless he took Bernardo to the hospital. And then he'd instantly felt better, no? So happy in love that he hadn't let himself worry about the viejo. A yanqui hospital, pues. Why should he have suspected anything? Now here he is draining tears of fear and guilt and pity into his hands, for himself as much as for the viejo. Hijo de cien mil putas, he's hardly given Bernardo another thought ever since he found out he'd been sent home! Though he's told Joaquina all about the viejo. All about how it was Bernardo who'd practically driven him from the ship so that he could meet her, challenging his pride. That crazy viejo with all his fussy doting and his sad stories and his wrapped snapshots and his pedantic lessons and his sitting cat and his ridiculous dreams of chicken incubators! This can't be, no? What did they do with Bernardo? Puta, *why?*

"What do you think happened?" Esteban asks the Ship Visitor, when he can finally bear to look out from behind his hands, sitting there with Joaquina's arms tightly wrapped around him.

"I don't know, Esteban," the Ship Visitor answers. "I'm just as baffled as you are. What we really need to do is find this Elias and this Mark."

After the Ship Visitor leaves the salon, Gonzalo announces that he's closing up early because of the snow. Esteban wakes late in the afternoon in Joaquina's room, under a blanket on the bed, clutching her body against him. He buries his nose in the soft place between her upper arm and her chest, breathes in deeply . . . Bernardo *Puyano*. He feels terrible now that he hadn't been warmer with the viejo. But Bernardo's effusive and dogged love was so generously and at times so stiflingly given that Esteban always felt blocked from showing him much affection in return. Or maybe love had just stopped flowing inside him, until he met Joaquina . . . And trying to comprehend or even imagine this mysterious abyss that has somehow swallowed Bernardo, he suddenly realizes that it isn't something that has been done only to Bernardo. It's something that's been done to all of them, and that they never even knew or suspected the truth makes it all the more terrifying. And makes it also too much like what happened to la Marta and to how many compas, everyone he's lost so far, another thing he's never understood until right now . . .

It's night when he finally feels ready to walk to the ship. There's plenty of time left. He puts the roll of quarters he's saved for this occasion into the pocket of his wool jacket, pulls on his stocking cap. From a pay phone on the corner outside he calls in sick at the fábrica for the first time ever, and then he makes all his other phone calls, leafing through the little address book with fingers numbed and aching from the cold. When he's finished he stands staring at the receiver for a moment through the clouds of his breathing, wishing there was a way he could track down and phone Milton in Miami, just to talk to him. He listens to the crunching of tires through the packed snow on the avenue, hears shovels scraping pavement everywhere. It's stopped snowing now. Everywhere, this sparkling white sugar. The avenue has been strung with Christmas lights and tinselly banners.

3

"IT'S STOPPED SNOWING." ELIAS TURNS FROM THE WINDOW AND LOOKS AT Kate, who's nursing their baby. Hector. Two weeks old. The Law of Similars. Like cures like. Therefore, those nearly ten pounds of pure and innocent flesh cure the father.

Kate's disappointed in him, of course. Very disappointed. She thinks he's a total fuck-up. But Mark absconded with all the money, what could he do? Kate has always thought there was something slimy about Mark Baker. She hopes Elias has learned something from all this. These risky ventures have their charm, but really, Elias, it's time to get serious. He's explained the "technicalities" to Kate: The crew is still on the boat. Sooner or later federal marshals will seize the ship, there'll be an auction, the crew will be paid and sent home. Tough break for everybody, all around, but it's the way things work. In the maritime industry.

Where'd the wanker go? And where'd the old waiter go? Bernardo.

He's waiting to find out. He's been waiting for six weeks now, to find out. And feeling sick with *fright*.

But they won't find his name on a single piece of paper. And the Panamanian Registry has no legal culpability, because they were never licensed seamen. He made sure that the "Oath of Officer or Agent of an Incorporated Company" was signed on behalf of Achuar Corp. of Panama City by Mr. Mark Baker. And Mr. Mark Baker has apparently vanished off the face of the earth. And who's going to force the Panamanian Registry to turn over even that piece of paper?

It's easy to hide. Ayahuasca can make you feel invisible. In the rain forest people saw ghosts, the spirits of the ancestors, *tunshi* they called them: elongated shapes of pale mist floating out of the jungle at night. And if you see one, it can give you a case of *manchari*—fright. Long-lasting fright, inside you like a wasting disease. Children, especially, can die of it. They can catch manchari from a reflection in a puddle, especially the reflection of a rainbow; or from a shock, or from suddenly falling down—that initial moment of fright billowing inside them and staying, a sickness. Unless you go to a shaman. Cumpashín could cure children of manchari, blowing wild tobacco smoke all over them, the magic smoke wafting their fright away. People came to Cumpashín from all over, to cure their children of fright. The river people were especially afraid of rainbows. Clothes left out to dry when a rainbow came out had to be washed again. That's the world they live in, the world they know and understand. Terrified of rainbows. And he lived there, among them, for many years.

And now he's afraid to look his baby in the eye. He's afraid of giving him fright. He worries that he has mal de ojo.

So don't look over at Daddy, Hector, whatever you do, because he suspects he has the evil eye, he could give you fright—but Hector never does. His wrinkled little prune face is buried in Kate's breast, and her head is bent over him, and she's cooing.

In a truly legitimate business, he thinks angrily, there are rules, very definite rules to follow, which create accountability. Such as malpractice suits. Such a threat keeps a güey out of trouble, doesn't it?

The other day he went by Mark's apartment, climbed the dark stairs, six flights, feeling full of fright. He was remembering a girl he'd known long, long ago, back when he'd just met Kate and was still living on Mark and Sue's couch. She'd lived in a depressing little apartment like Mark's, and she owned a German shepherd, like Mark's, named, he'll never be able to forget, Spoon. She died of a heroin overdose and for days no one knew, until the smell, and when they broke down the door because of the smell, they discovered that Spoon had eaten a portion of her body. Her dog had eaten her face. That gave him fright. But outside the wanker's depressing, caca-hued apartment door, there was no smell. And he went downstairs and knocked on Mark's super's door, and spoke to him in Spanish, except the super turned out to be Moroccan. The super said that Mark didn't live there anymore. That just days ago movers had come by and taken everything away in a truck, and the super didn't know where to, and no, Mark hadn't been there, it was just the movers. And Mark hadn't left a forwarding address.

I suppose I could trace him through his credit card receipts or cash machine withdrawals, thinks Elias, if I were the law. But I'm not the law. Not that kind of law. The Law of Similars. But he can't even look into his own baby's eyes. Kate thinks he's just having one of those new-father freak-outs—mortality, the end of youth, that sort of thing.

He gets up and goes into the bathroom and shuts the door and looks at himself in the mirror. He looks into his own reddened and wounded—yes, wounded—eyes, which others have always found so—well, his best feature—tender and intelligent. His best feature, his eyes. He can hear Hector crying now, and Kate's low, soothing murmurs.

It's too easy to hide. But you I won't be able to hide from, Hector. He wonders if he's just being sentimentally overwrought, or appropriately overwrought—isn't it appropriate for a father to look at his two-week-old-son and think, From you, I won't be able to hide? Not until you're old enough, Hector, to start hiding from yourself, anyway. Which is why all guilty souls fear the open gaze of little children.

Moira Meer has no idea where Mark is either, and neither does Sue. He does love sweet Moira. He loves Moira Meer and couldn't ever bear to hurt her and so will go on loving her until she finds the right man, someone who can replace him well enough in her heart, and who, of course, will be free to give Moira so much more of himself. Certainly not Mark. She never thought so for a second, poor deluded wanker. But she's not interested in Phil either. He went to see Yoriko the other night—turned out to be the night before the day Kate went into the allopaths' maternity ward. Yoriko was leaving for Japan with her boyfriend in another few days, bringing him home to spend Christmas with her parents. With the baby expected any day, he'd figured it was his last chance to see Yoriko, and so he'd told Kate he was going to the health club and gone over. She showed them those snapshots she'd taken, him and Mark and Haley out on the deck of the *Urus* during the tow to New York, hoisting their champagne glasses to the future, high times! high hopes! Really, just having tried to make it work nearly excuses everything, doesn't it? Nearly. Because trying to get ahead, to innovate, to make something of yourself, güey, is honorable. There's an implicit honor in just the bloody fucking effort, that's all. And if that doesn't quite excuse everything, it ties you, binds, connects you to all those who've come before who've made such an effort also, the successes as well as the failures. Because it's what the world's been fucking built on. So if there's no honor in that, even in failure, then there's nothing at all. Because success and failure are bonded by effort and risk. And what's the difference between a failure and a success? Maybe just the slightest alteration in one's DNA, a lucky break here, an unlucky one there, a stupid decision that was almost brilliant, a ruthless decision that, had it worked, would have been seen as fair and even uplifting (what if they *had* sailed? If the crew *had* been paid every cent they were owed, every *cent*!)—basically the effort, the intention, are the same. I've been successful, he thinks. I've married Kate. I'm not some spineless wanker who's taken the easiest, most obvious path, who's never done or seen anything. But I'm sorry I've disappointed Kate.

And he leaves the bathroom and crosses the big, empty space of the loft and looks out the window at the clean, snowy street, feeling the cold through the glass, listening to the cold-muffled shouts of teenagers, watching them having a snowball fight—a very *ironic* snowball fight, no doubt, given the character of the barrio. They're still out there, on the ship, in the snow, all those poor güeyes. Where the fuck is Bernardo? Where did Mark really take him? How could he be dead? I keep waiting to see his *tunshi*. I'm wasting away with fright.

He turns and looks at his wife, her bare shoulder whitely smoldering above the slipped-down black robe, her long, twirly black hair falling over her chest, her head bent over the baby snuggling there.

"Kate, my sweet," he says. And she looks up at him, with a slim smile, a tender, Madonna smile, of course. "I'm going to be a good father to Hector. I hope I will be. I'll give it every effort, Kate. That's one thing, being a father, that I'm never going to let you down on."

And Kate's dark eyes hold his for so long, so long, as if she knows that's just what he needs, as if she's drawing his fright out of him like smoke with her own invulnerable gaze, as if she's telling him with her eyes that of course he doesn't have the evil eye; he feels a sob welling in his throat, though he never, ever weeps.

Kate says, "Oh honey, of course you will be." Oh honey! He's full of honey, not fright!

And he walks right up to Kate and takes the baby from her arms and holds him up in his little white jammies, his hands spread around his fragile little ribs, and he looks right into his tiny, squinty, unrecognizing, raisin eyes and he says:

"Be fearless, Hector. Be a big-hearted, fearless cabrón!"

4

FOR THE LAST TIME, ESTEBAN MAKES THE LONG WALK DOWN TO THE waterfront and to the ship, his boots squeaking through the snow. When he comes into the lot behind the grain elevator, he realizes that the sound he's been following from a long way off is the chugging of the generator on the pier. But the black Mazda isn't parked there, nor is any other car. The generator's yellow steel, locked shield has been crowbarred off, cables run from it up onto the darkened ship. He climbs the ladder and looking around the deck, sees no one. He looks into the mess, into the cabins, and sees no one, and follows the cables over the deck, behind the deckhouse, and sees them descending into the open hatch over the engine room, and hears the louder chugging coming up out of it, distinct from the noise of the generator on the pier. The open hatch is a square of soft, diffuse light. He looks down over the coamings and sees Cabezón, Canario, and Caratumba hurrying back and forth across the wet, leaf-strewn bottom of the engine room's lower level, and José Mateo standing there beside them holding Elias and Mark's yellow flashlight. There are a few of the plumber's lamps hanging. He sees the rest of the crew arrayed along the catwalk, sitting and standing in dark shadows.

"Vos, we're going home!" Tomaso Tostado shouts over the noise of the generator when Esteban has come into the engine room, onto the catwalk.

He sees the stereo that Elias and Mark had always kept locked up on the bridge set down on the catwalk too. The red eye is glowing, but you can't hear anything for the noise. He looks dumbly at Tomaso Tostado, who now shouts, "You know about Bernardo?"

Esteban nods. And then Tomaso shouts, "That's why we're stealing this fucking ship! Get that hijo de puta capitán in even more trouble!"

Stealing the ship?

He sees Panzón laughing his lugubrious laugh, though he can't hear him. And now Panzón shouts, "Cabezón thinks he can get this thing going. He's built a bridge!"

"We're going home!" shouts Tomaso Tostado again, laughing, his gold tooth glinting.

Cabezón is hot-wiring the engine. He's built a bridge: bypassing their nonexistent main circuit breakers by wiring one of the ship's generators directly to the copper bus bars at the back of the switchboard, connected to the smaller circuit breakers powering the pumps. Everything else on the ship that uses electricity will stay dead. He's started up the engine room generator with power from the portable generator on the pier. Bypassing the main circuit breakers means that there's no modulation of the amperage, the output of electricity is constant and uncontrolled. It could even start a big fire. But he thinks it will work. There's still water in the boilers and tanks and easily enough fuel. Everything's been properly maintained, the pipelines drained, we've tinkered with this thing for months. There *won't* be a fire. It should take a few hours before the engine cranks over. Fuel pump settings set. The transfer pumps sending diesel fuel now to the settling tank, and then through the system until purified and heated to flash point. All he has to do now is go up into the control room and throw the lever. Eventually the rods will start moving up from the crankshaft, the pistons will fire off in order. And finally the propeller will begin to turn. A ship with no one at the controls and without any steering mechanism, with no one at the helm . . .

Now the uproar in the engine room is deafening, all along the catwalk they hold their hands over their ears, but no one leaves, even the solvent sniffers are mesmerized. This rhythmic, iron clanging and clatter. This entire iron cavern of a ship beginning to vibrate. And when Cabezón finally orders them out, they can even feel the icy deck vibrating under their feet as they cross it, sliding, falling, some of them charging down the ladder to the pier to undo the mooring lines, they'll leave the lines trailing in the water. By the time they're back on deck, the ship is already drifting away from the pier on the current.

They make their way up the foredeck to watch. Esteban stands at the rail, looking around at the cove, the ruins transformed by snow. The smashed pier extending from the old terminal, snow layered over its collapsed and broken slanting timbers, looks like a long line of Chinese writing against the black water.

Water rumbles against the ship's faraway bottom, the whole ship seems to shiver and groan as the propeller begins to churn more than four hundred feet aft, beneath the stern. The ship moves forward, so indiscernibly at first it feels like a slight dizzy spell. But suddenly Esteban sees the pier sliding away behind them. And then the ship begins slowly to turn sideways inside the tide.

5

WHEN THE SHIP VISITOR COMES AROUND THE GRAIN ELEVATOR IN HIS VAN, this is what he sees: an empty pier. The shock of that moment will remain inside him like a silent explosion forever. For a split second, he thinks that somehow some great and mysterious fraud has been perpetrated on him; the ship never had anything wrong with her, and has just sailed away. He glances in the side mirror at the graffitied walls of the grain elevator behind and then out across the gray-green water at the ship run aground, her immense, rusted prow driven up over the pilings and against the collapsed wooden terminal, the top of her mud-caked black propeller sticking up through the water. Her mooring lines dangling, and the accommodation ladder hanging down the hull like a broken prosthetic arm. He sees the wreckage and debris of the now utterly smashed old spice terminal's pier floating in the water, driven up against pilings, bobbing around the hull. And on this now empty pier, he sees the generator with its shield torn open, cables running off it, across the pier, down into the water . . .

He gets out of the van and slowly begins to pick his way around the snow-covered ruins of the basin. When he reaches the other side, he stands beneath the immense wall of the prow, trying to comprehend the tidal wave that has somehow driven the ship up over the pilings. A drop ladder hangs from the rail midship, descending to the rubble. This ship, he thinks, already owes nearly fifty thousand dollars in berthing fees alone. And now the cost of hauling her out of here? She'll bring in seventy thou, sixty-five, if she's lucky, when she's auctioned for scrap. They can say good-bye to their pay. Losers, a completely mediocre situation, I just don't see how, Johnny, you can spend your life around people like that, complete dupes, people so incapable of helping themselves—that's what Ariadne said the other night, when he was telling her the story of the *Urus* and her abandoned crew and the kid who'd found a novia.

He calls up, and no one answers. He waits awhile. And then he grabs onto the drop ladder, and with much leaping, grunting, and effort finally hoists himself up onto its bottom rung and begins to climb to the rail. The slanted deck is treacherous, and he makes his way along it clutching the rail with both hands, calling out. And then he sees one of the crew, one of the smaller kids who always look worse than even the others do, sitting against the back of the deckhouse, sobbing, a little rag clutched in his hand.

"Qué pasó?" he asks.

The kid squints up at him through his small red eyes, his dirty little face tear streaked. He shakes his head.

"He wouldn't take me," he says breathlessly, and then he starts sobbing again, falling over on his side.

He goes around to the side of the deckhouse, past the plastic sheeting stretched over the mess doorway, looks in through the one open porthole, and sees the tattooed kid and two more—the kind of handsome, hollow-eyed guy who'd raved at him in front of the gangway—sitting against the wall, blankets wrapped around them.

"Qué pasó?" he asks. "Where'd everyone go?"

One of the kids responds with some sort of unintelligible muttering. And then he hears someone calling to him from above, and he looks up at the wing, and sees the older guy, the slit-eyed cook, waving to him.

He climbs the switchback stairs four flights to the bridge, and when he goes into the bare wheelhouse, he sees the kid with a big head stretched out on a mattress with his hands clasped behind his head, his arms and face and even recently donated clothes smeared with black lubricating grease. And the cook is standing there with one hand grabbing onto the helmsman's wheel.

The pumpkin-headed kid on the mattress grins at him. And the Ship Visitor demands to know what has happened, and the kid tells him, while the cook just stands there chortling through his teeth. "We didn't get very far," says Cabezón. "Pero, bueno, we didn't do too badly, no?"

"And where's everybody else?" the Ship Visitor asks.

"They went with Esteban," says José Mateo. "They all decided to take a chance, and if it doesn't work, then they can still go home penniless later, no? He has friends in the city who've offered to put them all up for a while. The drug addicts wanted to go too, but Esteban wouldn't take them, pues. He said he couldn't do that to his friends in the city." The cook shrugs. "Me? I'm too old for that. I'll go home for a little rest, and then I'll look for another job."

"Los drogados." The mechanic who built a bridge to bypass the circuit breakers grins. "Pobres. Cómo sufren, no?"

And the cook impassively says, "They're suffering, sí pues."

"Cómo *suuuuu*fren," the mechanic quietly sings out, and then he snaps his tongue against the back of his teeth.

"But what about you?" the Ship Visitor asks him.

"Me?" says Cabezón. "I have to go home. I'm getting married, pues."

Riding the PATH train back to Manhattan and Ariadne from the Seafarers' Institute that night the Ship Visitor replays that moment of utter surprise over and over in his mind: driving onto the pier and seeing the ship not there, and then looking over and seeing the ship run aground. And he thinks, Well, I've sure as hell got a story for her tonight . . . And I'll begin it like this: Think of a pier, Ariadne, any old pier, maybe one as old as the century, but paved and sturdy. And no ship berthed there. And then think of what this so concrete object, a pier, represents, evokes: All the ships that have ever berthed there and all the ships that ever will, and all the faraway ports those ships have come from and are headed to, and all the hidden lives on those ships. And then think of that pier again when it's empty. A pier with no ship berthed there. An emptiness, but a certain kind of emptiness. Kind of like love without lovers. Because in a way that's what love's like, Ariadne, like that pier, and you and I, our love, our love is just one of the ships that have called there. And this Esteban, his is another . . . Well, that's what I think of when I stand on an empty pier. A ship visitor's gotta find his poetry where he can get it, right? And today, when I drove onto that pier in the van to collect that abandoned crew, the ship was gone.

Acknowledgments

IN NOVEMBER OF 1982 A NEWS STORY BURIED IN THE INNER PAGES OF THE New York *Daily News* caught my eye: "Sailors abandoned" was the headline. The reporter's name was Suzanne Golubski, and her story reported: "Seventeen abandoned sailors have been living in a floating hellhole on the Brooklyn waterfront for months, aboard a rat-infested mystery ship without heat, plumbing or electricity, an international seamen's organization charged yesterday . . . The sailors had been lured here from Central America with the promise of good wages but instead found themselves abandoned, unpaid and trapped on the ship of horrors . . . When they ventured off the ship to escape the nightmare situation . . . a number of the men were hit over the head with pipes and beaten up by neighborhood thugs." And so on. The ship was registered under a flag of convenience, and the owner's identity was unknown.

I was just back from a nearly two-year stay in Central America, balancing fiction writing with journalism and living in Manhattan, so it was the Central American connection that first drew my attention. A friend and I immediately drove out to the ship.

The crew had already been evacuated and were being temporarily housed at the Seamen's Church Institute's facilities in lower Manhattan. But when we reached the pier there was an automobile parked there, and the ship's ladder was down. We went up onboard and found a middle-aged man in a blue windbreaker leaning on the rail, smoking. The man approached and asked what we wanted. I answered that we were interested in buying the ship. He shrugged and said that he was just the ship's chief engineer, hired to oversee its repair. We explored the ship, and a while later he approached us again and confided that he *could* in fact sell us the ship and asked how much we'd be willing to pay. I must have answered with a ridiculous sum: he told us we had to leave the ship.

I went next to the Seamen's Church Institute and spoke to Reverend Paul Chapman, the director of the Institute's Center for Seafarers' Rights. My story confirmed what he'd suspected all along, that the man we'd met was in business with the ownership, or the owner himself. I also, briefly, met the crew. They were mostly young, Costa Rican and Nicaraguan—though there were at least two older members, the cook and waiter. Our conversation—a few hours in the Institute's basement cafeteria—took place so many years ago now that I remember very little of what we actually talked about, though some of the things they told me have been a part of my attempts to reimagine the story from the start. I owe a special debt to the waiter, Bernardo Iván Carrasco M. He wrote a twelve-page account of the travail, which he titled "Los Ultimos dias de un viejo lobo de mar," and gave it to me, urging me to make good use of it. (This was especially helpful in its explanation of how he and some of the others had originally been hired.) The *Urus*'s Bernardo Puyano meets a far more tragic fate than Bernardo Iván Carrasco M. did. Needless to say, I've paid the real-life Bernardo the token tribute of lending his first name to his entirely fictional counterpart.

So I'd wanted to write this story for a long time. In a certain way, I've pursued it all over the world. I spent the 1980s dividing my time between Central America and New York—whenever I could, down there, I'd stop in port towns and talk to people, especially the seamen you could always encounter in the usual raunchy nightspots. When a dear, late friend of mine, Bruce Johnson, worked briefly as a ship's chandler in Puerto Barrios, Guatemala, I went with him as his "assistant"—there, I boarded some working ships for the first time. In the 1990s, when I was living in Mexico, I made many trips to Veracruz: late one night I found myself drinking alone in a cavernous, high-ceilinged "seamen's bar" whose madam was about to move her business to another establishment in a midnight dash. I ended up risking my neck for that madam: climbing a long, rickety ladder—a few of her girls held it from below—to snatch nautical pennants from the rafters so that she could take them to her new center of operations. That was the highest, most unstable ladder I've ever scaled. We became friends. She had a lover, a captain of a ship then in port undergoing repairs. He'd given her a port pass, and she lent it to me, on the condition that, once past the port gates, I'd distribute flyers advertising her new "Seaman bar," leaving them in stacks by the gangways of every ship I managed to board.

In the meantime, Rev. Paul Chapman had written and published an excellent account of the sometimes horrifying exploitation faced by international seafarers in the maritime industry: *Trouble on Board* (Cornell University Press). In it, he tells the story of the abandoned crew and ship that had first captured my attention in the news years before. The "phantom owners" of that ship escaped legal prosecution, but they were banned by the Liberian Registry from ever again registering under that flag of convenience. Amazingly, the ship, once seized and auctioned off as scrap to a machinery company in Brooklyn, was repurchased by those hapless owners; sometime later they were caught trying to work the same scam, with the same ship, in Staten Island; and then again in the Caribbean. (Perhaps the *Urus* is on her way to a similar destiny.)

Reverend Chapman's book led me to Capt. W. A. Chadwick, chief investigator for the Liberian Registry. The Liberian Registry is unique among "flag of convenience" registries: it is operated as an independent business out of headquarters in Reston, Virginia, unaffected by whatever government happens to be in power in strife-ridden Liberia at the time, though a share of the registry's profits go to that nation's treasury. The Liberian Registry, probably more than any other flag of convenience, tries to enforce international maritime laws and standards aboard its ships—thus the investigation, and subsequent banning, of the phantom owners of the aforementioned ship. I spent two days talking to Captain Chadwick in Reston in the autumn of '94, and I am very grateful for both his generous hospitality and the information he gave me.

In January of '95 I moved, again, from Brooklyn, New York, to Mexico City. I was feeling a bit shipwrecked in my own life, and perhaps that provided the impulse to set aside another project I'd been working on for a few years and plunge into this novel. I still felt I lacked a true feeling for shipboard life, but I trusted that my imagination would be able to fabricate something coherent out of the bits and pieces I'd been able to pick up during the thirteen years I'd been hunting this story down. At least, since the story was about a ship that never moves, I wouldn't need to know very much about navigation.

Work went slowly. In the fall of '95 a lucky break changed everything. I met Miguel Angel Merodio in a Colonia Condesa restaurant. We struck up a conversation, during which it came out that his "primo hermano," Juan Carlos Merodio, is the head maritime lawyer at Transportación Marítima Mexicana, TMM, Mexico's largest shipping line. It's a long story, but in the end, thanks to Miguel Angel and Lic. Juan Carlos Merodio, as well as Lic. Fernando Ruiz of TMM, I found myself, in November of '95, departing from Veracruz aboard the TMM ship *Mitla*. We stopped at various ports before I finally left the ship in Barcelona, after a nearly monthlong voyage. I now believe that I'd been incredibly naive to think that I could ever have written this book without having gone to sea. Many thanks to Capitán de Alta Mar Guillermo Cárdenas, Chief Engineer José Millán, and the rest of the officers and crew of the *Mitla*. I am also grateful to Chief Engineer Tom McHugh of Baltimore, Maryland, to the Nicaraguan war hero Noél Talavera, and to Reverend Jean Smith, of the Seamen's Church Institute. Alvaro Mutis lent me precious books on tramp steamers and shipping and exhorted, and trusted, me to write this story for "both of us." Nothing could have meant more. To Alvaro and Carmen, my deepest thanks and cariño.

Morgan Entrekin is the most supportive editor any writer could hope for, and also a great friend. Thanks for the office space, too, Morgan. The whole crew at Grove/Atlantic—Elisabeth Schmitz, Eric Price, Judy Hottensen, Miwa Messer, Carla Lalli, John Gall, Tom Ehas, Kenn Russell, and everyone else. Thanks, also, to Bex Brian and Jon Lee Anderson. Amanda Urban is my own "Queen of Luck" and a good friend of many years.

I owe so much to Veronica Macias, "Musa de Desastres y más . . ."